THE
LITTLE
PEOPLE

THE
LITTLE
PEOPLE

by MacDonald Harris

WILLIAM MORROW AND COMPANY, INC.
NEW YORK

Library of Congress Cataloging in Publication Data

Harris, MacDonald, 1921–
The little people.

I. Title.
PS3558.E458L5   1986   813'.54   85-13855
ISBN 0-688-06132-X

Printed in the United States of America

First Edition

1 2 3 4 5 6 7 8 9 10

BOOK DESIGN BY ELLEN LO GIUDICE

This book is
for my friends that
I've only imagined,
especially Mic, Pat,
Robbie, Tom, and
Linda.

I cannot render the pleasure that I felt in the midst of these charming beings who were dear to me even though I knew them not. They were like a primitive and celestial family, whose smiling eyes sought mine with a gentle compassion. I began weeping hot tears, as though at the memory of a lost paradise. I felt bitterly that I was only a visitor in this land at once so strange and so beloved, and I trembled at the thought that I had to return to life. In vain, they pressed around me as though to retain me. Already their delightful forms were dissolving into vapors; the fair faces paled; the distinctive features, the shining eyes were lost in a shadow in which only the last ray of a smile still lingered . . .

—GÉRARD DE NERVAL, *Aurélia*

One

The van, glistening like opal in a rare day of summer sunshine, turned in off Praed Street, picked its way among the standing taxis, and came to a stop in front of Paddington Station. It was a brand-new van, enameled a pale green with the words Villa Felicity on the door under the driver's window. Bonner stepped out and stood on the pavement looking around him, and Julie got out from behind the steering wheel on the other side, went round to the rear of the van, opened the door, and took out his suitcase, which she set on the pavement.

He didn't pick up the suitcase immediately; he was still looking around him at the traffic and the busy crowd pouring in and out of the station.

"Are you sure you'll be all right?"

He nodded.

"Is there anything else I can help you with?"

"No. I'll be fine."

"I'd come to the train with you and help you with your bag except that I can't leave the van parked here."

"Please don't bother."

"Do you know how to buy the ticket?"

"Oh yes."

"I just thought that since you're an American you perhaps weren't familiar with our trains."

"Oh no. I've traveled a good deal on British Rail."

She looked around and hesitated. A traffic warden was already moving up with her notebook and pencil. "Well, goodbye then."

She offered her hand and he took it. He had half expected her to embrace him, and he had even imagined the efficient, brisk, and yet feminine and fragrant sensation of her body pressed briefly against his own, but they only held hands for a moment and then dropped them awkwardly. She was friendly and pleasant but professional, just as she had been in the Villa Felicity. When he went off with his suitcase he turned once and saw she was still watching him; they exchanged smiles and he went on into the station.

Inside he stopped, bewildered and bemused by the colorful buzz and activity all around him after his months in the rest home. Groups of people brushed by him with their baggage; lines of travelers waiting for their trains had formed at the barriers. There was a flower shop, a buffet restaurant with steamy windows, and kiosks offering books and magazines, photo supplies, and travel information. Everything was brightly colored, noisy, and in animated motion. He was absorbed by this for a few moments and almost forgot why he had come. He was reminded only by the weight of the suitcase in his hand. He smiled and went on to the departure board to look for the next train to Waldon.

It was scheduled to leave in only a few minutes and the gate was already open. He bought a ticket and went in through the barrier with his suitcase along with a straggling line of other people. On the platform he walked along until he found a car that didn't seem to have too many people in it, turned toward the open door, and then stopped, a little intimidated by the solid steel wall punctuated by its row of square windows. Then, getting a grip on himself, he climbed into the car and bumped down the aisle looking for an empty seat. He felt a little queasy, as he had expected he would on the train. He found a seat, lifted his suitcase into the rack over it, and sat down. Almost immediately there was a little lurch and the platform outside, with a porter pushing an empty cart and a trainman watching, began moving slowly backward. There was no sound at all. The platform slid away more rapidly and the train came out into the sunshine. He leaned back onto the seat and closed his eyes, with only a light malaise at the sensation of being enclosed inside the steel walls of the train.

To distract himself from this unpleasant feeling he began thinking about the enjoyable time he was going to have visiting his friends the Boswins at their place in the country. The house was by a river, he had been told; there were pleasant walks to take and an unspoiled village nearby. There was even a forest not far away where there might be wild animals, rabbits and foxes, he supposed, perhaps even deer. He had very little experience of English country life and his notions of it were rather fanciful, coming mainly from poetry. "And all the air a solemn stillness holds, save where the beetle wheels his droning flight, and drowsy tinklings lull the distant folds." Perhaps James even kept sheep. He imagined the changing of the seasons, Gray's plowman homeward plodding his weary way, the river like Burns' sweet Afton flowing placidly through grassy meadows with overarching trees along its banks. And there would be two young women in the house, Sylvie and Stasha, James's daughters. Perhaps he could go on walks in the forest with them, especially with Sylvie, the quiet and thoughtful one, who probably had more feeling for nature than her prattling and fun-loving sister. Lulled by these soothing thoughts, he dozed off to sleep for a while, then woke again, then napped intermittently with a sound like running water washing softly over his ear.

It was a couple of hours later, he was awake, and the train was rushing over the countryside at great speed. This part of England was pleasant broken land of hills and woods, with farms scattered here and there in the flat land along the railway. The fleeting train made no sound but a kind of muted hush or murmur, most of which probably came from the ventilating system. There was nobody else in the block of four seats with its small table which he was occupying and for all purposes he was alone; the other passengers were bent over, mysteriously murmuring to each other or immersed in their newspapers. He watched the landscape racing by for a while and then the train plunged into a tunnel. The lights in the car went on and for a few seconds he caught a glimpse of himself in the flickering window-glass at his side. He was dressed in the clothes he had put on more or less at random that morning at the Villa Felicity: an old corduroy jacket, khaki pants, a dark purple shirt, and a necktie with a pattern of small pink roses. He was a smallish man with ginger hair, a short soft beard, quiet brown eyes with a nervous electricity to them, and a round body a little inclined to pudginess. Women found him attractive. He found them attractive too, but during his months in the rest home he had almost forgotten what they were like. Now he thought about Sylvie and tried to recall exactly what she looked like and whether she was pretty at all. It was odd that, although at one time he had seen her almost daily in the Boswins' flat in Belgravia, in the intervening months he had lost his mental picture of her, so that he could remember only her qualities, her kindness and understanding, her subdued sense of humor, the funny little pauses she made in speaking. Did she have blue eyes or brown? Did she wear her hair long or short? He couldn't remember. His reflection flickered at him from the window; he smiled at it but succeeded only in making a kind of pallid grimace. Then the train fled out of the tunnel into the sunshine again.

He sighed, stretched, sat up in the seat, and looked out the window again in the hope of catching a glimpse of a tree. There were a few trees going by but they were only a blur; the train destroyed them with its velocity. He craved to get out and touch one, to embrace it. He felt affectionate toward trees and liked having them around him, or being among them. A tree whose hungry mouth is prest, against the earth's sweet flowing breast. God, what a rotten poem, he thought. Still it was true. A tree was a natural thing, it grew, it was made up of cells like people and flowers, and you could feel a kind of kinship with it. Some trees even had a sex life. He greatly preferred trees to the products of modern industrialism, as useful as some of them were. Iron, the iron the train was made of, was not natural; it was something that blackened and sweating men had beaten and burned with fire until it turned black itself and was so hard that even the men who made it could no longer make a dent or imprint in it; it was harder than their own flesh and totally lacking in pity. Chains and shackles were made of iron, as were weapons, bullets, knives, the engines that thundered in factories, and the nails that held Christ to the Cross. As for trains, it wasn't the form of the train but its substance that he disliked; he would willingly and with pleasure have ridden in trains when the carriages were made of wood. Or even in a bronze train, if such a thing could be imagined.

If he could only be more like other people and not dwell so much on these depressing thoughts. He looked around at his fellow passengers, who had scarcely attracted his attention up to this time. Halfway down the car was a young woman with a pair of children, one of whom had decided for some reason to occupy a seat across the aisle from her, so that a lot of banal complaints, touristical remarks, requests for another sweet and so on had to be passed through the air from a considerable distance, making them clearly audible to the other passengers. "Mum can't ah hev just anuvver." "Nao you can't." Farther ahead, a fat woman traveling alone and an Anglican priest with a dignified head of gray hair, the only feature that could be discerned from the rear. In the seat ahead of Bonner was a man with a dog. He hadn't realized you could bring dogs with you into a train. It was an Airedale sort of animal, which yawned at the end of its leash out of sheer boredom. At that moment it turned around and looked over the seat at him with an expression of unmistakable complicity. He had always had a certain rapport with dogs. He understood their language, so to speak, and they understood him. He knew a lot about dogs that nobody else knew. As a matter of fact, he had never had a dog of his own. He had very few possessions except for books and an old Remington typewriter, the tools of his trade as a scholar.

Ahead of him in another seat across the aisle was a cello-colored man, an Indian or a Pakistani from the look of him. He had a large bundle wrapped in paisley cloth on the seat beside him and he kept his hand on it at all times. Perhaps it was his supper, in which case he ate an enormous supper, or possibly it was the dismembered corpse of his wife which he was taking into the country in the hope of finding a place to dispose of it in the woods. Bonner was fond of making up stories about strangers, or rather he wasn't fond of it, he just found himself doing it now and then without being able to stop. The cello-colored man had cut up his wife in the bathtub, in order not to stain the floor, and had intended to boil her to the point where she could be flushed away down the toilet, but found this was impossible with the head. In the end he had just bundled everything into the paisley cloth and got onto the train with it. As Bonner watched, the cello-colored man furtively untied one end of the parcel, reached into it and took out a small object wrapped in waxed paper, removed the paper revealing a piece of pita bread stuffed with vegetables, and began eating it. After that came a stalk of celery. Turning around, he caught Bonner's eye and looked away. Perhaps he thought that although you could take dogs onto trains in this part of the world you could not eat your supper on them. Nobody else was doing this in spite of the little tables provided. From the rear, Bonner watched his maxillary muscles pulse in and out as he chewed.

"Effie stop picking your nose," ordered the harassed mother. In the seat behind the ashamed brown diner was a girl who looked like a student, reading a paperback Thomas Hardy novel, and sitting across from Bonner and one seat ahead of him was a lean bony man wearing a tweed jacket with elbow patches, corduroy breeches, and boots. He seemed to be taking a considerable interest in Bonner and was wearing a look of light amusement.

There was something about him that struck Bonner as vaguely familiar, although he didn't think it was anyone he had ever met before. He had a long face like a hare, with a prominent nose and large protruding eyes. Perhaps it was just that he looked a little like Prince Charles, whose picture he was always seeing in the papers; he had the same air of cheerful and toothy satisfaction with himself. Making up a story about him to pass the time, Bonner decided he was a gamekeeper who had been down to London to visit his unmarried sister, who had a cast in one eye. He knew nothing whatsoever about gamekeepers but didn't see any other reason why someone would go around wearing corduroy breeches and boots. He thought probably the reason he visited his sister in London was to torment her for not being married. It wasn't her fault if she had a cast, the poor creature.

Sitting crossways on the seat with his arm over the back, the man was still staring at him. It was possible he was someone he had met on an earlier trip to Britain, there were hundreds of such people, or someone who had seen his picture on a book jacket. On the other hand he might be just a nosy gamekeeper who liked to stare at people on trains. However he was showing no interest in anyone else in the car, and he seemed more amused than curious. Finally he spoke, in a thin voice with a little drawl in it that Bonner associated with the British landed classes.

"Hallo there. It's funny the people you meet on trains, isn't it. I often wonder who makes these arrangements. Some Supreme Station Master no doubt. Would you believe it, I once sat for a full hour on a train behind a woman before I recognized her as my own sister."

Bonner smiled weakly and said nothing.

"Since fate has thrown us together, we might as well talk. H'mm?"

Not wishing to be impolite, he tried to think of some banality to offer in reply. "So you believe in fate?"

"How can one *not*. Such odd things happen, don't they. Although the poet has it the wrong way around. He says there's a destiny that shapes our ends, rough-hew them how we will. Actually it's fate that rough-hews them, don't you think, and we're only allowed to make the little finishing touches."

He had a somewhat affected way of expressing himself. Perhaps he was a homosexual, he thought, which would account for his striking up an acquaintance so vigorously. Bonner proceeded warily.

"Hamlet. And I believe he said divinity, not fate."

The gamekeeper seemed pleased at finding himself corrected by Bonner. "I can see you're a well-read man."

"I don't think I believe in fate. What we imagine as significance in our lives is probably all just a story that we're telling to ourselves."

"A story? I beg your pardon." He seemed most interested in this theory. He smiled, showing his small sharp teeth like those of a rabbit in a children's book.

"Yes. You see, the life of any one person is pretty much at random. But we're unable to accept our own unimportance in the world, and so we make up stories in which we play the part of hero. We also invent stories about other people, in order to explain their appearance or their actions to ourselves. For example, sitting here on the train just a few minutes ago I made up a story about you."

"You did?"

"Yes, I decided you were a gamekeeper."

"Ha ha! Well, that's not so far off the mark."

"And you had been to London to visit your sister who has a cast in her eye."

"Ah well, that wasn't quite it. Of course, I do have a sister. She used to live in London at one time but she doesn't now. Surely you know who I am?"

Perhaps he *was* someone whose picture he had seen in the paper, an actor or other minor celebrity. "No, I don't know who you are. I haven't the least interest in the subject." He was feeling better now, distracted from his dislike of the train by this stimulating conversation on a subject he had thought a lot about. "Experience is subjective. There's your reality and my reality. It doesn't matter to me whether the stories I make up about you are true to you, as long as they're true to me."

From the seat ahead the man with the dog turned around. "You're American, aren't you?"

"Why do you say that? Because of the way I talk?"

"No, you talk like anybody else. It's on account of your bloody necktie. It looks like a flaming botanical garden, or one of your fruit salads. Believe me I've been to America and I know what I'm talking about."

Farther ahead in the car the cello-colored man turned around to look at Bonner's necktie. He was making a mental note not to buy one like it. It was obviously disadvantageous to go around looking like a flaming botanical garden. At least in England. If he went to America, it might be the kind to wear.

"It's just a floral pattern. Lots of people wear them. It has nothing to do with fruit salad."

The man with the dog turned away, showing the back of his neck with two small red ears. Then he turned around again. "You Americans think you're better than us, don't you?" he said in a voice that could be heard up and down the car.

"We do?"

"I don't ask out of hostility. I just ask as a point of information. I'd like to know whether you think you're better than us. A lot of people think you think that."

Practically all the heads in the car turned at this point. "Well," said Bonner, "I think we're better in some ways and worse in others."

"Better in some ways how?"

"Well, we're open and friendly, for one thing. We speak to people in trains. You English are cold and reserved. You don't do that."

"Oh I say." This seemed to take him aback. He didn't know whether Bonner was joking or not.

"And also your cooking is terrible."

"Our what?"

It was hard to conduct a conversation from seat to seat over the noise of the train, as subdued as it was; it was a low hum that seemed to interfere with the acoustics in some way and had the effect of isolating each passenger from the others. He raised his voice. "COOKING. You overcook your meat and you don't understand vegetables."

The Airedale dog now began to take an interest in the conversation, perhaps because of the mention of meat. He sat up and looked at Bonner over the seat.

"That's nonsense," said the man with the dog. "My aunt is a very good cook. What you've just said is just a lot of bloody clichés. They're banal stereotypes. I don't know where in the hell you get such stuff anyhow. You must get them from those bloody American shows on the telly." He turned away in irritation, showing the backs of his ears again.

"As a matter of fact my aunt is a very good cook too," said the gamekeeper. "You'll enjoy her smoked mackerel pie."

"I don't expect to meet your aunt. You see," he went on, taking up the thread of the discussion at the point where it had been interrupted, "in a sense the world is only our mental construction. There's no real objective world out there that's the same for all of us, or if there is, we can't know about it. Everything that happens is in your mind. You can be happy in a concentration camp or miserable in a palace. It all depends on what kind of world your mind constructs for you."

Now the man with the dog joined in again. He had been following the whole thing, although all that was visible of him was the backs of his ears. He turned around and said, "That's nonsense. I don't believe in messing with your mind. Imagining all sorts of stories going on around you. There's a name for that. It's called paranoia." The cello-colored man, interested in this technical term from the culture he was doing his best to assimilate, turned and looked around. He had a slightly puzzled expression as though he wasn't following it all. "PARANOIA," the man with the dog shouted at him.

"Well, it might be a sort of benevolent paranoia," conceded Bonner. "What's wrong with that?"

"Of course, these things wouldn't really be happening, would they?" said the gamekeeper.

"I beg your pardon?"

He had to raise his voice too. "I say they WOULDN'T REALLY BE HAPPENING. IF IT'S ALL IN YOUR MIND."

Now the student with her Hardy novel turned to stare at them. The sensible thing would be for Bonner to move across the aisle and share the gamekeeper's seat, but he was sitting crossways in a way that took up the whole seat. And anyhow this might seem forward; Bonner didn't want to take the initiative in a relationship

17

that still had many mysteries to it, and a hint of something dubious.

"WHY DON'T YOU COME OVER HERE SO WE CAN TALK?" suggested the gamekeeper in a voice so loud that it made several heads turn again.

"Oh, it's more comfortable when we can both have a seat to ourselves."

"As you like."

"Anyhow we're almost to Waldon. It can't be far now."

"Not very far."

They both fell silent for a while, although the gamekeeper never left off watching him with his interested and lightly entertained expression. He looked out the window. The train was still running briskly through lightly wooded land with a river on one side and some hills on the other. It was dusk now and the lights in the train had come on. The train fled over a level crossing, watched by a boy waiting on a bicycle with one foot on the ground. For an instant he looked directly at Bonner, and this reflected glimpse of himself in the eyes of another reminded him that he was still in the train and had no way to get out. The euphoria induced by the conversation left him and he had a feeling he was going to be unwell.

He turned to the gamekeeper. "What's that river?"

"It's called the Val."

"Do you know this part of Britain well?"

He smiled, showing a glimpse of his small rabbit-teeth again. "Of course. Why should you ask that?"

"I don't know. It's just that . . ."

"Perhaps," suggested the other, "it's because you've not been well, and so you're not thinking very clearly."

Bonner held his gaze for a moment and then looked away. He felt definitely queer, as though small black particles of magnetism were forming and turning in his blood. He hoped he wasn't going to faint as he had once in the British Museum when he felt like this. Somehow he had to get out of this train, which at the moment was still hurtling along the tracks at great speed. He pawed at the window in the totally irrational hope of opening it, then looked around for the emergency stop lever. There was a fine for pulling it without a cause, a hundred pounds he thought, but he would gladly pay it if it would stop the train for only a few moments so he could get out of it. His pulse pounded. He half rose from his seat, groped around aimlessly, and then fell back onto it again. He glanced at the gamekeeper to see if he had noticed, but he was calmly looking out the window on the other side.

There was no sign of Waldon yet. The train was running at high speed along the Val, then it swayed as it began a broad curve to the left toward a bridge up ahead. The brakes gripped underneath, a little more violently than usual, and then all at once there was a screech, a lurch, and a great bumping and slamming that went on for some time. Everything in the car seemed to rise up like leaves in a whirlwind; the lights flickered and then went out. Bonner's heart leaped and flapped in terror and he had no idea what was happening except that he was surrounded by confusion, the yelping and screaming of the other passengers, and luggage falling down from overhead.

Wedged in his seat by the violent motion, he endeavored to free himself. The mother several seats ahead got up and moved to attend to her child across the aisle, then turned and fell heavily against the seat. Her legs flew into the air and he caught a glimpse of her underwear before she disappeared from sight. The Airedale yelped, fell into the aisle, and gazed at Bonner with a deeply penetrating, sorrowful look. The gamekeeper had disappeared totally down into his seat except for the top of his head.

The bumping gradually slowed, like a great ritardando at the end of a symphony, and the train came to a stop tilted over at a sick angle to the right. A long split had opened in the metal roof over Bonner's head, admitting a grayish sliver of light. Several windows were cracked and a good deal of luggage had fallen down from the racks overhead. It was suddenly quiet except for the sound of moaning.

There was a gust of fresh air from the opening over his head. His terror of a moment before was replaced by a burst of joy. It was clear that some of the other passengers were injured (he could still hear moans) but he could think of nothing except that the open air lay only a few feet from him and it was now possible for him to get to it, out of the train with its confining steel walls which thrummed gently and silently, exuding their waves of magnetism. He found his own suitcase and jerked it down from the rack. Holding it in one hand, he attempted to make his way down the aisle toward the door at the end. The aisle was full of luggage at all angles and the mother was lying in it whimpering with her two children bent over her. Her leg was at an odd angle impossible for the human anatomy to assume. With as much care as he could muster he stepped over her, his suitcase knocking against one of the children.

The cello-colored man was indignant. "Sir, can you not see that the lady is hurt?" He was still clutching his paisley bundle and gave the effect that he was leaning thirty degrees from the vertical, no doubt some national form he had of transcending gravity. He was fierce with righteousness. It was a pretty show, Bonner thought, for a man that had tried to boil his wife's head. "Sir, you are no gentleman from your behavior."

The man with the dog now joined in. "Here, what in blazes do you think you're doing? Stop treading on that woman and sit back down or I'll pop you one." He too was standing at a dizzy angle to the vertical. Bonner now realized that this was because the whole train and everybody in it was tilted at this angle to one side.

"Let me by please. I have to get out."

The mother moaned softly. The older child said, "It's all right, Mum, they'll get a doctor."

With a final effort Bonner managed to get clear of the woman lying under his feet. He lurched on down the aisle, pushing the cello-colored man out of his way, followed by a chorus of expostulations and indignant comments.

"Did you ever see the like."

"He's a Yank," said someone by way of explanation.

"He's a flaming egotist is what he is. He needs a pop in the eye."

"Somebody stop him."

"I'll stop him, proper. Here, you."

He reached the end of the car, leaving the chorus of condemnation behind. What he feared most was that the door of the carriage might have been jammed by the accident so that it wouldn't open. As a matter of fact it was just the opposite; the shock of the derailing had flung it open and it was hanging down like a broken bird's wing. He jumped down with his suitcase, striking the ground a little more violently than he had expected. People were now trickling out of the train onto the roadbed. Some of the carriages were still upright, but one up ahead was lying on its side. There was a confused mumble of voices, a kind of insect buzzing, curiously calm. Holding his suitcase, he strode rapidly across the roadbed and scrambled up an embankment into the meadow.

It would be dark in a half an hour or so; the sun had set and there was a rusty glow staining the lower edges of the clouds to the west. He was walking along a ledge of grassy ground a few feet higher than the tracks. Behind him the railway line made a long curve to the left and crossed the Val on a concrete bridge. The derailed train was lying in fragments on the curve, like a snake that somebody had chopped up. Beyond the bridge the river meandered on through a swampy bottomland until it disappeared in a clump of woods. Across the river there were more meadows, stretching away to a set of lumpish shapes and tiny points of light on the horizon that must be Waldon, the county town and a good-sized industrial center. On his side of the river there was a narrow ledge of meadow a few hundred yards wide, then the land sloped up sharply into the hills. This high land above was thickly wooded; in the failing light it gave the impression of a black and impenetrable forest. Along the Val, and over the meadow that ran along its bank, a few lights had come on. The air was chill and fresh.

He continued on across the meadow in the direction of the lights. He felt a keen uplifting, an exultation, a sense of joy and release. At the same time he felt a slight sense of guilt which he couldn't quite account for; in fact he couldn't account for either of these two conflicting emotions. The guilt was not on account of abandoning the train or of the woman with the broken leg he had so carefully stepped over. It was perhaps merely a sense of guilt at feeling so happy when he didn't know why. It swarmed in him like wine and made his lungs tingle. He was keenly aware of every sensation, every corpuscle that pulsed in his body, every detail of the unknown and darkening landscape around him. Through his shoes he could feel each tiny blade of the grass he walked on. His vision was abnormally acute. On the slope of the meadow ahead of him a shape crossed in the twilight, undulating a little as though it was descending into hollows and then emerging again. It gave the impression of a doll, a figure in a shooting gallery, an undersized man wearing a queer hat and a coat with floating tails. It was perhaps only an animal, a badger or a fox, distorted by some trick of the light. Bonner was delighted with all this. He felt as though in escaping from the train he had entered a realm of friendly darkness, a kingdom of magic where all kinds of good things might happen to him and there would be many other diverting visions of this sort. The moving shape ahead was no longer visible; perhaps it had vanished into the trees. The darkness around him winked with diamonds.

He was by no means sure where he was going, although he had some vague notion of the directions. The house of his Anglo-American friends the Boswins lay somewhere along the river. There was a village near it called Pense Coombe, and the whole business was not very far from Waldon. In fact the derailing of the train had probably left him nearer to the house than it would have been if it had brought him to the Waldon station. To go from the house to the village you went along the river to a place where a canal intersected it. This much he had been told. The lights ahead were perhaps those of the village, or of the house itself. There wouldn't be any difficulty. He could ask someone. The Boswins might be worried about him when he was late; they had arranged that he would telephone from the station. Their worry didn't trouble him, since it was groundless after all and he was perfectly safe. It would even be fun to surprise them, walking in along the river in this way with his suitcase.

After going on for another quarter of a mile he began to feel that he was perhaps lost. There was no moon; a thin whitish starlight illuminated the meadow around him. He hadn't come to the house and the lights ahead seemed no nearer, although they had slowly drawn apart from one another so that they no longer provided any kind of precise goal to walk toward. He had lost sight of the river; it was somewhere over to his left, but its meander had taken it away from the meadow for a stretch and there was nothing around him to give any indication of the direction he ought to take. He wasn't bothered by this either; he would surely find the house sooner or later, or make his way into the village where he could phone the Boswins, and meanwhile he was enjoying himself and still filled with this curious well-being that tickled in the particles of his blood.

Without knowing exactly when it had happened he found there was a path under his feet. In his abnormal sensitivity he detected through his shoes that he was no longer walking on grass but on a ribbon of beaten earth, a path so narrow that the ferns and bracken brushed against his ankles on both sides. If there was a path it ought to lead somewhere, probably to a place of human habitation. He went on along it, guiding himself by the sensations of vegetation brushing against his ankles. Presently he caught sight of another creature taking form in the darkness ahead of him, although this one was unmistakably not an animal in a funny hat. It was a young woman, who had been coming toward him along the path, and had now stopped at a point where a pair of trees formed a kind of sylvan gateway marking the place where a hedge crossed the meadow. She stopped, resting her hand on the tree.

She seemed to be wearing a curious costume, a kind of flimsy frock that came to her ankles. No doubt it was something the locals wore in this part of the world. Under it her feet were bare. She had a shawl of some sort around her shoulders. In the milky starlight he could make out her features well enough to see that she was smiling. As he approached her she did an unexpected thing. She slipped abruptly away from the gate of trees and darted out over the meadow, trailing the shawl after her. There she stopped. Her smile had not changed. Adjusting the shawl over her shoulders again, she gazed at him fixedly, but without alarm and without real curiosity, in the way that a tame animal will gaze at a human who, it is sure, will cause it no harm.

I beg your pardon.

As well as he could see in the starlight she seemed not so much fearful as playfully unwilling to come any closer. He saw now that she was smaller than he had thought. Perhaps she was only a child. Half-reflexively he looked for signs of breasts, but the loose dress revealed nothing. She was quite pretty; there was a fragility to her, a birdlike charm that was enhanced by her flighty, playful, mocking manner. He now detected a flaw; her limbs were somewhat shorter than usual, her torso the normal size. It was these short arms and legs that had made her seem small.

Could you tell me how to get to Byrd Mill?

His own voice rang curiously in the starlight, as though he was hearing it in his head rather than in the outside air.

Ah, the Mill. You're bringing corn to grind? She laughed, looking at the suitcase in his hand. Other folk live there now. They don't grind corn anymore.

He smiled back at her. The thought struck him that she was perhaps mentally retarded. It was consistent with the short limbs and the fixed smile. There was something artificial and contrived about her archaic turn of language; she gave the impression that she could speak like anyone else if she chose but spoke in this folk-loric way as a game, or as though she were acting a part in a play.

Yes, I know. They're friends of mine.

This made her laugh again.

Friends?

Yes, friends of mine. She was definitely an idiot, but she seemed to be a harmless one and he was enjoying the encounter. You see, my train had an accident, and so I'm going on foot to the Mill.

Bringing your corn in your bag.

Bringing my corn in my bag, and I hope you can tell me how to get there, because I'm already late for supper and my friends will be worried about me.

She waited for a long moment. Then she said crisply, as though she were reciting, dropping her smile, There's a path off there toward the Val. She pointed behind her, at the other side of the hedge. When you come to the water, turn and go along it until you come to the footbridge across the weir. Then you cross it to the Mill, but don't fall in.

I won't. Do you come from the village?

From the Coombe? Oh no. She laughed again. You won't see the likes of us there. Except late at night when everyone's asleep. Are you . . . She hesitated again. Are you Bonner?

You've heard of me?

Instead of answering, she said, It's a nice name. It sounds like a bell.

Bong, bong. I'll leave you now. Thanks for the directions.

When he started toward the gate of trees, this brought him a little closer to her, and she moved swiftly back. She was almost invisible now in the lactic darkness.

Bonner.

He heard her laugh again. She was probably someone who did housework for the Boswins, he thought, or lived nearby and had somehow heard he was coming.

What's your name, by the way?

She had vanished. He went through the gate of trees and turned left along the path to the river, feeling thoroughly pleased by this encounter. The idea occurred to him that it might be a good idea not to tell the Boswins about it, at least for the moment.

The creature might be interesting to cultivate. Was this a lustful thought? He thought not. Why then didn't he want to tell the Boswins about her? As frequently happened, he was not quite sure about his motives. He only knew that he was in excellent humor and that whatever it was that pulsed in him was a honey very like that of love. He heard the river before he saw it. Along its bank, as promised, was a path that led to a louder sound of plashing, the water falling with perseverance over the ancient and disused weir. Across the footbridge he saw the brightly lighted windows of the house.

Two

It was a little after nine o'clock on a pleasant summer day, and James was having breakfast in the morning room with Sylvie and Stasha. Tita had not come down yet, and her brother Drood had gone for a walk. The morning room was on the river side of the house, which was the back really, although it was the side that had the best view and where they spent most of their time. The large paned windows looked out onto an expanse of lawn scattered with beeches and sycamores running down to the Val. To the right you could catch a glimpse of the Mill Cottage, an old stone building with two small narrow windows like eyes. Across the Val there was a stretch of meadow, then the land rose up into some low grassy hills which almost immediately became thickly wooded. This was Waldon Forest, still in its unspoiled state even though it was only a few miles from a good-sized industrial town, rescued from exploitation by a far-sighted National Trust. There was only one road into it and that was on the other side of the hills, invisible from the windows of the morning room. The windows looked out across the river onto a forest that might have been that of a pristine and virginal England before the age of factories and cities. They, in the family, could reach it easily by crossing the footbridge over the weir and walking for ten minutes or so across the meadow. Since there was no road into it on this side, the forest was for all practical purposes a part of their land. Cassie, the unmarried aunt of Tita and Drood, often walked there, carrying her stick and coming back with a wildflower or a pocketful of mushrooms. James was too busy with his affairs to have much time for walks, and Drood kept his habits to himself. Since he often disappeared from the house on foot for long periods of time, and since there was no place else to walk except into the village a mile or so down the river, it was possible that he spent a good deal of time in the forest. There was a National Trust keeper but he, for the most part, kept to the public house in Pense Coombe, where he regaled the locals with tales of the improbable fauna to be found in the depths of the forest. These stories were always good for a drink. The pub was called the Arm & Hammer. But back to the house and the gentlefolk.

James Boswin was a lean and wiry man with an angular smile and a network of fine red veins on his face. He might have been taken for English until he began talking and revealed his flat Philadelphia accent; he had been born in Pennsylvania and spent most of his life in America managing a chain of small-town newspapers which he had inherited from his father. A few years ago he had retired from this business and moved to Britain with his English wife and his two daughters, first to London and then to Waldshire, to the house of his wife's family the Cromlechs. The arrangements for this move involved his transfusing a good many American dollars into the Cromlech family fortunes, which were on the decline, with the result that James ended up in possession of the eighteenth-century house with its extensive grounds and outbuildings. Since he had moved to Byrd Mill he had made a good many improvements to the house and grounds and was thoroughly enjoying his new life. In only a few short months he had succeeded in converting himself, at least in his own mind, into a thorough-going English country gentleman. In this new life he modeled himself on the English as much as he could, from the routine of meals he established in the house down to the details of his dress. This morning, at breakfast with his daughters in the morning room, he was wearing a smoking-jacket, flannel trousers, and a scarf knotted neatly in the open collar of his shirt.

Bonner, who had arrived the night before, was not yet up, and James and the girls were talking about him and also about an article in the Waldon Blade which James had open on the large oaken table in front of him.

"What did he say when he came in? The whole thing is very queer. If he's expected at a certain hour he could at least phone. He was going to call from the station." James had spent the evening in Waldon, at a meeting of the county council at which the Byrd Mill dairy was discussed. He didn't want to go on with the dairy, since there were only six cows and it was a nuisance taking care of them, but the council said that if they didn't have a dairy the property wouldn't be a farm and would lose the tax advantages enjoyed by agricultural enterprises. "And when I got back at eleven he had already gone to bed. And none of you seems to have got a straight story out of him about what happened."

"Oh, he had nothing much to say. You know how he is. He speaks so queerly. He said the train stopped and wouldn't go on, so he took his suitcase and walked."

"Someone must have given him a ride."

"Well," said Stasha, "he didn't come in along the road. He came through the meadow and crossed over the weir. I saw him."

"He always does these extravagant things and then everyone apologizes for him by saying that he's not well. I think it's nonsense about his being ill. He's always been perfectly reasonable when I've talked to him. He's a professor, a brilliant man. He has an international reputation as a medievalist. He's a pleasant person to talk to. He's just got it into his head that there's something interesting about behaving in bizarre ways and pretending that he can detect iron inside walls. Bonner would be perfectly all right if he would just leave his mind alone and behave a little more like everyone else."

"But we wouldn't want him like everybody else, would we?"

Stasha said, "I could just eat him up. When I saw his little beard and his fuzzy head coming across the footbridge. How lucky you are to have got him, Sylvie."

"Oh, I haven't got him exactly. I'm not sure Bonner is the sort that can be got, really. I'm not sure what you mean by got."

"Oh, he likes you better. I'm sure of that."

"It's no doubt just the ancient custom that the elder daughter has to be courted first," said James. "You can read about it in Jane Austen. If a man courts the younger daughter first, he's behaving like a cad."

James half believed in things like this. Over the years he had made himself into an expert on British civilization and customs. No one was quite sure whether he had a sense of humor or not. If he did, then remarks like this might be taken as ironic. If not, then he really believed them. Probably it was a little of both. He went on in a good humor, "If you want him, Sylvie, I'll get him. I don't seé why you can't do a little bit for yourself once in a while. We've known him for over a year after all. He was always hanging around the flat in London. A young woman needs to throw a hint in a man's way, if the idea doesn't occur to him," he said, still thinking of Jane Austen.

"Oh good heavens. What am I supposed to do?"

"Cast shy glances at him from under your parasol," said Stasha. "Send him forbidden notes by the maids. Let him catch a glimpse of your bloomers while playing croquet."

"I don't have a parasol," sighed Sylvie. "I don't wear bloomers. I'm not sure Bonner's interested in that sort of thing anyhow."

"They all are."

"Neither of you is taking this seriously," said James. He contemplated his daughters, as he always did at the ritual of breakfast, with a pleasant sense of possession, of intimacy, and yet the slight bafflement of a man who does not entirely understand women even when he has been living with them for most of a lifetime. The girls seemed to have little to do, in their appearance and temperament, either with him or with Tita, and moreover they were so different from each other in every way that it was hard to believe they had the same parents. Sylvie, the elder, was an ethereal wisp of a creature, always deep in her private thoughts. Her figure was sparse and flat-chested; in costume she might have been taken for one of those boy-actors who play girls in Shakespeare's plays. Natalia, called Stasha in the family, was a constant and irreverent prattler, with a voluptuous body which she flaunted, maliciously but innocently as it were, like a child brandishing a toy. Sylvie, who was fond of poetry and a talented musician, had graduated in English from the University of Pennsylvania. Stasha had taken courses in theater arts for two years and then quit at the time they had left for England, bored with studies. Whatever was to become of them, he wondered. Having paid for their scarlet fever and whooping cough, given them French lessons, straightened their teeth, and seen to their education, he was evidently now called upon to find them husbands, starting with Sylvie according to the principle elucidated in Jane Austen's novels.

"Bonner's always been fond of you both, especially Sylvie. And now he's going to be living in the same house with you. You have a good chance to—become better acquainted with him—to show yourselves at your best advantage—you know perfectly well what

I'm talking about. After all, when a man is sleeping under the same roof with a pair of attractive young women for months. I wish he'd stayed up last night until I got home; I was meaning to have a talk with him. He must have said something about the derailing," he went on, reverting to Bonner's deliberately bizarre behavior. "How on earth can a train derail itself in this day and age anyhow. The Blade said something about a person on the tracks. Where is that article anyhow?"

But Stasha had taken the paper before he was finished with it, a practice that annoyed him, and was looking at it at her place across the table.

"Service on the London to Waldon line of British Rail"—she had a gift for mimicry and fell effortlessly into the voice of a BBC announcer—"was interrupted for over five hours on Wednesday evening owing to the derailing of a train on a curve south of New Bridge, Waldshire. Although there were no fatalities, there were a number of injuries in the accident. Passenger Cecily Blaine, 23, was admitted to King Edward VII Hospital in Waldon for treatment of a broken leg. She is said to be in excellent condition and has given birth in hospital to three children and a healthy male orangutan."

"Oh, let me read it." Sylvie attempted to take the paper from her.

She snatched it away from her sister and went on. "Investigators are still uncertain as to the cause of the derailment. A spokesman explained that British Rail are still uncertain what makes trains run. The engine driver, Mr. William Lacey, 62, of Maidenhead—"

"What an old-fashioned expression, engine driver."

"That's what they're called," said James. "It's the official designation of British Rail."

" . . . of Maidenhead, what a ridiculous name for a town, stated that he was proceeding normally when, coming around the turn about three miles south of Waldon, he caught sight of a small man on the tracks ahead and braked violently to stop the train. Police carried out a search for the trespasser on the roadway, but this was abandoned when it turned up no trace. British Rail authorities and the police have so far found no fault with Mr. Lacey on account of the accident. A spokesman explained that it is quite customary to employ victims of senile dementia as engine drivers."

"Why on earth should he say a small man?"

"Perhaps he meant a child."

"Why didn't he say so then?"

"Well, he was a bit rattled. Wouldn't you be if you had just derailed a train with several hundred people on it on account of a mirage on the tracks."

"The Blade didn't say it was a mirage. They just said the police couldn't find anyone."

"It was probably Bonner himself. Got out of the train and ran ahead and derailed it, just for a lark."

"James, will you stop it about Bonner."

"Oh, I have a great admiration for Bonner. He just does rather bizarre things now and then, that's all."

"Why don't you do something bizarre just once, James. You're so predictable. Like a figure in a Swiss clock. You come out daily and announce the hours, then you disappear into your study again. Good morning, Tita dear."

The girls had been trained to call their parents by their first names. James would rather have been called Father, or perhaps Pater, since he was such a thorough-going Anglophile. It was Tita who had decided they were all to behave in this way like a family out of Noel Coward. As tots in their cradles in their Philadelphia home, barely able to lisp, the girls had called their parents Tita and James. Tita served herself smoked haddock, toast, and tea from the sideboard and sat down without a word. She was a nocturnal creature, in her own view of herself, and didn't function very well in the morning. Her eyelids, which were unusually large, were painted a grayish silver. Her wrapper was oriental and polychrome. Even in the morning she wore small diamonds in her ear-lobes. In a characteristic gesture she reached up to touch behind both ears simultaneously to verify that the jewels were still there and firmly screwed into place. Then she began picking at her breakfast.

"Any sign of Bonner getting up?" James asked her. "It's almost ten."

"I don't prowl around the doors of sleeping male guests."

"Perhaps you ought to," he said heartily. "Give you something to do, and it'd be entertaining for them. What they expect from British country life."

"Does the paper say anything about Bonner's accident?"

"Yes it does. It says a lady's leg was broken, and the whole thing was caused by a gremlin on the tracks."

"Stasha, will you please give me back that paper? I can't start the day off right if I don't have the Blade with my breakfast. Are you going to finish reading the story, or do I have to come across the table and commit an act of violence against you?"

"Oh, that *would* be out of character. Investigation into the incident is continuing," Stasha went on. "In the meantime Mr. Lacey, the engine driver, has been temporarily suspended from his duties and set to picking lint in Paddington Station for bandages of the injured passengers."

"Why should they suspend him from his duties if he wasn't at fault?"

"Perhaps it wasn't because of the accident but on account of his seeing gremlins. Ah, here he is. Good morning, Bonner."

Bonner stood awkwardly at the entrance to the room. He had never been in the house before and wasn't sure whether he was supposed to sit down at the table or go directly to help himself at the sideboard.

"Coffee or tea, Bonner?"

"It really doesn't matter."

"We have both."

"Coffee then."

"I'll go make it," said Sylvie swiftly. "There's some in the kitchen."

Bonner was appalled at what he had said. It was a little awkward anyhow accepting the Boswins' hospitality at a time when everybody knew he was not well and had just come from a rest home. Above all he wanted to be inconspicuous and not put anybody to trouble. Now it seemed his chance remark was causing Sylvie to leave the room and do something special for him, something that nobody else in the family required. "Tea, tea," he said hastily. "Please don't bother. Either will do."

"You tell us about the accident to the train, Bonner," said James. "I can't get a straight story out of anybody about what happened. I wasn't here last night when you came in. There's a story in the local paper about it but Stasha won't let me see it. She mixed it all up with her schoolgirl jokes and I can't make head nor tail out of it."

"Oh, I . . ." Finding the family together at the breakfast table, he had forgotten that he hadn't paid his respects to James the night before. "How do you do, James. It's good to see you again."

He offered his hand; James half rose, holding his napkin, and took it briefly. Bonner always found James an attractive person and yet a little bit intimidating. His angular and ironic smile was friendly enough when he wanted it to be, but it could also indicate a sarcastic displeasure when things weren't done his way. When he had known him in London he had always dressed formally, in gray suits from Savile Row and narrow ties. But he had been transformed by his move to the country, as though he had changed costume for the second act of a play, and was now wearing a smoking-jacket and a foulard knotted in the open collar of his shirt. He said in his flat Pennsylvania voice, "You don't have to be so darned formal. You're one of the family almost."

"James," said Tita, "don't exaggerate. Bonner is a valued family friend. I wouldn't say he is a member of the family."

"I'm so very grateful for the distinction," said Bonner.

"Well, don't fly off the handle," said James. "You are practically a member of the family. We knew you so well in London. We want you to feel welcome here and stay as long as you want. Make the house your own. You'll find it's quite comfortable. If there's anything special you require in the way of meals or anything else just let us know." After having complained to the others earlier about Bonner's eccentricities, now he was all solicitousness and hospitality. He made up for it in this way. He was a fair-minded man and besides he was genuinely fond of Bonner.

"I don't require anything special. Please, I—"

"You haven't told us what happened about the train."

"Didn't I last night?"

"I wasn't here last night," said James patiently. "According to the girls, you just said the train stopped so you got off and walked."

"Well, I was very tired when I got here. The thing went off the rails and came to a stop. Since it didn't seem very likely that it would be going on any further, I got out and walked the rest of the way to the house."

"How on earth did you find it?"

"Oh, I had a general idea. And I asked someone."

"The paper says a lady broke her leg."

"Yes, I had to step over her to get out."

"James says," put in Tita maliciously, "that you probably caused the accident yourself."

"I very likely did. I feel guilty about all sorts of things."

He caught Sylvie's eye and they both smiled. Then he looked at her again, sitting across from him in a white summer dress that left the bones of her throat bare. He had lost his visual image of her in the months since he had seen her, but now it all came back in a flash. In London her thin sort of beauty had always seemed to him childish and wispy, but she seemed to have matured prodigiously since the family moved to the country. There was a new presence and assurance about her, a sense of self, of being her own person. She said, "Help yourself at the sideboard, Bonner."

He got some eggs, a kipper, and toast and marmalade for himself and sat down. He didn't really want a heavy English breakfast, but it was what they were all having and he didn't want to seem ungrateful for their hospitality. The house was certainly a pleasant place. The morning room was light and cheerful, with skyblue opaline walls and white boiseries. He was on the side of the table that faced toward the windows with their view of the river and the forest. Some white fluffy clouds that had evidently escaped from a painting by Rubens were piled up to the east, waiting for a pink overweight lady to arrange herself in front of them. The lawn that ran down to the Val was an intense green, and in the morning sunlight the trees cast a dappled light onto it. Around the edges of the lawn were some statues of classical or pastoral subjects, much worn by the elements. The sooty patches on the marble were only partly washed off by the rain. Here and there an eye was crumbled or an ear worn away. A light mist lay along the water. Across the river he saw a man coming slowly down the slope over the broad expanse of meadow. He was still a good distance away and he could make out nothing of his details. Beyond was the forest where, as he had earlier imagined on the train, he could go for walks with the girls, or with Sylvie alone. When he turned away from the window he found her eyes were still fixed on him. She said, "It's good to have you here, Bonner."

A little rush of attraction filled him, of desire, although it was too pure to be described exactly by that term. Pretending to eat his kipper, he secretly contemplated her honey-colored and silky, somewhat sparse straight hair, which she wore tied with a black velvet ribbon at the back. There was a nacreous elegance about her, he now saw, that stirred in him the admiration you might feel for a priceless work of art, a Vermeer or a Parthenon fragment, or one of those objects in nature that closely simulate works of art; a rare seashell, porcelain-white on the outside with orifices of pink— here his desire did become physical, quite independently of his will, and his napkin stirred in his lap. He blushed and drank his tea.

He looked out the window at the pleasant view again. The man advancing across the meadow had almost reached the weir now and was coming along the path as though he meant to cross on the footbridge. He was wearing corduroy breeches, a tweed jacket with patches on the elbows, and boots. With a little shock Bonner recognized the man he had talked to on the train. Somehow he got it into his head that the gamekeeper had escaped from the train too, but there had been some difficulty, so he had only got here at ten o'clock in the morning. He had followed Bonner because he wanted to go on with their conversation about fate, story-telling, and the subjectivism of our perceptions of the external world.

He came across the footbridge and strode negligently up the lawn toward the house as though he owned the place. The others, who could see him clearly through the window, hardly paid any attention. Bonner now saw that he was carrying a stick, a gnarled oak-burl. To his knowledge he hadn't had that on the train. Bonner had an impulse to flee from him, or to go out on the lawn and prevent him from coming into the house.

Having crossed the lawn, the man disappeared and evidently entered the door of a kind of orangery at the right. He reappeared in the door of the morning room.

"Hello, Drood. Have you breakfasted yet? Have a kipper. There's still one left."

"Oh, I had a crust before I left. I don't require much."

"You're Drood?"

"Oh, I forgot. You two haven't met," said Sylvie.

"Oh yes. We met on the train," said Drood, smiling to show his small neat hare-teeth. "How strange. How bizarre. And what a coincidence."

"That's a line from a play by Ionesco."

"Only a B, Professor, unless you can name the play."

"I believe it's *The Bald Soprano*."

Drood didn't go on to give him the promised A. He said, "Bonner and I had a delightful conversation which whiled away the tedious train journey. Unfortunately it was interrupted by a pest with an Airedale, and then by the train going off the rails."

"Why didn't you identify yourself?" said Bonner irritably.

"I thought you recognized me, at first. Then when I saw you didn't I didn't want to embarrass you."

"How could I recognize you if I've never met you."

"On the train?" frowned James. "What is this all about?"

"I just went down to London in the morning. I had some business to attend to. As it happened, I came back on the same train as Bonner."

No one in the house had missed him. Drood sometimes disappeared from the house for days at a time, without taking a bag with him or telling anyone where he was going. Tita believed he had a mistress somewhere, in Waldon or in London. As for James, he doubted whether Drood was capable of having a mistress.

"What then is your account of the incident that happened to the train?" he asked him a little stiffly.

"Oh, nothing much. The train went off the rails while going around a curve. I managed to get jammed under a seat and was having difficulty extricating myself, so I didn't say goodbye to Bonner when he left. I did notice that he stepped on an injured woman on his way out. When we finally got out of the train, everyone stood about on the rails talking about it for an hour or so, and then British Rail sent some coaches to take us in to Waldon. It was all very efficient. We were treated to free cocoa and buns in the station buffet. Then I walked home from the Waldon station as I often do."

"Free cocoa and buns. You see Bonner, you should have stayed with the others."

"I didn't step on her. I stepped carefully over her. I believe I did hit one of the children with the suitcase."

"Children?"

"Oh yes, she was a mother and the whole business."

"How thoughtless of you, Bonner."

"That's exactly the word," he conceded.

"I still don't feel that this whole thing makes sense," said James. "Why didn't you come along in the coach with the others,

Bonner? And it strains belief a little that you were both on the same train and in the same car. What did you say you had gone down to London for, Drood?"

"I didn't say. What is it you do all day in your study, James?"

"I'm sure you wouldn't be interested in what I do in the study. I have a lot of details to attend to. Managing the house, and telephoning to America."

"I think it's perfectly natural that Drood and I were on the same train," said Bonner. For some reason he felt a kind of complicity with Drood, a need to defend their odd way of meeting and the *odi-et-amo* nature of their relationship, if that was what it was. "We were both in London, and there's only one train to Waldon in the afternoon. As for being in the same car, that's the part of it that was written by Ionesco."

As a matter of fact, he powerfully shared James's curiosity. The figure of Drood interested him, not for what lay on the surface but for the mysteries he seemed to conceal; there was something he knew, Bonner sensed, something harmless but interesting and infinitely complex, perhaps something about the family or about Bonner himself. It lay just behind the little smile that showed his sharp neat teeth, behind his good-natured pretence of naivete and chumminess. Then a revelation struck him. He saw now that there was a strong family resemblance shared by all the Cromlechs. It had never before occurred to him that Sylvie and Stasha resembled each other, since their types were so different. But now with their uncle as a common denominator, so to speak, the familiar pattern could be clearly seen. In the case of Sylvie, the resemblance to hares took the form of a shy but resolute resemblance to Virginia Woolf, with her long chin, her large eyes, and her clear and serene brow. It was there again in Stasha's wiggly mouth and its grooved upper lip, her protuberant eyes, her skittishness of a woodland creature who at any moment was about to scuttle away and induce pursuit. Of course, the girls were half Boswin. In Tita, who was Drood's sister and pure Cromlech, the angles and knobs had been worn away by some erosive process like the ones that had blasted the statues on the lawn, leaving the details blurred except for the eyes, which had resisted and remained at the original level, slightly popped. Drood was the archetype, the mold from which the others had been cast.

Sylvie caught his eye again. "You're not eating much, Bonner."

He had hardly touched his kipper or the toast and marmalade. "Oh, I'm not really very hungry."

She was kind and solicitous, determined to be the perfect hostess, since James was so brusque and Tita downright rude.

"Does the tableware bother you?"

"I beg your pardon?"

"The knives, forks, and spoons."

"Oh no. They're silver."

"Can you be sure?"

"Oh yes. If they were iron I'd know it immediately."

"Let's try. Stasha, cover his eyes."

Stasha got up and came to him at his place at the table. He felt a coolness slipping over his eyes and penetrating into the green shadowy depth of his mind, and at the same time he heard Sylvie leave the room and then return. Now she was approaching the table.

"Is this iron or silver?"

"Don't, please." He tried to pull Stasha's hands away.

"Which?"

"It's iron." He pulled the hands away from his eyes and saw Sylvie holding out to him a carving knife with a gleaming steel blade. He got up from the table and stood trembling lightly, holding his napkin.

"Oh, I'm sorry. I didn't know it would bother you so much. Can you find iron if it's hidden?"

"Of course."

He felt uncomfortable and wished she would leave off. But Sylvie, who had been so solicitous only a few moments before, was carried away now with the fun of the game. When the two sisters were together a malicious streak often showed in them. "Stasha, you take him out into the hall."

When the two were gone from the room she looked around, considered the sideboard and the armchairs against the wall, then lifted the tablecloth and put the knife in a drawer of the table. "Now bring him back in again, Stasha."

Stasha came into the room with Bonner following her.

"What am I to do?"

"Where's the knife?"

"It's in this room?"

"Yes."

He moved to the center of the room, sensing a dark conelike power radiating to him from the table. He felt an intense discomfort. Clenching his teeth and half shutting his eyes, he hardened his will against the adversary. He advanced a few more paces toward the table, struggling in his inner mind against the sense of encroaching blackness that was invading him.

There was a clang and a tinkle like shattering glass that made them all jump. Sylvie lifted the cloth, opened the drawer, and took out the knife with both hands. The blade was broken off cleanly just by the handle; on the two fractured ends the bare metal gleamed brightly.

She put the two pieces away in the sideboard. She seemed a little shaken.

James looked around at the others in the room. The network of red veins on his face stood out sharply. After a moment he said, "Which one of you is responsible for this trick?"

No one replied.

"Is this one of your jokes, Stasha?"

"Me? I wasn't anywhere near the thing."

"That's not what I asked."

There was a silence. After a while he said, "It's an old knife. It probably had some flaw in it. One of you must have kicked the table with your knee." When no one said anything he added, "It might have been internally stressed all the time. Some knives aren't properly annealed. And then some slight atmospheric change might have set it off."

"That's certainly likely," said Drood.

"It's not likely, but it's the only explanation."

"I think Bonner broke it with his mind," said Sylvie.

James considered this theory skeptically. The red veins on his face had subsided, but he was still angry. He resumed his thin angular smile. "He'd probably like us to think so. Bonner, you're our guest and we're happy to have you in the house, but I wish you would stop deliberately behaving like a cuckoo."

Bonner felt pleased with himself. With a kind of elation he inwardly treasured this minor triumph over the incubus that had haunted him for so many months. His mind wasn't like other people's; this was clear, and so far it had been a defect. But now he found he could do things with his mind that other people couldn't.

He got up from the table, setting down his napkin, and said with aplomb, "James, I'll pay for the knife."

"Oh, don't be ridiculous. You're our guest."

"I am not a cuckoo, James."

"Oh, it's just an expression. For God's sake don't be so darned touchy," he said jovially. He put his arm around him. "Come on, I'll show you around the place."

Three

They started with the kitchen, presided over by a certain Rhondda, who served as cook, housekeeper, and maid-of-all-work. The only other domestic, explained James, was Miles, who lived in the former mews over the garage and took care of the cars, in addition to a little gardening and anything else of a handyman nature that was necessary. The kitchen, a large whitewashed room with a high ceiling, was full of hanging onions and burnished copper pans. It was scrupulously clean and neat. Rhondda was a dour woman of perhaps forty with a gypsy look to her, a little haggard. She watched in dark silence as James explained that the copper pans were authentic from the eighteenth century and had been meticulously restored to their original condition. "If you think it's easy finding a tinker these days," he said with heavy satisfaction.

Perhaps Rhondda's taciturnity was connected with the fact that it was not really very much fun cooking in pans from the eighteenth century. They left her and went on to the dining room, which had paneled walls and was full of heavy dark Victorian furniture. There was an ornate Murano chandelier over the table, reflecting like diamonds in the polished mahogany surface. The room was quiet and smelled of linen and floor wax. Here the family took their meals in the winter; in the summer the morning room was more pleasant. They left the dining room and went on into the hall beyond.

James, in a benevolent and proprietory mood, explained things as they went. The house, in the traditional H shape of an eighteenth-century country house, had been built symmetrically around this large and high-ceilinged hall. Bonner noticed a massive stone fireplace, a good deal of period furniture but also a leather sofa that was evidently Victorian, and a heavy double oaken entry-door like that of a castle in a movie. The decorations were conventional hunting prints and Derby scenes. On one wall was a mounted stag's head, and facing it symmetrically across the room was a pair of crossed shotguns.

"When they first built the house this was where the family sat in the evenings. Then when they came down in their fortunes they couldn't afford to keep such a big fire and they moved into the gallery beyond."

This was a room on the river side of the house, sharing its chimney with the hall. The fireplace itself was smaller, and the room was narrow, only a kind of strip along the back of the house with windows facing the river. The furniture was modern and comfortable. There were a dozen or so pictures, mostly portraits.

"These are the family ancestors. I got them at Christie's." Occasionally James permitted himself a joke. "Not all of them though. That old gentleman there is an authentic Cromlech, the one who built the house."

He indicated a large picture in the late eighteenth-century portrait manner, a kind of inferior Lawrence or Reynolds. Its subject was a sexagenarian in knee-breeches and a cocked hat, leaning on a stick much like Drood's, with a glimpse of the Mill Cottage and the forest in the background. With interest Bonner noted his long upper lip, his protruding teeth, and his large exophthalmic eyes with their Cromlech rabbit-look. He seemed angry at the twentieth century; he gazed out at James and Bonner with a frown of annoyance. The picture badly needed cleaning. "We tried to have it cleaned, but the whole ancestor began to come off with the varnish. Nothing can be done. The painter didn't prepare his surface right." Bonner would have remarked that this was strong evidence the picture was a modern forgery, except that the figure was so unmistakably a Cromlech, and somehow so unmistakably of the eighteenth century.

"Sir Fellows Cromlech. Only a lifetime title, unfortunately, so it wasn't passed along."

Perhaps James imagined he could have assumed it. There was little else of interest in the gallery. Magazines were scattered around on tables, and there was a bookcase with fine bindings, uniform editions of Walter Scott and that sort of thing. There were also a good many modern books, including a copy of Bonner's own *Explorations in Dawnland* which he had given James in London.

"I do want to get around to reading that sometime, Bonner," said James. "Come here now. You're interested in old things. What do you think of this?"

At one end of the room was a long glass cabinet like one in a museum, filled with prehistoric artifacts of various sorts. Bonner inspected amulets, bone needles, a tiny stick-pin of gold, horn implements, thin spindly bronze knives, wooden plates, a few shards of pottery. It was the usual stuff found in provincial museums. He felt drawn to the collection because, as he noticed after a moment, there was no iron in it.

"This cabinet is Drood's hobby. Most of these things came from the Long Barrow across the river. They're valuable, I suppose. Here's a spooky one."

He pointed to a horn incised with what appeared to be a group of sticklike human figures, one of them wearing a stag's head and raising his arms in a <u>hieratic</u> gesture. At first Bonner got the idea that the other figures on the horn were chasing him and that there was an arrow sticking into his abdomen at an upright angle. Looking closer, he saw that it was an erect member. What he had taken for bellicose stances in the other figures were gestures of worship.

"Curious."

"It's more than that, it's obscene. Well, come on. Enough of this. I'll show you around the grounds."

He led him out into the passage, pointing out the music room on the way. Through the door Bonner could hear Sylvie practicing a Chopin étude with a difficult cadenza. She kept sallying into it, attacking it with verve and doggedness, and always getting stuck at the same point and starting over. She had played the piano in London, he remembered. "She practices every day," said James briefly. "But she's lazy. I have to keep her at it." They went on through the orangery, a steamy glassed-in room heavy with the odor of humus, full of tropical plants and exotics. At the far end of the orangery was a door leading out onto the terrace at the side of the house.

"This place has been inhabited from the very earliest times," said James.

They were standing on the terrace looking down to the river and the stone Mill Cottage with its two eyelike windows.

"There's always been a mill here. The local belief is that it was the Romans who built the first one, but no one really knows. When the present weir was built, in the sixteenth century, some Roman coins were found in the foundations of the old one." He launched easily into a lecture which he seemed to know by heart. He would have made an excellent history professor of a rather old-fashioned tedious sort, Bonner thought. "Byrd Mill is mentioned in the Domesday Book. At that time, in the eleventh century, it was owned by a miller named Wilyam Byrd, although nothing is known about him but his name. The Cromlechs acquired the property in the seventeenth century. They weren't millers, of course. They were local farmers who were deprived of their land under the Commonwealth because they supported the Royalists, and then became prosperous again at the time of the Restoration. They bought the mill because it was a well-built stone house in a pleasant spot on the river, and they lived in it for almost a century. Sir Fellows Cromlech was the founder of the modern family. It was he who began the building of the modern house, although he never lived to move into it. He died of ague, toward the end of the eighteenth century, in his bedroom in the Mill Cottage, as the Cromlechs called it after they began living in it. He's the one whose picture we've got in the house." It was a rather grandiose portrait, Bonner thought, for a man who had died in a small damp room in a medieval mill.

James gazed expansively around at the Mill Cottage and the house with its pleasant lawn sloping down to the Val. "These people were on the point of turning all this over to the National Trust before I came along. Can you imagine that? Hordes of tourists tramping through taking pictures, writing their names on the walls, sitting down in the park to have picnics. I saved the place from all that. But to hear them talk, you'd think I was some kind of thief who came along and took what belongs to them."

"Who talks like that?"

"Oh, Drood and the others. They don't really say it but that's what they think. I imagine they think I didn't restore it authentically. I've done some modernizing there in the cottage, and I've put in my study." He pointed to a room he had added to the house. The ham-colored brick of the rest of the house had been matched perfectly; it was hardly noticeable from the outside. "But it wouldn't be possible to restore the place authentically in any case. There's no one period you could restore it to. The mill is medieval and the house is eighteenth century. And some things are even older. Come on, I'll show you the park."

He led the way across the terrace to a hedge with a gate leading through it. The gate seemed to be brand new and had been artificially rusticated with some sort of stain. James opened it and they went through into an expanse of grass scattered with trees, mostly beeches and elms. It was quite different from the lawn at the back of the house. Where the lawn was neatly mowed, the coarser grass of the park gave the impression that it had been cropped by sheep. It was large, stretching for a considerable distance around the Mill Cottage and along the river beyond. After they had walked across it for a few minutes Bonner saw with a start what it was that had cropped the grass. In the distance, half-hidden by the trees and the occasional clumps of underbrush, were a half-dozen or more reddish-brown shapes. A moment later he saw more moving through the trees beyond. The first group consisted of a stag, a pair of younger males, and a small harem of does. As the men approached the stag raised his head, holding his array of antlers motionless, and stared straight at them with a foreleg bent. Then he turned and moved away, and the others followed him. Bonner heard the soft thud of their hooves on the grass and the wheezy muted sigh of their breathing.

"These are not your ordinary park deer," said James. "Those are fallow deer usually. These are great red deer. The medieval kings used to hunt them. I believe the royals still do in Scotland. They're very rare here in England. I went to a great deal of trouble to acquire them. You won't find deer like this in any other park in England."

"Don't they try to break out through the hedge?"

"Oh no. They don't need to be fenced in, really. I don't think they'd run away. But if you let them into the garden they'd eat the rosebuds."

"Really?"

"A couple of them got out once and they did."

Bonner found himself pleased by this thought. He liked the deer and wished he could get closer to them, to inspect them more carefully and perhaps feed them rosebuds. He had the irrational notion that it was only because James was along that they had shied and walked away. If he came alone, perhaps they wouldn't be afraid of him.

"Are there deer in the forest?"

"Where? Oh, Waldon forest." The wooded highland across the river was hidden now by the trees. "No, there are no deer in the forest. There may have been at one time, but that would have been centuries ago."

He pointed out the dairy, just beyond the end of the park. It was built at the far end of the estate so that the odor wouldn't be noticed from the house. Bonner made out a low modern building with a galvanized-iron roof. There was another gate out of the park into the dairy pasture. A man came twice a day from a nearby farm to attend to the cows, milk them and do whatever was necessary. James was a little vague on what you did to take care of dairy cows.

"Come on," he said. "I've saved the best thing for last."

They went out through the gate again and down the terrace toward the Mill Cottage. The entrance was around the corner of the building on the side facing the river. The old mill race had been filled in with gravel, and between the river and the cottage there was a decrepit sunken pond, full of dried leaves, with a statue in the middle of it which had once spouted water. It was a round-hatted sort of figure with one leg upraised, much like the so-called Eros on the pillar in Piccadilly Circus. Probably this had been added by the Cromlechs when they converted the mill into a habitation for living. Just beyond this was the door to the cottage, which was unlocked. James opened it and they went in.

For some reason, perhaps connected with the flow of water to the millstone, the floor of the good-sized room inside was sunken below ground level, almost at the level of the river. James reached up and switched on a light. The two of them were standing on a kind of landing ending in a low fluted wooden railing, looking down into the brightly lighted room. In the center of it the old mill wheel lay on its side, looking like a piece of abstract modern sculpture, a somewhat rougher than usual Henry Moore. The rest of the room was full of complicated pieces of machinery, with rods, cranks, and adjusting-wheels protruding from them. The machines were all meant to do the same thing, and after a moment Bonner puzzled out what it was; they were printing presses. Some of them seemed to be very old, others were modern. They weren't very large; the biggest was the size of a billiard table. There were perhaps a dozen of them arranged in rows with a brass-framed sign on each one, exactly as in a real museum.

"Where did all these things come from?"

"Oh, I've been collecting them for years. In America, and later in London, I had to keep them in storage. Now I have a proper place to keep them." Earlier in the morning he had been alternatingly friendly, stiff, and ironic with Bonner; now he was overcome with boyish good humor and pride in his collection. "Come on down; I'll show you a couple."

Bonner followed him down the steps onto the floor of the room. The walls had been whitewashed or plastered and there was no sign of dampness. The fluorescent lamps overhead filled the room with a clear bluish glare, leaving no shadows except directly under the machines.

James went briskly around the room from press to press, explaining each one in turn. Bonner followed along behind him. His explanations in almost every case were identical to the descriptions on the signs in their brass frames. Since he had written the signs himself, he had little to add to the information they conveyed; he was like a professor teaching out of a textbook he himself had written.

"This is the oldest of them." He stopped before a towering machine which looked something like a gallows. "An English Box-Hose Common Press of 1650. There's a complete type-font, all black-letter." Next came a Blaeu's wooden hand-press, and then a Stanhope press of 1810, the first all-metal press. "This is the only one in the world in private hands," he explained, repeating the information on the sign. He went on to a Pyne & Sons Albion hand-press and another small Albion of 1860. The presses were variously powered by lever-handles, cranks, foot treadles, and engines. The most striking perhaps was an 1824 Columbian hand-press which was copiously decorated with dragons, wreaths, flowers, and what appeared to be a caduceus in silver, gold, and colored enamel. All these machines gave Bonner a vague sense of foreboding, perhaps because of their blackness, or because they were made of iron. It was true that the black Columbian was decorated and gilded, but this only made it look like a French funeral hearse. Of course, he reflected, if it weren't for printing presses, he and all the other scholars and critics who made their living from literature would be out of a job.

"All these presses are in working order," said James. "And most of them have their fonts, more or less complete."

"Then you could print things here?"

James smiled. He led him to the last press in the room, directly under the stone stairs where they had entered. It was about the size of a bed, with a large cylinder at one end and a double arm with claw-fingers at the other end. On the side in gilded letters was the inscription "Winterthur 1902."

"As you know, I inherited the newspaper business from my father. This is the first press he ever owned. It belonged to the Altoona Clarion, which he bought in 1922 when he was only twenty-four years old. I went to a great deal of trouble to find it and restore it. It's the only one like it in the world. It has a unique paper-feed mechanism. Winterthur was an eccentric Pennsylvania mechanic and built these things according to his own notions, or visions as you might say."

It was an odd way of describing what was only a piece of machinery. Still the Winterthur was an extraordinary-looking apparatus. It was driven by a primitive electric motor, and the feeding-arm on top looked like something that would be more appropriate to a hay-baler. It actually had a stock of paper neatly stacked at one end, with the feeding-arm poised over it.

"You stay here," said James.

Bonner was standing by the side of the press. He had not felt well every since he came into this room full of iron machines, and now he felt even worse. James wound his way around through the other presses and mounted the short flight of stairs. The red button to switch on the Winterthur was overhead on the landing near the light switch. "Stand out of the way now. The switch is up here so that nobody will get caught up in that thing when it starts up."

Bonner cautiously backed away a little. James reached up and pushed the red button over his head. The Winterthur gave a groan, a snap, and launched into motion. The fingers on the feeding-arm seized a sheet of paper, lifted it into the air, and slammed it onto the bed, where it was caught by the rotating cylinder and pressed onto the type underneath. The cylinder reversed with a clank and spewed out the sheet, and the feeding-arm dexterously caught it and turned it over. This time it went through upside down and was printed from another part of the type-bed lying between the frame. The cylinder ejected the sheet a second time, and it was caught up in an arrangement of rods that folded it and dropped it with a final thud onto the iron table at the end of the press. The whining of the motor died out and the clanking ended.

"A facsimile of the first paper my father published. Have a look at it."

Bonner was hesitant.

"Go ahead. The thing is turned off now."

He picked up the folded newspaper from the table and examined it, holding it by the margins so as not to get the fresh ink on his fingers. It was a copy of the Altoona Clarion for May 28, 1922. A little bemused, he glanced over this synthetic and clumsy artifact from the past. On that day President Warren G. Harding made a speech claiming that things were going splendidly and the country was well on the way to normalcy. The stock market was doing well. "Bull Market Taxes Nerves of Brokers. Long Hours For Clerks." In local news, an Altoona woman had been injured in a crash with an ice truck, and the city council had denounced graft by policemen. An editorial decried labor agitators who were attempting to infiltrate local industry. There were advertisements for vacuum cleaners, cod liver oil, and Ford cars.

"You can keep it," said James. "I always make one for guests as a souvenir."

Bonner folded it up, finally getting ink on his fingers in the process, and stuck it into his back pocket. He didn't know what printer's ink was made of but he strongly suspected it was made by dissolving iron in some kind of acid. He saw now that there was a door at the far end of the museum leading to the other rooms of the mill.

"What's in there?"

"Oh, nothing much."

They made a brief inspection of the other rooms, James switching on the lights as they went. They consisted of three or four windowless stone cubicles with connecting doors. Originally these had been storerooms where the miller kept his supplies, such as bags, twine, and tallow to lubricate the great stone wheel. Then the Cromlechs had lived in them before they built the house, using the large mill-room as a hall. Two of the rooms still had rustic wooden beds in them. There were signs of more recent habitation, however. One of the rooms was fitted up as a kitchen with a hand pump that still worked, and there was a bare bulb in the ceiling and electrical outlets in the walls. There were no windows, but it was cool and perfectly quiet; the rooms were insulated from the outside world by the thick stone walls. It was a relief also to get out of the museum with its machines radiating their lightly throbbing black waves.

"You know, I could move in here myself, James."

"Here? In the Mill Cottage?"

"There's everything I need. There are beds and there are things to cook with."

"Why would you want to do that?"

"It would be fun. I'd be all by myself and I could fix my own meals. I wouldn't need to bother anybody in the house. I could even bring my papers in here and work on my book."

"It's rather damp." It was clear that he thought this was one of Bonner's eccentric ideas, reflecting a small flaw in his character. Bonner himself was rather taken by the idea. Even if James didn't approve, he thought he might just sneak into the place some night and bring his things down.

James's study, the room he had added to the house, was a pleasant sunny place with comfortable modern furniture. At one end of it was a desk surrounded by various items of technical equipment: a telex terminal, a microcomputer, a telephone machine with automatic dialing buttons, and a Japanese shortwave radio. Above the desk was a pair of digital clocks with red neon readouts, one set on British time and one on U.S. Eastern Standard.

James opened the bar and took out bottles, glasses, and ice. "What can I offer you?"

"Nothing, thanks." Bonner had been forbidden to drink by his London doctor Lovejoy. He had to hang onto whatever tenuous reality he could cling to, without weakening his grasp with this subtle chemical. It was all right for James; he had an excellent grasp of reality.

"Suit yourself." He poured himself a gin-and-tonic and they both sat down, James behind the desk and Bonner in a modern Swedish chair of leather and aluminum.

Bonner looked around at the technical equipment. The red clocks winked and silently changed minutes: 12:03 in Britain, 7:03 in America. "What do you do in here anyhow, James?"

"Oh, I have to keep in touch with things. I still have interests in the States, you know, even though I'm officially retired." After a contemplative pause, and a sip of his drink, he said, "I'm glad you like the place." Bonner hadn't said he liked it but he did rather, except for the collection of presses. Still in an expansive mood, James began philosophizing. "We have a darned good life here, you know. It's a lot better than it was in America. Better for the girls. America is raw and new; there's no sense of the past. And London wasn't quite right either. It isn't really English, you know. It's an international city; it's too much like America. It's changed since I first knew it too; it's full of Pakis and colonials now. Here in the country we can live a life that's genuinely English. There's a sense of the past in the country; a feeling of history, of the imbedded tradition of the land. Tita didn't like it in London, you know. She's deeply attached to the English countryside."

"She is?"

He was a little startled. It was a little difficult to imagine silver-lidded Tita being attached to anything so bucolic as a countryside. He had always thought of her as a creature of the town, of brittle conversation and cocktail parties. In London, when he had first met the family, she had presided over a kind of salon that gathered in the Boswin flat in Belgravia on Sunday afternoons.

"Oh yes. She was born here, you know, and raised in this house. It was only an accident that we happened to meet in London."

"She lived for a long time in America."

"She never really adjusted herself to life in the States. She's English to the bone; all the Cromlechs are. Now she's come back to her own place. The Cromlechs have lived on the land here in Waldshire for centuries. And of course I'm English too by blood. My people only came to the States in the nineteenth century; before that they were farmers in Devon. So you see, it's my own past I'm rescuing and preserving here, along with theirs."

Bonner didn't contest all this. He felt it was nonsense, but harmless nonsense as long as it resulted only in James's fixing up an old house and persuading himself he was an Englishman. "It is very nice here."

"You're darned right it is. It's better for the girls," he said again. "You see Bonner, as you get older your ideas turn away from personal success to the happiness of your children. I have the means now and I'm determined to give the girls everything they need, everything they want. Sylvie is going to become a concert pianist, and Stasha a fashion model. The classy kind you know, international Vogue and all that."

Bonner raised an eyebrow at this, and James smiled. "That's what they want and I'm ready to get it for them. I don't question their foibles. I don't tell them how to be happy. If they want it, that's enough."

"You're very liberal."

"I'm modern. Times change and well-brought-up girls do all kinds of things."

It seemed to him there was a certain confusion in all this. America was raw and new, so James moved to London and then to the English countryside, but James was modern, he had liberal ideas, and his study was full of electronics and Swedish furniture. Still it all fitted into a pattern; James felt it was modern to like old things and tradition and to have a sense of the past.

"Whatever they want, I'll get it for them." Here his sinewy glance fell on Bonner himself. He contemplated him thoughtfully over the top of his glass, then took another sip. He was not quite so jovial now.

"You know, Bonner, I still don't like that trick with the knife."

"I'm sorry. I didn't want to do it. It was Sylvie that egged me on to it."

"I wouldn't try to blame it on someone else if I were you. You know, you have a brilliant mind, Bonner. But a mind is like a piece of complicated electronic equipment." He set his hand on the microcomputer beside him. "This computer is a marvelous machine. But I don't want to know what goes on inside it. I wouldn't dream of taking the cover off and tinkering with it myself. If something goes wrong I consult an expert. I'd advise you to do the same with your mind."

"Yes. It was you who sent me to Dr. Lovejoy. I appreciate it."

James smiled. He was capable of mercurial adjustments of

mood. "Lovejoy's a good friend of the family. He has an excellent reputation. If you have a medical problem we want you to have the best treatment available." He paused, and made an invisible inner transition of the kind common to the computer he so much admired. "I am fond of you, Bonner. We all are. You know, I take a great deal of satisfaction in my family. The girls are wonderful young women and I'm proud of them. I'm sure they'll do well in the world. But a man does want to have a son, doesn't he?"

"I don't know. I've never felt that impulse. Maybe I will later."

"It's a very fundamental impulse. It's an idea that grips you at a deeper place than all these modern ideas about the equality of women. Oh hell, I share those ideas too. I'm as up-to-date as anyone else. But daughters aren't as satisfying, not for a man. He wants a son. He wants someone he can put his arm around and talk to. A man isn't really close to his daughters in the way that . . . I don't know." He made his one-sided smile and sipped from his glass. "You'll find that most men think they know all about women until they have a couple of daughters, and then they find they don't know anything at all."

"There is something a little mysterious about them. I think we prefer it that way, don't you?"

James didn't have any opinion on this. He passed the remark over and went on to what he was really interested in. "I own all this now, you see Bonner." Deep in the chair with his legs crossed, he waved his hand to indicate the house, the grounds, and the land stretching along the river. "These people were on the point of bankruptcy and I came along and bailed them out. I fixed the place up and restored the house. I put a lot of money into it, as you can see. If something happened to me now, it would all go to Tita, who would probably end by giving it back to the Cromlechs." His tone implied that this was an unthinkable alternative.

"Unless," he added, "someone else were to come along."

Bonner was embarrassed. He stood up and turned as if to leave the room. James got slowly up too and finished his drink. "We're glad to have you here in the house, Bonner. Stay as long as you like. We consider you practically one of the family." He was still in an expansive mood, but now it had assumed a tone of intimacy and mysterious seriousness. He put his arm around Bonner and they made their way toward the door. "I've always admired you, Bonner. In London I saw right away that you were a person of exceptional promise. You've already achieved a great deal for your age and you have a brilliant mind. I know there's a wonderful future ahead for you."

Four

Lunch, like breakfast, was served in the morning room. This was a more elaborate and formal meal, with Aunt Cassie in charge and dark-eyed Rhondda helping to serve. Bonner had never met Aunt Cassie, although he had heard her talked about a great deal, and now he got his first look at her. She was a small woman with a shock of cropped gray hair, narrow shoulders, and a thin bony face covered with a network of fine lines like an old glove. She had the Cromlech mouth, small and triangular, with teeth that appeared now and then in the opening. The vertical ridges above her lip were prominent. He saw now that she, not Drood, was the avatar of the family hare-look; compared to her Drood was only a softened imitation. She supervised Rhondda's setting about of the dishes and then sat down herself.

Cassie was the sister of Persejohn Cromlech, who had presided over the decline of the family in the years culminating in the Second World War. He died in 1945 of a cardiac attack, and his wife Abbie, née Birdsell, in 1947 of renal infection complicated by endocarditis. These were the parents of Tita and Drood. God had removed them from the family as superfluous, as a novelist often does with characters not necessary to his story. The family worked quite well without them. Bonner thought of God primarily as a storyteller, rather than a stern judge, a dispenser of judicial tablets, a kindly uncle straightening things out, or an x-ray cop spying on masturbators, the usual anthropomorphisms of the Judeo-Christian tradition. Cassie had a modest air of being totally in charge of the lunch and anything else she touched. He found himself staring with curiosity at her clothes: a man's jacket and shirt with a black string tie, a gray woolen skirt, and stout walking boots.

Following his glance, Sylvie explained deftly, "When Aunt Cassie is in the country she dresses country."

James said, "Cassie is always in the country."

"Don't you ever go into London, Miss—what shall I call you?"

"Aunt Cassie."

"Don't you ever go into London, Aunt Cassie?"

"Oh yes. Now and then. I was in London at the time of the Royal Wedding."

"And—did you enjoy the wedding?"

"Oh, I didn't go near it. I went to Smith and Sons in New Oxford Street and bought an umbrella. You can't get a decent umbrella in Waldon. They're all made in Taiwan."

"Aunt Cassie's idea of a decent umbrella is something built like the Shield of Hercules that never wears out."

"Black," said Cassie. "I don't believe the Shield of Hercules was black."

Sylvie said, "The Cromlechs all wear funny clothes. The more Cromlech you are, the funnier your clothes. The original Cromlech must have been a scream."

"Dressed in skins and painted with woad," Stasha chimed in.

Bonner said, "Doesn't the name Cromlech mean something?"

Cassie inspected him for a moment. Her slightly bulging eyes were wrapped about in eyelids wrinkled and scaled like those of an interesting reptile. "Indeed it does. It's the name of our family."

"But doesn't it have some other significance?"

"I'm sure it has all sorts of significance."

Rhondda came in to take away the soup plates and serve the second course. She set down a smoked mackerel pie, along with a dish of vegetables and home-baked bread with butter from the Byrd Mill dairy. For some reason Cassie got up from her chair and helped her as she did all this, adjusting a dish here and there and straightening the bread on the plate. Only when Rhondda had disappeared into the kitchen did she sit down again. The lunch was excellent. Bonner remembered that Drood had promised him Aunt Cassie's mackerel pie on the train.

Now, since he had made the mistake of attracting her attention by addressing her during the soup course, she pressed home the attack herself.

"Do you plan to work while you are here, Mr.—what shall *I* call *you?*"

"Bonner, please."

"Do you plan to work while you're here, or only convalesce and recover from your mental wounds, or whatever they are?"

"I—I haven't thought about it. Perhaps I'll do some work."

Stasha said, "I always forget, Bonner. What's your book going to be about?"

"It's a study of the *Ancren Wisse,* a thirteenth-century handbook for anchorites. However, Professor Kölbing is inclined to place the Corpus Christi manuscript about the middle of the twelfth century."

"I'm sorry I asked."

"The *Ancren Wisse* is a rather interesting book," he told her. "You might enjoy it. It says, for example, that a female hermit shouldn't keep a cow, because it would distract her from things of the spirit, and besides she might become involved with the cowherd."

"Well, I never."

"And then too," said Cassie, "a cow would remind her of reproduction and motherhood. Just what she's expected to forget."

"Exactly." He was getting along better with Cassie now. She seemed harmless enough, only a little cranky and odd in her ways.

"I suppose I'm a sort of an anchorite myself," she went on. "I've never married. I've passed my whole life in this isolated part of the world."

"And *why* did you do this?" he asked her.

"I beg your pardon?"

"Did you choose to live such a life?"

"I'm not sure we choose the basic elements of our existence. Did you choose to be born in America? Did you choose to write a book on an obscure medieval text nobody's ever heard of? Did you choose to be barmy?"

He had to grin at this. "Perhaps I did. At least so Lovejoy says."

"Who?"

"He's my doctor in London. He says my problems would go

away if I just willed them to. He says I prefer being ill to being well."

"He's perfectly right," said James. "A brilliant man, Lovejoy."

"He gets annoyed with me from time to time. To punish me for not taking a realistic view of things, he sent me to the rest home in Wimbledon, although it was a pleasant enough place as a matter of fact."

"I think it's rather narrow-minded of you," said Cassie, "to reproach someone for being a spinster, when you're not in command of the decisions of your own life."

"I didn't reproach you with anything. It was you yourself that said you had never married."

"As a matter of fact, although I don't own a cow, I do have relations with six cows. Fred Baines brings the milk to the doorstep every morning in his little truck, and Rhondda and I do not only the bread-making but the butter-making."

"Does that remind you of reproduction and motherhood?"

"I wouldn't say that, but these fundamental things are very satisfying. I'm sure you know that, Mr.—Bonner, if that's what you wish to be called."

"Aunt Cassie is very fundamental," said Sylvie.

"She is a matriarchal figure."

"She is symbolic rather than real."

"She presides over the kitchen and sees to our nourishment."

"Only she can make the butter come in the churn, and she knows the mystery of yeast."

"She knows how to sex chickens."

"Oh, I don't either. I can't even tell girls and boys apart these days." The old woman wrinkled into a grin, showing her Cromlech incisors. "You probably mean that I can candle eggs. It's just a way of telling whether they're spoiled."

"We call Aunt Cassie the Great Mother of Us All. That includes James, who only married into the family."

"I'm conscious of my inferior status," said James, who entered into this banter good-naturedly. He had changed for lunch and was wearing a tweed jacket with a solid red necktie. In this he did look something like a country gentleman in a magazine. He was adept at camouflage, like those butterflies who mimic other insects too bitter to be eaten.

"I would think Tita would be the mother of the family."

"Oh, bother motherhood and the whole bloody business," said Tita. "If Aunt Cassie wants to muck about making butter she's welcome to it. I don't care to be fundamental."

"James says you are deeply attached to the English countryside," said Bonner maliciously.

"I wish you wouldn't repeat things I tell you in a private conversation, Bonner."

"Oh, bugger the countryside," said Tita. "This is a pleasant enough place if you don't go outdoors. The view from the window is lovely."

"Tita went for a walk once as far as the pasture," said Drood. "She stepped on a cow-pad. That's what she's referring to."

"It was the park, and it was a deer-dropping."

James said, "This is all bosh, Tita. We all enjoy taking walks. You know you love it here in the country. The Cromlechs have lived here for centuries."

"Far too long, in my opinion." She gazed at Bonner languidly. "Are you the sort that likes to take walks, Bonner, or do you prefer to stay indoors and shuffle your old manuscripts? I don't remember from London."

"I do like to take walks. I like nature and all that sort of thing."

"You ought to let me show you my orchids in the orangery. They're quite beautiful, and they have the advantage that you don't have to walk to them."

He hadn't known that the orangery was Tita's realm, but it all fitted in. "I'd love to see them."

To finish off the lunch there were small horny pears, spotted like dogs on the outside but juicy and surprisingly succulent when you cut into them. Drood, Bonner, and the girls had coffee, James a sherry, and Tita some cognac in a large balloon glass. Aunt Cassie had disappeared.

Only a few moments later Bonner, standing in the morning room with his coffee cup in his hand, caught sight of her crossing the lawn toward the weir and the footbridge. She had added to her costume a shapeless gray felt hat and she was carrying a stick. She had a direct short-stepped way of pacing; there was nothing the least senile about her motions or her posture, although she must be at least eighty, Bonner thought. She was headed straight in the direction of the forest. Evidently it was she who was going for a walk, while the others just talked about it. He looked after her with regret; he would have enjoyed going with her but she hadn't asked him. Of course, in the private reverie he had built up in his mind, it was Sylvie who went with him on a walk in the forest. Cassie wasn't the companion he would have chosen, but he might have settled for her. She passed through the gate of trees on the opposite bank and disappeared from his view.

Cassie continued along the path over the meadow toward the wooded uplands in the distance. Perspiring a little, she mounted up the slope and passed in under the shadows of the trees where it was cooler. In only a little while she came to a clearing with three large blocks of bluish stone in it, two upright and one fallen over on its side. With scarcely a glance at them she continued on up through the trees, which grew larger now, immense over-arching oaks and beeches. Sometimes she had to push away a hanging branch to continue on her way. Ferns and bracken grew profusely to the height of her waist. The path grew more obscure; sometimes it dwindled away to scarcely more than a sliver of dead leaves through the ferns, or disappeared entirely, but she had been here many times and knew her way. A gray squirrel nipped out of her path and scuttled up a trunk; a hedgehog lumbered inexpertly along the leaves ahead and finally broke into a clumsy run. Every so often she came to a clearing, a level spot with a little circle of grass, as though these were set deliberately in her path to give her a little rest now and then. Then the slope rose upward again and she climbed, puffing a little through her set teeth. Her perspiration oozed from her clothing and its odor mingled with the other odors of the forest, the sharp perfume of the conifers and the faint stink of squirrel-droppings.

As she came up into the clearing she slowed a little. The opening was larger than the others, like a good-sized room in a house. The arching foliage of the oaks overhead allowed a little greenish sunlight to penetrate, flickering lazily and dappled with shadows. There was no sound but the buzz of insects and the crepitation of leaves under her feet. She stopped.

In the tangle of foliage ahead of her, in the play of shadows, she caught sight of a motion like a disturbance under the surface of the sea. It passed along from right to left at a leisurely pace. A shadow turned into a russet polygon with a gleam of sunlight on it. A reddish-brown flank appeared and disappeared, and an immense set of antlers took form in the opening of the leaves. The head turned toward her and the limpid and liquid large brown eyes gazed at her thoughtfully. The stag's smell, a pungent musk, was added to the others in the forest.

The large nostrils closed and opened again. A fly or two stirred in the shaggy reddish hair on the massive neck. Then he lifted a foreleg and turned slowly away. The brown phantom disappeared into the foliage with a rustle of leaves. Cassie said, "Pretty fellow."

"What would you like to do this afternoon, Bonner?"

"Oh, nothing in particular." Of course, he had wanted to go to the forest.

"I have to go to the village on some errands. Would you like to come along?"

"I suppose so. Yes. That would be very nice."

Sylvie had changed after lunch and was now wearing a pair of linen trousers tapering to her ankles, with a blouse and scarf. He was still in his old corduroy jacket and pants. They went out through the front door and crossed the graveled drive to the garage. Here he got his first look at Miles, the chauffeur and handyman who lived over the garage. He was a lanky slow-moving man who might have been Rhondda's cousin; he had the same black aggrieved look to him. He had to come down from his room and shift the cars so Sylvie could get hers out. There were three cars: James's vast Daimler, Sylvie's small Morgan sports car, and an old estate wagon which had belonged to the Cromlechs before James moved to the country. Sylvie's car was the same one she had had in London, a pale-yellow roadster with tooled leather seats and a walnut dashboard. The doors were cut so low that if you dropped your handkerchief or your gloves you could circle around and pick them up without getting out of the car. Miles grudgingly opened the garage door for them and then stood with a cigarette dangling while they got into the car.

Sylvie turned the key and the engine started with a competent burr like a sewing machine. She was evidently in a good humor. Instead of looking where she was going she turned and smiled at Bonner as she drove out of the garage, across the gravel, and down the short lane to the road, as though inviting him to admire her skill in driving. She turned to the right and drove on down the narrow country road at a moderate pace.

"Watch where you're going, Sylvie. Where *are* we going, by the way?"

"I told you. Into the village. I have some things to buy, and anyhow I wanted to get you away from the others so that I could have you to myself."

He enjoyed being with her too. The small open car was cozy and intimate, the sun trickled down intermittently through the trees that lined the road, and the air smelled pleasantly of farms and stagnant water.

"Does the car bother you?"

"What? Oh, because it's iron. It doesn't seem to."

"It's almost entirely aluminum according to the brochure. The engine is iron, I suppose."

"I suppose."

The road ran for a short distance along the Val with a row of poplars on one side. Then they came to the canal, which he had heard about. After they crossed it on a concrete bridge the road turned to the right and continued on along the canal with a stone quay at one side like that of an old Norman port, lined with cannons set into the stones. It was quite charming. A little farther on was the village of Pense Coombe. There wasn't very much to it: a row of shops, a single side street, and a stone-paved car park which again resembled the square of a small French town. A market was held here on Wednesday. Today was Thursday. There was a quite nice market cross in the Gothic manner, actually a Victorian imitation. The only human beings in sight were some old black-clad men drowsing in the sun, propped on canes. Sylvie parked the car, or rather she just abandoned it in the empty square, and they got out.

"You're looking very nice today."

"Oh, this?" Like all women she began deprecating her clothing in order to be complimented again. "Just an old pair of pants, they really belong to Stasha. And the scarf—" She dangled it with her fingers. "Well, it is a new scarf. I put it on for you."

"I'm flattered."

He stared at her smiling, and she laughed. In the warm sunshine, with the still water of the canal playing like molten silver nearby, he felt pleasantly amorous. Her thinness and boyishness were part of the complicated attraction. What he felt for her at the moment was something like the innocent homosexual reveries that men sometimes have in their unguarded thoughts; a longing for a chum, a companion, a loyal and fresh-cheeked young follower, narrow-hipped and bashful, who would follow you everywhere and, still bashful, share your bed in wayside inns and the bunks of freighters. He put his arm around her shoulder and attempted to nuzzle her behind the ear, an attractive part of her revealed, perhaps deliberately, by the way she wore her hair tied with a ribbon in the back.

"Oh don't, Bonner. You know I don't like that sort of thing. Especially in public."

She pulled away from him and rearranged her hair in its velvet ribbon, which he hadn't touched.

"I am fond of you. We all are. You know, I couldn't go to sleep last night. I just lay there thinking, it's so strange, Bonner is *under this roof.*"

Now he was baffled. She had always been a little cool and difficult, even in London. But today she had dressed to please him, she had admitted it. Still, after she had said she was fond of him, she quickly added, "We all are," as if to reject any erotic element in her affection. As James said, women were rather mysterious.

They had stopped in front of the chemist's. "Please *don't* come in here with me, Bonner. I have to buy something personal."

Her period was coming on, he thought. That was why she was so skittish. Still she seemed to be in an excellent humor. Left alone in the street, he inspected the other shops. There was a nice-looking pub, a bakery, and a newsvendor's which also served as a branch post-office. In front of the tobacconist's next door was a wooden painted Highlander holding a flask of snuff, the English equivalent of an American cigar-store Indian. It was obviously modern. There was something a little fake about this charmingly authentic English village, he now began to see. It had the air of something in a museum, how our forefathers lived in the eighteenth century, with authentic shops and a simulated pavement. Sylvie came out of the chemist's with her parcel and they went into the bakery, where she seemed to be on friendly terms with the dark old hag presiding. "How are you today, Mrs. Thrane, a dozen rock cakes if you please, some of those little pastries, they look delicious, and some scones, do you have any scones?" The old woman spoke not a word as Sylvie paid for her purchases. He took the bags with the scones, the rock cakes, and the pastries and they went out through the glass-paned door which tinkled as it opened and shut.

"This village would be charming if I could believe it was real."

"Oh, it's real all right. You have to pay real money for the scones. I know what you mean though. When I first came here from London it all seemed like something in a movie set. Too too picturesque. But England is like that, as soon as you get out of the city."

He went into the paper bag, took out a rock cake, and began eating it. He offered one to her. She shook her head. "They're called rock cakes not because they're hard but because they look like stones. They are hard though."

"What next?"

"Tea. And yeast for Aunt Cassie."

The small grocery shop had the same tinkling door as the bakery. Sylvie bought Ceylon tea, the yeast, and a tin of curry powder, and began discussing sultanas with the girl. Bonner took pleasure in watching the back of her neck for a while, and then he turned his attention to the contents of the shop. There were the usual Carr's biscuits, Weetabix, oatmeal, and marmalade. In the open-backed shelf by the door where the sunlight struck them were some jars of honey, apparently produced locally since the label was only a slip of paper with the price on it in pencil.

He hadn't tasted honey in years. For some reason the good weather and the bucolic odors of the village were producing in him a longing for simple and innocent sensuous pleasures. He stood by the shelf looking at the honey. It was a rich light-brown liqueur with tints of gold where the sunlight struck it. He remembered the delight he had taken as a child in the consistency and the deep woody flavor of honey, its heaviness and opulence. Although he didn't touch it now, he remembered how it flowed heavily in the jar when you tipped it, varying in translucence from the palest gold to a deep opaque umber. The joy of the stickiness on your fingers. He hoped that Sylvie would want to buy a jar of honey, but she had finished her purchases and was standing waiting.

"Fallen into dreams? That's all. We can go now."

They went back to the car and he stowed the various parcels behind the seats. He got into the car by vaulting over the low door rather than opening it. "Oh, Bonner." She sighed and started the engine. With the small car making its usual burring noise she drove out of the square, steered deftly around the bends that followed the elbows of the canal, and drove on down the road with the Val on the left. The house was visible in the distance now a half mile or so ahead. She slowed down and then turned off the road at a place where the poplars provided a little shade just at the edge of the water. Here she switched off the engine and sat looking out at the river with her delicate little smile. The warm engine clicked faintly. It was so quiet that they could hear the purling of the water along the stones under the bank.

His hand crept out to enfold hers on the parking-brake of the car which lay between them. She didn't remove her hand and showed no sign that she had noticed. Then, turning, she bent and touched her lips to his for a moment. He was aware of the slightly bifurcated coolness of her mouth, which remained open only because she always had a little difficulty closing it over her Cromblech teeth. In a moment it was over. He was left with a swarm of sensations in which a soft tingling pleasure and an intense frustration were the main elements.

She withdrew her hand but didn't start the car up yet. After a moment she said, "There. But you've got to kiss all the other females in the family in order to distribute yourself evenly. Stasha and Tita. And even Aunt Cassie, I imagine."

With this mention of the family a thought struck him, a suspicion that was perhaps unworthy but which rose darkly in his mind all the same. "Did James tell you to take me out in your car?"

"What do you mean?"

"He says he wants you to be happy. To have everything you want."

"I don't know what you're talking about."

"You know what I'm talking about."

"I think it's the most preposterous thing I've ever heard. How can you . . ."

"Well, did he?"

"Oh Bonner, let's not quarrel."

"It's such a nice day."

"Isn't it."

Bored, with nothing to do, he inspected his room. It was neatly but sparsely furnished, with no personal possessions in it; evidently it was used only as a guest room. His half-dozen books were arranged on top of the dresser. In the drawers, the contents of his suitcase were already neatly stowed away. In the wardrobe there was nothing but his own corduroy jacket and an old belt which somebody had forgotten, dangling from a hanger, dusty and brittle. There was a musty and disused, slightly medicinal odor to the room; unlike the other odors of the village and the surrounding farms it was not really very pleasant. It was probably some disinfectant or something used to clean the room. Tiny motes of dust hung in the rays of the later afternoon sun that came in through the window.

From outside he heard the two girls on the lawn, chirping and chortling to each other like two songbirds. He wondered if he ought to to out and join them instead of mooching about like a troglodyte in the room. Perhaps he found the room unpleasant because inside him somewhere he didn't really like the idea of sleeping under James's roof, a notion which had been suggested to him by Sylvie's remark that he had been under it last night. What did he have against James anyhow? He was a friendly enough fellow, generous and hospitable. Bonner thought of the collection of printing presses, which was a harmless enough hobby after all for a man who had been in the newspaper business. The recollection of them made him feel a little faint again, a sensation as though if he persisted in thinking about them things might go black. But perhaps the faintness was caused not by the presses but by the fact of being kissed by Sylvie in the car parked along the river. He was still not really well, he had to admit. It might have been better for him to stay a few more weeks in the Villa Felicity. He shook his head and reached up to smooth down his curly ginger hair. It would be nice if they had a pitcher of water and a glass in his room; it was supposed to be a feature of English country life.

Back to the inspection of the room. He didn't know what he was looking for; perhaps some clue to the house and what James had made of it, or his own fate in it. There was a kind of foot-locker against the wall opposite the bed, but it contained only spare blankets. To his surprise the drawer of the small nightstand by the bed was full of things. This gave him pleasure. Idly he riffled through the contents, a half-empty and stale pack of cigarettes, some elastic bands, a theatre ticket, a pocket-knife, a brown and brittle flower, a stick of grease for lubricating doors. Turning these things over with his fingers, he caught a gleam of bright metallic yellow, which disappeared again like a fish in the sea. This, possibly a coin, eluded him, but his fingers encountered something else, a patent fingernail-clipper.

His nails did need clipping. He sat down on the bed to do a neat job of it. He cut off each fingernail in a neat crescent, wincing a little at the sharp snapping bite of the steel. As he worked he laid the clippings in a neat row on top of the nightstand, five and five. When he was done he gathered them into his hand and slipped them into the pocket of his shirt. He didn't like to leave his fingernail or toenail clippings in some strange place that wasn't his own, because if anyone took possession of your fingernail or toenail clippings they in a sense took possession of a portion of yourself, even though an unwanted portion that had been discarded because it was no longer of use to you; but it might be of use to *them,* that unseen and omnipresent *them* that hovers so disconcertingly over our lives. In fact, he didn't even like to leave them in a place that was his own, since the "places that were his own" in recent years had tended to be provisional and temporary shelters in which he had no real right of possession—hotel rooms, service flats, the Villa Felicity. It was better to dispose of them by putting them away in some safe place, such as down the toilet; although heaven knew what complicated and perhaps ominous things might happen to them after the waters took them away into that maze of pipes that lay under our modern civilization. He left the clippings for now in his pocket. Later he would dispose of them in the forest or somewhere. He still had a strong desire to go to the forest.

Five

Bonner had met the Boswins in the previous summer when he came to London on a Fulbright to do research for his book on the *Ancren Wisse.* He was on leave from his position at Johns Hopkins and expected to go back the following June. He heard about them from a friend named Conan, who was an expert on early Renaissance music and was also in London for a year. Conan had told him only that they were Americans who had a flat in Belgravia and held open house on Sunday afternoons. The people who came were academics, writers, artists, poets, in short interesting people. "The music is not really at a very high level," warned Conan. At first he wasn't interested; it sounded like a banal sort of amateur salon of the kind he was familiar with from Baltimore. But he found after a while that there was not very much to do in London on Sunday afternoons; most shops and stores were closed and he didn't care for going to concerts or movies alone. You could of course go to the National Gallery or the Tate, but that palled after a couple of weeks. Perhaps, he thought, pondering it over in his solitary flat in Kensington, he might make friends at the Boswins, even meet a girl who would be someone to go out with in London. He went for the first time with Conan; after that he was free to come on his own.

Conan hadn't told him about Tita, who presided over the Sundays; an odd, heavy-lidded, bejeweled creature given to bizarre and exotic costumes, full of a powerful menopausal sexuality that seemed to have no place to expend itself. She greeted him in a throaty insinuating voice and then introduced him to her other guests: a pair of London University lecturers, a female BBC programmer with a long solemn face, a landscape painter who looked like a sheepdog, and a fluffy-haired literary agent trailing after her an Indian lady who wrote cookbooks. The two London University lecturers examined him curiously, exchanging glances with each other. One was the usual tweedy literary academic, the other was in blazer and flannels with a regimental necktie.

"Are you the Foley who wrote *The Learned Plowman*?"

"That's right."

"And *Grendel's Dam*? And *Anti-Skeat*?"

Bonner smiled and shrugged, a little embarrassed at this list of his accomplishments.

"And the Clark Lectures. I'm sorry I don't remember the title. I'm not a medievalist myself but I found the book brilliant."

"Explorations in Dawnland."

"Yes. You do go in for titles, don't you?"

"What's all this?"

Someone else had joined the circle. Bonner had the impression of a slender man perhaps sixty, with a bent smile and a thin redlined face, dressed in a well-cut suit with a handkerchief in the breast pocket.

"Ah, James," said Blazer-and-Flannels. "Our host. James, have you met Professor Foley? We were just talking to him about his books. A brilliant medievalist. Well known on this side of the Atlantic."

"Ah," said James. "Medieval studies. Highly interesting. These days so few people have a feeling for the past. So you're a professor at—"

"Johns Hopkins, in Baltimore."

"Ah," said James again.

The two academics continued the conversation with Bonner while the others in the circle listened.

"I wonder," said Tweeds, "if we couldn't get you to come round to the University of London and give a lecture. Or just talk to a seminar if you prefer. We have a fund for that."

"Oh, I don't think so. I'm here in Britain to write a book. I ought to keep at it."

They were instantly attentive. "What's the book about?" inquired Blazer-and-Flannels.

"I'd rather not say. Until I get it finished."

One by one the others in the room joined the conversation until there was a good-sized circle of people around him, one or two of them asking questions and the others listening.

"Are you going to continue," pressed Tweeds, "along that interesting line you developed in *Grendel's Dam,* of applying Jungian archetypes and myth concepts to medieval texts?"

"Oh, I don't think so. I've pretty well exhausted that. I'd rather go on to other things."

"And *The Learned Plowman.* As I remember, your thesis was that the author of *Piers Plowman* was not the rather shadowy William Langland at all but a committee of monks who filled it full of all sorts of biblical and classical allusions."

"That was more or less it."

"Stunningly argued as I remember."

"Oh—" began Bonner deprecatingly.

James took him by the elbow. "You know, Professor Foley—what's your first name by the way?"

"Bonner."

"Do you mind if I call you that?"

"Not at all."

"You know, Bonner, there's somebody I'd like you to meet." Holding him by the elbow, James led him delicately with thumb and forefinger across the room. "So you're at Hopkins."

"Yes."

"D'you know Hugh Kenner there? And John Barth?"

"Oh yes. Slightly."

For an expatriate James seemed extraordinarily well informed about American universities. Still guiding him by the elbow, he led him up to a bison-shaped man who was nursing his drink alone by a window. "Bonner, this is Dr. Lovejoy. Doctor, Professor Foley."

Dr. Lovejoy, who seemed to be a half a head taller than ordinary men, was distinguished mainly by his bulk. He filled a large tweed suit to the last crevice, and he had a mane of salt-and-pepper hair that made his head seem even larger. His glasses were oversized with thick lenses. As he turned toward Bonner two crystalline stars glinted in them, reflections from the lighting in the room.

"Charmed."

"Professor Foley has written a number of books in his field."

"And what is that field?"

"Medieval literature."

"Ah well," said Lovejoy, inspecting Bonner with interest and glinting at him through the eyeglasses, "if you'll come up to Regents Park some morning we'll quickly cure you of that."

"Why Regents Park? Are you a zoo-keeper?"

James reddened a little at this irreverence of Bonner's. "Dr. Lovejoy has a psychiatry practice in Prince Albert Road."

Lovejoy himself was unperturbed. "I deal," he said, "in diseased souls, which I succor by leading them out of the morass of delusion and back to reality."

"I'm not quite following. Am I to understand that you consider medieval literature a delusion?"

"Everything except the solid world is delusion. The past is delusion. The future is delusion. Thoughts are delusion. Practically everyone is deluded in one way or another."

"Except you, of course, who cure them."

Lovejoy only smiled at this.

"You must have a prosperous practice."

"I do." Lovejoy seemed to be enjoying the banter. "People like you I can deal with in a week or two of treatment. Serious madmen, those who believe that the world can be improved or that human nature can be changed, take a little longer. You'll find my fees are reasonable. I take all major credit cards and offer a discount to academics, clergy, and pensioners. Why don't you take one of my cards. Do I have a card?" He went through an elaborate pantomime, patting through his pockets for a card.

Bonner grinned. "I don't expect to need psychiatric treatment."

"Have you met the girls?" Lovejoy asked him. "If there is anything that for a certainty is not delusion, it is a pretty young woman. Two are even better. I would recommend it in your case."

Although it was natural at the time, afterward it seemed curious to him that it was Lovejoy who had introduced him to the girls and not Tita or James. He stood rather awkwardly while Lovejoy explained which was which. Then, for some reason, Lovejoy simply drew away and disappeared; he somehow became invisible in the large and crowded flat in spite of his bulk. Bonner was left with the girls. They were so different that it was hard to believe they were sisters and could wear the same clothes. Sylvie, the elder, was a thin wispy girl with fine golden hair, flat-chested and as straight as a board except for her little jutting hips. In spite of this elfin body she seemed not entirely free of feminine vanity; she tied her hair in a simple black ribbon in the back to expose her ears and the fine bones of her skull behind the ears, a part of her so fragile and delicate that leaving it bare seemed almost an embarrassment. Stasha, her sister, had the body of a model in an indecent magazine for males: a small neat rear, cupcake breasts, a little triangular mouth like a cherry picked by birds, and a flash of electric bronze hair.

He attempted to make conversation with them. "Do you—do something clever?" he asked Sylvie. "Write or paint or something?"

"Not exactly. I studied—English at college."

"Which one?"

"The—U. Penn. We lived in Philadelphia then."

"I'm at Johns Hopkins you know."

She murmured "Yes" as though she was familiar with his name and knew him by reputation.

"What did you specialize in?"

"Oh—poetry." She seemed embarrassed; a little roseate flush spread from her ears and crept slowly over her cheeks. She seemed to hesitate, opened her mouth as though she was going to say something more, and instead turned away and melted into the crowd, with a final brief glance at him over her shoulder.

He was a little intrigued. "What was the matter with her?" he asked Stasha.

"Oh, she's just shy."

"Shy?"

"Shy. She's probably fallen in love with you," Stasha prattled on in a thin fluty voice. "She fell in love with all her professors at Penn."

"Did you go there too?"

"Oh, I just fooled around for a couple of years. In theatre arts."

"And did you fall in love with your professors?"

"It was the other way around. Bonner," she went on with a slapdash intimacy as though she had known him for years, "are you really going to spend your whole life studying that dusty old stuff?"

"What dusty old stuff?"

"Mee-dieval litrachewer." She was standing very close to him in the crowded room; he felt the tickle of her bronze hair.

"Of course."

"Why?"

He smiled. "It interests me." He looked around the room to see where Sylvie had disappeared to, but she like Lovejoy had become invisible. "And besides," he went on still a little distracted, "I'm richly paid by the university, and now I have a grant to spend a year in England." He imagined that this was the only thing that would impress this attractive but evidently idiotic young creature, who was wearing a silver lamé dress that sparkled whenever she moved.

"Oh good grief. What hideous materialism. Well, we'll straighten you out with our Sundays. Is that your drink?" It was standing behind him on a bookshelf where he had set it for the moment.

"Yes."

She took the glass and sipped a little. "James won't let me drink so I just have a little out of other people's glasses." She passed the glass back to him, then she too was gone, swallowed up in the crowd of guests like Lovejoy and Sylvie, leaving a smell of scent and a faint sexual electricity in the air behind her.

There was tea for those who wanted it, also Pimm's Cup, punch, and kir, which was what Bonner was drinking. The little sandwiches of cucumber, cress, cream cheese, smoked salmon, and caviar had evidently come from Harrods, to judge from the fancy paper cups in which they rested like jewels in plush. Sylvie played Chopin, there were charades and literary games, and the more talented passed around the parts of *Mourning Becomes Electra* and read them while the others served as audience. There was a self-conscious quality about the whole business, as though the Boswins had heard about this sort of thing, or read about it, or as though they were all playing parts in a play, attempting to ape the gestures of a fashionable tea or a literary salon without really grasping what the point of it was, like savages staging a coronation. Still he came back a second and a third time, he wasn't quite sure why. It was amusing and it filled up his Sundays. The Boswins were interesting people, even though banal, and they attracted his curiosity. He was studying them as a diversion. Or so he told himself. It was possible that there was something more to it, that he was becoming attached to the family in a way that couldn't be explained in terms of ordinary friendships.

By the time of his third or fourth visit it was clear that he was on a more privileged standing than the other guests. Silver-lidded Tita offered him more than the usual number of her smoky glances and brushed her bracelets against him when she handed him his drink, and James treated him with great courtesy and bonhomie considering their difference in ages—he seemed to be about sixty. By this time Bonner had given him a copy of his *Explorations in Dawnland,* the one of his seven books that was the most suitable for laymen, even though it was rather tough going for most. James seemed to be quite impressed by this and to value the gift. He mentioned it frequently at later meetings, even though he didn't say he had read it, and he began treating him as though he was a friend of the family rather than just another of the interchangeable guests who thronged the flat on Sunday afternoons.

"I'd like to have you up to our place in the country, you know. We go there now and then."

"You've bought a place?"

"Not exactly. Tita's family lives there. It's up in Waldshire. They've lived there for centuries. An old county family. But the place is run-down and I've been fixing it up. When I'm done we may move there with the girls."

"In Waldshire?"

"Yes. A place called Byrd Mill. Beautiful coutryside. A forest nearby."

"It sounds rather remote."

"It's three hours from London."

"Do you think the girls will like that?"

"Oh yes. They'll like it well enough. They're half English, you know. It's in their blood. Anyhow that's where we're going to live."

"And Tita's family—don't mind?"

"Mind?"

"I understood you to say that it belongs to them."

"I said they live there. It belongs to me now. They've run through their money, you know. All these old county families have done the same thing. They flourish for a few centuries and then the blood begins to get thin. They get fuzzy and don't know how to manage things." He seemed to feel that this was a peculiarly English institution, which he admired along with all the others. "At that point, it's time for someone new to step in."

"Is it a large place?"

"Oh yes. Private park. A dairy, two houses, a lot of land. A nice little village within walking distance, Pense Coombe. Completely unspoiled. The shops are all exactly as they were in the eighteenth century. Restored by the National Trust."

"I hope you won't move soon."

"Why not?"

"I mean I've enjoyed your Sundays."

"Oh, you can come and visit us in the country, Bonner. That's what I'm trying to explain to you. I'm sure you'd like it. The house and the village, the countryside, the local antiquities. Everything has been there for centuries. There's a medieval mill on the property, stone walls a couple of feet thick. I'm fixing it up as a museum. I know you're a man with a feeling for tradition. A sense of the past. You'd have to be in your academic specialty."

"Everything is the past, isn't it? There's only the present moment which is a knife-edge, and everything else is past."

James had never thought of that. "I suppose it is." It wasn't what he had meant by the past.

Later on that same Sunday he had an interesting conversation with Sylvie which revealed things about her he had never detected before. She had always seemed to him a model daughter, helping Tita with the sandwiches and drinks, playing the piano for the guests, taking her part in the play-reading, even though with the slight touch of irony with which she did everything. Now a burst of mutiny came out, a discontent that left creases on the sides of her small neat mouth. She perched on the arm of the sofa next to him and signed.

"Enjoying yourself, Bonner?"

"Yes. Aren't you?"

"Oh, I'm so bored. The whole family is captive of this thing."

"Thing?"

"These Sundays. They don't make any progress. They're circular, like something in Dante. The same people every week and they're so repetitive, so mechanical. I don't mean you of course," she put in quickly. "How many times have we read plays together. I always play the same Chopin mazurka. I try others but they ask for the same one. They drink the same drinks and Tita and James always say the same things." There was a genuine fretfulness in all this that was quite at odds with her usual calm and cool composure.

"I always enjoy them."

"Do you want to go for a walk?"

"Won't the others miss us?"

"Oh no. Just to the park. We'll only be gone for a few minutes. Come on, come *on*."

She took him by the hand. Stealing out of the flat unnoticed by James, they came out into a luminous London afternoon with the pale sun hanging in the haze to the west. The flat was in Wilton Crescent. They went up Wilton Place past the small St. Paul's church, ran hand-in-hand across Knightsbridge dodging busses like two naughty children, and crossed into Hyde Park. Here they slowed down, Sylvie panting a little from the dash.

When she recovered her breath she said, "Are you still working on your book?"

"Oh yes."

"How do you write a book? I imagine you poring over dusty old tomes by lamplight."

He laughed, feeling good at being out of the house and walking in the park with a pretty girl. "More or less. I go to the British Museum and check out books and sit in the reading room making notes, like Karl Marx."

"Dull dusty old Bonner. Can I come with you?"

"No, you have to have a reader's card."

She hardly seemed interested in these technicalities; she was talking only to make conversation. They went on along the Serpentine. There was no one in sight anywhere around them at the moment, a curious accident for a fine Sunday afternoon in the fall. There had been some other walkers but they had left them all behind.

"James says you're going to move to the country."

"What? Oh, yes."

"I'll miss seeing you on Sunday afternoons."

"Will you?"

"Yes, I've become quite fond of—the family." He had been about to say *you*, and then decided on this formula instead. "I'd be sorry to see you go away."

She looked at him fixedly and her manner changed; her eyes

glowed and a touch of color appeared on her cheeks. She said, "Oh Bonner, I just love you, do you know that?"

He was a little startled. "I don't understand the word just."

"I mean, I don't want to do anything about it, possess you, or . . ." Here came one of her weak trailings-off . . . "anything else. I just love having you around and knowing you exist."

He couldn't say whether he loved her too in this special and complicated way she was delineating. He had become attached to the Boswins almost as though they were his own family, and his feelings toward them were ambivalent as one's feelings toward a real family are, composed partly of affection and partly of a wary and fractious instinct to flight. In this crypto-family Sylvie played the part of a sister of whom he was quite fond; and yet, since she wasn't really a sister but only a crypto-sister, he was permitted to feel desire for her. But she, being a sister even in that limited sense, was forbidden to feel any desire for him—the *anything else* she referred to in her Delphic announcement. It was all very complicated. He didn't really care for games and puzzles, yet when the prize was such an attractive, fragile, and expensive porcelain figure you had to take an interest.

Without noticing what they were doing they had walked all the way along the Serpentine, across the bridge, and into Kensington Gardens, and now they found themselves at the Peter Pan statue, a work of art that Bonner had always been fond of in spite of its undeniable corniness.

She laughed and said, "Clap hands if you believe in fairies."

He took her hand. For an instant they were both totally and perfectly happy, standing before the bronze figure transparent at the edges where the afternoon sunlight touched it, and yet there was something strange. There was a disembodied, a buzzing and slightly unreal quality to their happiness; to his happiness, he couldn't be sure of hers. It was not quite happiness yet; it was the premonition, the elusive promise that he *might* be happy at some time in the future, that an unnameable bliss lay somewhere just out of his touch, yet even the hint itself that such things might be made him happy, if only for a fleeting instant. In that instant he imagined himself turning to her, touching her cheek which would be cool and firm, and applying his lips to the cool resistant flower of her mouth. He didn't do it. Instead they turned and went back along the path, holding hands like brother and sister.

* * *

When they got back to the flat in Wilton Crescent the play-reading—today it was Strindberg's *Ghost Sonata*—was over and people had gone back to talking in little clusters, looking around furtively for the last remnants of the little sandwiches which had almost disappeared and had not been replenished. James detected them instantly coming in through the door and stared at them fixedly out of his red-lined face.

"Where have you been, Sylvie? Everyone's missed your music. Play your mazurka."

"I've already played it today."

"Then the little thing by Scriabin."

In all this James said not one word to Bonner. He only gave him a long stare, without hostility but reflectively, as though he were weighing something in his mind. Then he turned back to the group he was talking to, in which the bulky figure of Lovejoy loomed large, and resumed his conversation. Sylvie sat down at the piano and began playing the Scriaban, an étude that seemed to be played mainly on the black keys and looked extremely difficult.

Bonner sat in an armchair listening to her for a while, then behind him he was aware of a familiar odor of something at once infantile and heady, perhaps heliotrope.

"Naughty Bonner," said Stasha. "Stole off with Number One Sister and went for walk in park."

"How did you know?"

"To the Peter Pan statue. That's where she always goes when she's fed up with things."

"And you tattle on her, I'll bet."

"Oh James doesn't need me. He knows where we are at all times. Would you like another sandwich? I know where they are."

"No thank you."

"Oh, don't be so cold and aloof. You get that way when you're with Sylvie too much." She pulled him away into the kitchen. The unwashed glasses and the trays that had held the sandwiches were strewn around on the counter, and Tita had gone back into the drawing room for another load. In the crumpled Harrods papers and crumbs on one tray there were still two sandwiches left, tiny triangles of thinly sliced white bread no bigger than postage stamps, filled with caviar. She held the tray out to him.

"I'm really not hungry."

She took one and ate it herself, licking the salty black dots from the corners of her mouth and gazing at him with suppressed mirth. She took up the other sandwich in her fingers and held it out to him.

"No really."

"Oh come on."

She attempted to put it in his mouth; he turned away fretfully. Finally she grabbed him and, giggling, held his nose in a childish game so that he had to open his mouth or suffocate. In that instant she stuffed in the sandwich, and when he attempted to spew it out she pressed it back into his mouth with her small and agile pink fingers. When he finished it she held out her finger and he licked the last of the caviar off it. It was good and he was hungry.

He knew now that he was deeply and mysteriously attached to the Boswins; at the same time he began to wonder whether they were really good for him. The task of attempting to grasp the intricacies of his relation to the family was a strain on his intellectual powers, if not his nerves. And probably it was not normal for a young male in full possession of his powers to linger for weeks, for months, in the bosom of a family with two nubile daughters without defining his position more precisely. That was why, in previous times, the father of the family had at a certain point demanded of such a young man what his intentions were. What were his intentions? What were James's intentions? That is, what were James's intentions in regard to him? He had all kinds of ideas on this subject. Some of them he didn't care for, and others were pleasant to think about but he didn't fully examine them in the shadows at the back of his mind where he relegated them for the present.

He had been in London for three months now and he should have been well along with his book, but his work in the British Museum was not going very well. He had been brooding over the plans for his book and making copious notes for it but he didn't know what the point of it was going to be. He felt overtwanged and inelastic, and he had difficulty concentrating; he began to suspect that his social life was beginning to interfere with the more serious matter of his book. His social life, of course, consisted entirely of his visits to the Boswins; he ignored all other invitations and spent his evenings except for Sundays in his own flat in Kensington, reading or listening to music. There was definitely something wrong with him. Whatever it was—overwork, the onset of the dull British winter, the unhealthiness of a diet of books rather than the nourishing food of real life—it was beginning to affect his eyesight; he had difficulty making out the words on the page and often had to go back and reread a paragraph which he had totally failed to grasp.

Sitting one November day in the Reading Room of the British Museum, surrounded by the dozens of other assiduous bent-over scholars, he had a premonition all at once of something unpleasant, a feeling as though the lights in the room were dimming or twilight was coming on. This went on for a few minutes while he tried to continue working. The thought occurred to him that perhaps he had been reading too much and ought to have his eyes examined. Then this visual dimming, harmless enough even though it interfered with his work, was replaced by a far more upsetting sensation. As though the great dome overhead and the walls of the room had become transparent, he was suddenly aware of the iron reinforcing rods imbedded in them at close intervals. It was not that he *saw* the buried iron bars, since his head was still bent over facing the wavering page in front of him, but he was conscious of their exact pattern and outline all around him, a reticulated shape like a birdcage, enclosing him in a contracting network of magnetism. Their color was black and their smell was acidic and dark, the odor of an animal carcass. They radiated a faint inky energy that vibrated in the particles of his blood. He tried to rise from the desk but found he couldn't; it was as though his limbs had lost their strength. For a while, a moment or perhaps longer, he even lost consciousness.

When he came to himself his head was on his desk on his crossed arms and he was looking sideways at the wall of the room out of his open eyes; he was covered with a clammy perspiration. His fellow scholars were staring at him curiously. One rose from his desk and came over to look at him with mingled sympathy and caution; it was a man named Cotswater, an Australian scholar that he knew slightly.

"Are you all right?"

He nodded without a word, conscious that every eye in the room was on him. He collected the material from his desk, turned in his books, and left. In Tottenham Court Road he went automatically and without thinking, as he always did, into the Underground station. Then he hesitated at the ticket barrier, feeling a premonition of the same queer sensation again. With his eyes fixed on the floor, he clearly perceived every detail of the complex reticulated pattern of iron rods in the walls around him. He felt faint; he barely made his way out before things went black. Outside in the street the traffic of Tottenham Court Road quivered and roared about him, all pistons, cogs, and levers. A bus went by radiating a black vibration that almost overcame him; he stepped farther back onto the pavement. No point in trying to take a taxi either. In the end he walked back to his flat in Kensington, by Oxford Street, Park Lane, Knightsbridge, and the Cromwell Road, arriving after an hour and a half footsore and fatigued. Luckily his flat in Cornwall Gardens was in an old Victorian house, solidly built of masonry and plaster without iron in the walls.

Six

It was a day or two later and he was sitting in the office of Dr. Lovejoy in Prince Albert Road across from Regents Park. Lovejoy gave a somewhat different impression in his office than he had at the Sundays in Wilton Crescent; he was less jocular and bantering, more serious and rational, and seemed genuinely sympathetic to Bonner's problems. He was still bulky, but behind the desk his bulk became a professional attribute, an emblem of his authority as a physician, rather than the zoolike and slightly comic quality it had in a social gathering. He slumped in a comfortable position in the chair, toying with a pencil, glinting at Bonner through the glasses, explaining things in a calm and heavy baritone.

"Hemoglobin, a basic constituent of blood, contains a large element of iron. It's possible that a person of abnormal sensitivity like you can detect magnetism with the particles of his blood. In the brains of some migratory birds, like bobolinks, scientists have found minute grains of iron oxide attached to the fine nerve endings. It's likely that these birds can detect the lines of the earth's magnetic field around them in the air and use them to navigate on their annual migration from one hemisphere to another."

He stopped to see if he was following. Bonner said nothing and only shifted in his chair. He looked around; there didn't seem to be any reinforcing rods in the walls. He thought he could detect iron somewhere in the room though.

"There are even tiny plankton that have specks of magnetic oxide in them to guide them to their food. It's believed that they use the dip of the earth's field, or its inclination from the horizontal, to find their way to the bottom of lakes and ponds. They of course are a very low order of animal. Among humans, at least those in good health, the phenomenon is less common but not unknown. You are perhaps such a case. It has considerable medical interest."

He smiled. "Iron *does* send out lines of force, you know. It's a fact of physics."

Turning to the cabinet behind him, he took out a small aluminum canister and poured some filings onto a white paper on the desk. Bonner cringed at the sight of the ominous black powder. From the desk drawer came a small magnet of the kind used as a toy for children, painted red and black. This he slid under the paper. The filings rustled and erected, and immediately sprang into an arabesque of graceful curves around the invisible poles of the magnet underneath. Bonner stared, fascinated. The tracery was as exact as a mathematical diagram, and it followed across the paper with a gritty sound as Lovejoy moved the magnet underneath.

"Please don't do that."

Lovejoy seemed pleased at the discovery that this phenomenon was unbearable to him. He removed the magnet and shook the filings back into a random disorder. He set the paper with the filings onto the cabinet behind him, and then he put the magnet away into the drawer of the desk. Next, he took the paper of filings and, with a sly smile, set it back onto the surface of the desk. The filings rustled only slightly as though sleepy. He tapped the paper. The filings scratched. He tapped a little harder with the pencil, with a touch of irritation, it seemed to Bonner. The filings at last crawled into a fuzzy and off-focus version of their former arabesque symmetry around the pole-points of the invisible horseshoe.

He made his lightly sinister smile again, the eyeglasses glinting. "The magnet is now at a distance of, perhaps, twenty centimeters from the filings. The influence is still perceptible. More powerful magnets can exert an effect at even greater distances. The earth itself, which is a magnet, can form a pattern in subatomic particles thousands of miles out in space."

"Don't speak of it."

"So you see, Bonner," said Lovejoy, "there's nothing to be afraid of."

"The lines are always there. Invisible lines. In the air."

"Yes. There's nothing to be afraid of. Now, I want you to become familiar with these things. This piece of paper, this tin of filings, this little magnet. I want you to become friendly with them." He lifted the paper and made a crease at one edge, and then tipped it so that the filings slid into the canister. He took the magnet out of the drawer and set it next to the paper and the canister. "I want you to take these things into your pocket, and now and then get them out and perform this little educational game as I have demonstrated."

"In my pocket?"

"Yes. Twice or three times a day—say before meals—" he gave a little laugh at this medical joke—"take out the paper, sprinkle the filings on it, and amuse yourself by wiggling the magnet underneath. This will demonstrate to you gradually that the forces that disturb you are perfectly natural, that they can be made visible, that in their visible form they are perceptible to everyone, and that your perception of them when they are invisible is just an exceptional sensitivity, nothing to be disturbed about, in short it demonstrates no more than the fact that you have superior nerves."

"I couldn't possibly put them in my pocket."

Lovejoy found a brown-paper folder and put the canister of filings, the piece of white paper, and the magnet into it. He tied the folder with its brown string. "Let me tell you something, Bonner. There are two worlds that we can live in. The first is the real world, the world of reality, and it's the same for all of us. The second is the world of fantasy and reverie, the world of delusion, and for each person that's a private world that he invents for himself. He may consciously invent it—that's called reverie—or he may generate it unconsciously, so that he isn't aware of its source and imagines it to be real. That's called delusion. For most people"—he corrected himself, toying with the pencil, considering Bonner with a calm and ponderous thoughtfulness—"for people like you, it's usually the second."

"I'm not quite sure I follow you."

"You're not well, Bonner."

"I know that."

"But you imagine that your illness consists simply of your not feeling very good—of nausea, darkening vision, weakness of limbs. But you would be unwell even if you didn't have these symptoms.

You would be unwell if you simply went around the world believing you could detect iron in walls."

"But I can."

"Yes you can. As I've explained, you no doubt have tiny specks of magnetic material on your nerve-ends. We all do, but in your case there's some neurological connection with the imagination that doesn't exist in most people. My job is to cure you of this special power which only makes you fearful. I think I know how to do that. But I can only do it with your help."

"What must I do?"

"The first thing is that you must wish to be cured. From one point of view mental illness is simply a failure of nerve. All your problems would go away if you just willed them to. These special powers that you have are on the borderline between mental illness and paranormal experience. In fact there may be no difference; what we call paranormal experience may be simply a form of mental illness. In the Middle Ages people who were deranged saw the Blessed Virgin; now they see saucers with little green men. The form your illness takes is that you perceive invisible things around you made of iron and you are fearful of them. What I want you to do is embrace your fear. When you close your arms on it, you will find there is nothing there." He fixed a meaning glance on him. "Here is your little therapy kit."

Lovejoy handed him the brown folder and he took it. In Prince Albert Road outside the office he dropped it into the first dustbin he came to. But after a few yards he went back and, gritting his teeth, took the folder out of the dustbin again. It was only a brown-paper folder. There was nothing magical or portentous about it. You could buy one in any stationery store. Carrying it in his hand, he went with a slight feeling of faintness into the St. John's Wood station. He still didn't care at all for the idea of riding an Underground train but he accepted Lovejoy's suggestion of applying a little will to his problems. On the platform he waited for his train to come, got onto it, and slipped gingerly into a seat. When he set the brown-paper folder down next to his knee it sprang to the wall of the train and clutched it like an octopus.

On his next visit Lovejoy had something even more ominous to show him, a collection of guns. He had evidently staged this display for Bonner's personal benefit because he surely didn't keep all these guns in his desk drawer for use with every patient. He took them out of the drawer and arranged them in a row on the desk: two or three heavy black revolvers, a small nickeled automatic pistol, a Colt six-shooter of the kind used by movie cowboys to blast their enemies, and a Smith and Wesson .38 special.

"What do you think of them?"

"I don't like them."

"What do you think of this one?" He pointed to one of the three heavy black revolvers, the one in the middle.

"Not much."

"Take it up. Feel it. Here." He picked it up and insisted on thrusting it into his hands. Bonner took it and had a dizzying and disorienting sensation; the gun rose in his hands as though it was full of helium, and would rise if he let go of it until it bumped gently against the ceiling. It was light as a feather. He examined it more carefully, his aversion to it dissipating only gradually.

It turned out to be made of wood. "It's a very clever facsimile, made by a convict in a prison who used it to overpower his guards and escape. He worked in the paint shop, you see, so he was able to put this beautiful black matte finish on it."

"Clever."

"You would think," said Lovejoy, "that such a person would be able to make a good living in the world at an honest task, as a woodworker or even a gunsmith. But some people are just basically criminal." He made his cackled laugh, which was beginning to irritate Bonner, and stared at him with enlarged eyes through his lenses. Perhaps he thought that Bonner was one of those who would be better off as an honest woodworker. Unlike James, and almost alone among the guests at the Sundays, he had never seemed impressed by Bonner's achievements as a medievalist.

He took the wooden gun away from him and shuffled all the guns around on the desk again, like a carnival operator arranging the materials for a shell game. "Here, try again."

This time he almost fell out of his chair onto the floor. The object in his hand was cold and heavy; something pulled it downward in his grasp with tremendous force. The waves from the metal reverberated and stung in his flesh. It wasn't the wooden gun at all; Lovejoy had switched them. He let go of it and it clattered onto the floor. He sprang up from the chair and stood looking at it, trembling.

"Now, I'm going to put these guns into a folder," said Lovejoy. "I want you to take both of them home, and . . ."

This new development in Bonner's life, his not being well as everyone put it, seemed to give him a new status among the Boswins. James was still respectful, even though a little stiffly now, it seemed to him; he treated him warily but with ceremony, as though he were a firework that might go off unexpectedly at any moment. Stasha was affectionate in a new tender, less facetious way, and Sylvie, donning a mantle of illuminated wisdom, seemed to grasp exactly what was wrong with him.

She drew him apart from the others. "I'm sorry you haven't been well. I do enjoy it when you come on the Sundays. You see, Bonner, we all . . ."

"I know. You're all very fond of me."

"No, I didn't mean that. I don't mean us in the family. I mean all of us. We all have the sense that there are dark things about us from time to time. That there are shadows in the air, or other things—goblins that lurk in holes. At least—if we're more sensitive than the others—I'm not making very good sense, am I?"

"You're making very good sense. That's what Lovejoy told me, that I'm more sensitive than the others."

"Yes, but I'm not sure he means that as a compliment. He doesn't approve of me either. He told James I was vaporous. That was his word."

"What an old-fashioned term."

"He's right of course. You see, you and I . . ." She hesitated.

"Yes."

"You and I are the . . . are the . . ."

He waited for her to find the right word.

"Familiars of spirits. Bonner," she went on hastily as though frightened of this phrase, "don't you remember the time when we walked in the park and stopped by Peter Pan?"

"Of course." It was only a few weeks before.

"You took my hand. I felt that something good had happened, that there was something in the air about us that was benevolent and would protect us from the darkness. It was there when you

touched me, but only if you *just* touched me. If you had done anything more . . ."

"Yes." But he hadn't.

"So, if you are frightened of things that aren't there, perhaps
there are friendly spirits that . . ." She broke off. "When you were a
child, did you have an imaginary friend?"

"Yes."

"So did I. He was called Professor Twist. I was quite precocious
and my imaginary friend was a professor. He was very queer and
funny and used to explain to me all kinds of things I didn't understand, like what adults did and . . ." Here she trailed off again in
the way that she had. "All sorts of things I didn't understand, but
he had such a funny way of explaining them, so that even the bad
things didn't seem frightening and instead they made me laugh, we
both laughed at them, he was so queer and had an odd way of expressing himself. And then, when you came to London, I recognized you and saw that . . . you were Professor Twist."

"I'm so queer and funny."

"Yes. I just love you, Bonner. We all do."

A week or so after this—it was December now, halfway through his
planned year in London—he went out in the middle of the morning to go to his session with Lovejoy and found the pavement in
front of the house obstructed by a good deal of confusion. Painters
were getting ready to paint the outside of the house, and other men
were unloading large bundles of iron pipes from a van along with
hundreds of little clamps. He sidestepped around all this ruckus
and set out on his walk, which took him by Kensington Gardens
and Regents Park to Lovejoy's office in Prince Albert Road. It was
a cold gray day, the temperature only a little above freezing, and
the trees in the park were leafless. He arrived a little late for his ap-
pointment, which may have annoyed Lovejoy slightly although it
was hard to tell because he seldom showed any emotion. He settled
into the chair behind his desk and glinted at him through his eyeglasses in his usual way.

"Well?"

Bonner shrugged and smiled.

"Progress?"

"Not much."

"How are you feeling today?"

"Not so bad. I walked—"

Lovejoy interrupted him abruptly, trampling over his planned description of how he had found the leafless trees in the cold park consoling and comforting somehow. "I think we're on the wrong track, Bonner. We've been approaching this thing from the wrong direction. You can detect iron bars in walls and this makes you nervous. Fine. So far we've been trying to accustom you to being friendly with iron. But why do you have this affliction in the first place? Why *do* the magnetic particles in your nerve-ends connect in a pathological way to your imagination? What's the fundamental source of your illness? That's what interests me now."

"You said it was a failure of will."

Lovejoy reflected. He toyed with his pencil, holding it in one hand while he rocked it rhythmically with the other. "You've told me nothing at all about your family or your childhood."

"There's nothing to tell. It was quite ordinary. My parents are still living in Illinois. I was an only child. Nothing special happened to me when I was growing up."

You would think that a competent psychiatrist would home in on this statement and mine it as a rich vein, devoting a dozen or more sessions to demonstrating that this apparently innocuous childhood was actually riddled with traumas, neuroses, and suppressed incest. But Lovejoy hardly seemed interested in the subject of his family. His mind had already sped on to something that interested him more.

"You're not married of course?"

"No."

"How do you get on with the Boswins?"

"Very well, I think."

"Trying to make out with the girls, are you?"

"Now really!" He felt hot and the blood rushed to his face.

"Well why not? They're both charming creatures. I wouldn't mind having a go at them myself. Stasha in particular, I'd say. Sylvie is a little vaporous. But they're both nice."

"I don't care to discuss the matter."

"But you haven't succeeded yet, have you?"

He burst out angrily, "Look. I didn't come here to—"

"The idea makes you fly into a flurry, doesn't it? Just a little medical test I was administering, Bonner. And I found out what I wanted to know. We're on the right track now."

"We are?"

"I'm sure of it. What I said just a moment ago produced the first powerful emotion I've seen in you. And! Ha ha!" He cackled maliciously. "The secret of your trouble surfaces like a whale. There's only one thing wrong with you, and that is you're not getting enough pussy. A man needs female companionship. If he doesn't get it by the time he's your age, it turns him a little queer."

"I'm not queer."

"You are though. Like those old nuts who tried to live without women—hermits and monks. Crazy as bedbugs, all of them. Your biological nature is unfulfilled, and in your case this causes an abnormal connection between the iron particles in your nerve-ends and the visionary part of your mind. At the bottom your problem is nothing but a pair of overswollen seminal vesicles."

"That's too simple."

"No it isn't. It's very profound. It goes to the heart of man's being and the human condition, if you'll pardon the expression. You see Bonner, at the bottom your fear of sex is really just a fear of death."

"Sex and death? I don't see the connection."

"It's because you don't see the connection that you're not well." Slumped in the chair, he tilted his pencil and gazed over it philosophically at his patient. "You see, biologically speaking, sex is necessary because there is death, and death is necessary because there is sex. Single-celled organisms, dividing without sex, never die and are for all purposes immortal. It was when sexual reproduction was introduced into evolution somewhere along the line that we all became mortal. If we were still amoebae, we wouldn't have sex, we wouldn't be afraid of death, and we wouldn't be neurotic."

Bonner tried without success to visualize this mentally healthy microorganism. "What am I supposed to do then? I can't become an amoeba."

"Accept your mortality. You haven't done this yet; you're still living in the world of a child who believes he'll never die. Once you accept your mortality you'll be free to enjoy all the pleasure of the world. Or if you prefer you can do it the other way round. Accept sex and you'll also accept the idea of your own death. You'll become mortal like the rest of us."

"Accept sex? How can I do that?"

"If you can't make it with the Boswin girls perhaps you need professional help. You might find someone along Shaftesbury Avenue after eleven in the evening. Or in Greek Street in Soho. My fellow practitioners. You'll find they're quite skillful."

Bonner stared back at him morosely. "You don't charge for the referral?"

"No, that's fee-splitting. It's against medical ethics." Lovejoy smiled and got up heavily from the chair, indicating that the visit was over. He did have a sense of humor. Bonner wondered if he was married himself, and if not whether he sought the kind of professional help he recommended. He tried for a moment to imagine Lovejoy in the arms of a Shaftesbury Avenue tart. The attempt failed, probably because he was unable to remove his glittering eyeglasses.

Later, in the street, he considered this theory quite objectively and without prejudice. Could it be that all his troubles were at the bottom only suppressed randiness? It was a very mechanical explanation. It turned him into an animated doll who only needed to be jiggered a bit to start working properly. Perhaps he should give it a try. He wouldn't even have to think about what he was doing and it would be over in fifteen minutes. Up the stairs of a bedsitter in Soho, pay her a fiver, and go home. It was a good deal less than he was paying Lovejoy. He didn't really believe in it. And anyhow the treatment would have to go on week after week; it was a dreary prospect.

He walked back to Kensington by the same route he had come, stopping on the way at a Lebanese café to buy a falafel which he ate as he walked through the park. He dropped the paper neatly into a dustbin in the Gloucester Road and turned the corner into Cornwall Gardens.

The old white pilastered house on the square was transformed. While he was gone the men with the van had erected around it a complicated scaffolding of iron pipes held together with little clamps. The structure was intricate and bewildering; it was like one of those drawings by Escher in which any attempt to ascend the stairs only brings you back to your original level. It was difficult to believe that this was still his old house with his mailbox in the hall and his flat on the second floor. The painters had already set planks on the scaffolding and were passing up their drop-cloths and cans of paint.

Lovejoy had said that he should embrace his fear; when he closed his arms on it he would find there was nothing there. Gritting his teeth, he mustered all the forces of his will. He ducked resolutely through the scaffolding and went through the street door into the hall, past the mailboxes. Immediately he knew it was futile; even before he reached the foot of the stairs he felt tingled and disoriented, as though the tiny ferrous molecules in his brain were eating like worms at the nerve-ends. He barely made it out into the street, clammy with sweat, before his vision began going dark.

Out on the pavement he considered his predicament. He examined his pockets; he had some money but not enough to go to a hotel. He also had an Underground pass, but he was pretty sure that he wasn't capable now of going down into the station with its ironbound walls any more than he had been of entering the house with the scaffolding around it. Still, central London was fairly compact and you could get around most of it on foot. Now where? To Shaftesbury Avenue? The idea made him sick. Anyhow it was far too early; it was only the middle of the afternoon. To the Boswins' flat in Belgravia? Probably they would take him in, and the eighteenth-century house, solidly built of stone and masonry, was no doubt devoid of iron.

He set off in the direction of Knightsbridge, but when he came to Wilton Place he changed his mind, or rather he saw the impossibility of explaining to the Boswins, to James for example, that he was unable to go home to his flat because there was a scaffolding around it. He continued on past Hyde Park Corner and along Piccadilly to the Green Park, where he turned in through the gate.

The park was almost deserted in this freezing grayish weather; there was only a single nurse pushing a pram with a bundled-up infant in it, and a muffled man in gloves walking a dog. After wandering around aimlessly on the paths for a while he found a bed of leaves under a tree and scratched a hole for himself. Scrunching down into it, he found it was comfortable and even fairly warm. There he stayed until long after dark, dozing now and then and waking up to bury himself deeper in the leaves. He was tired from all his walking and it was a good chance to catch up on his sleep.

At one point—he was not certain of the time but it must have been late because the enormous city around the park was quiet as a tomb—he got up and made his way down the winding path toward the gate where he had come in. There was a full moon and the park was clearly illuminated, with silver-frosted glass and the black skeletons of trees. When he got to the entrance he found that the gate was shut and chained. On either side of it was a high iron fence with a row of spikes at the top.

He retraced his way to his leafy lair under the tree again and burrowed under the leaves. He spent the rest of the night in an indeterminate state between waking and sleep. An hour or two before daylight he was awakened by the murmur of voices, and discovered black-clad figures standing over him discussing his fate in an atmosphere from which the moon had disappeared. However there was nothing supernatural about their enormous rounded heads with metallic gleams on them; they were only the helmets of two police constables. It was some time before he was able to identify himself or give any account of why he was unable to sleep in his flat like other people, but at a certain point he found himself sitting in a pleasant green room in a police station over a cup of tea, with Lovejoy sitting across the table from him.

"Do you have any friends in London, Bonner?"

"The Boswins of course."

"I mean apart from them."

"Not really. Why do you ask?"

He was evidently annoyed at being roused out of bed so early in the morning. He glinted at Bonner without sympathy. "Because you have got to the point where you can't take care of yourself any longer. If you had some friends in London, not the Boswins, friends of your own type, perhaps you could stay with them. Lacking that, I think the best thing is for you to stay for a while with some very nice people in Wimbledon I know who are specially trained to take care of you."

"Am I being committed?"

"Oh no. It's perfectly voluntary. I will say, however, that you can't wander about a large metropolitan city in this way with no clear purpose in mind and not being able to explain who you are. It's against the law to sleep in the park. There *is* a real world, you know, and it might be defined as one where you have to take account of policemen."

"The police were very kind and helpful. They called me sir and gave me a cup of tea, as you can see."

"You had a reader's card in your pocket for the British Museum. You know, I am beginning to wonder whether at the bottom—at the very botton"—he glinted at him meaningfully—"your problems come not from all these other sources we've been discussing but from your profession as a medievalist. It isn't natural to spend your life studying obscure old texts in dead languages. The choice of such a profession," he said, "is a deliberate rejection of reality."

"It is?"

"It's more than that. It's a rejection of responsibility. And so is mental illness. In fact, in your case the two are one and the same thing."

"What will happen to me in the . . . in this place. I don't know what you call it."

"Well, you won't be allowed to read books in Anglo-Saxon. You won't be allowed any books at all. Nothing much will happen. You'll have a nice rest and a nourishing diet. They may ask you to take a pill now and then. As you know, our perception of the external world depends very largely on what's coursing about through the endocrine system."

"Will I be free to leave when I want?"

"I'll take you in my car. It's just outside. Before we go, where are my two guns and my magnet kit?"

"I threw the magnet kit away. The guns are still in my flat. I never touched them."

"I need them for another patient," said Lovejoy.

Bonner spent several pleasant months in the Villa Felicity in Wimbledon. He wasn't allowed any books and as a matter of fact he didn't miss them. While he was there winter passed, it turned to spring, and summer came on. In March the Boswins left London and moved to their country house at Byrd Mill. He heard from them now and then; Sylvie sent a get-well note, and Stasha a facetious postcard showing a man with an enormous belly saying to a boy, "So you're Little Willy. I had a Little Willy once but I haven't seen him for years." He didn't answer either of these communications. He didn't have anything to say to them and he felt the note and the postcard were purely formal and mechanical, mere expressions of etiquette rather than signs of an intimacy that probably no longer existed. And at the same time—and this was funny or more properly mysterious—he had to recognize that as soon as he was well enough to leave the rest home he would see the Boswins again and matters would take up as they had in the past. No, it couldn't be the same as it was in the past but matters would take up again in some way. In spite of the ambiguity that hung over his memories of the family, he felt himself drawn to them by a kind of magnetism. Of course, magnetism was his enemy. It was possible that the Boswins were his enemies in this new world he had come to inhabit which was full of silent and invisible watching presences. The attraction these four people exerted on him, out of all the other billions of people on the face of the earth, was extraordinary. It was an attraction not specifically to any one of them but to the whole family, and moreover—this was curious—in order for him to be attracted to them he had to imagine them in a place, in the flat in Belgravia. If they had been living in a hotel he wouldn't have been interested in them. He tried without success to imagine them in another place, the house at Byrd Mill that he had never seen.

The Villa Felicity was a pleasant place set in a green lawn with a large white building opposite. It was possible that this was the tennis palace where the famous Wimbledon matches were held; at least there were people coming in and out of it in white clothing. After a while he fell across a more obvious explanation, that the white building was a hospital and the people coming in and out of it were doctors and nurses. If that was so, then perhaps the Villa Felicity was only a wing or branch of this institution. It didn't matter; the food was good, there was music and television in the evenings, and there was Julie with whom he played Scrabble, brushing her wrist accidentally with his fingers now and then when their hands met on the board. Julie, he began to suspect after a while, was part of his treatment, arousing in him a mild and no doubt therapeutic eroticism, a possibility that there might be more to existence than rooms with cretonne curtains disguising the fact that the windows were barred, colored pills, and meals taken on schedule, a world outside where you could wander around as you pleased looking at things in shop windows and taking pretty girls to tea at Brown's or the Savoy. He was never quite sure what the Villa Felicity was trying to do with him, or whether the people who ran it knew this themselves or had any plan for him at all. Perhaps they just thought of it as a pleasant place for him to rest for a few months. At any rate it was very expensive, so they must have known what they were doing.

During his months there he didn't entirely get over his aversion to iron, but the medical director Dr. Lohengrin was very kind about providing him with sterling tableware for his meals and removing bed-trays, scissors, and other ferrous objects from his room. By July, in the full flare of a gorgeous English summer, he was deemed well enough to attempt life on his own in the outside world. Everyone concerned—Dr. Lohengren, Lovejoy, the Boswins, and Bonner himself—agreed that the fresh air and quiet of the country would be good for him.

Seven

Bonner left the house by the door of the orangery, closing it carefully after him, and stole off under the trees across the lawn. It was possible that somebody might see him crossing the lawn, but he didn't think it was likely, and anyhow they would only think he was going for a walk along the river. He crossed the weir on the footbridge and set off on the path toward the forest a mile or so away. It was a clear windless morning. Across the river to his right the stone bulk of the Mill Cottage stood deserted in the sunlight, gazing out blankly from its two high windows like eyes. As far as he could tell he had left the house and the grounds unnoticed by anyone.

After five minutes' walk he left the gate of trees behind him and continued on with the Val on one side and the first trees of the forest on the other. A little farther on he passed something he hadn't noticed in the gathering darkness on the night a week or so ago when he first came to the house: a long and narrow earthen mound, the length of a railway car but not as high, overgrown with grass and showing signs of recent digging at one end. This was the Long Barrow, the source according to James of the collection of artifacts in the glass cabinet in the house. Perhaps Drood would bring him along sometime and let him join in the amateur archaeology. He found himself powerfully interested in the objects in the cabinet, especially since, as he understood it, they were all pre-Iron Age. He had left his wristwatch behind and had been careful not to bring anything else of ferrous metal, like a pocket-knife, on this first clandestine expedition into the forest.

After a half a mile or so the path in the grass divided; to the right it continued on along the Val and to the left it mounted up through the rising land into the forest. He hesitated. It was a little farther on, he thought, not far from the curve of the tracks where the train had derailed, that he had seen the small indistinct figure disappearing into the trees. After another moment he decided to take the path to the left anyhow. From where he stood he could see that it rose up through alders and low shrubbery into the deeper green of the forest, where it disappeared.

He began climbing through the alders and into the oaks and beeches beyond. He was perspiring a little now but it was cooler in the shadows of the larger overarching trees. A little farther on he came out into a clearing, a shallow round concavity in the forest so symmetrical that it looked almost as though it had been formed by human hands. In the middle of it two immense upright blocks of stone, overgrown with mosses and lichens, stood at a right angle to each other with flies buzzing around them. Near them a third had fallen down and lay half hidden in the thick growth of ferns and bracken. There were no natural deposits of this blue sandstone anywhere in Waldshire; it occurred only in the chalk downs far to the west. He stood looking at the sarsens reflectively for a few moments while sunlight trickled through the branches and insects hummed. Thinking of something he had almost forgotten, he slipped his hand into his shirt pocket and scattered the fingernail clippings in the undergrowth at the side of the fallen sarsens. Then he left the clearing and continued on into the forest on the other side.

The trees here were larger, immense giants that formed a shadowy green ceiling high over his head. He was deep in the forest now. There was no sound from the farmland behind him or from the town beyond. In the windless morning he was aware only of the buzz of insects and of the crackling of his feet in the twigs and leaves along the path. He was climbing up through a ravine or rising cleft in the mountain, with a trickle of water running in it and the forest sloping up steeply on right and left. Then he reached the top of the rise and came out into another small clearing, almost level and the size of a small room, covered with a carpet of grass. The air was cool and dank and smelled faintly of rotting vegetation. In the middle of the clearing was a scattered growth of mushrooms, irregular in size but forming a circle as precise as though it had been drawn with a geometrical instrument. There was a perfectly natural explanation of this: consuming the nourishment in the soil, they had grown evenly outward form the center where the spores first happened to fall, perhaps a century ago. Some people called them fairy rings. He paused for a moment, catching his breath from his climb.

It was at this moment, standing in the clearing with the sweat drying on him, that he was first aware of a low murmur echoing through the trees, or coming from the trees themselves. He stood listening, motionless and careful not to make a sound. It was like the slow purling of a river, rhythmic and liquid. After a time he identified it as the sound of voices. As he listened he made out a song in slow tempo, each word emphasized delicately and, it seemed to him, with slight irony. He caught fragments and the rest slipped away from him elusively

> *Wood-land . . .*
> *. . . deep . . .*
> *Love . . .*
> *. . . a-sleep . . .*

He advanced a little across the clearing. The sound seemed to be coming from that direction, from the forest above and beyond him. At the edge of the clearing he climbed up a little into the green shadows of the trees, standing waist-deep in the ferns. From here he could hear it more distinctly. A word now and then escaped him, but he could clearly make out the pattern of the song.

> *Dew-drops . . .*
> *. . . ears . . . ,*
> *Pre-cious dia-monds . . .*
> *. . . are her tears . . .*

The song passed through an odd turn of harmony, then it sank down and ended on a minor note that left a thinly edged echo tremoring in the air. He was sure that the singing was coming from above him and to his left, and not very far away. Heedless now of the noise he made, he pushed his way through the crackling branches and scrambled up the slope. The undergrowth was almost impenetrable; twigs struck him in the face and roots tripped him underfoot. He burst out of it in a place where the growth was a little thinner and saw there was someone watching him from only a few yards away.

It was a barefoot girl in a long gray dress with a tinge of violet to it and a shawl around her shoulders. She was small, hardly more than a child. He moved toward her and she disappeared in the leaves. But there were others, showing fragments of themselves mockingly in the maze of branches about him.

> *Bon . . .*
> > *. . . ner!*
> *Bon . . .*
> > *ner!*

He heard a laugh. He followed on after them as they flitted away, disappearing behind tree-trunks and then floating into view again in the middle distance. The whole forest echoed with the song; it came in a soft almost imperceptible chant from every direction.

> *Wood-land dark . . .*
> > *wood-land deep, . . .*
> *Shel-ter now my . . .*
> > *love a-sleep . . .*

He burst out of the branches and found them all facing him in a little semicircle. He stopped, perspiring and breathless, feeling a little foolish. There were a dozen or more of them, barefoot, in long flimsy gray dresses each with a different pastel tint to it: blue, orange, pink, magenta, violet, green. They were all pretty, all perfectly formed, except that their arms and legs were short, a doll-like feature he found attractive. One of them he recognized as the queer little person he had met at the gate of trees on the night he first came to Byrd Mill.

Hello Bonner.

She smiled, shy and solemnly mischievous at the same time. There were titters from the hidden shadows in the trees.

Still panting, with a foolish smile, he looked around him more carefully. Now others had appeared, men in tight-buttoned shirts and trousers that ended a little below their knees. They too were barefoot, their feet tough and knobby. The women had long flimsy shawls over their shoulders, and sometimes they slipped them off and floated them playfully in the air. The men wore various head-gear: stocking caps, battered bowlers, felts with wavy brims, flat vi-sored caps like Danish sailors, a knitted cap with a long tapering tail that came almost to the ground. One, who seemed older than the others, wore a tailcoat of shabby gray. On his head he had an old topper with a flaring crown and a narrow brim, a sort of hat that hadn't been worn for years.

I'm John Greene, said the one with the topper. His shabby tailcoat, in fact, had a tinge of forest leaves to it.

The others named themselves one by one, with smiles.

Elof.

Norn.

Trig.

Gondal.

Bork.

The one who had met him at the gate of trees was Jenny Stone.

And this is Lara, and Flicka, and Penny, and Cobold, don't have anything to do with him, he's a crazy fellow.

They were all laughing, at themselves or at him.

I'm Bonner.

Their voices echoed quaintly and so did his, as though their thoughts came alive in the air without any effort of their throats.

Of course. We know that. Look you, what exactly might the name Bonner mean now? inquired John Greene.

It's French for happiness.

Is that so. Well, I don't know Frinch, that's after my time, said John Greene with a waggish look at the others. But you, Bonner, look now, you're a learned man, a Clark.

A Clark? Ah, a clerk. It was the old word for scholar, he re-membered. The Clerk of Oxenford. Gladly wolde he learne, and gladly teche.

Now see here, Bonner, said John Green, you wouldn't happen to have a bit of iron about you, would you?

No.

That's good. You never know. People come up into the forest and bring all kinds of things, guns and knives, cannon-balls for all I know.

There was a fellow back some years ago, said Elof, who brought up some iron traps into the forest and set them. A poacher he was.

He looked around at the others. D'ye remember?

They all nodded, tittering.

Well, he got himself in a fix.

What happened?

Got his leg caught in his own trap, he did. Something or other touched it and the thing snapped shut, just as he was setting it. Such a shame it was. He lived for four days, tugging at the thing, until at last he grew faint from hunger and expired totally.

I don't believe that.

They thought this was hilarious too. You don't be-lieve it. Look here, John Greene, he doesn't be-lieve it.

We'll show you his bo-ones.

Bo-ones, echoed the others dismally.

With the trap still on them.

What made the trap spring just as he was setting it?

A fly lit on it, perhaps.

It was a moth, said another solemnly.

I don't care for iron myself, said Bonner.

Oh yes, we know that.

I still don't believe your story, he said, laughing himself now.

Ohhh, you're a terrible septic.

We'll put him in the septic tank.

This seemed to be one of their jokes among themselves. The others all joined in.

They've got one in the village, in Pense Coombe.

A filthy thing it is.

We'll put Bonner in it until he's more cred-ulous. A great thing for inducing cred-ulity, the septic tank is.

Do you go into the village much?

They looked at one another.

Now why should you ask that, Bonner? said John Greene.

Just to make conversation. Shouldn't I have said it?

We go into the village now and then. But only in the dark of night. They won't have the likes of us in the daytime, you see.

And Waldon. Do you ever go there?

This provoked more sideways looks among them.

We used to in years gone by, said John Greene. But now. He looked at the others. They tittered. A smothered laugh escaped here and there. But now. You see. He was trying not to laugh himself. We don't go anymore, because we can't cross the iron rails.

They all burst out in laughter, some of them until their eyes watered. Swinging their arms, they broke into a polyphonic chant like a crazy fugue of Bach.

We can't cross the rails.

We'd like to go.

And pinch the girls.

And tug their curls.

And have a feed.

Or a pint of mead.

But it's no avail.

Cause we can't cross the rail.

So we have to make do with Pense Coombe, which has everything a body could need, concluded John Greene. They all got out cloths and wiped their eyes. But we only go there at night.

I should think you might lose your way in the forest at night.

Lose our way?

They looked around, clutching at one another in mock alarm.

Lose our way.

We might lose our way in the forest.

They all began trembling. Yes sir, we lose our way all the time. It's a feer-ful place, the forest. There's no way a body can find his way in it. You'd get lost in no time.

Wander around in circles.

Bump into trees and stun yourself.

Tumble into pitfalls.

Get eaten by wild creeturs.

Well, I'm sorry, said Bonner laughing. Excuse me for mentioning it.

They all cheered up. Look you, Bonner, said John Greene. You're a good fellow. You know the ways of the world and you're a Clark. It's a good thing you've come to enlighten us in our feer-ful ignorance.

Bonner was enjoying his talk with this merry gang. He felt cosy and secure with them, a glow of good feeling that spread through his body. He had felt good almost from the time he had first caught sight of them.

Bonner could tell us all kinds of things, said one.

How wheels work.

How to grind corn in a mill.

How to break into honey shops.

How to cross the rails and go to Waldon.

How to speak Frinch.

How to write things with pen and paper like the Sassenachs.

They tittered and punched one another. Yes, we could write large tomes about the sarsens and the Long Barrow, things like that. We know all sorts of things about them.

The mention of the iron rails reminded Bonner of something.

Do you ever go walking along the rails? he asked John Greene.

Along the rails?

Yes. You know what I mean.

Only at the side of them, like. If you go walking along the rails, look you, a train might come by. That's the point, you see.

And what would happen then?

Oh, it might cause a mis-fortune of some kind. You never can tell.

No, you never can tell. You know, the night I came to Byrd Mill, there was a terrible thing happened to the train.

A terrible thing?

They exchanged looks.

What terrible thing, Bonner?

I think you know. He faced John Greene squarely. The engine driver said you were standing on the rail.

Hurrying away from it, perhaps. I wouldn't put my foot on the filthy thing.

A woman broke her leg.

Ah well, the poor creetur. You wanted out of the train, didn't you? For you to get out of it, somebody would have to stop it. That might happen if somebody stood by the rail and threw the engine driver into a fright.

Bonner laughed. Aren't you remorseful for all these tricks?

Tricks, Bonner. John Greene seemed baffled. What are these tricks you're speaking of? Do any of the rest of you know of any tricks?

They all shook their heads.

If there were any tricks . . .

It must have been Bonner himself who was doing them.

He's a sly fellow, that's clear.

He told me, said Jenny Stone, that he was carrying corn in his bag to be ground at the Mill. She tittered. But I'm sure that's not true.

I'm a terrible liar, that's so, said Bonner. But it was Jenny who said I was carrying corn in my bag. She knew about the Mill and set me on the right path to it.

Oh, she's a kind body. Helpful to strangers.

Bonner pressed them. Do you know the people at the house then?

The house?

The house at Byrd Mill.

Oh, we only go down that way at night, said John Greene broadly. He seemed to want to pass on from this subject. Look you, Bonner, the women, vain as they are, you know the creeturs, want you to listen to their song.

I think I've already heard it.

Oh, you haven't heard it all.

There was a flurry of mirthful activity. Bork produced a wooden flute and tried a few notes on it. The girls, except for Lara, assembled together and arranged themselves on some gnarled roots. The slim and dreamy Lara in her magenta dress stretched out on the bed of leaves before them. Bork raised the flute to his lips and the song began.

> Wood-land dark, wood-land deep,
> Shel-ter now my love a-sleep . . .
> Let the hid-den fire-fly gleam,
> In the for-est of her dream.

Their voices were thin and childish but perfect in pitch. Flicka in her violet dress, still singing but drawing apart form the others, capered around Lara streaming her shawl after her in the greenish air. She extended her hand; a tiny diamond gleamed and flared on her finger. Lara shut her eyes and smiled tremulously.

> Make her clad in rai-ments fair,
> Gold her gar-ments, gold her hair . . .
> Pearls are dew-drops in her ears,
> Pre-cious dia-monds are her tears.

Now the others rose and circled about Lara too with their shawls drifting after them. Some strewed mistletoe in her hair and over her dress, and others slipped off to a nearby spring and came back with their fingers dripping. The drops fell onto the face of the sleeping girl and trickled down her cheeks.

> *are . . .*
> *her . . .*
> *tears.*

Each syllable was lightly emphasized and distinct from the others, floating in the air like a flower-petal until it gradually dissolved; each stanza ended by dropping to the same minor and slightly dissonant note. The soft chant continued as the mimers circled around the sleeping girl.

> *Soft the dan-de-lion fall,*
> *Au-tumn leaves her par-a-sol . . .*
> *Wed-ding gown the sum-mer cloud,*
> *Win-ter snow can be her shroud.*

The clever Flicka held a dead dandelion in the air and blew at it lightly; the tiny grayish particles drifted in a cloud over the magenta-tinted dress. Others flung the petals of wildflowers over the recumbent figure. A handful of white blossoms floated slowly around her and sank to the forest floor.

The mimers wove in and out, the shawls intermingling and then separating again into their pastel green, violet, and orange. As each one passed she bent low over Lara and caressed the sleeping face with the tips of her fingers.

> *Touch her here and touch her there,*
> *Touch her eye-lids and her hair . . .*
> *Let her slum-ber till she's born,*
> *Wake her with a shep-herd's horn-nnn!*

As the song died away the flute broke into a miniature fanfare. Lara sprang up from the bed of leaves and laughed, a little peal of delight that burst out of her almost in spite of herself. She brushed off the dandelions and the white blossoms and shook her hair free of the mistletoe.

Did you like our song, Bonner?

She floated playfully toward him and touched her fingers to his face in the way the others had caressed her as she lay in the leaves. He felt a prickle of cool delight. The others circled around him and did the same one by one; some touched his cheeks, others his hands, others passed the points of their small sharp nails over his clothing. Flicka slipped her fingers over his eyes, covering them for an instant, and then darted away. With light mockery they strewed flowers over him as they had over Lara. There was a little tinkle of laughter from one, then another.

A warm glow of felicity swept over him, tremoring on his skin like butterflies. He was aware only of pastel shapes passing before his eyes and of a light, heady aroma of crushed flowers. He moved forward after a violet-tinted dress and it vanished into the trees. Running after it, he seized it and found himself embracing the laughing Flicka. Her small soft shoulder dissolved in his fingers and she eluded him. A magenta-tinted dress floated into his vision and he grasped it; it was the slender and owlish Lara. The form he felt under his fingers was that of a child, short-legged and short-armed, yet with disquieting contours of womanhood here and there. She too broke away from him with a hard little smile.

He groped for the others one by one. Each small supple form struggled for a few seconds in his hands and then escaped, sometimes with a gasp, sometimes with a ghost of a laugh. The green-tinted dress of Penny floated by him; he stopped her by seizing her waist rudely and slid his hand upward until it met a soft and babyish swelling like a seashell. A cry like broken glass came from her, a kind of alarmed tinkle, and she slipped from his embrace.

Panting, he stood and looked about him. The others had all collected and were watching him, men and women intermingled. Flicka's dress was torn at the shoulder and she repaired it with a thorn without taking her eyes from him. With shame he realized that he was in an aroused state and that this was showing through his clothing. He was aware of the musklike odor of his own body.

Look you, Bonner.

John Greene had a queer expression on his face, not disapproving exactly but solemn and serious. He had assumed a curious dignity in spite of his small stature and his battered topper.

You see, you're a good fellow. But you've been down there among the Sassenachs and you still have their ways. The gels don't like it, you see.

I'm sorry.

We know the thing you have in mind, said Trig in a deep bass voice.

Oh yes, agreed John Greene. We know of it. But it's a mortal thing to do, look you, Bonner. And when you think of it, it's not a nice thing, is it?

He said nothing. His face was still flushed and burning and his body stank. He had not quite recovered his breath.

A body might love and cosset you and still not want her dress torn, said Flicka quietly.

The Sassenachs caress folk inside their bodies. That's not a nice thing to do, said Lara with her private smile. She seemed more amused than resentful about the whole thing.

All the beasts do it, said Trig, still in his deep voice. The coneys and the hares. I've seen 'em, more'n once.

This entertained the others. Evidently Trig was a simple figure and often the butt of their fun.

Oh, the dear beasts.

They don't know any better, the sweet creeturs.

They do all sorts of things.

The coneys eat their own droppings.

Why don't you chase after 'em and ask 'em, Trig, they might show you how.

Oh, leave off now, said the deep voice.

The subject had changed and the obloquy, bantering as it was, had turned upon Trig. Bonner was grateful. He swallowed and looked around him. The perspiration dried slowly on his body.

Now Bonner, look you, don't take it hard, said John Greene. It's a thing you didn't know. You're a great friend of ours, so we'll overlook it. It was just that, he decided, cheering up, the gels sang their song so prettily that you were carried away. He laughed and glanced around in his roguish way at the others.

Bonner thought of something.

You don't have children.

No, we don't, said John Greene agreeably. He seemed to have recovered his good humor entirely. They're a mortal thing, children. For look you, Bonner. If you have a child you become a father. And if that child grows up, he may have a child too, and you become a grandfather. And what happens then? You turn into an old man, and you must perish utterly. It's a mortal thing, Bonner.

He wanted to question him more but the words clung in his throat and wouldn't form; he wasn't sure what he wanted to ask. He felt a note of the ominous; a coolness, a touch of shade fell over the forest as though the light was fading. He looked around bewildered and saw that the shadows were deeply slanted in the forest. He had left the house in mid-morning and now it seemed to be late afternoon, although this was hardly possible. Perhaps he had slept, after the song, and had forgotten it.

John Greene. What time . . .

They looked at one another and then at him. They all laughed. He laughed too; he hadn't really expected one of them to have a watch.

The sun is as you see it, said John Greene.

I'll have to leave now.

Aye, you'd best be down before dark.

The others nodded vigorously.

In the dark you might lose your way, said Bork.

Bump into a tree and stun yourself.

A fox might eat you, intoned Trig solemnly in his basso.

He felt a sense of genuine regret at leaving them, almost a panic. There was a lump in his throat. He wondered whether he might come back and whether they would still be here in the same place if he came. He wanted to ask, but John Greene had turned away from him and the others had fallen silent. He fixed his mind on trying to memorize how he had come up through the forest in the morning past the two clearings.

They set off down the path with John Greene leading the way sturdily on his short legs, with Bonner following at his elbow and the rest of them loping along behind like spotted dogs after a coach.

Look you, Bonner, said John Greene as he marched, you must come back to us again, for it's good to have you with us. You're a learned man, a Clark, and you can help us with your knowledge. There's things we can't do, you see, without the knowledge of a learned man like you. You still have a bit of your Sassenach ways but that's not your fault. See now Bonner, we all grieve for you when we know you're not well in your head.

When I'm what?

We know you're a good fellow. It's the iron that makes folks not well in the head. It comes from the factories in the plain. A terrible day it was that men found out about iron. They ought to have left it in the earth where it was and not come digging and disturbing it.

Yes.

If you're not well in your head you must come to us, said the little man, reaching up to set his topper straight.

They had passed the dell with its circle of mushrooms and were going on down the ravine that led to the sarsens, with the small brook trickling and seeping under their feet. They clambered down the rocks that served as steps at the steeper places, then the path leveled and came out into the lower clearing with its three immense stones.

Here John Greene lagged and then stopped; the others came up to him and stopped too. They stood looking at one another all smiles and surmises, with a touch of their slyness.

John Greene considered.

Well now, what do you think?

They all chortled at once.

I think we might.

We've got lots.

Bonner's a good soul.

And they're fond of them down there below.

Simple Trig seemed undecided. Well, I don't know. They're pretty things and we're fond of 'em. He looked about at the others. What's one when we've got so many? he agreed finally in his voice like a bass viol.

He could use it for all kinds of things.

He could buy honey with it.

He could parade about and show it to folks.

He could give it to his girl, tittered Flicka.

Well then, to work, all of you, said John Greene.

The men disappeared in different directions into the forest. The women remained behind, forming a circle around Bonner and staring at him in their slightly malicious way, suppressing their giggles. In the middle of the circle he was immobilized. He smiled at them, not sure what was happening.

When the men came back each one was carrying a stick, a branch, or the trunk of a small tree. They went to the fallen sarsen half-hidden in the ferns and wiggled and pushed the sticks under its side. After a few heaves and grunts they pried the enormous stone off the ground enough so that John Greene could reach under it and extract an ordinary earthenware cooking-pot with a lid. He brushed the earth and grass from it and pulled out a leather bag with a drawstring. Feeling into this with his small broad hand, he took out something and gave it to Bonner.

He looked at it. It was a bright coin with some kind of leaping animal on it in bas-relief, perhaps a springbok, and below it was the legend, "1 oz.—Fine Gold."

They were all smiling in a shy and self-satisfied way. John Greene put the bag away in the pot and tucked the pot into its hole under the stone. On a signal, the others removed their sticks and the sarsen fell back into place with a thump.

None of them said anything and Bonner was silent too. He put the coin in his pocket and turned away from them. At the edge of the clearing, just before he reached the trees, he looked back. The clump of figures had not moved. John Greene was still watching him, and at his shoulder was Lara with her subdued and dreamy, her wise, owlish and curious, her innocent and blank, her childishly mysterious smile.

Eight

He woke up and found that he was lying in bed in his room as usual and that it was a quite ordinary morning in the country. Lying lazily in the bed and still only half awake, he was aware of familiar sounds: voices from downstairs, a clink of crockery from the kitchen, the distant faint lowing of cows from the pasture. He lay listening to all this for a while and then a thought struck him; he got up quickly and pulled open the drawer of the nightstand by the bed.

He turned over the stale pack of cigarettes, the theatre ticket, the dead flower. At the bottom of the drawer was the Krugerrand; he took it out and inspected it. It gave the impression that it might have been in the drawer for some time; it was covered with a light film of dust. Of course it might have become dusty from the other things in the drawer; everything in it was filthy and mixed up with the stale grains of tobacco from the cigarettes.

It was late in the morning; he could hear Sylvie practicing downstairs in the music room. He had mislaid his watch somehow and wasn't sure what time it was. He dressed, went across the passage to the bathroom, and shaved himself with an electric razor, trimming his beard afterward with the scissors. When he came back to his room the coin was still lying on the nightstand. He slipped it into his pocket and went downstairs.

The morning room was deserted; the others had already had their breakfast and left his on the sideboard for him. Hurriedly and without appetite he ate a piece of toast and drank a cup of lukewarm tea; he wanted to have a talk with Sylvie about something.

When he was finished he went down the passage to the music room and opened the door.

Sylvie was sitting at an old Broadwood piano, a heavy dark instrument with intricately carved legs; there was a lamp at one side illuminating the music on the stand and providing an attractive Vermeer-like chiaroscuro. The piece she was playing was something baroque with intricate fingering and many trills and decorations; she frowned with concentration and chewed the edge of her lip as she played. Her hair was tied in the back with its usual velvet ribbon, and she was as pretty as always in a dress that showed the small knobs of the vertebrae on her back. As she turned to glance at him her long Cromlech chin was dented with a little crease of vexation. Perhaps she didn't like people to watch her when she was practicing.

He looked over her shoulder at the music on the stand; it was a violin partita of Bach transcribed for piano by Busoni. Sylvie worked at it diligently, glancing only occasionally at the music and keeping her eyes for the most part on her hands. Now and then she broke off and, without interrupting the tempo, played a passage over until she got it right. The thing came to an end in a flurry of flying fingers. She took her hands from the keys and dropped them into her lap, breathing heavily.

"Brava."

She smiled thinly without replying.

"It sounds very difficult."

"It is. It's been my bugbear for weeks."

"You seem to have mastered it now."

"It's full of mistakes. I've got to have it ready soon. I'm going to have a recital in London in November."

"Yes, James told me."

"He's hiring the Wigmore Hall for me. And this is to be the program. The Bach-Busoni"—she took it from the stand and replaced it with another piece of music—"and this little trifle of Martinů, and this boring old César Franck, and some waltzes of Ravel, the music is around here somewhere but I've mislaid it, and finally an étude of Saint-Saëns"—she flopped the music onto the stand and played a little of it, fluently and with only a single mistake when her hand seemed to trip over her thumb. Her hands at the ends of her thin forearms were muscular. In fact they seemed slightly unnatural, now that he looked at them more closely in the strong lamplight, like the hands of those famine victims in photos which have remained strong in some way in spite of the broomstick emaciation of the arms.

"I thought you enjoyed your music."

"Oh, I do. It's just this old piano. The action is so stiff—it fights back at me. And I have to do this for two hours a day. People don't realize that playing a piano is tiring."

"You play so beautifully."

"You don't understand technique, Bonner."

She picked up something from the piano. It was a plaster cast of the hand of Chopin, with the fingers stretched as if to play an octave chord.

"My London teacher Nigel Farrington gave me this. It's to remind me to work hard." She held it up and showed him the unnatural separation of the fingers. "To be a pianist you have to mutilate your hand. Do you know the story of Schumann's hand? He got a machine that held up the other fingers while each one struck the keyboard, to stretch the web of the hand. Instead he broke something in his hand and paralyzed it. After a while he could play the piano again, but not well enough to be a concert performer. So instead," she concluded, "he became a composer."

She put the plaster cast back on the piano and got up, trailing her fingers over the piano as she left it. The room was a pleasant one, with an oriental rug under the piano and a pair of Chinese vases on stands. The old paneling was evidently genuine and there was a drawing in a walnut frame of Brahms playing the piano. The curtains were drawn; the room was dark except for the lamp on the piano.

She flopped into an armchair and closed her eyes. She was in a curious mood; he had never known her to be so restless and out of sorts. She didn't seem to be annoyed with him, however; it was something else, or a number of things. He slipped onto the piano bench and began idly fingering the keyboard with his right hand. He wasn't very much of a pianist, although he had taken lessons as a child like everybody else.

"James says he wants to do everything he can to help you with your career. He says you're determined to become a concert pianist."

"James always decides what he wants us to do, and then says we want it."

"He says Stasha is going to become a fashion model."

"Stasha could never be a model. She can't hold still long enough."

"An actress then." He tinkered out the first phrase of the forest song, as well as he could remember it, ending, as he discovered after some groping, on an F. The next line was similar except that it dropped to an A flat, a slightly dissonant effect.

Slumped in the chair, she opened her eyes. "What *is* that?"

"Heard melodies are sweet, those unheard are sweeter. How," he asked her, "can you be a concert pianist and Stasha a model if you're living here in the country?"

"You can't."

"James tried to explain to me why you moved to the country. He said you girls would like it. It was in your blood because you're half English."

"Balls. I hate it here. In London we had a Steinway, at least a decent instrument I could practice on. Here we have this antique torture machine."

He was startled; he had never heard her use so vulgar an expression. "Well, perhaps James would get you another piano." He went on fingering out the song. Each of the four phrases mounted up a little higher on the keyboard. He had started in C minor, but the thing ended as far as he could tell on an E natural, an impossible note.

"Did you make that up?"

"What would you say if I did?"

"That you have a queer imagination. I don't believe you made it up. I have the feeling I've heard it before—that odd turn at the end."

"It's probably just a mistake I'm making." He got up from the piano and turned to her. "Sylvie, I want to tell you something. Something that happened to me yesterday when I went to the forest. I know I'm not well. I'll explain it to you, and then you can tell me whether—"

The door opened and Stasha came in. Finding them in a conventional dramatic pose, Sylvie in the armchair and Bonner with spread arms launching into his speech, she tittered. "Am I interrupting something? Oh, I see that I am. I'll leave."

He felt only a momentary annoyance; he had something he wanted to say to Sylvie but it could wait until later, and he did like

Stasha too. This morning she was wearing a tank-top that showed an enticing edge of her breast, shorts, and white moccasins. She went directly to the piano and seized the plaster cast, arching her back and stretching langorously. "Oh, touche-moi, Frédéric. Embrasse-moi." She caressed herself up and down with the white fingers, with particular attention to her breasts. "Oh Frédéric, comme tu me fais amoureuse."

"Oh Stasha, don't be tiresome." Sylvie took the cast away from her and put it back on the piano.

"It *is* a boring morning."

"It was until you came along," said Bonner. "Now everything's brightened up. You're such a charming creature."

"Why don't we do something. We could walk to the pub in the village. Heavens, we can't do that, it isn't even noon yet. Or feed the deer."

"We're interrupting Sylvie's practicing."

"No," she said with a sigh, "I've been at it for my two hours. Let's go out."

They found apples in the pantry and stuffed them into their pockets. It was a sparkling summer morning, with a hint that it would be hot later. They crossed the lawn and entered the park through the simulated-rustic gate. There was no sign of the deer. The big trees stood motionless in the sun, emitting faint clicks that perhaps came from insects in their branches.

"The deer are shy at this time of the day," said Sylvie. "You have to come here at daybreak. Then they're quite tame and you can walk right up to them and touch them."

"Do you come here at daybreak?"

"Sometimes."

"I came here once with James in the middle of the morning. We saw them then."

"He probably summoned them with his authority. Everybody has to obey James, even the deer."

"Oh deer, my possessions, come forth so that I, James, may inspect you and see that you have your rabies shots and have not been fornicating or lying down during working hours. James," said Stasha, "is very good with animals. He goes every day to the dairy to bark at the cows about production, and sure enough every day they produce milk."

"Stasha, don't chatter so. You'll scare them away."

They were almost at the end of the park. In the distance, beyond it, he could see the galvanized-iron roof of the dairy.

"I don't think we're going to see them."

"Shhh. There they are."

They got out the small cider apples from their pockets, wrinkled and crabbed, reddish-brown with streaks of black. The deer appeared in the undergrowth only a little farther on. The old stag was there; he stopped and stared at them over the top of a bush. Following him were a half-dozen or so does.

"Now be quiet," said Sylvie.

She advanced slowly, holding out the apple. The stag raised his head and sniffed. Sylvie stopped. From behind her Bonner caught a glimpse of porcelain neck where her hair was caught up with the ribbon. Her narrow body was erect and patient, motionless. The stag stamped lightly with his forefoot and half turned away.

"I, James's servant and delegate, command you to eat an apple, you dumb critter," said Stasha. She went forward holding out hers. "Oh, Sylvie, they're going away. They're such cowards. What a bore."

"It's the wrong time of day," said Sylvie.

They turned and walked back under the overspreading elms and beeches. Stasha bit into her apple and so did Bonner. After a while Sylvie followed their example. They were sour and tough but surprisingly good. He remembered that he hadn't eaten much breakfast. He finished off the apple, nibbling around the edges and tossing the core away into the grass.

"Let's go look at the museum."

"I've already seen it," said Bonner.

"We all have. Let's go look at it again."

They went down along the hedge and met Drood, who was coming up the lawn from the footbridge across the river. He was wearing his usual tweed jacket and boots and he had a light knapsack slung over his back. As he drew up to them he took off the knapsack and dangled it by one strap.

"Scaring the deer, were you?"

"How did you know?"

"I saw you from across the river."

"We were just going to the museum and look at the presses."

"All right."

The four of them wound around the corner of the Mill Cottage and past the sunken pond and its statue, Drood bringing up the rear with his knapsack. They pushed open the unlocked door and entered; Drood came in after them and switched on the light.

Bonner found that the iron in the room didn't bother him so much when he was with Drood and the girls; still he didn't go down to the floor of the museum. He sat down on the landing and stuck his legs through the low wooden railing, with his feet dangling over the presses below. The others did the same.

"This is so *boring*," said Stasha. "Why didn't we go to the village?"

"But if no one ever comes to look at the presses then it won't be a real museum and James will be disappointed."

"Well then why doesn't he *tell* people about it. Put notices in the papers and so on."

"Oh, he doesn't want just anybody to come."

"But he wants it to be a real museum. That's inconsistent."

"Yes but it's very human."

"Oh, James is very human."

"Does anybody ever come to look at the presses except the family?" inquired Bonner.

"Oh yes, Fred Baines came to look at them once. He's the man that takes care of the cows."

"What did he think of them?"

"I don't think he thought they were as interesting as cows."

"Well they're not," said Bonner. "Look how interesting a cow is. How complex. A printing press is just something mechanical after all."

"Only God can make a cow."

"Yes, exactly." He remembered again the bad poem by Joyce Kilmer and how true it was. "I wish James had just restored the mill the way it was in the Middle Ages. That would be interesting. Does a mill have any iron in it?

"Not very much. Even the axle in the wheel was probably wooden."

"James says there's always been a mill here."

"Well, I don't know about that," said Drood. "You see, originally there was just a shallow place in the river here. In prehistoric times it was a convenient place to ford the Val. People from the valley beyond, where Waldon now is, crossed the river here on their way to the sarsens. And once people start to ford a stream at a certain place, somebody else is sure to build a house there to sell them something. Beer, honey, or wick-lamps. Or just to charge a coin as the price of crossing. And once there's a house at a ford, sooner or later someone will get the idea of damming up the water and turning it to some useful purpose."

"Why did they come from the valley to the sarsens?"

"No one is sure exactly. It may have had something to do with astronomy, or with some ceremony of the seasons. Perhaps they sacrificed goats there, or other people's children. Nothing is known about the sarsens except that they are very old and that the stone came from somewhere else. Did you know that the spire of Lady Church in Waldon and this mill and the Long Barrow and the sarsens are exactly in a line? You can draw a pencil-mark through them on the map."

"No, I didn't know that. But if they are it's called a ley."

Drood look at him curiously. "Ah, so you know about them."

"Not much."

"What's a ley?" inquired Sylvie.

"All over Britain there are alignments of this kind, usually of churches, old stones, or spots that were believed to be sacred. A man named Watkins wrote a book about them. Some people think that early man used them to find his way through the forest. Other people believe that the leys follow some sort of invisible lines of power across the countryside, and that prehistoric people learned to harness these forces in some way by erecting stones or cairns along them."

"They could be landing strips for UFO's," said Stasha.

"They could be but they weren't."

"How could the Lady Church be a sacred place for prehistoric people?" said Sylvie. "It wasn't even built."

"Early Christian churches were often built in places that had been sacred to the local inhabitants for centuries."

"Do you believe in leys?" Bonner asked him.

"I didn't say that."

"Then you don't believe in them?"

"I didn't say that either. People have constructed maps showing hundreds of them all over Britain. It isn't very difficult. If you get out the average map you're sure to find at least three or four points that can be connected up with a ruler."

"So," summarized Bonner, "primitive people traipsed back

and forth, wading across the Val here on their way to the sarsens, and then someone built a house and charged them a coin to cross, and then someone else turned the house into a mill, and then the miller moved out and the Cromlechs moved in, and then the Cromlechs moved out too and built the present house, and then James came along and bought the whole thing and made it into a museum for printing presses. And the Lady Church and the mill and the Long Barrow and the sarsens are all on a line you can draw on the map."

"If you say so."

"What a rigmarole," said Sylvie. "Drood, I think you've made all this up."

"Perhaps James has learned to tap invisible lines of force running over the earth and that's why he's rich."

Drood grinned and showed his rabbit-teeth. "Very likely."

Stasha kicked her feet. "Oh, this is all so *boring*. Why don't we start up that thing, whatchamacallit, the Altoona Clarion. Bonner, make us a paper."

He looked questioningly at Drood, who shrugged. Bonner stood up and pushed the red button overhead and then sat down with the others again. The Winterthur press below them groaned and started into motion. The large double feeding-arm rose into the air, came down, and grabbed a sheet of paper from the stack.

"I don't think James wants us to do this."

"Oh look, it's doing it," exclaimed Stasha excitedly. She leaned over to watch the complicated clanking of the arms, levers, and cylinders, lost her balance, and almost fell over the low railing. She gave a frightened squeak and grabbed at the railing. Her moccasin, dangling on the end of her foot, fell from her toe. "Oh fuck, I've lost my shoe."

Bonner, looking down, caught a glimpse of the white moccasin jammed under the feeding-arm and being relentlessly thrust under the cylinder. It disappeared into the machinery which groaned and slowed, but finally managed to spew it out on the other side.

"Oh Bonner. Get it for me, will you? I'm afraid it's ruined."

He felt giddy. He got up and took Sylvie's hand, pulling her up after him. "Let's go."

They sat down on the river-bank with their feet dangling over the water, a little upstream from the Mill Cottage at a place where they were half hidden by the trees. Behind them they had left Stasha and Drood trying to extract the moccasin from the press.

"Why is it," said Sylvie, "that when I'm with you I always feel I'm doing something naughty. Something that James would disapprove of. It's a rather nice feeling really."

"I bring out the naughty in people."

"Professor Twist. Why have you brought me here anyhow? Are you going to seduce me? Under these wicked old trees."

They were perfectly ordinary poplars. "I don't think I'll do that just now. I wish you'd be serious, Sylvie. You're always like this after you've been with Stasha. She brings out the silliness in you."

"Oh, we bring it out in each other. Sisters always do."

"They're going to find us in a minute." He toyed with a coin in his pocket, took it out, and found he was holding the Krugerrand. He put it away again. "Listen, Sylvie. I was trying to tell you something in the house. About what happened yesterday. I went to the forest and—I don't know how to explain this." He stopped and started over. "Look, Sylvie. Suppose I told you that I've had a dream. About another kind of people, different from us. They live in some other place, but we can go there. They wear different clothes from us, and they . . . they're gentle and loving and magic. They aren't crass and selfish like the rest of us. They aren't lustful. They—"

"You dreamed this?"

"Not exactly. They have everything they need. They don't have anything made of iron; they don't need it. They're merry and full of fun. They play all kinds of pranks. You have to laugh. They—"

"Bonner."

"I know. I know that I'm not well. But they're—they make music, Sylvie. They make the most beautiful music. You know—that song I tried to play for you on the piano just now. It's strange and . . . I want you to know them," he concluded, a little dumbfounded at his own burst of eloquence.

She said quietly, "You know that can't be, Bonner. They belong to you."

He turned to her with a kind of urgency. She was watching him calmly out of her large eyes. He reached out and touched her just below the waist. The long oval of her face seemed to swim and blur in the greenish reflection from the water. "Sylvie. If you could come with me and see them too. It would mean that . . . how the hell can I explain this. I don't understand it myself."

"Oh you two," broke in Stasha's voice. "There he is with his hand on her snatch."

"Almost," said Drood.

He jerked his hand away as though Sylvie's body were a white-hot iron. The invaders came toward them on the river path, and Stasha showed them the moccasin. It was bent double and covered with ink from the machine. On the stained white leather a fragment of headline could be read, "ULL MARKET TAXES NER."

"A rare edition. It might be worth money. You should save it," said Bonner.

"Bonner was just telling me about a dream he had," said Sylvie.

He vehemently wished she would shut up. He gritted his teeth and turned away from her.

"Oh, dreams are so boring," said Stasha.

Bonner never did get to finish his conversation with Sylvie. After the four of them went back up to the house the girls got into Sylvie's small Morgan, which would only hold two, and went to the village. Bonner wandered into the hall after Drood, who was still dangling his knapsack by the strap. His attention was caught by the antlered head on the wall, directly facing the crossed shotguns across the room.

"Did James shoot the stag?"

"Oh no. That's quite old. It was here in the house when I was a boy."

"How about the shotguns?"

"James bought them when he moved in here. There used to be some crossed swords there; I don't know where they are now. In general James has kept things pretty much as they were."

"Chekhov says that if there's a gun on the wall it will be used before the end of the play."

"These are only loaded with birdshot. They could hardly hurt anybody."

"Does James shoot?"

"Not that I know of."

"Why does he have them then?"

"He has the impression it's something you do if you live in the

122

country. You know, I have a great deal of sympathy for James. He wants so badly to be an English gentleman. But it's difficult. The first requirement for being a gentleman is that you shouldn't want anything that badly."

"Drood, why did you people surrender to James anyhow?"

"Surrender?"

"Just look at you. You people used to be the gentry here. Now you don't amount to anything anymore. You're just his possessions. He's come and taken over your house and put Swedish furniture in it, and filled it with guns."

"You exaggerate so, Bonner."

"You didn't have to surrender to him. You could have simply walked out of the house and gone to London and got jobs. Instead you threw Tita in his path, so that he would come here and buy the house with his money. Now you're just his possessions."

Drood contemplated him languidly and smiled. "That's just the way the world is, Bonner. James is just the world. If it hadn't been him it would have been someone else. You see, everyone admires the English, and they don't just admire us, they want to *be* English. James wants to be just like us. He's not doing very well at it now, but perhaps his children will, or his children's children. You Americans are just the last wave of foreigners who have invaded us. First there were the Romans, and then the Danes, and the Anglo-Saxons, and the Normans. We just assimilate them all and in time they become English. Perhaps the next wave will be Chinese, I don't know. We'll assimilate them too, and you won't be able to tell them from the English. We're pretty good at this. We've been doing it for two thousand years."

He lifted the knapsack, which he had lowered to the floor while they were talking, and went through into the gallery. Bonner followed him.

"What's in the bag?"

"Just some trifles. I was digging a little in the Long Barrow this morning. I saw you going off yesterday for a walk yourself, by the way."

He was a little flustered. "Yes. I went for a walk in the forest."

"And what did you see there?"

"Oh you know, the usual things you see in the forest. Shy woodland creatures."

"Strange folk flitting from trunk to trunk?"

Bonner flushed. He felt a warm wave of surmise. "Then you believe there are such things?"

"I didn't say that."

"You didn't say you *didn't* believe it. It's like the leys."

"Exactly. If there were such things, you would be the one who would be able to see them, I imagine. It's much more likely that you made the story up. You know, when we met on the train, you told me the world is our own mental construction."

"Did I?"

"You also said that everything that happens is in our mind."

"Well it is, I suppose." He came to his senses now and decided not to reveal to Drood what he had seen in the forest; he would only open himself up to ridicule.

"That story you made up about my being a gamekeeper. There's something childish about you, Bonner. I don't say it's un-attractive but it's still childish."

He unlocked the glass cabinet and slid back the top.

"That's quite a collection you have. How long have you been keeping it?"

"Oh, I began when I was a boy."

"Have you ever studied archaeology?"

"No." A little smile.

"Don't these things belong to the National Trust?"

"That's right." Identical smile.

The things in the knapsack didn't amount to much. He set them one by one into the cabinet, displacing the other objects to make room for them. A pair of bone needles, a broken comb, a few scraps of pottery, and a tiny pierced object of bronze no bigger than a candy mint, the kind called Life Savers in America and Polos in Britain.

"What is that thing anyhow?"

"A clitoris-ring."

"That's ridiculous."

"Well, what do you think it is?"

Ignoring the tiny bronze doughnut, Bonner reached into the cabinet and took out the decorated stag-horn. The figures on it were cut with some crude tool like a sharp stone, but with consider-able skill; they covered the surface of the horn completely and you had to turn it to see them all.

"What do you think this is?"

"It's a horn with incised figures showing traces of pigment."

"I mean what's it a picture of. This one character is wearing a stag's head, or else he's a stag standing on his hind legs. The others are bowing down to him."

"Totemism is very common in prehistoric art."

"So is fetish, the confusion of the signifier and the thing signified, according to Derrida. Maybe the horn itself was blown in some ritual to summon the faithful. Dieu! que le son du Cor est triste au fond des bois!"

"Alfred de Vigny. Maybe, except the tip of it isn't bored out so you can't blow it."

"You're very well read for a gamekeeper. It never occurred to me before that an animal's horn and a horn you blow are the same thing."

"The first musical instrument. You know, you and I get on fairly well, Bonner. I don't know whether it's because you're dotty or because I have a feeling for the past."

"The eminent Dr. Lovejoy says it's the same thing."

"Lovejoy has all sorts of theories about you. Some of them are quite sound, and others I think are wildly fanciful."

"Then you know him too?" Drood's remark was a little disturbing. He had thought of Lovejoy as part of his London life and Drood as part of his life in the country; he didn't like it when people he kept in separate parts of his mind turned out to have joined hands behind his back.

"Oh yes. James told me the whole business about your being under treatment and going to the rest home. Did you ever wonder why I was on the train with you that evening when you first came here?"

"You said it was a coincidence."

"Actually I had several pieces of business in London that day, but while I was about it I called on Lovejoy. Since you were going to be a guest in the house, I was naturally curious about you. He rambled on for some time about your various ailments and his theories about them. He said you stole a magnet from him, and also had guns in your possession."

"I didn't want the things. He forced them on me."

"It's true that he connected the form your illness took to your profession as a medievalist. But he didn't feel it started from that. He felt it started from something else. Did he ever advise you to seek out a woman of the streets or anything of that kind?"

"I don't think I care to discuss what he told me."

"It used to be called green sickness when it occurred in languishing maidens. It's rarer in males, he says, but it occurs now and then. He says that Van Gogh was a typical case. In him, sexual denial took the form of hallucinatory visions which he transcribed in his very strange pictures."

"What right on earth did Lovejoy have to talk about the case of a patient under his care with you, a perfect stranger?"

"Oh well, he's a friend of the family. I told him I was James's brother-in-law. I don't say I'm entirely convinced by his theory. Like all psychiatrists he overemphasizes sex. But it did make me wonder why you happened to come to Byrd Mill when you got out of the rest home or whatever it was, out of all the thousands of places in the world where you could have gone."

"I came here because James invited me."

"That doesn't really answer the question, does it? Why did James invite you?"

"Because he likes me, I imagine. I like him too. I like all of you."

"Yes, we're all so likable. Everyone likes us. Sylvie is a charming creature. And Stasha."

"What are you getting at, Drood?"

"You were asking me a moment ago why we surrendered to James. You yourself said we were his possessions. James likes to acquire things. It's really not so unpleasant being acquired by James. He's after all an intelligent sensitive man and one who takes good care of his possessions. Polishes them and dusts them and keeps them in a well-lighted room. He even starts them up now and then and makes them do their thing, to show to visitors. I for example am the eccentric country gentleman on whom he is attempting to model himself. I rather enjoy it. Perhaps you'll like it too, being a member of the family."

"I don't know that I have any plans to become a member of the family. It's true that I was trying to kiss Sylvie just now, when you and Stasha surprised us, but she wouldn't let me. That sort of thing doesn't mean much nowadays. People do it all the time."

"James is a man who usually gets what he sets out to get. I myself would rather enjoy having you one of us. You're a pleasant chap. You're interested in these things." With a final glance at the glass cabinet, he slid it shut and locked it, pocketing the key. "Maybe I could be the family expert on shards and bone needles, and you on strange folk flitting from trunk to trunk."

Nine

Bonner stole furtively out of the house and crossed the gravel toward the garage, the former mews. It was another fine day with the soft English sun playing over the kitchen garden and the orchard. Over to the right there was an abandoned tennis lawn with a sagging fence and weeds springing in the grass; he hadn't noticed that before. He opened the garage and allowed the sunlight to flood in on the three cars. The Daimler and the Morgan were side by side and the old estate wagon behind them. As far as he could tell, nobody ever drove the estate wagon. Drood walked everywhere, and it was impossible to imagine Cassie driving a car of any kind. Perhaps Rhondda used it to go to the village for groceries. He opened the door of the Morgan and in that instant saw lanky dour Miles watching him from the shadows at the rear of the garage.

"Got the keys out of your mum's purse did you."

"I don't think that's any of your business."

"I'll tell them up at the house that you've got the car."

"You do that. It's a nice little car, isn't it? I believe it's all aluminum except the engine."

"The engine's aluminium too. The block and the head. The valves and all that are iron probably. I understand you're addled about iron."

"Who told you that?"

"Oh the servants do talk below stairs."

Bonner looked at him. He seemed incapable of humor; perhaps he was mentally deficient. He did seem to understand cars though.

"Is there gas in this thing?"

"What?"

"Petrol."

"Oh yes."

He reached into his shirt-pocket for a Players and lit it without taking his eyes off Bonner. He had the black look of all the locals around Pense Coombe, and probably all of Waldshire.

"Know how to drive or do you want a lesson."

Bonner ignored him. He inserted the key and after a couple of tries got the car started. It ran with a pleasant clicking sound, coughing only a little because it was cold. "Yank, are you?" said Miles. Bonner drove it out of the garage and turned onto the right-hand edge of the lane that led out to the road. "IN THIS COUNTRY WE DRIVE ON THE LEFT!" Miles shouted after him.

On the road outside, which was called the Canal Road, he drove for about five miles until he found a place to get onto the Motorway. Here he quickly pushed his speed up until the wind sang in his ears; the traffic was light and the small open car flew along as lightly as a dart. It was a lot better than the train. He felt only the light presence of the ticking iron valves in the engine, and the car was open to the air, the clear pure empty sky and the yellow sunshine. A turnoff for petrol went by, a cluster of road-signs, a chalky hillside in the distance; the car mounted effortlessly over rises and sang down the slopes on the other side.

The fleeing black ribbon went through woods with a grove of ancient oaks on one side, and he smiled. Why did the sight give him this little twinge of pleasure? He remembered and thought: *I have seen the Little People.* He had never dared to pronounce these words even to himself, but in thinking them even silently in this way he brought a new hard and opaque reality to what had happened, as though before it had been only a dream or a vision and now it sprang out before him in solid and living flesh. An excitement came over him, an exultation. He was one of the privileged few who had seen these elusive and magic friendly creatures ... and yet, had he or not? A doubt assailed him, a flaw in his happiness. Had they really been there? And what exactly did he mean by "there"? There in his head or *really* there, outside him in the objective world?

It was on this point that he was seriously muddled, or rather ambivalent as he preferred to think of it. He had to retain this ambivalence if he was going to cling to the slippery tail of his belief that he had seen them, because clearly, by any rational argument, he had not. It was simply the old problem of the elusiveness of reality: a Mandarin fell asleep and dreamed that he was a butterfly, but then on awakening, was unable to decide whether he was a Mandarin who had dreamed of a butterfly or a butterfly who was now dreaming he was a Mandarin. It was possible, from a philosophical point of view, that two such systems of reality could exist in alternation but not at the same time, just as you can't see both sides of a piece of paper at the same time.

This, however, was rather too sophisticated an explanation for what was probably only a symptom of mild mental illness. The rational explanation was that they were only hallucinations, harmless enough but lacking any true permanence or reality. If so, they were astonishingly clear and had all the solidity of real objects in the real world. He could hardly believe that the speaking and moving figures he had seen, singing in silver voices, touching his emotions, brushing their fingers over his eyelids, were only poppy-dreams and moonshine, the figments of an overfevered imagination. What exactly was meant by the word hallucination? It meant seeing something that was not there. But how do you know that it is not there? Because other people can't see it. But that's not satisfactory. St. Teresa of Avila didn't have hallucinations. She had visions. Why do we believe this? Because we believe that what she saw was real.

Of course, he went on taking up the other side of it, as though he were Bertrand Russell arguing with a lunatic, it was easy enough to induce all sorts of minor visual disturbances through modifying your physical conditions, such as the stars or fried eggs you could produce by pushing your thumbs onto your eyelids. And there were optical illusions, and effects produced by drugs, and the pink elephants and other entertainments seen by alcoholics. Just because you saw it didn't mean it was there. But, Mr. Russell, what about Yeats, and Conan Doyle—*they* saw them, and so did other intelligent people, poets, seers and mystics, even innocent children; books were written about them, and some people even claimed to have photographed them.

The thing was, he *wanted to believe.* It would help if he could find somebody else who had seen what he had seen, or at least thought he had. He had almost achieved this with Drood; he had been on the point of asking him flatly if he had seen the Little People and then he had held back at the last moment, filled with a sudden unresolve, a fear that Drood's witty bantering might destroy these fleeting visions that he clung to so longingly. He did not intend to make this mistake again. He looked forward with excitement to the rendezvous he was headed for, with a person who did not know he was coming and was unaware of his existence. This afternoon he would know for sure, or he would know that it had *not* been real, that what he had seen was only hallucination.

When he came off the Motorway on the outskirts of London he drew over to the side of the road and consulted a map he found in the glove box. With its help he began working his way around the great spiderweb of the metropolis. After several mistakes and wrong turnings, he got himself onto the North Circular Road and threaded his way through East Acton and Ealing to the M4 Motorway leading west into Berkshire. Once he was on this, it was only ten minutes to the Maidenhead turnoff. In Maidenhead he stopped again and consulted the slip of paper with the address he had got from British Rail. Twenty-four Borndon Road. He had to ask a boy on a bicycle about the street, but after that he found the number easily enough. It was a well-kept brick house, more prosperous than he had expected. He rang the doorbell.

The door was opened by a gaunt woman whose hair was done up in a bun with a fine net over it. There was a cameo on the bosom of her print dress. She stared at him, taking in his old corduroy jacket and his shoes with turned-over heels.

"Mr. Lacey, please."

To this she replied not a word. Perhaps she was deaf. She was certainly not frail; there was a large-limbed elemental strength about her. Her face, craggy like the rest of her, was covered with a reticulation of fine wrinkles, as though the hair-net had been drawn over it too.

"Excuse me. I'm looking for Mr. William Lacey. I've been given this address."

"I am Mrs. Boatright."

"I see. Does Mr. Lacey live here?"

"Who are you?"

"My name is Foley. I—"

"Mr. Lacey can see no one."

"I'm sorry. Is he not well?"

"Who are you?"

"I tried to tell you but you interrupted me. My name is Foley. I—"

"Are you from the Rail?"

"I beg your pardon? I want to see Mr. Lacey on a personal matter. I don't want to disturb him. I represent no one. My name is Bonner Foley. I'm a perfectly harmless person, an American, with a doctorate in medieval studies. I've written a number of books that are in any library in case you'd like to consult them. I've recently been institutionalized but I'm quit well now, and I have some friends named Boswin who are persons of substance and would be glad to verify my identity and speak for my character. Is Mr. Lacey in?"

Without another word and without changing her expression, she opened the door a few inches more, and he passed after her into the vestibule of the house. She called out in a fluted voice, oddly birdlike coming from her gaunt and rangy frame, "Emma!"

The two of them stood silently in the vestibule waiting for Emma to come. She seemed to be evaluating his jacket-button, and he inspected the print dress and the cameo more carefully. When Emma appeared she was a kind of duplicate of Mrs. Boatright made on an inferior copying machine, fuzzy around the edges and indeterminate in color. She too wore a print dress, in a finer pattern and more somber. In place of the cameo there was a simple onyx pin. Her hair was done in a different pattern, fitting her head like a small helmet, but with the same net over it.

"What is it, Elodie?"

Mrs. Boatright, or Elodie, only inclined her head toward Bonner. Emma fixed her eyes on him as though she had not up to then noticed him standing in the vestibule. In spite of their outward similarities the two women were quite different. Emma had none of Elodie's formidable presence and imperturbability. Something quivered just under her surface, rendering her eyes liquid and causing a faint tremor at the corners of her mouth. She was a smaller woman and gave an impression of fragility, of flightiness, as though she were a chronic invalid or a mystic who led a withdrawn spirtual life.

"Excuse me. My name is Bonner Foley. I've come to call on Mr. Lacey. Is he in?"

"What was it in regard?"

"A personal matter."

"I don't believe William has any such friends. I don't remember you."

Her voice was thin and unsteady, with a little catarrhal thread as though she needed to clear her throat. She looked at Elodie for support. The two women exchanged a glance and then they both went back to staring at him.

"I've come as a friend. I'm not his friend, but I've come as such, and I'd appreciate your letting me see him. If not, please say so at once and I'll go away. I don't intend to make a pest of myself. If you'll excuse me for saying so, I've heard that the English were reserved but I didn't know they were rude."

This extreme language seemed to provoke them, even though reluctantly, into a spasm of conventional behavior.

"We're not, I'm sure. It's just that William—"

"Is nervous."

"He has very few visitors. He doesn't go out much. We've encouraged him to have more friends. I'm sure you're just as you say, a medieval doctor. Is that your little car in the road?"

"Yes."

"It's a little yellow car," explained Elodie to Emma. "If you'd like to come this way."

The two women led him through a number of passages and turnings to the rear of the house. There Elodie opened a door and motioned for him to enter, without altering the severe expression which was evidently a permanent feature of her face, even when she was trying to be gracious. He went in through the door and the two women followed after him. Lacey was sitting in an armchair watching a television only a few feet away from him across the room. The crawling red, green, and yellow colors on the screen were dimly reflected in his face. He turned his head as they came in and then went back to watching the program.

"William, this is Mr. Bonner."

"Mr. Foley. Mr. Lacey, excuse me for bothering you. I wanted to make your acquaintance because—"

"What?"

Bonner went to the television and switched it off. The picture on the screen winced, drew inward to the middle, and turned black. The scratchy voice from the speaker ended. Lacey turned in the chair and inspected him with a frown.

133

"My name is Bonner Foley."

Lacey got up from the chair, looked at him and made as if to offer his hand, changed his mind, turned around like a dog preparing a place to lie down, and sat down in the armchair again. He was lanky of limb, slow, deliberate, and a little suspicious in manner. He appeared to be in his sixties, although his complexion was fresh and pink; he had a bald head and a cranium with a ridge along it like the roof of a house. He blinked at even intervals, about every five seconds.

"Who did you say you were?"

"My name's Foley. I was a passenger on the train—"

"I don't want anything to do with you. I don't want to talk to you."

The two women exchanged a glance. They went back to following the conversation attentively.

"Mr. Lacey, I'm not from British Rail, and I'm not from the insurance company and I'm not from the press. I've just come to see you personally. I'd like to have a friendly chat with you."

"William," said Emma, "we don't know anything about Mr. Bonner. He just came here. Came in a little car. We don't know where he's from. You don't have to talk to him."

Bonner wisely said nothing. He began to suspect now that this was the way to get Lacey on his side.

Elodie said, "You shouldn't tire yourself, William. Although we have encouraged you to have friends."

"If you like we'll ask him to go. We did, but he wouldn't go. He said he wanted to see you."

Lacey stirred himself in his chair. He looked at Bonner more carefully. "What did you want to see me about?"

"I just wanted to have a friendly chat."

"Mr. Bonner—"

"His name is Foley, Emma. He said so several times."

"I wish you'd call me Bonner. May I call you William? It's a way we Americans have. It sounds funny at first but it's friendly and you get used to it."

"Bonner," pronounced Lacey experimentally.

"I imagine you're out of a job, since you're here at home. I saw something about it in the paper. I'm sorry about that."

"The papers didn't tell the whole story," Lacey told him gloomily.

"I'm sure they didn't. They never do. You see, I was a passenger on the train—"

"He *might* be from the insurance, William. He might not be telling the truth."

"William, do you suppose we could have a quiet little talk together, just the two of us? We might have interesting things to tell each other. It's been a great pleasure meeting Mrs. Boatright, and also Mrs. Lacey—I assume it's Mrs. Lacey—" he looked around at them and they all three stared back at him. "But I was hoping for a friendly chat with just the two of us. Later, perhaps, we could all sit down and have a chat about what a nice day it is and how we've all enjoyed meeting one another."

"Emma," said William, "why don t you see to something in the kitchen. Or run your sucking-machine around on the floor. I'm sure there are so many things for you to do. You're always telling me how much work there is in the house."

The two women exchanged another of their glances. Elodie fixed Bonner in her stare again, no more hostile or no less stonelike than all the others, and then she withdrew, followed by Emma. Bonner and William watched the door-handle click upward into its closed position.

"Emma is my wife," said William. "Elodie is her sister. She's a widow. Drove her husband to drink and ruined his liver. A fine young chap was Boatright. He worked for the town council, an architect. This is her house."

"It's very nice."

"When we were married, you see, I wanted us to have a place of our own. But Emma wanted to be near her sister, so we moved into this house and we've lived here ever since. She's never charged us anything, you know."

"That's very generous of her."

"Elodie is a fine woman. She has very high principles. Hardly anyone can come up to Elodie's principles. And if you try, then she raises the principles."

"So they've put you on leave, have they?"

"Yes. Trains were my whole life, you know. I worked for the Great Northern, and then the British Rail after they changed the name, for fifty years. Now I've got nothing to do but sit here and watch this trash on the telly."

"You don't look that old."

"I began as a boy, going up and down the tracks picking up bolts."

"Picking up what?"

"Bolts. The trains lose bolts, you see, as they go down the rails, and someone has got to pick them up."

"Do they put them back on the trains afterwards?"

"I can't say. It was someone else's job. I worked for forty years before they made me an engine driver. They said my reflexes weren't quick enough. And there was a written test. That was difficult. But I persisted, don't you see, and finally they made me an engine driver after all. By that time, this was ten years or so ago, they were having trouble getting enough young chaps to apply for engine drivers, because the wages were so low. And so they made me one after all."

"William, is all this true?"

"What do you mean?"

"All this you're telling me about British Rail. About bolts falling off the trains. About the wages. I can hardly believe they would make a man an engine driver when his reflexes were too slow, just because nobody else wanted the job."

"You said you wanted to have a friendly chat."

"I'm sorry. I believe everything you told me."

"That was a crack train on the Waldon line. Those things go too fast, really. Of course, on that day I was only substituting for another chap."

"William, how did the thing happen to go off the rails anyhow?"

"Well." He started to give his account of it. There was a knock on the door and immediately, without waiting for an answer, Emma came in with some things on a tray. "It's time for your tea, William." On the tray were a small teapot, a single cup, a napkin, and an egg cup with a blue-and-white capsule in it. She set these things on a table by William's side, filled the cup, and handed it to him. He took the cup, looked at it as though it were a strange object he was recognizing only with difficulty, and sipped a little. There was nothing for Bonner; there was only one cup on the tray.

Elodie put her head in the door. "And the—don't forget, Emma."

"Yes." She took the capsule from the egg cup and placed it in William's outstretched hand. He put it in his mouth, took a sip of tea, and then spat the capsule out from the side of his mouth and inconspicuously slipped it into the pocket of his sweater.

"You were telling me about the derailing."

"Yes. Thank you, Em." He turned and stared straight at her until she left the room. He set the teacup aside. "You see, I was coming along just entering the Waldon section and I saw the New Bridge ahead."

There was a clatter and a sound like a low-flying airplane from just outside the door. Elodie's sucking-machine was evidently an old one but powerful. It hummed up and down the passage, bumping against the walls and the door to the room.

"Just about then I—"

Bonner moved his chair closer so that he could hear.

"... I was coming along and I could see the New Bridge ahead, you know. There's a curve at that point." A doubt overcame him. "I don't know whether I ought to tell you all this."

The door opened, this time without a preliminary knock, and Elodie came in briskly. "William, you shouldn't overtire yourself. It's almost five and there's another good thing on the telly. It's that game, you know? The one you like so well. The one where all the people wear baby clothes. Mr. Foley will be leaving soon. Emma, stop hoovering because William wants to watch the telly." She switched on the television and waited until it flickered bluely, jumped, and sprang into a picture of a young woman explaining that a bomb had gone off in Lebanon. When this melted in favor of the game host in a pinafore holding a microphone, she left the room.

Bonner got up and switched the televison off. "Why don't you want to tell me about it?"

"I don't know. That's all past and gone. There's no point in dragging it up again. How did you find where I was anyhow?"

"I saw the story in the Waldon paper. Your name was in it and I got your address from British Rail. I just wondered whether you could tell me—"

The door opened again and Elodie said, "I'm going out to get some things. What would you like for supper, William? I'll get a nice bloater. I know you like bloater."

"Anything."

"Emma will be here in case you want anything. I'll leave the door open."

Bonner went to the door to shut it and found Emma watching him from the end of the passage. He sat down again, leaving the door open.

"William, who don't we step around the corner to the public house. I'm sure there's one in the neighborhood."

"I don't drink."

"You don't have to. We can just have a little talk."

"The women will have supper ready in a while."

"Elodie has just gone out for the bloater. She won't be back for some time."

"I don't go out much anymore." He fingered at the buttons on his sweater, hesitated, and got slowly out of the chair. "I'll tell you what. I'll have to step out for a moment to the lav. It's the tea, you know." He started for the door, but took Bonner by the elbow and pulled him after him, nodding mutely. Under Emma's eyes they went together down the passage and he opened the door of the bathroom. He pushed Bonner and pointed to another door at the end of the passage. "You go out there."

Bonner went to the door cautiously and opened it. It led onto a stairway at the side of the house, ending in a lane. From the lane he made his way out to the road in front of the house. Presently the stooped hurrying figure of William appeared at the door and came down the stairs. His escape was covered by the gushing of the old-fashioned toilet. For the first time Bonner noticed that William was wearing a pair of worn carpet slippers instead of shoes. When he caught up with him he took his elbow again. "It's just down the road there at the corner."

In the Orange Tree, a pleasant dark pub with almost nobody in it, Bonner got two pints of bitter and brought them to the table where William was waiting. They both sat down and took a long sip from their glasses before either of them said anything.

"I don't suppose that Emma and Elodie drink."

"Oh no. They're temperance."

"But you slip out now and then and have a drop at the Orange Tree, is that it?"

"Now and again as you might say. Sometimes Emma takes a nap in the daytime, and if Elodie happens to go out at the same time I can manage to nip. But the women can smell the stuff on your breath, you know. I can't do much of it."

"Elodie is the elder, I imagine."

"D'you know." He seemed puzzled. "I've never known that. It's likely Elodie is the elder. But perhaps not. Maybe they were twins. I've never known that," he said again in a puzzled tone.

"And you've been married for—"

"For thirty years."

"For thirty years." Bonner contemplated the long face, the lugubrious frame, with a new curiosity. "Do you have children, William?"

"No, you see Bonner, she wouldn't let me."

"Let you?"

"She wouldn't let me. Wouldn't ever let me touch her. Her mother was opposed to it, and Elodie kept a watch on us. You know, it makes a chap nervous after a while, when you're living with a woman and she won't let you touch her."

"It might. Do you mean to say you've lived with her for thirty years and you never . . ."

"Well, the two of them were very close. I might have been able to talk to her if we were alone, but Elodie was always there."

Bonner pondered over this and studied William's face, which offered no clues to the rather improbable history of his life. "Elodie is a funny name. Is it French?"

"It was their mother's idea. Emma and Elodie. Put them together and they spell melody. It worked pretty well. I've never been able to separate them and neither has anybody else."

He had finished his pint and he looked around hopefully for more. Bonner's was almost gone too and he went back for two more pints.

He waited until William had drunk a little of the fresh glass. Then he said, in as casual a tone as he could muster, "About the derailing. The people of British Rail told the press that you braked because you saw a small man on the tracks."

"Yes." Or perhaps, "Yes?" William's tone was vague and his eye wandered.

"What did you mean, a small man?"

"Just a little chap."

"And he was not on the tracks, he was standing by the side of the tracks. Isn't that right?"

"He might have been. I only caught a glimpse of him, you know."

"Was he wearing a hat?"

"A hat?" William thought and became furtive. "He might have been wearing a hat."

"Well, what kind of a hat was it?"

"What kind of a hat? I don't quite see what you're driving at."

"I mean, tell me about the hat. It was a funny hat, wasn't it? Was it a topper?"

"It could have been. It very likely was." He seemed very dubious and looked nervously about the empty room. "That's an old-fashioned sort of hat. Why, nobody has worn a topper for years."

"And he was wearing an old-fashioned coat too, wasn't he? A tailcoat."

"He was only a little chap. The light was so poor I couldn't see much."

"But you saw enough so that you applied the brakes."

"I didn't want to run over the little chap, after all."

Bonner began to see that he had made a terrible mistake in asking him all these leading questions about hats and other clothing. He was probably only putting thoughts in his mind. William gave every sign of being a very suggestible person. Now he would never be able to get a straight story out of him.

He tried another tactic. "If he was a young chap he must have been fairly agile." William hadn't said he was a young chap, he had said he was a little chap. But William didn't correct him. "Enough to get out of the way of the train," he persisted. "What was it about him that unnerved you?"

"That what?"

"That caused you to go into this panic reaction and jam on the brakes and derail a whole train full of people, all of whom just wanted to get on to Waldon and go about their business."

William turned and looked at him fixedly. There was a spot of foam from the beer on either side of his mouth. "Mr. Foley, I knew what it was all right. The thing is, I'm afraid to tell anyone else about it."

Bonner waited. He was aware of his own heartbeat, pulsing softly in his chest like a cunning animal waiting to spring.

"You would think it was silly. People would say I was not right in the head. I wouldn't want to tell them."

When Bonner still said nothing, he went on in his rambling way with many repeats, the manner of a man who has spent his life talking to people who weren't listening to him. "I knew what it was all right. But people would think it was silly. Take you, should I tell you or not. I've got nothing against you personally. But I'm older than you and I've been around for some time. You see a lot of rum things in a lifetime. But there are some things that, if you see them, it's better not to talk about them. People don't take it right. They only think you've gone dotty or something."

"You don't mean me, do you?"

"Oh no. You're a friendly enough young chap. But I don't like to talk about things to anybody, very much. People always take it wrong."

He stopped there. It didn't appear likely that he was going to say much more. He had finished off his second pint and Bonner wasn't sure it would be good for him to have more. He already had a vitreous look about the eye and his chin had descended an inch or so below its normal position.

"Perhaps we'd better go."

"Well, I don't look forward to it."

"To what?"

"To going back to them, you know." He fixed Bonner with his slack and mournful eye. Probably he wanted Bonner to buy him another drink.

A sudden idea struck him. He had intended only to interview William to find out what it was he had seen on the tracks, but now he decided to rescue him from these two frigid and disapproving scolds who made his life a misery. He was conscious all the while of the danger of messing around with other people's lives, but once this idea had come to him it was fixed; it dropped like a billiard ball into a pocket.

"I'll tell you what, William. Why don't you just not go back. You can come and stay with me in the country."

"In the country?"

"I live in the country with friends. It's a large place. There's plenty of room."

He looked dubious. "Well, I don't know. I'd have to go back and pack a grip. And the women, you know, wouldn't let me."

"They can't stop you if you don't go back. You can come just as you are. You don't need anything at all."

"I haven't got my things. Toothbrush. The women—"

"You don't need anything."

"I couldn't do that."

He allowed himself to be led passively out of the pub and down the road. "You see, they'll be expecting me for supper." Groping absently in the pocket of his sweater, he encountered something and threw a small blue-and-white particle into a bush.

"What was that capsule anyhow?"

"They're for depression. They make me jittery and also they make the depression worse."

"Don't take them then."

"I really ought to go back. You know, they give me those things three times a day."

When they reached the car in front of the house they both got into it, William's long knees jutting up in the small cockpit. Bonner started it up and pulled away without, as far as he could tell, being detected from the house.

William looked around at the tooled leather seats and the walnut dashboard. "Is this your car?"

"Yep. It's a fine machine, isn't it. It's all aluminum, even the engine. The valves are iron."

"You don't say so."

"Do you like working with things made of iron?"

"Of iron?" He seemed mystified.

"You worked for the railway for fifty years. Trains are made of iron, of course. Did you like that?"

"I don't know. I don't know what else you'd make them out of."

"Aluminum, for example. Like this car. It's a very fine piece of machinery." He got it onto the M4 and accelerated until the wind began to whistle about their ears. "You see? It runs beautifully. Ordinarily I don't care for cars but I really like this one."

William's hair at the sides of his head fluttered up and down. He set the palm of his hand on his bald spot. "Where is this place in the country?"

"In Waldshire. Near Pense Coombe."

"Why, that's right near where I—where the train went off the rails."

"That's right. I got out and walked from there to the house. You see, I saw him too."

"Who?"

"The little chap in the topper."

William stared straight ahead and said nothing.

Darkness fell over them on the Motorway long before they got to Byrd Mill. As the house loomed up on the right Bonner turned in off the road and followed the blond beam of the lights down the short lane. When he stopped on the gravel the ticking of the engine echoed loudly in the silence. He opened the garage door and put the car away, backing it in neatly so that he left it exactly as it was before. There was no sign of Miles or anyone else. A single light was on in the kitchen; the other windows of the house were dark. A dog barked somewhere in the distance.

With William following him he made his way along the drive, with the gravel crunching noisily under their feet. They came to the quieter grass at the side of the house. Seeming to sense the clandestine nature of what they were doing, William said nothing and made almost no sound. They reached the hedge and felt their way along it in the darkness, then turned the corner of the old stone wall.

"What's this place?" came a hoarse whisper in the darkness. "Shh."

"That looks like the house back there."

"It is. We're not going to the house. This is the Mill Cottage."

Inside on the landing he didn't turn on the light. A thin starlight penetrated into the museum from the open door behind, barely revealing the shapes of the machines in the room. He led William by the hand and went forward extending the other hand ahead of him like a blind man. It encountered a rough door; he pushed it open and they went on into the room beyond.

"You don't have a match in your pocket, do you?"

"A match?" repeated the quavering voice in the darkness.

As far as he could recall the arrangement of the rooms, they were in the kitchen. He could smell the water in the old brass pump. He groped around and finally found the switch that turned on the small weak bulb in the ceiling overhead. William was revealed blinking and looking around at everything with an unsurprised air.

"You see, there's everything you need here. There's a bed in the next room."

He went in and turned on the lamp, a spindly little thing with a parchment shade. The bed was provided with a straw mattress and some shabby blankets, and the lamp was on a table at its side. There were no windows in any of these rooms; the walls were damp and there were flaky excrescences on them. Blotches of moisture covered the ceiling. In spite of this dungeonlike atmosphere, he felt oddly secure and comfortable in the old mill, and apparently William did too. It was something about its isolation and privacy, its dumb stony exclusion of the outside world. William inspected the place with his lank eye, ending with the crude wooden door.

"This is an interesting place. It looks like something in some old story. I like to read old stories, you know."

"You do? What kind of stories?"

"Oh, stories about bygone times. Some of them rather odd. That kind of stories. But Em and Elodie don't like to catch me reading. They say it gives me ideas. They'd rather have me watch the telly."

"I'll see if I can't get some books for you."

"Oh, it's all right. I enjoy being alone. After—you know—mm." He seemed reluctant to criticize Emma and Elodie, even now at a distance from them.

"Yes. You'll be snug in here. No one will bother you. I'll go and find you something to eat."

He groped his way out through the dark museum again, then crossed the lawn and entered the house. By this time it was almost midnight and everyone had gone to bed. The light was still on in the kitchen. He found a saucepan and went about collecting things in it: a couple of eggs, a tin of sardines, a tomato, the end of a loaf of bread. He was looking around for some coffee or perhaps a bottle of beer when he sensed the presence of another person in the room. He turned and found Rhondda considering him from only a few feet away. She had entered the room without a sound, wearing a long black gown that had the look of a nightdress.

"What are you looking for, Mr. Foley?"

"I'm looking for a bite to eat."

"What do you want? I'll make it for you."

"No, I was just looking for a snack. Don't bother, please."

"Then why do you have that saucepan?"

"I thought I would take some things up to my room and fix them there."

"There's no electric ring in your room."

"There's one in the Mill Cottage," he said recklessly. "I'll go down and get it."

"Yes, I saw you just now coming up from the river. And didn't I see you earlier, going down the lawn with someone else?"

"Someone else?"

"Yes, another person."

"Who was it?"

"I can't say. I'm not even sure you were with another person. I just had that impression."

"Perhaps it was my shadow. Or an old Cromlech ghost."

She greeted this suggestion with her black skepticism. Perhaps it was her way of being amused; he had never seen her smile.

"You're a remarkably attentive woman, Rhondda."

"Attentive?"

"Yes. You notice what's going on in the house."

"I wouldn't say that. Sometimes I can't sleep, that's all, so I stand and look out the window."

"You must see a good many things."

"Oh, anybody will see a good many things if they stand at a window long enough."

"You've been in this house a long time, haven't you, Rhondda?"

"Oh yes."

"Before James came."

"Oh yes. Long before that."

"Are you from the region?"

"I beg your pardon?"

"Did you grow up around here?"

"My people had a farm just down the Val. I left it when I was fifteen and went into service. I don't think my personal history is of any interest to you, Mr. Foley."

As far as he could tell she was free of rancor. She simply radiated darkness, like one of those astronomical phenomena into which everything falls and goes black. He felt that he too might fall into her pit if she stood there watching him much longer in her dark dress.

"If you'll excuse me, I'll take these things away and I won't bother you any further. Is there a bottle of beer perhaps?"

She got it out of the refrigerator for him and he put it in

his pocket. There wasn't room for anything more in the small saucepan.

"Mind you don't start a fire," she advised him. "The walls are stone but there's all that old wooden furniture."

"I'll be careful."

Ten

It was a week later. William was safely installed in the Mill Cottage and Bonner brought him food stolen from the kitchen from time to time. He also found him some books, including James's copy of *Explorations in Dawnland* which he filched from the bookshelf in the house. William appeared quite content; he was able to cook on the electric ring or at least to warm up the food that Bonner brought him, and he spent most of his time reading. He also slept a great deal and seemed to have no impulse to leave his hiding place. There was an earth-closet in one of the small stone rooms and he took care of his needs there. Bonner felt a sense of secret and mysterious pleasure in this new possession of his, the engine driver in the mill. Earlier in the evening he had taken him a cold mutton-chop left over from the family dinner, and had left him puttering about in the kitchen warming it on the electric ring. Then he had retired to his own room in the house to go over his well-thumbed copy of the *Ancren Wisse* and make notes in the margin. It was Tolkien's edition of the Corpus Christi manuscript, which he had carried around in his suitcase for months but hadn't been allowed to look at in the Villa Felicity. He had not actually gone back to writing his book yet; that would require an effort of the will and imagination that he didn't yet feel able to muster, but he had at least got to the point of making pencil notes in the margin of the text. His other research materials, the notes from the British Museum, were still in his flat in Kensington. He surrendered himself to this task for two hours or more, with the happy sense of privilege of an expert working in a specialized field that he understands thoroughly.

When it was after midnight he folded up his book, yawned, went across the passage to the bathroom and micturated without any very impressive result, and roamed around the upper floor of the house. The girls had gone earlier to a cinema in Waldon but they were back now and had gone to bed. The rest of them too retired early in the country. Everybody seemed to be asleep except for James, whose light was still on. He slept in a small room by himself, while Tita occupied the large bedroom at the end of the house. There was no sound except for the inconspicuous rustle of James clearing his throat. Probably he was reading in bed.

Bonner descended the stairs into the darkened house below. No one was astir down here either. He turned on the light in the kitchen and rummaged through the cupboards one by one but found nothing in particular that enticed him. He had a craving for something sweet, a reversion to the forgotten desires of his childhood. The family didn't really have very many sweets with their meals, although sometimes Aunt Cassie made a trifle. He sampled a bland tea-biscuit from a box, put it away in the cupboard again, and went restlessly out of the house onto the lawn.

It was a clear warm night. The moon hung in the west like a shadowy orange, just touching the horizon. The trees on the lawn, the Mill Cottage, and the river were illuminated in a grayish wash that blurred their outlines and yet lent them a vivid sharpness, like a knife seen through half-closed eyes. Without having any very clear idea in mind he went on down the lawn toward the river, followed the bank past the Mill Cottage for a few yards, and came to the weir with its footbridge.

After a hesitation he set off across it, picking his way carefully; the wooden plank bridge was narrow and there was only a wobbly railing on one side for support. Below his feet he could see tiny pearls of phosphorescence stirring and bubbling in the water flowing over the stones. On the other bank he set off on the path over the rising ground of the meadow.

After a short while he realized he had lost his way and missed the fork on the left leading into the forest. He stopped. Below on his right he could hear the Val purling and mumbling, and on the other side was the slope scattered with alders. He couldn't tell whether he had passed the fork in the path or not yet come to it.

He turned and looked back the way he had come. Behind him he could see the Val curving along under the meadow and the whitish cube of the Mill Cottage. The house itself, hidden in the trees, was harder to see. Beyond it, visible over the house because of his slight elevation, was the outline of Waldon on the horizon. After some searching he managed to make out the spire of Lady Church, a small needle silhouetted against the loom from the setting moon. To find the ley that led into the forest he had only to line this up with the Mill Cottage. He started off again over the meadow, glancing over his shoulder at the spire creeping leftward toward the stone building in the trees. When the two were exactly aligned he found the path and followed it without much trouble even in the darkness. In only a little while he passed the Long Barrow, an indistinct shape smelling of damp earth. He looked behind him; the spire, the Mill Cottage, and the barrow were precisely in line. The light from the setting moon was fading and in only a few minutes he would no longer have been able to see the spire.

He entered the first trees of the forest and came out into the clearing where the sarsens glowed in the starlight. Giving them only a passing glance, he continued up the rising cleft in the mountain. His progress was a good deal more difficult than in the daytime; he stumbled continually in the bracken and bumped into unseen branches. He held his arms in a protective shield around his head and blundered on. Finally, after a number of wrong turnings and a good deal of groping, he came out into the second clearing where he had seen the circle of mushrooms, although they were invisible now.

The trees overhead were black and the forest floor under his feet was inky; only a thin lactic light seemed to float in the air, illuminating nothing, as though the particles of the air itself were glowing faintly. There was no sign of anything moving in the forest and no sound except the munching of his own feet in the dried leaves and now and then the call of some nightbird, a lugubrious double note that sank at the end. It was probably an owl. He pushed on through shoulder-high ferns, less sure of his way now because he had gone beyond the farthest point of his daylight visit to the forest.

After a while he stopped and listened. He heard the owl-note again. After a moment it was repeated, and then came a fragment of song in a thin falsetto voice.

Weave. A. Cir. Cle.

He stood motionless, holding his breath to hear more clearly.

Round. Him. Thrice.

The fragment trailed away and there was a tinkle of laughter, from more than one voice. He pushed his way through the ferns and came upon a blur of indistinct forms in the shadows. There was a white flash of teeth, the glow of eyes, and more stifled laughter. He identified Lara by the graceful line of her cheek when it caught the starlight. The other girls he didn't recognize. With them was a small squarish man holding something in his hand.

I heard you singing.

They laughed again. That wasn't us. That was Bork. He's such a caution.

He mocks us by singing. Do it, Bork.

Another giggle. The second girl he recognized by her voice as Flicka. Bork, or his shadow, clapped vines over his head to make a wig. He set his fingers on his chest, drew erect, and sang in a sweet falsetto uncannily like the voices of the girls.

> *Oh John my son*
> *why doan you cum to hame . . .*

Bonner laughed too. Have you lost your flute then, Bork?

My forest pipe? Ah no, I've got it right heer.

He raised it and made the owl-sound. The two girls joined in their thin harmony, on the same dying fall.

> *To wit, to-woo,*
> *He cries the mid-night for-est through . . .*

They broke off, interrupted by a chatter like baby birds. There were others in the clearing now; he recognized Jenny Stone and the clumsy and simple Trig with his bass voice. Bork with the flute to his mouth leaped lightly through the ferns and started down the path, and the others followed. Bonner fled along with them, Lara at his side and Flicka just ahead. There seemed to be a dozen or more of them; behind him he caught sight of John Greene's topper bobbing rhythmically in the darkness like a dolphin plunging in the waves. But this time John Greene said nothing and hurried along with the others, allowing Bork with his flute to lead the way.

With these jolly guides for his escorts he had no difficulty finding his way down the cleft in the mountain he had come up with such difficulty only a short time before. The shawls of the girls floated like wraiths in the starlight; the various hats of the men bobbed up and down as they ran. For all their leaping and chorusing they made remarkably little noise. The laughter and snatches of song were a liquid murmur like water splashing; their feet touched lightly on the forest floor. Only Bonner's feet crackled in the dry leaves and bracken; the Little People seemed weightless, as though their feet were only touching the ground intermittently to guide them in their headlong descent down the mountain. People often said that a hurrying person flew or that his feet hardly touched the ground; the Little People semed to be playfully illustrating these locutions, with smirks at Bonner and stifled laughs.

Don't make such a crash with your feet, Bonner our friend. You'll awaken all the creeturs in the forest.

And the Sassenachs below. They'll call the alarm and come at us with pitchforks.

Do they ever come at you with pitchforks? he panted.

They might except they can't find us, said John Greene, who was now running along at his side holding onto his topper. We've learnt to tread lightly, look you. That's why we're still about after all this time. Some folk don't even believe we're here in the forest.

I'm not so sure myself, laughed Bonner. His breath was short and his limbs ached from the mad pace of the descent through the forest, but he was blissfully happy and at peace.

He's a terrible septic!

They all chanted:

> *The septic tank!*
> *The septic tank!*
> *We'll put him in the septic tank!*

They burst out into a clearing and back into the darkness of the trees again, guided by an occasional flute-note from the invisible Bork up ahead. They fled past the sarasens, not stopping this time to dig up a coin for Bonner, and emerged in a straggling band onto the meadow.

In the open starlight he could see them more clearly. All about him fine silken hair swirled, the dresses rustled and fluttered, the shawls glittered with tiny pastel sparks. There was clownish Co-bold, clever Flicka in her violet dress, serious May Brown, and old Quare who had a light stubble of a beard. Fingers brushed him playfully, and he reached out and touched the undulating figures at his side as he ran; it was like grasping gossamer or soft curls of smoke. They were loping along with the Val at their left, a dark curving thread under the meadow. Across it he could see the park and the grounds, and dim pink fragments of the house through the trees. Everything was transformed, enchanted, as though the house had been reconstructed for a stage play or portrayed by a slightly deranged artist. The Little People stopped, piling together in a soft bunch, and stared across the river with mock solemnity. They nod-ded to one another, rolling their eyes; they glanced at Bonner meaningfully. A spurt of laughter broke the transfixed quiet of the starlight.

Is your sweetheart awake, Bonner? We could call her to come with us.

It was dreamy Lara, who had replaced John Greene at his side.

She's asleep. And she's not my sweetheart.

A repressed titter or two. They went on over the meadow to-ward a clump of trees in the distance. Bonner had never explored this bank of the Val beyond the house and he was not sure of the way. The path continued along the river-bank, through a couple of unlocked gates which they crowded through with little hurrahs and left swinging behind them, and onto a road which they in-spected solemnly and carefully in both directions before they set foot on it. They crossed a road bridge over the Val, stopping to point down into the water with a chorus of birdlike chatter at something that had caught their interest, perhaps a fish invisible to mortal eyes. Bork was still in the lead but his flute-note was no longer necessary to keep them together now that they were in the open. They were coming to the first houses of the village. The win-dows were dark and the cars parked along the road were covered with a film of dew; the village slept in a thick silence. The footsteps of the Little People rustled softly like leaves along the pavement. The arrangement of the band kept flowing and shifting; Bonner was usually somewhere toward the middle but those at his side kept changing. Now it was Jenny Brown, a shy creature who ap-peared about to flee whenever he looked at her.

He said, panting. Jenny. When I first met you—

First met me?

He waited until he had caught his breath a little. Yes. When I first met you. That night by the gate of trees. I asked you if you were from the village. And you said. I wouldn't see the likes of you there. Except at night when everyone's asleep.

Did I say that? Oh! Ha ha.

Do you come here often then?

Often?

Yes, he repeated patiently. Do you come here often.

She said playfully, We only come here with you.

He reached for her, if only to give her a little shake, but she eluded him with a laugh. In the best of spirits, suffering only from being out of breath, he loped with them down the road and into the square with its market cross and post-office. Here they spread out like birds circling for a place to settle, and came back together in a loose flowing clump. The swarmed up to the shops, setting their stubby fingers on the windows and peering through the glass.

The thing is, Bonner, said John Greene, we're not a violent people, you know, and we don't break things. You'll have to give it a tap yourself. Don't make too much noise. He passed Bonner a stone. We'll sing a song while you do it.

They sang, the men joining in their sweet falsetto.

Will you buy any tape,
Or lace for your cape,
My dainty duck, my dear-a?

After several ineffective taps with the stone he broke a pane of the door. There was a fine tinkle of falling glass, hardly audible over the song. With care not to cut himself he reached through the broken pane and turned the handle. The men took off their hats and waved them over their heads with a tiny cheer. The door swung open and they all streamed in, Bonner following after them.

There was hardly room for everyone inside the small shop. They jammed together and all talked at once, their small cool bodies pressing against his own.

Oh, look at all the fine things.

It's good we have a friend like Bonner.

We couldn't come here by ourselves. Ha ha.

We don't meddle with locks and latches. Hee hee.

All this was for his benefit, with grins and glances; they were not really talking to one another. After streaming around inside the shop for a while they all crowded over to the shelves by the window. A thin light from the streetlamp outside illuminated the jars with their handwritten labels. Bonner was the first to take a jar from the shelf. The Little People pulled down others for themselves with chuckles of glee. Some of them had difficulty unscrewing the lids with their stubby hands and he helped them. Lara dipped a finger in her jar and licked it off sensuously, smiling in her dreamy way.

He tipped his jar and drank a long sip. The slow-moving fluid was the color of gold, heavy and viscous, clinging stickily to the lips. The taste was heavenly. All the passionate cravings of his childhood came back to him with a rush and were sated in the flow of sweet melting liquid under his tongue. The flavor spread through him until his bones and sinews seemed to dissolve in an exquisite and buzzing warmth. He raised his hand to wipe his lips and succeeded only in getting the hand sticky too.

When they had sated themselves the men began taking down more jars from the shelves and stowing them away deftly in the capacious pockets of their trousers. Each of the girls took at least one. Bonner as an afterthought slipped the coin from his pocket and left it on the shelf. They all rattled out into the square, slightly drunk with sweetness. Now they no longer hurried; they streamed down the road in a straggling band under the poplars standing like gloomy guards in the starlight. Their rustling feet hardly made a sound on the pavement. From the canal a frog croaked and then another: *dribbit dribbit.* Nothing else stirred in the phosphorescent night. The village was behind them and they were headed down the road toward the bridge, with Bork still in the lead. He took the flute from his pocket and played a tune ending low on a minor note. Flicka took up the song in her silvery voice.

> *Beware!*
> *Beware!*
> *His flash-ing eyes, his float-ing hair!*

Bork looked around with the flute still at his mouth. He couldn't smile while playing the flute but his eyes were merry. The others joined in the song, a round of repeated lines to a mocking little ironic melody.

> *Beware! Beware!*
> *His flash-ing eyes, his float-ing hair!*
> *Weave a cir-cle round him thrice,*
> *And close your eyes with hol-y dread,*
> *For he on hon-ey dew hath fed,*
> *And drunk the milk of Par-a-dise!*

Bonner laughed and clasped them to him, cool and snuggling fragrant forms, as many as he could hold in his arms. They went on together down the road in the starlight. A fragment of the song still trembled in the air.

> *Round him thrice . . .*
> *Par . . .*
>   *a . . .*
>   *dise.*

It ended and there was only the sound of their rushing feet, their gasps and sighs.

He woke up to find sunlight streaming through the window and an insistent tapping in his ears, like someone pounding nails with a small hammer.

> Knock knock knock knock knock.
> Knock knock knock knock knock.

He sat up under the bedclothes.
"What is it?"
"It's me. James. There's something I want to talk to you about."
"Go away."
He lay down and pulled the sheets over his head. James came in anyhow. Out of one eye, through a gap in the sheets, Bonner saw him crossing the room with his grim angular smile and going

directly to the nightstand. He opened the drawer and searched through it, setting its contents on top of the stand, and then put everything away again.

"Did you take something from this drawer?"

"Take something? What?"

"You know what it was. It was there last week and it isn't now."

Bonner sat up sleepily with the bedclothes still wound around him.

"Why did you put the coin in there anyhow?"

"I didn't say I put one in the drawer. I just said there was something in the drawer last week. How did you know it was a coin?"

"All these games of yours, James. What's the point of them?"

"It was just a little study of character that I'm making. The coin was in there last week. I wanted to see if you'd taken it out, and you have."

"Well?"

Instead of replying James began searching around through the rest of the room. In the wardrobe he found an empty glass jar with a handwritten label on it. He looked at it and set it back on the shelf, wiping his sticky fingers afterward on one of Bonner's shirts. He found the shoes Bonner had worn the night before and inspected the soles, putting them down exactly where they had been.

"How are you feeling this morning?"

"All right."

"Came in late did you?"

"Yes. I couldn't sleep and I took a walk down the road. It was a lovely evening. What have you concluded about my character?"

"Get up, Bonner. Don't just lie there like a slug. The rest of us are having our breakfast. You know, I've always had a great admiration for you. You're intelligent and witty and you have a powerful imagination. But there's a clownish side of you that causes you to do bizarre things. You do it just to attract attention, I think. You're like a little boy who wants to show us his bottom for a penny. But we've all seen little boys' bottoms before."

"I don't care for the metaphor."

"We're all fond of you, Bonner. You do have an engaging sense of humor. Derailing trains and stepping on mothers to get out. Stealing magnets from Lovejoy. Keeping guns in your flat. Are you still afraid of iron? Here." He found a pair of scissors and tossed them into the bed.

"Don't."

Carefully avoiding the scissors, he sprang up off the bed and wandered around the room in his underwear, picking up whatever he saw and putting it on. He buttoned his shirt and then struggled with the pants, hopping on one foot. "I'm not familiar with the etiquette of country houses. Is it customary for the host to burst into the rooms of guests before they're awake and then watch them while they dress?"

"You're not a guest, Bonner. You're practically a member of the family. If you're looking for your shoes they're over here. They have honey on them too. You must have been treading in the stuff up to your ankles. You know, I'm really concerned about you, Bonner. We all are." He glanced at the nightstand. "For the time being we won't say anything about this to anyone else. It will be strictly between us."

"So you can hold it over me later."

"Oh for heaven's sake, Bonner. You know I have the greatest good will toward you. We all do. That's why we wanted to have you here in the country, so you could have a nice rest and get over these things that were bothering you. You're someone very special to us, Bonner. We're on your side. Remember that."

"You know, James. You *have* seen my bottom. So how about giving me a penny."

"Oh, Bonner." He grinned indulgently and put his arm around his shoulder. "You didn't really mind my coming into your room, did you? After all we know each other so well. I'm just an ancient paternal figure, perfectly harmless. I think of you as a son." He was still smiling in his narrow way as he followed Bonner down the stairs.

The rest of them were at the table in the morning room talking in low voices. They stopped and looked up as Bonner came into the room, helped himself at the sideboard, and took his place at the table. James sat down too and poured himself some tea.

They took up their conversation again, talking over his head as though he weren't there. Drood was interrogating Sylvie about something. "So you think he—h'mm."

Sylvie caught Bonner's eye briefly and turned back to Drood with a placid little smile. "Oh, he knew it was there all right. I saw him looking at the jars when he came into the shop with me."

Stasha said, "Are you hungry this morning, Bonner?"

"Not very." He had taken only tea and a scrap of dry toast, but he hardly had an appetite for that. He felt a little queasy.

"How much is a Krugerrand, Drood?"

"Well over two hundred pounds. Enough to buy the shop and everything in it."

"But where did he *get* it."

"Perhaps he's found a pot of them in the forest."

The two girls were unsuccessfully suppressing their mirth; Drood was matter-of-fact. Tita paid no attention to the conversation and seemed not to understand what they were talking about; she was methodically buttering a muffin and then spreading a thin layer of marmalade on it. James sat drinking his tea and looking from one to the other as they talked.

"But if a person *pays* for something," said Stasha, "then he hasn't *stolen* it, has he?"

"He shouldn't have broken the window."

"It wasn't a window. It was a glass pane in the door."

"But he had to break the glass," said Sylvie. "Otherwise how could he have got in?"

Bonner looked around at them warily. "Where are you getting all these details?"

"Aunt Cassie has been to the village. They're all talking about it there."

"Twenty or thirty jars, they say. What could he have done with it all?"

Stasha said, "He's got a cache of it hidden somewhere, so he can go back to it like a bear in a book."

"Oh, funny Professor Twist."

He said nothing. He didn't feel like explaining to all of them at the breakfast table that he had done it along with some friends of his who lived in the forest and sang songs from Coleridge; this didn't seem very plausible to him either.

"And then he tracked honey on the carpet," said Sylvie primly. "That wasn't very considerate."

"Well it sounds like *fun*. I don't know why he didn't take one of us along."

"I wish you girls wouldn't talk such nonsense," said James. "Bonner is embarrassed about this. You're only making it worse."

Silver-lidded Tita unexpectedly broke into speech. She was still eating her muffin and she chewed what she had in her mouth and swallowed it as she talked. "I remember once when I was a girl growing up right here in this house. I must have been twelve or so. I took the money from the kitchen jar and went to the village and spent it all on cream-cakes. I could never get enough of them. I put all the money on the glass counter at Thrane's and said I wanted cream-cakes for it. I got two large bags of them. I started down the road eating them but I couldn't eat a third of them. Just then I met a boy who asked me what was in the bags. I gave him some of the cream-cakes, and after he had eaten them he took me under a hedge along the canal. I haven't been interested in cream-cakes since then. After that I was interested in boys." She finished the last of the muffin, tucking it in her mouth with her little finger.

"Who was the boy?" asked Drood.

"Oh, it was Lud Wexen, you know. The son of Wexen who married that Egyptian woman. They called him Black Lud."

"Oh, he was a terror," said Drood. "Used to drown cats in the cistern. Police had him up several times for breaking into houses. Finally got a girl in trouble and left town. Went to Australia and became an opal miner." Drood knew all the local folklore.

"It all came from eating cream-cakes. A warning to us all."

"Perhaps, Tita, you're still doing it," said James. "Rhondda tells me there's money missing from the grocery jar in the kitchen."

No one said anything.

"On more than one occasion. I don't suppose any of you know anything about this?"

"Oh, here's something in the paper," Stasha interrupted him. She was immersed in the Waldon Blade at her place across the table from James and had found a small article on an inside page. "It's about the man that saw the gremlins. Mr. William Lacey, a British Rail engine driver who was involved in the unexplained derailing of a London-to-Waldon train in July, has disappeared mysteriously from his home in Maidenhead, Berks."

"Stasha," said James.

"I *know* you like to look at the paper first, James, but you didn't take it and it's such fun. According to a relative, Mrs. Elodie Boatright, Mr. Lacey was visited by a man she described as a 'medieval doctor' shortly before his disappearance. He left his Maidenhead residence on August 4 taking nothing with him and clad in indoor clothing. He is believed to have no money with him and perhaps to be suffering from mental confusion. Authorities speculated that Mr. Lacey may have taken refuge in Waldon forest, where he is nourishing himself on mushrooms and on nuts given him by squirrels. Mrs. Boatright has bought a compass and sun hat and is organizing an expedition into the forest."

"Oh, she's not."

"I see," said James. "This is the fellow who was driving the train that Bonner was on."

"Oh, you're so quick, James. The very same one. Do you know what I think? I think it was that small man he saw on the tracks who enticed him."

"Small man?"

"He saw a small man on the tracks and so he derailed the train to chase him into the forest. He couldn't find him then so he's run away from Maidenhead to look again. Now they're in the forest together living on nuts and acorns."

"I wish you wouldn't mix up the news with your cock-and-bull stories, Stasha," said James. "When you do that we can't tell what's what."

Bonner got up and left the table. No one paid any particular attention except James who followed him with his eyes. The rest of them went on talking and chatting around the table. Outside he headed for the Mill Cottage, but when he saw James following him he swerved abruptly and crossed the lawn toward the deer park.

James caught up to him and laid a hand on his shoulder, slowing him down. He smiled his thin bent smile.

"Why did you leave the table so abruptly?"

"I was finished with breakfast. I wasn't very hungry."

"I wasn't suggesting that you stole the money from the grocery jar. Did you think that was what I meant?"

"Oh no."

"Was it something the girls said? You shouldn't let them bother you, Bonner. They're silly creatures sometimes."

"It wasn't that."

He opened the gate and set off briskly across the park with James at his side. He would much have preferred to be alone; he had meant to go and check on what William was doing in the Mill Cottage, but since that was impossible he felt like communing with the deer, if he could get close enough to these timid creatures to make friends with them, or simply walking in the park by himself. He thought he caught a glimpse of an antler in a clump of trees in the distance, distracting him from what James was saying.

"You have to take Sylvie in a rather special way," James went on in his jovial tone that nevertheless always had a touch of the querulous in it. "She seems younger than her age sometimes. Her schoolgirlish ways. Her jokes. Her fits of moodiness. A lot of this is just the silliness that comes out when two girls are together too much."

"I am fond of her. I'm fond of you all."

"She's a very precious thing, Bonner. She's like a fine watch. Fragile. Complex. Easily put out of adjustment. She needs taking care of in a very special way. But she's going to be a treasure for some man. What a charming creature. Sometimes I wish I were twenty years younger myself, and not her father."

The naivete of this remark astounded Bonner. If it was not naive it was tremendous. Perhaps it *was* a tremendous remark, a Sophoclean profundity, transcending all morals and going directly to the heart of the matter. It was possible that he had underestimated James.

"Sylvie is not just for anyone. I've thought a great deal about this matter. What is needed is a man of imagination and vision—someone who has character and a place in the world, and yet someone who will respect these very special qualities of hers, this fragility, this vulnerability. Someone with compassion and sensitivity."

"A place in the world?"

"And then there's her career," James went on, ignoring him. "She's going to be a concert pianist of course. She has a great deal of talent; all her teachers have said so. But she's lazy sometimes and doesn't apply herself. She needs someone constantly around to make her toe the line. I've tried to do that—I've paid for her lessons and helped her all I could. But I'm not musical and I don't understand these matters very well. She needs someone who is sensitive to the arts, someone to support and encourage her, to give her the inspiration she needs to become a great performing artist."

"I see this hypothetical person only indistinctly."

"Don't be coy, Bonner. The others have just melted away. It's amazing how many people you think you have for a given purpose, and when you start examining them more carefully none of them will do for one reason or another."

"You shouldn't have taken her away from London. She can't meet very many people here in the country."

"I imagine her married to someone—an Oxford don perhaps. Tell me—I've never quite understood. What is your status at Hopkins just now?"

"Why do you ask?"

Without changing his expression James parried in his canny way. "I've always been interested in your career. Your position at the university. Your achievement as a scholar. You know that."

"I went on leave from Hopkins to take the Fulbright. Then when I didn't go back I was given another year's leave for medical reasons. That expires at the end of this academic year."

"And will you go back?"

"I don't know. It depends on a number of things."

"Why couldn't you get a position in an English university? Oxford or Cambridge."

"That's ridiculous, James."

"Why?"

"I'm quite happy at Hopkins. Anyhow I wouldn't care to live in Cambridge. It's rather remote and the people are stuffy there."

"Oxford then."

"Same thing."

"How about the University of London. Aylesworth and Doggenbank speak very highly of you. You know, you met them at the Sundays."

It was Tweeds and Blazer-and-Flannels. He had never known their names. "What's the point of all this, James?"

"It's just that I'm fond of you and have a great admiration for you. I want the best for you. I want you to be happy. I like to imagine you as a university don here in England, with a nice house and—"

"Wife and children."

"I didn't say that. That might go along with it of course. I'm very fond of Sylvie as I am of you. I want her to be happy too. And if . . ."

"You forget that I'm not well."

"I've been talking to Lovejoy. I was in London the other day and I went to his office and had a chat with him. He says it's very likely that your troubles—I don't recall exactly how he put it but I remember the gist—are just the result of your being deprived of things that are normal for a man of your age."

"I wish Lovejoy would keep his mouth shut about my green sickness."

James appeared not to notice his annoyance. "And then there's all this," he went on, waving expansively at the park, the grounds, and the house half hidden in the trees. "It's a priceless heritage. A responsibility. It's important that it should be preserved. And I won't be around forever. I'm concerned that there should be someone . . ."

"Drood is only fifty. Maybe he'll get married."

"I don't want the Cromlechs to have it. They're finished. You see, Bonner." He breathed heavily, made a little grimace, and then resumed his angular smile. "I'm looking for a son-in-law. It's a deep need, a biological need, as profound and pressing as any sexual desire. I've got over that, you see—the demands of the flesh. Now this thing has replaced it. It's on my mind night and day. It's the only thing that's lacking now in my life. I've got everything else."

"James, that coin in the nightstand."

"What about it?"

"You know it was there and you waited to see if I'd take it; you said you were testing my character. Now you're throwing Sylvie at me in just the same way. Then when I take her you'll slap my hand."

James smiled in a kind of amazement and put his arm around Bonner's shoulder. "You've got it all wrong, Bonner. I wouldn't dream of playing tricks of that sort on you. I like you and I respect you. You're like a son to me. I hope you always will be."

"I could tell you things about me, places that I've been, things that I've done, that would completely change your opinion of me."

"Oh, I can imagine what you're referring to. We've all had our adventures. I myself—"

"You haven't any idea what I'm referring to. It's as though you were offering Sylvie to a saint, a madman, a criminal. You don't know what you're getting."

"Don't make it into a novel by Dostoevski. You dramatize yourself too much, Bonner. You think you're the only one in the

163

world who's got any imagination. You and I are much alike after all. That's why I think of you as a son. You have a sense of tradition, you have a feeling for the past, you have vision. Only you, I think, can appreciate what I've done to this place and why I've done it."

They had made a circle through the park and were coming back to the gate in the hedge. If James hadn't talked so much, he thought, they might have seen the deer. James was so proud of them and yet he talked them off into the far corners of the park whenever he set foot in it. Bonner couldn't help glancing at the Mill Cottage as they went up the lawn. It was quiet and there was no sign of life, although the door to the museum was ajar. He himself was always careful to shut it when he went in and out. James also turned his eyes toward the half-open door.

"I thought I saw someone prowling around here the other day. Did you ever see anyone going into the museum?"

"It's open to the public, isn't it?"

"It is and it isn't. The museum is open to the public, but you have to cross over my property to get to it, and it isn't open to the public."

"Who was it that you saw?"

"I didn't notice. Perhaps it wasn't anybody at all. I just wondered if you'd seen anyone."

"Maybe it was one of the Cromlechs. It's their priceless heritage too."

James grinned and put his arm around him again. "What a logic-chopper you are. I suppose you learn that around a university. You do like to be contrary, don't you?" They walked along together toward the house. "Do you have an appetite for lunch? You probably need a good purge after your escapade last night. I'll bet Cassie has something."

Silver-lidded Tita, turning to ponder him thoughtfully, lit a Marlboro and shook out the match. She said, "I'm fond of you, Bonner. You know, we all are."

"Everyone keeps saying that. You all keep saying that you're fond of me, and I keep saying that I'm fond of all of you. What's the point of all that?"

"There doesn't have to be any point to being fond of someone. One just is, that's all."

"Yes, but it seems such a program in this family."

They were sitting in folding canvas chairs on the lawn looking down toward the river. They had taken their coffee out after lunch, and the cups were posed on small white plastic tables that flared on the green lawn like doves. Tita was wearing a mauve gown so sheer that it showed the straps of her underwear, with white stockings and violet shoes. Along with this went a large Dolly Varden hat with flowers on it and the brim turned down on one side, even though there was hardly any sun in the shade under the trees. As usual she was encrusted with jewels like a Maharani.

"What were you and James talking about? On you long intimate walk."

"Oh, nothing in particular."

"Was he upbraiding you for your orgy last night?"

"Oh, no."

"James *is* fond of you."

"I wouldn't say that. He has a kind of blind belief in me that nothing can undermine. At times he seems to be thinking of someone else entirely, and has the mistaken belief that it's me."

"When James has decided on something nothing can be done. You might as well try to push an elephant off a bun."

"Yes. He seems to have decided that I'm a brilliant person, and an Oxford don, and a prospective son-in-law."

"Well, I think that would be a very good arrangement. James likes to collect things and now he's thinking of collecting a professor. We're all fond of you, you know."

"Will you stop saying that? James says that Sylvie is like a fine watch."

"Oh she is. I'm sure of it. I wouldn't go monkeying around with her watchworks if I were you."

Conscious that he was talking to her mother, he said cautiously, "I have an enormous respect for Sylvie."

"It would be a *mariage blanc* of course. Do you know what a *mariage blanc* is?"

"Yes, it's a highball with the whisky left out."

"Well, a glass of nice cool water is good for you."

"With a twist of lemon."

"Oh, don't be malicious. of course, young men of your age do have certain needs."

"Yes, so James told me. He also told me—"

"I can pretty much imagine what he told you. He is a somewhat predictable mechanism. I've lived with him for a long time and I always understand pretty much what he is thinking at all times. You see, he has left all his vices behind him and now concerns himself only with the dynasty he imagines he is founding. But I haven't reached that fortunate state yet. I'm a good deal younger than he is, you know."

She must be if she says so herself, he thought, although she didn't entirely look it. What was this leading up to?

"And you know, Bonner—but I mustn't say that I'm fond of you, must I? It makes you angry. But I am. And so, if you were to become this son-in-law that James envisions, perhaps we could work out some scheme useful to all. You know, I have this enormous four-poster all satin and damask. I don't know whether you've noticed it. I roam about in it all alone like a bark in the sea. James sleeps at the other end of the house."

"Good heavens, Tita."

"I don't think I'm such a hag. Do you? And Sylvie is—you know. If you tinkered with such a fine watch you'd surely break it. It's not much of a picnic for you. It would be a good arrangement for all concerned, wouldn't it?"

"For Sylvie?"

"Why not? She wouldn't know about it, and anyhow we wouldn't be taking anything away from her that she wanted."

"I hardly think that any woman likes to imagine her husband in the arms of another."

"But surely when it's her own mother."

"I've never thought of you and Sylvie as close."

"What's that got to do with it?"

"According to James, Sylvie is a sensitive creature who is easily put out of adjustment. She needs to be carefully taken care of."

"Exactly. The two of you will be perfectly suited to each other. It will be a union of the spirit."

"But surely James . . ."

"Oh, James is tired of my nagging him about it. I and my needs are only an annoyance to him. He'd be happy to have me take them to Fred Baines the dairyman if I chose to."

More and more James seemed to him like the Serpent in the Garden, and also the Angel who would chase him out when he had taken the apple. "I think what you are saying is absolutely preposterous, Tita. It's out of the question. It's ludicrous on the face of it. You may be prepared to tell lies and deceive and betray the people you live with every day of your life, but I'm not. You *are* an old hag, you know. An attractive one perhaps but you're far too old for me. I'm not the sort to get involved in some incestuous stew with my mother-in-law. I'm no Hippolytus."

"Oh, very well," she said. She was not at all offended. "It seemed a convenient arrangement to me. If you're not interested that's all there is to be said."

Eleven

In November the mild autumn weather ended and it turned suddenly cold. There were no storms and no winds; the air was still as death and the sun burned feebly through the mist like a circle cut from Christmas paper. The cows in the pasture moved over the fields trailing streamers of vapor, and cars going along the Canal Road left white caterpillars behind them that dissolved only slowly in the sunshine. In the absolute calm the leaves turned on the trees and then fell directly downward in the motionless air, so that each tree was surrounded by its own round carpet in various colors: yellow, scarlet, brown, ochre, russet. The rooks cawed in the bare branches.

In the village of Pense Coombe the square was deserted except for the usual two or three black-clad old men propped on their canes and gazing with curiosity at St. Clongowes Chapel across the way, a small stone structure with a copper steeple. These Oedipal tripods (what has three legs in the evening?) had been fixed in place for some time, but the chapel was frozen in the mist. Now and again a faint groan of music came from inside, now a kind of bump as through spirits enclosed in the stone wanted to get out. St. Clongowes, like so many other churchs in the region, had been built on the site of a ruined Roman temple, and no one was sure what had been there before that. A little yellow sports car, a Daimler, a shabby estate wagon, and a baby-blue Ford Escort stood by the chapel accumulating dew on their surfaces. A tattered black-and-white cat, a familiar of the square, leapt onto the bonnet of the Daimler, found it warm as he had expected, and settled down onto it with his chin wound into his elbows.

Finally there were signs that something was stirring in the chapel. The sounds changed; there were murmurings and the scraping of chairs. A verger flung open the doors and came out in black with a white dickey. After an interval a small procession emerged to the strains of a creaky organ playing Mendelssohn. First Bonner and Sylvie came out holding hands, Bonner in a morning coat and striped pants hired from a shop in Waldon, a rig he swore he'd never wear, and Sylvie in an old gown that had belonged to her Grandmother Birdsell, all organdy and lace, fastened with blue ribbons in the front. Next came Father Maidan in a cassock and surplice with a narrow black scarf, trailed by a pair of altar boys in frocks; then James in another hired morning coat, Tita in a sheath of dark taffeta trimmed with pearls, Drood and Cassie in their usual county garb, and Stasha in a long nylon gown with a band of eyelets around the waist through which her apricot skin showed in little dots. Lacking a cape, she flung an old mackintosh over it as she came out of the chapel. She reached into the pocket of the mackintosh and found a toffee which she unwrapped and ate. Finally came Miles and after him Rhondda. Miles lit a cigarette, surveyed the square in a leisurely way, and dropped the match on the pavement. He caught sight of the cat on the Daimler and shooed it off with a negligent gesture of his arm.

The strains of Mendelssohn died away. It was cold in the square and those without coats shivered. The fog seemed to crepitate very faintly, a sound like insects chewing. They all shook hands and embraced in silence. While the tripods across the square watched, Bonner and Sylvie self-consciously got into the Morgan and he started the engine; the pipe at its rump responded with a spout of steam. He put it in gear and started out of the square. Everyone had forgotten rice and Stasha flung the toffee wrapper after them.

Father Maidan was ordinarily attached to the Lady Church in Waldon; he came to Pense Coombe only on special occasions. He demanded a certain minimum level of ceremony; thus the two altar boys. James passed him an envelope which disappeared unobtrusively into the cassock. Then, lifting his skirts, he got into the Ford Escort with the altar boys and drove away.

The estate wagon with Drood and Cassie was next, leaving only the Daimler. Miles, with a final look around the square, took out his cigarette, dropped it to the pavement, and crushed it with his foot. Then he got in behind the wheel. Rhondda served as footman; that is, she helped James, Tita, and Stasha into the various doors of the car which she then shut. Then she got into the front seat next to Miles and shut her own door. The Daimler dwindled noiselessly off down the Canal Road trailing its caterpillar.

Thoroughly chilled, Bonner and Sylvie changed in the large bedroom at the side of the house, which had been hers and Stasha's and would now be theirs. It contained two narrow dark-wood beds, a wardrobe, and antique chest of drawers, and escritoire in which Bonner could store his clothing, and a massive oaken cheval glass. He got his first glimpse of Sylvie in a state other than totally dressed, that is in her slip without a bra underneath, so that a pair of pencil erasers appeared on the two shallow convexities like teacups. He turned his back on her and put on his old chino pants, purple shirt, and fruit-salad American necktie. When he turned around again she had disappeared behind a screen across the room and was tinkling into a chamber pot. He was thunderstruck by this and didn't know what to make of it; the bathroom was just outside in the passage. Perhaps it was an old family custom, although it seemed more Cromlech than Boswin. He felt the need to do the same himself but he certainly wasn't going to follow her example; instead he waited until she came out and put his arms around her and embraced her. He thought: here I am with my arms around Sylvie who is in her underwear. This—the thought not the action—produced the usual reflex, that coathanger in the pants which he always found so embarrassing, although perhaps no one really noticed it. She disengaged herself and reached into the wardrobe for her sensible gray skirt and jacket.

"Now I am Mrs. Foley."

"Madame Folie. It's French for crazy. You know, Tita is always telling me how fond we all are of each other. But I really am fond of you."

"I'm fond of you too, Bonner. But leave me alone now because I have to get dressed. We can't stay here in the room together much longer, can we?"

"Why not?"

"Because everyone knows we're in here. And if we don't come out soon they'll think . . ."

"Well let them."

"Oh Bonner, don't be dense. Besides we have to get to London before nightfall."

"Why?"

"Because that's the plan. I've got it all written down on a piece of paper somewhere. Oh, I'm frozen to the bone. I don't have a proper winter coat."

He had no coat at all. He found an old sweater and put it on with his corduroy jacket over it. Then he took his suitcase in one hand and hers in the other, and they went down the stairs into the hall. There was no one in sight anywhere. The emptiness of the rooms and the silence lent a creepy air to the place; where in the world was everyone? It was as though he and Sylvie were doing something shameful and the rest of the family had gone off to their rooms to ostracize them for it. The sound of running water and the clanking of pans indicated that Rhondda was in the kitchen, and James was no doubt in his study. The empty champagne bottles and the remains of canapés were strewn about in the hall where they had left them when they went up to change. Stasha appeared in the door of the gallery and tittered at them.

"Shut up, Stasha." He set the suitcases down and headed back up the stairs.

"I didn't say anything. Where are you going, Bonner?"

"I'm going to the lav," he said savagely. He had meant to use the downstairs bathroom, but Stasha was standing directly in front of the door and he hadn't wanted to make it so obvious what he was doing. "I stood in that frozen church for an hour with no chance to go, and then when we came back I drank all that champagne."

"Why do men do it standing up, Bonner?"

"Why not?"

"You spatter all over the place, and you leave the seat standing up so that we fall into the bowl and get stuck."

"I'm finding out all kinds of things about women that I didn't know before."

"Well, it's your wedding day," said Stasha. Sylvie remained aloof from this exchange. When Bonner came back downstairs he picked up the suitcases and the two of them went out without a word to the car.

He put the two suitcases into the tiny compartment at the rear and then decided to erect the top—the hood as it was called in Britain. It was an affair rather like a folding lawn chair except more complicated. Sylvie didn't know the least thing about it; in fact she had never known it was there on the car under its canvas cover behind the seats. Miles came down from the flat over the garage and watched him struggling with it for a few moments; then, putting his cigarette in his mouth and giving him a long stare, he reached in to grab two ribs of the apparatus and snapped it into place with a click. The two of them clamped the front of the thing to the windshield. There were some little canvas screens with celluloid windows that fitted onto the doors, and Miles showed him how to mount these. All this without a word. Miles took out his cigarette, examined it, and knocked off an inch-long ash.

At last they were in the car; Bonner started it and drove off under the skeptical eye of Miles leaning on his broomstick.

"I don't care for that man."

"He's an old family retainer. He's belonged to the Cromlechs since he was a child."

"He's a cold insolent son-of-a-bitch."

"Oh, he's *that.*"

Driving out along the gravel lane to the road, he glanced to the left and saw in a gap in the hedge a pale apparition of the kind that appears to children in dreams. Wreathed in fog, the melancholy face of William peered through the leaves with eyes that followed the car like wobegone sunflowers. He looked at Sylvie. She didn't seem to notice anything, although as far as he could tell her eyes had followed his own glance.

"At last we're alone."

"Yes, isn't it nice."

"I thought I saw someone in the hedge watching us."

"In the hedge? Funny Professor Twist."

He didn't know why he said this; it was as though he wanted to reveal the secret of William to someone, to Sylvie now that he had entered into the new intimacy of marriage with her, so that she could share this incubus that hung heavily on him with its constant sense of peril. For the moment he decided not to say more. He drove on down the road toward the Motorway through a mist that the small car parted as though it were a boat going through waves. From time to time he glanced at her profile; the aristocratic brow, the long chin, the moist and protruding Cromlech eye with its lash like a dark orchid when seen from the side. He could hardly believe that he possessed her. But how can one human being possess another? Did this mean that in some way she possessed him too? His mind failed to grasp the significance of this proposition. He was conscious of the iron ribs holding up the canvas over his head; as thin as they were they gave him a slight headache.

She said with her light irony, "Happy is the bride the sun shines on."

"There is a sun." He pointed to the yellow lemon halfway down the sky to the west. The car had a heater of course; he started it up and after a moment it began to send a thin thread of warm air over their knees. This was a mistake. Encouraged by this small creature-comfort the Beast rose in him again and almost overwhelmed him. Stop car at side of road? Out of the question. The sign indicating the entrance to the Motorway came up at him through an atmosphere of watered milk and he followed obediently around a cloverleaf. Awaiting his chance and peering out precariously through the amber distorting celluloid, he inserted the car into the stream of traffic and accelerated. The Motorway opened out before them like a black river, roaring.

The flat in Belgravia had been shut up for months and it was musty and close. It was also cold; he investigated the provisions for heating and found a kind of oil apparatus in a closet that, when switched on, began emitting stirrings and bubblings from its innards. Sylvie looked around as though it were a strange hotel where she had never been before.

"And what shall we do now?" he asked her.

"What does one do under these circumstances?"

The answer to this was so obvious that he could hardly believe she was referring to it. He came to her and enclosed her in his arms, and she slipped an arm around him with a gentle but crooked smile, a smile that, as he now saw, bore a familial resemblance to James's smile, but reflected, as it were, in a rippled and darkening feminine glass. He was caught all at once by her intense fragility, the thin silence of her eyes, the pain of her vulnerability which seemed about to open to him at any moment, petal by petal, as the spring rain opens a flower. At close range her face was no longer porcelain but had the slight porosity, the icy white coolness of a magnolia blossom, and something of the same odor, an absence of odor really which left behind it a trace of mint; clean, pure, invisible, childish, transparent. His mind fluttered with adjectives that struck her softly and fell like rose-petals, powerless to penetrate even a pore of her exquisite reserve, her self-contained presence of an animal too fine to enclose yet too timid and fragile to survive in the forest. Moved by instinct, aghast even in his own mind at what he was doing, he fingered the pencil-eraser in the mound under her jacket and was rewarded with a jerk as though she had been stabbed.

She pulled away and turned to the window, and yet he thought he detected the trace of a smile on her lips; the smile of an oracle, a Delphic seer of whom one has asked an improper question and yet who is not entirely displeased. Not to say that she won't wreak her wrath on you, yet there is that smile. Inside the oracle is a woman, if you could only get at it.

"Don't, Bonner."

"That's one of your favorite words. Why don't you have it printed on cards. Save you saying it so often."

"Don't let's quarrel. On this occasion above all."

"What *is* this occasion exactly?"

"It's our honeymoon. Here we are in this lovely flat in London with nothing to do except enjoy ourselves."

"Exactly." He sidled toward her and sprang, and she bolted. "The bedroom is in the other direction as I remember. I'm hoping that in time I can herd you toward it as though you were a flock of sheep. Don't go that way, it's blocked by the piano. If you'll turn around you'll see the door."

"I can't."

"I would be very gentle."

"No."

"You know," he told her, growing annoyed, "you can't really deny your nature. It's just an idea you've got hold of and it's a perverse one. You do have a body like other people. It's the human condition."

"Don't talk to me about your ghastly human condition."

"It's not my human condition."

"You make it seem as though it is somehow."

He made another attempt, this time cornering her as she skittered behind a piece of furniture. He himself was two persons; one of them wanted to do this, with an urgency like an express train slamming through a tunnel, and the other knew it was a thoroughly bad idea. This time she remained perfectly motionless under his touch; her mouth trembled and a glaze of tears filled her eyes. He took his hand away. He no longer felt desire; it was as though he had thrust a dagger into some soft and helpless creature that had trusted him and that he had previously treated gently and with affection. He felt in awe all at once of the strange sensitive glinting quality of her mind, like one of those women in Dostoevski who have been hurt in ways that can't be mentioned. He said, "I do love you you know. Sylvie. Oh Sylvie. I can't bear to wound you in any way at all."

"And I love you too. I wish I . . ."

"It's all right. It's just that I . . ."

"Don't you see, Professor Twist is someone who takes care of me. He's a funny man who amuses me and is wise and kind and protective, and doesn't bother me with things I don't want."

"Yes, that's what I—want to be. I want to be Professor Twist. I just want to take care of you."

"But Bonner—"

"Don't worry . . ."

They stammered mutually and this pleased them. It was an intimacy of particular poignance. She dried her eyes and smiled. "I'm sure I'm a silly goose. What would *you* like to do."

"Oh, anything at all."

"Except—"

"Of course. I except that."

"Oh, Bonner."

Instead they got into the car and went to Brown's Hotel in Albemarle Street for tea. There, in the thoroughly Edwardian atmosphere of chintz and taffeta, they sank into a comfortable sofa with a little table before them. The modern London was shut out: the streets swarming with pedestrians, the gassy busses, the traffic going by in Piccadilly only a short distance away. There was a discreet silence in the room broken only by murmurs. The tea was

Darjeeling; the sandwiches were small but interesting. The waiters went around with tea-cakes and scones, which arrived warm and at frequent intervals.

Sylvie poured. "Would you like some honey on your scone?" she asked playfully.

"No thanks."

"We could ask. I'm sure they'd have some," she persisted with slight malice.

"Please don't bother."

He ate avidly, compensating perhaps for the other carnal satisfaction he had just been denied. She only nibbled at the end of a sandwich and sampled a tea-cake, but seemed to take pleasure in them too. A large grandfather clock ticked steadily, marking off seconds no doubt in the year 1910.

"I do like it when we're alone together like this in . . . a nice place."

"On the river-bank at Byrd Mill."

"Yes."

"Parked in the car on the canal road under the poplars."

"Yes, wasn't that nice."

"There's no iron in this building. I'm sure there isn't. Sylvie, do you think I'm out of my head?"

"I don't know. You should be the best judge of that."

"I'm not sure that's true. But if I am, why did James let me marry you?"

"Perhaps he thought it would make you better."

"That's what he said. But I don't think he realized . . ."

"What?"

"That we wouldn't . . ."

"Please, Bonner."

Still that was the gist of the question. It was an unrewarding turn in the conversation and he wished he hadn't got onto it. "The fact is," he said, taking up another vein, "that reality is different for every one of us. I see a red wagon, and you see a red wagon, but who can say whether the red wagon we see is the same for both of us?"

"Oh Bonner, this is just freshman philosophy."

"Well we have to start somewhere. I've told you about my . . . friends. Or I tried to. You weren't listening very closely and besides we were interrupted by Drood and Stasha."

"Friends? Oh yes, I remember. But really, they aren't . . ."

"They *are*. They are there. I know they are, Sylvie. I've spoken to them and I've touched them, they're as solid as you and me. Please don't tell me they're all in my mind. Everything is in my mind—Drood, James, Tita, everything, London, and you sitting here next to me. They *are* there, in the forest. I've been to them, I've seen them and touched them and I've heard their voices, more than once. And I know I will again."

"Perhaps you should talk about it to Dr. Lovejoy."

"Only if I thought he could see them too. He seems far less real than them, far less solid and concrete. If I were an artist I would take a pencil right now and draw you pictures of them. I couldn't do that with Lovejoy. He seems blurry in my mind."

She seemed half convinced, or on the brink of being convinced; she turned solemn and looked at him thoughtfully, curiously. "What are they like? Tell me about them."

"They're gentle and loving and humorous, and . . ."

"No, I mean what do they look like."

"Oh. They're a little smaller than other people, but not much. They wear clothes that look as though they're gray at first, but each one has a different pastel hue. The men wear funny hats. The women . . ."

"Bonner, do you . . . you know, the women. In this dream you have about them."

"It's not a dream. No I don't. I tried to once but they don't care for it. They have other ways of being happy, and of making me happy. They sing, and they have beautiful voices."

"Yes, I remember your saying that."

"The song is quite strange."

"You were playing it on the piano at the house. Or trying to, you aren't much of a pianist. You know, the thing that troubles me is that you couldn't have made up that song. It's too odd and different and the harmony is too special."

"Why does it trouble you?"

"Because, if you didn't make it up—"

"Perhaps it came from my mind," he said, abruptly taking the other side of the argument. "After all I can think up music, even if I can't play the piano. I remember the words quite clearly too. I suppose I could have made them up, after all I did try to write poetry when I was younger. The silly thing is that later they began

177

singing the same music but the words were from Coleridge. *Kubla Khan.* You know, the part about the flashing eyes and floating hair. Of course I know the whole poem by heart. I memorized it when I was a student and I can still recite it. So it's likely that . . ." Then he thought of something. "But there's something funny about— you know—the way Coleridge composed it." He felt a cool prickle. He stared at her as though she were a mirror that would reveal to him what was happening in his own mind. "He didn't really compose it; it just came to him. He was alone at night in a lonely farmhouse and he had taken some laudanum. He fell into a kind of trance and the whole poem came to him. The words and the images; he saw the *things* as he heard the words. Then someone from Porlock knocked on the door and woke him, so that he never knew the rest of it. He didn't make it up. It came from his mind. Or from somewhere."

She was following all this intently. "Maybe he heard them singing it."

"What?" He stared at her. They were both calm but intent, facing each other on the sofa. There was a little tremor at the corner of her mouth. "Heard them singing it. Of course. He—Sylvie, how did you happen to think of this? He was living in the country at the time, with a forest around. They could easily have stolen into the room where he was dozing, or in a receptive state from the drug . . ." He felt his heart pounding; he looked around the room at the Edwardian furnishings, as though in mild bewilderment at discovering where he was, and then back at her.

"Bonner. Are you sure it's a good idea for you to talk about this?"

"But you—it was you who thought of the business about Coleridge."

"I didn't mean that they really came to him. He may have heard them, but that doesn't mean they were really there. You yourself said that reality is different for everyone. That everyone sees a different red wagon."

His heart sank again. "Then you don't believe me?"

"Of course I do. There's that song."

She looked at him in silence for a moment, then she smiled. She got up from the sofa and went to the old-fashioned cottage piano at the side of the room. It was draped with a Spanish shawl which she removed. Then, slipping onto the stool, she set her fingers onto the keys and played the four slow phrases with the queer and evocative, slightly dissonant note at the end. His neck prickled again. People in the room turned and stared curiously.

She came back and sat down beside him.

"Then you remember it."

"Oh, a pianist has a good ear. It sticks in the mind somehow."

"Sylvie, if you believe in the song—"

"I do believe in you. I don't think you're out of your head."

"No, I'm still in it, but the question is, are the things that are going on in it real or not."

"It's so pleasant here in Brown's. Let's not bother about Wittgensteinian propositions."

"Sylvie, if you knew how I—"

"Yes, I know. You're very fond of me. I'm fond of you too, Bonner. You invent these odd songs and say that Little People sang them to you, when it's so much more to your credit if you made them up."

"Did I call them Little People?"

"I'm not sure if you did. Perhaps that's what I call them in my mind."

"In your mind? Sylvie—"

"Have you noticed, in this whole conversation, we don't finish our sentences? We just leave them dangling. We start to say things and don't know how to end them."

"And then the other finishes for us."

"Let's try. I don't know if these things are in my—"

"Mind or not. Or if they're in your mind, whether they're—"

"Really in my mind or whether I'm only imagining them. Of course—"

"Everything is only in my mind, including you."

"And you for me. It's because our—"

"Two souls are one. Marriage of true minds. No impediments."

"It's so lovely. Why can't we just go on in this way, coming together in—"

"Each other's minds. Because I like to touch you, Sylvie. I like you to touch me."

"Well I don't mind touching you." She set down her teacup and set her fingers lightly on his face, exactly as he had an hour before at the flat. They kissed. The other people in the room, who had been puzzled by the song on the piano, stared at them again.

179

Both smiling, feeling pleased with themselves, they got up from the table and made their way slowly through the room to the hall of the hotel and the street outside. The waiter came after them and pointed out that they owed ten pounds fifty p. for the tea, enough to buy a good meal in a steakhouse. Bonner paid it without taking his eyes from Sylvie. They went on hand in hand down St. James's Street, around the Palace, and through the Green Park to Belgravia. He was exquisitely happy. In Wilton Crescent before the flat she looked around and said, "We forgot the car."

"I'll go for it tomorrow."

She laughed and they went into the house and took a bath together, like two innocent children in a painting by Maxfield Parrish.

That night, after dining on a hamburger at Strikes which they shared, since neither of them was hungry, they wandered about the city for an hour and then came back to the flat in Wilton Crescent. In the master bedroom, which had been Tita's when the family lived there, they disrobed and she put on a gown that came to her ankles and he a pair of yellow pyjamas with a hole in the elbow. Then they took their places on the bed and lay side by side, like some old bronze Crusader and his Lady on a sarcophagus in the crypt of some ancient church. He awoke after an hour or so and found that they were still in the same position, their noses erect and their toes pointed upward. Although he never slept on his back, he remained in this posture until morning, dozing lightly. He didn't want to turn away from her and he was afraid that if he turned toward her she might interpret it wrongly.

The next morning he went around to Albemarle Street for the car in front of Brown's. It had two parking tickets on it which he put into his pocket; then he took down the hood and folded it into its little compartment behind the seats. It was still cold in London, with a grayish mist clinging to things, but he preferred the cold to the sensation of the iron ribs arching over his head. He drove first to his old flat in Kensington and collected a few things: a carton of clothes, another cardboard box filled with the notes he had made in the British Museum, several armloads of books, and pencils and yellow lined pads. He also took some tea, rice, and canned goods he found in the kitchen, and an electric teakettle which he could give to William in his hideaway in the Mill Cottage. He ignored his typewriter, which sat on the table like a square robot emitting vibrations that made him feel a little queasy. He could write his book, or the rest of it, on the yellow lined pads.

Getting back into the car, he drove to the London University bookstore in Bloomsbury to get some commentaries on thirteenth-century Anglo-Saxon texts. He also went around to Foyle's to get some recent books on literary theory: Foucault, Derrida, Lacan. He had now recast his notion of the book he was writing. No longer was it to be a mere textual analysis; now he thought of a radically modern work, a futuristic work almost, in which he would brilliantly annoy his conservative critics by inserting into his criticism something that was anathema to them, the ultramodern theories of the phenomenologists and structuralists. It would be an unexpected, a stunning, a spectacular turn in his career. This would mean many more months of work, of course. He happily saw now a new vision of himself married to Sylvie, sleeping chastely with her in the bedroom at the side of the house at Byrd Mill, and spending his days writing his book in a little monkish cell he would fit out in the Mill Cottage next to William's room, so they could share the tea they made with the electric kettle. Since he had left the car open in Malet Street, someone stole his carton of clothes while he was in the university bookstore. This didn't bother him at all; the fewer possessions the better as far as he was concerned and you could only wear one set of clothes at a time. He was glad they hadn't stolen his research notes or the stack of yellow lined pads on which he planned to write his book.

Sylvie, deprived of her car, went about in taxis. She took one first to Chelsea for her piano lesson for which she always came into town on Tuesdays. The wedding had been planned this way, as a matter of fact, so that she could have her lesson while she was in London and Bonner could pick up his things in Kensington at the same time. Nigel was not very pleased with her playing because she hadn't been practicing enough, but this was often the case and she didn't let it bother her. When the lesson was over she flounced out confidently into Dilke Street. Not a taxi in sight. Never mind; the cold air and the search through the streets of Chelsea for another taxi exhilarated her. She remembered the events of the day before with a keen clarity, beginning with the cat drowsing on the warm car and ending with the two of them falling asleep together in the flat with the thin sounds of Belgravia penetrating faintly through the walls. She liked this dreamy ethereal funny childlike way of being married. She liked Bonner very much too; in fact she loved him. Why had she told herself that she liked him? She loved him. With a deep sense of bliss, of possession, she remembered his roly-poly body, his fair skin with freckles, his curly ginger hair so thin that you could see the freckled scalp through it. A spark came to life in her bosom and glowed at the thought of him. She found a taxi at last and told it to take her to Harrods, with the thought of buying him something expensive and extravagant, something he didn't need, something which would please him precisely because of its extravagance. She imagined his surprise, the look on his face, his pink pleasure, his stammers that it wasn't really necessary. She was happy turning all this over in her mind.

Getting out in front of the great red palace dreaming in the frozen mist under its flags, she went in and wandered without any definite plan down the aisles. He certainly didn't use cologne or any of the other male vanities advertised in magazines, nor did she imagine he would like a toilet kit with a little nailfile, a pair of fingernail scissors, and so on. Perhaps a long shoehorn with a golden tongue for a hundred pounds. And then the thought struck her all at once, why not give him what he *really* wants? It was a trifling thing after all. No worse than a trip to the dentist. As the French lady said, it gives them so much pleasure and us so little pain. Once when she was fourteen and had a persistent ache, Tita had taken her to a gynaecologist who had thrust a silver instrument into her, cold and creepy, slightly oiled. It was no more than that. She had decided. She would surprise him with it, this unexpected, priceless, and exquisite gift. She smiled and went on into the next hall of the store.

It was full of male mannikins standing about stiffly in tweed suits. Their faces were waxen and their chins lifted arrogantly; from the cuffs of their sleeves they dangled tags showing their expensive prices. One after another they stared at her with their glittering waxy eyes as she passed. Her mood changed abruptly. She didn't care for their hidalgo superiority, their cold and smooth egos, and she certainly wasn't going to buy a cologne or a shoehorn for one of *them*. She stamped away into the next department.

It was populated with female mannikins wearing the clothes provided for their sex, in this case smart tailored suits with narrow skirts. There was something odd and improbable about the skirts which she at first could not pin down in her mind, something vaguely disquieting. It was perhaps because she had come directly into this room from the men's section. Comparing the men's clothes with the women's, she was struck with the thought that trousers were very rational after all. They exactly fitted the human form, they kept the legs warm, they were comfortable, and they were convenient for disposing of the waste products of the body. A skirt was an indecent instrument invented no doubt by men, or at any rate worn for their pleasure, if you could call such a vile fascination a pleasure. It was as though it were designed for men to peep surreptitiously into. If you sat down in it—in a train, or anywhere else, on a low chair or a sofa—it was a gymnastic trick to do so without exposing yourself. And you had to stand about in a certain way; you couldn't stand in just any way, but in the way that women were supposed to stand while wearing skirts. The mannikins were all posed in a posture common to mannikins, legs apart and one foot turned out, a position borrowed from ballet. Looking more closely, she saw that they would have fallen down if each one had not been supported by a strong chromium rod which, coming up from the round base on the floor, disappeared into their skirts at the rear. This no doubt accounted for the slightly glazed cheerfulness which they offered to the world. The similarity to the gynaecologist's shiny instrument was unmistakable.

I can't bear to wound you in any way, he said. Catching a glimpse of herself in a pier-glass, she saw reflected her moist eyes, her hair drawn back in its black velvet ribbon, her special grace of things fragile and not intended for common use. And indeed, she thought, this particular wound, so intimate and somehow in spite of nature's necessity so grotesque and humiliating, was patently unsuited for a person of such sensitivity and refinement, of such carefully balanced talent, of a beauty which depended as much on a momentary angle of glance, on the chance passing of a featherlike thought, as it did on the features themselves. And if that angle of glance, that feather, were disturbed by a mad and angry penetration of her being's most delicate intimacy, what would be left? Wouldn't it all fall into the center, like the walls of a sacked and pillaged town? She was not made for that somehow. Life was brutal and the means we have been given to perpetuate life still retained their primordial brutality; they still depended on the thrusting of a blunt weapon into a trembling and half-willing victim. In spite of all nature, this victim could not be Sylvie.

Frowning darkly, she fled off into costume jewelry to buy something expensive and extravagant for herself. For was not she herself the one who deserved to be consoled, to be recompensed, for this insupportable arrangement? Angrily, rebelliously, with an impudence toward the universe, she flung open her purse. After considering several other things she bought an antique cameo brooch for a hundred pounds, no more than a shoehorn. On it a kind of Diana-figure was seated on a tree stump, holding a sceptre or staff. The stone was white on the surface and red underneath where the tool had cut it, like the human body itself.

"May I wear it?"

"Only if you carry the sales receipt in your hand, mum."

She pinned the brooch to her throat like a badge. Flaunting the piece of paper, she went out of the store into the icy gray wilderness of Knightsbridge.

Twelve

The newly wedded pair drove back that afternoon to Waldshire, Sylvie wearing her new brooch and Bonner with his books and research materials, which he left in the car in the garage for the time being. After dinner he planned to install these things in his new workroom in the Mill Cottage so that he could start working on the new idea for his book the next day. During dinner, of course, there was a certain amount of badinage about what had happened on the honeymoon, most of it from Stasha, although James and even Drood also permitted themselves to be witty on this subject. This irritated Bonner, or at least made him fretful, and he got up from the table while the others were still finishing their coffee.

In the colder weather they were now taking their meals in the dining room, which faced out toward the garage and the lane beyond. Bonner gazed moodily into the darkness, impenetrable except for the first few feet illuminated by the light from the house. Through the window he caught a glimpse of something moving in this band of half-light. At first the notion occurred to him that one of the deer had got loose from the park. He went closer to the window and looked out to one side, in the direction the object had disappeared. In the dim light from the house he made out an ungainly shape standing in the shrubbery and peering into the window of the hall, which was adjacent to the dining room. The light was coming mainly from the window where he was standing, so that William was outlined in profile, a beaky and bony figure like a stork. Catching some intuition that he had been noticed—a slight noise or a change in the light from the window—he melted into the shrubbery and disappeared. One moment he was there and the next he was not. He didn't crouch down into the shrubbery or move away sideways; he simply vanished.

Bonner said nothing to the others, who had paid no attention to him when he got up from the table. He wondered if William was something that only he could see, like the Little People. Murmuring some excuse to the others, who scarcely looked up, he went out to the garage and cautiously opened the door. When he switched on the light and looked around there was no sign of Miles. He had never before lived in a house where there were servants and he found them a pain in the neck. You could see why people in old novels were always shutting doors and talking in undertones so they wouldn't be overheard. He got the carton of research materials and the box of kitchen things out of the car and set them on the floor, then he looked around for something to hold the loose books. There were boxes and cartons stacked against the wall, some empty and some full of the usual junk found in garages. He got an empty one and began putting the books into it.

In the pile of cartons he noticed one marked "Household— Save." It was full of electrical appliances for the most part: a flat-iron, a portable hair dryer, a bunch of extension cords, and an immersion heater. Nothing very interesting. He was just closing it up again when he saw Miles watching him from the rear of the garage, his hands in his pockets and a cigarette in his mouth as usual.

He took the cigarette out and said, "There's a sandwich grill in there. The old fellow could use that."

"Thanks." He felt a sense of deep annoyance combined with peril. There was no way he could retreat now from what he was doing. "Anything else?"

"No, the rest is pretty much junk."

He put the sandwich grill in the carton with the other kitchen things and hoisted the three cartons heavily, getting a good deal of dust on his clothing. Miles, drawing on his cigarette, watched him go in an interested way. Then he threw the cigarette onto the floor and disappeared up the stairway to his flat.

At the Mill Cottage, which gave every appearance of being deserted in the chill autumn night, Bonner held the three piled-up cartons on his knee while he pushed open the door. He went first to the empty room he planned to use as a workroom and groped for the lamp to switch on the light. He set the three cartons on the table and brushed the dust from his clothing, then he looked around. The room, in addition to the bed and table, contained a chair and a lamp on a three-legged stool which served as night-stand. He moved the lamp from the stool to the table and arranged the yellow lined pads, the pencils, and the books neatly under it. Out in the museum he found some left-over paving stones on the floor and he utilized a couple of these as bookends. When he was finished he was pleased with the effect. The room was sparsely fur-nished but clean and neat. With its windowless stone walls it re-sembled the cell of a medieval monk-scholar, a scriptorium, except for the yellow pencils in place of quills. He might try writing with feathers to see if it would improve his style. Of course the electric light was also a modern note. It would be too much to try to write by candlelight. It would ruin his eyes, and he might set the place on fire. A certain amount of anachronism had to be accepted if you were going to live and breathe in the twentieth century.

Carrying the box of kitchen stuff, he went into the next room where William was lying on the bed with his slippers off, his nose in a book. He went on reading as Bonner entered.

"How are you getting along, William?"

"Oh, all right enough." He looked up briefly and then turned back to his book. Bonner had expected a little more companionship from William; or rather he didn't know what to expect from him. His lanky melancholy, his pale and thoughtful blinking, were al-ways the same no matter what the external conditions of his life. A conversation with him was a dialogue of the deaf, with little scraps of meaning that one snatched at. He didn't seem unhappy. In his way he gave the impression of being grateful to Bonner for rescuing him from the virtuous Maidenhead sisters and providing him with his lair.

Bonner began unloading the things from the carton. "I've brought you an electric kettle."

"Yes, I can see that. You can heat up water in a pan, you know."

"A sandwich grill. And some things to eat. Tea. Some rice, it's a special kind that cooks quickly. Saltines. And do you like canned peaches?"

"What? Oh, tinned. Tinned peaches. Yes, they're all right."

"Is there anything else you need?"

"Not particularly. I'm snug enough in here with my books. The

187

only trouble is it makes a chap costive, sitting in here all day with no exercise. I don't move regular. You don't suppose there would be some psyllium seed up at the house, do you?"

"Psyllium seed?"

"Little seeds that swell up. You mix them with water and they keep you regular. I took a little every day when I was home."

"I'll see if I can find some." He had meant to tell William the news that he had got married since he had last seen him, but he couldn't find a way to work it into the conversation. William was interested in very little but himself and his own affairs.

"So you're doing a lot of reading, are you?"

Bonner turned over the books he found on the table. Some of them were from the library in the house but others he didn't recognize. There was a paperback with a shiny cover called *The Secrets of the Land*. It was a nicely done book with photos on front and back, one a set of menhirs in a green coutryside and the other a view of Stonehenge from the air. He leafed through it while William watched without expression, the pulse in the top of his skull beating softly. It was about what you would expect from the title. There were chapters on prehistoric burial sites, on leys and other strange marks on the land, on various kinds of standing stones, and on white hillside figures like the Uffington Horse and the Cerne Abbas Giant. Another chapter explained that Stonehenge was a prehistoric landing place for visitors from outer space.

"Where did you get this?"

"Oh, I go into Waldon once in a while. There's a nice bookstore. There's a bus you can catch in the road. I drop in at the pub while I'm about it. I couldn't do that when I was with Em and Elodie, you know. They can smell it on your breath."

It was not clear where he had got hold of enough money even for the bus, let alone for the books. Surely he hadn't had much with him when he had stolen out of the house in Maidenhead in his carpet slippers.

"William, I can bring you anything you want. You needn't go out of here at all. It's a little dangerous. Does anybody see you when you leave to go to Waldon?"

"I don't think so. I skulk along under the hedge, you know."

"You have to go right by the garage. I think the chaffeur has seen you. He made some remark to me just now when I was in the garage."

"Oh, Miles. He's all right. He's a straight enough chap. You won't have any trouble with him. I stop and have a chat with him now and then."

"You do?"

"Oh yes. He's the sort of chap you can talk to."

"Who did you tell him you were?"

"I didn't tell him anything. He didn't ask. He speaks very highly of you. He said you were a brilliant man, a professor. I hadn't known that."

Not only had he made himself acquainted with Miles, but it was an entirely different Miles from the one Bonner knew. Perhaps this other Miles had given William money, for some reason best known to himself. Then another thought struck him. Perhaps the money William had was a Krugerrand.

"William, do you ever walk the other way?"

"The other way?"

"Across the river. You go over the footbridge, and then there's a path that leads across the meadow to the forest."

"I couldn't do that, could I. They'd see me from the house."

"If you go on for a while you pass the Long Barrow, then you turn off into the forest and the path comes to a clearing with some stones in it." His eye caught the book on the table again; he picked it up and then set it down. "Sarsens. Two are standing and one is lying on its side. They're very old. And then—" He struggled to keep his voice natural, conscious of his rising excitement. He was very desirous of knowing whether William had seen the Little People too, or whether he was capable of seeing them. "And then, if you go on a little farther, up through a cleft in the mountain, you come to another clearing where—"

William didn't appear to be listening to what he was saying. He guarded his private movements jealously and didn't care to discuss them. "They'd see me from the house, you see Bonner. So I couldn't go across the river."

Bonner smiled thoughtfully over his defeat. Then he said, "They're going to see you from the house anyhow if you're not more careful. I saw you looking into the window of the hall, an hour or so ago when we were having dinner."

William was shifty; he got up from the bed and shuffled around the books on the table. "How could you have seen me?"

"It was very simple. I looked out the window of the dining

room, and there you were standing in the shrubbery looking into the hall."

"It was dark."

"Yes it was, but there was light from the house."

William frowned; he sat down at the chair before the table, chewing his lip. "I wish you'd leave me alone and not interfere in my affairs."

"What are you talking about, William? It *is* my affair if you go wandering around the grounds and people see you. I was the one who brought you here."

"I only go to the forest at night."

Bonner stared at him. "You go there at night?"

"I mean, I couldn't go across the river in the daytime, because they'd see me from the house. I mainly go out at night. The trouble is, the bookstore in Waldon isn't open at night. So I have to go there in the daytime."

It was hopeless trying to get any kind of connected story out of him. Bonner went back to his own workroom and shuffled about with his papers for a while, arranging them in order and setting them in neat stacks on the table. From time to time he looked to see if the bar of light was still showing under William's door. It still was after a couple of hours. Eventually, he knew, he would have to tell James and the others about William and what he was doing there. It was perfectly natural; he was a friend of Bonner's and there was plenty of room for him in the Mill Cottage. He didn't eat much, and if there was a question about that Bonner could pay for his board. After all William wasn't a criminal; he was a harmless old fellow who had no place else to go. He imagined himself discussing all this with James. He decided not to tell him quite yet. He remembered now the reason why William had derailed the train, because he had seen a little fellow in a topper on the tracks. James might start questioning him about that and the whole business of the Little People would all come out.

Thirteen

When Bonner was gone William inspected the things he had left. The electric kettle would be handy; it didn't heat the water up any more quickly but it was more convenient for pouring the water into the teapot after it was boiling. The rice would be useful too, although it wasn't really of very much interest to him that it cooked in seven minutes as it said on the packet; he had plenty of time. He didn't care for tinned peaches. He prepared himself a little meal: a sausage which he fried in a pan, tinned peas, saltines, and tea. He didn't have much appetite living the way he did and only a little would do him.

After he had finished the meal he washed up and put everything away neatly in the cavelike kitchen. He got out his railroad watch and found it was after eleven. Taking off his slippers again, he settled onto the bed and went back to reading *The Secrets of the Land* at the place where he had left off, which he had marked by turning down the corner of a page.

The notion of a fairy as a small winged creature with feminine attributes flitting about with a wand is a modern invention. Traditionally the Little People are described by those who have seen them as much like ordinary humans except slightly smaller in stature, of both sexes, and having odd coloration. They are thought to dwell in the forest or underground, and to be intimate with birds and animals. They are depicted as fond of music and as skilled musicians; there are numerous sites in Britain where the piping or singing of the Little People has been reported, usually in forests or at the sites of ancient mounds. The Little People are frequently associated with two natural substances, gold and honey. The first of these is the only metal found in its pure form in nature and therefore accessible to societies without technology; its use antedates iron and even bronze by many millennia. Honey is also found in its pure form in nature and was an important source of food for nomadic and gathering peoples before the invention of agriculture. These facts suggest a very ancient origin for the tradition of the Little People.

With satisfaction he went on leafing through the book at a leisurely pace, not really applying his mind to what he read with any vigor. The words trickled through his mind like a warm and friendly brook, or a leak in a boat which filled it only slowly. The railroad watch in his pocket ticked away faintly. In this new life of his in the mill the minutes and hours were identical to one another and without distinguishing characteristics, since night and day didn't penetrate the windowless rooms in the old stone building and he ate his meals and went to bed whenever the impulse struck him. Some time after midnight he finished *The Secrets of the Land* and went back to read parts of it over again. There was a chapter toward the middle, he remembered, that had interested him particularly, and there were also pictures. If a chap took a photograph of a thing and it was printed in a book, that pretty much meant that it had to be real. There they were, all marching around in a circle with the things on their heads. The text under the picture gave a devious but electrifying explanation of what this was all about.

Herne the Hunter, a figure out of the far archetypal past, is said to haunt an oak forest near Windsor Castle. There have been a number of sightings in modern times; he is described as a wild spectral figure more or less human in form, wearing a cloak of deerskin and bearing on his head a large pair of antlers. He is surrounded by a blue phosphorescent light. Are these horn dancers, photographed at Avebury in Wiltshire, perhaps disciples or worshippers of his strange rite?

William very much enjoyed reading. He could keep at it endlessly as long as he had a good book. It was now after three o'clock, and he arose from the bed with his joints creaking and put on his slippers. He finished off the cold tea in the pot, then opened the door and went to the earth closet in the next room. In the light from the open door behind him he urinated a brief trickling stream, and then turned around, sat down, and tried the other thing. No results after sitting for ten minutes. He got up, fastened his trousers, and went to the kitchen where he ran a trickle of water over each hand in succession while he pumped with the other hand. Then he dried his hands, went back to his room for a small electric torch which he slipped into his pocket, and went out.

It was a moonlight night and overcast, so that the way across the lawn lay through pitch blackness. William had found out some time before how to get into the house. Feeling his way up through the shrubbery to the glass wall of the orangery, he slid his flattened hands along it until he came to the door. This was fastened with a simple spring-latch. He took from his pocket a plastic straight-edge he had bought in Waldon, and with this inserted into the edge of the door he was able to push back the weak bolt after only a little fumbling. The door swung open and he passed stealthily into the dark and warm jungle of the orangery.

No need for the torch yet, since by this time he knew the interior of the house well. First to the downstairs lavatory off the passage. Holding the torch inside his almost closed fist, he allowed a needle of light to penetrate through his fingers. In the cabinet he quickly found what he was looking for: a small jar of psyllium seed. It probably belonged to the old lady with the boots and the man's hat. He found a tumbler and a teaspoon, stirred a spoonful of the seeds into a glass of water, and drank it in a single long draught. He filled the tumbler again and drank a second glass of water. Then he put everything away, drying the tumbler and the spoon carefully on the towel. The tiny seeds soaked up water like miniature Japanese flowers; he thought with satisfaction of their swelling into a yeasty and gelatinous lump and following their way down through his innards. Leaving the lavatory, he went off through the pitch-black house to the kitchen.

There he turned on the torch again and enclosed it in his fist. On the pantry shelf he found a few bags of Twining's English

Breakfast tea, which was a good deal better than the cheap job-lot stuff that Bonner had brought him. He was careful not to take too much. About a third of what there was there was his rule. Then, in a household with a number of different people using the kitchen, it wouldn't be missed. He passed by a tin of anchovies, since these made his gout flare up, and pocketed a jar of olives, a tin of potted beef, and a handful of spaghetti which stuck up out of his back pocket like a fan.

Next he got down the money jar. This was in its usual place on top of the cupboard, just above the level of his head. It was an affair of white faience with decorations of a pastoral sort, satyrs pursuing nymphs and so on. He took off the lid and inspected the contents in the needle of light from his fist. There were two fivers, a dozen or so crumpled pound notes, and a lot of coins. He took four of the pounds—his principle of never taking more than third of what there was—and a handful of coins. These last he distributed into various pockets so that they wouldn't make a noise; two of them went into the rear pocket with the fan of spaghetti. He replaced the jar on top of the cupboard where he had found it.

Moving now with cumbersome steps on account of these objects bulging in his pockets, he went on through the morning room into the gallery. The streak of light from the torch passed over Sir Fellows with his varnished frown of petulance, flickered over the other portraits, illuminated the furniture with its antimacassars and its worn pillows, and came to a stop on the glass cabinet at the end of the room. When he turned the ribbon of light downward into the cabinet a portion of it was reflected in the glass, causing a small pale circle to waver back and forth on the ceiling. In this faint light he caught a glimpse of his own face reflected in the glass, a bony cheek and a long brow limned in chiaroscuro as though by a melancholy Flemish master. He directed the ray of light onto the objects in the cabinet: amulets, needles, a scrap of gold ornament. At the end it fell onto the incised horn.

He puzzled over this for some time. The needle of light in his fist wavered unsteadily; he made an effort to keep it focussed on its object. In this illumination as capricious as a butterfly he studied the details incised on the horn by an anonymous prehistoric hand. There were crude animals, geometric shapes like triangles and diamonds, and a number of animated stick-men who seemed to be celebrants of some sort. He held his fist steadier and the needle of light vibrated like a fly's antenna. The stag-headed figure, twice as large as the others, had his stick-arms raised as though he was radiating energy from his palms. The limb which protruded from his fork was erected almost to the vertical, and in proportion to the rest of him it was the size of a pick-handle. The light in William's fist tremored. He felt a wave of excitement, a feverish and guilty sense of discovery unmatched since the day when, as a child, he had benefited from his mother's absence from the house to rifle through the drawer where she kept her underwear.

He searched carefully over the rest of the horn with his tiny pinprick of light. There was nothing more of any interest. All the other stick-figures had fallen on their faces and were prostrate with their hands stretched out toward the giant. Either they had no choice or they benefited in some way from the emanations that radiated from his hands. William switched off the torch and stood for a while in the darkness, wrapped in his thoughts which seemed curious even to him. Then he began feeling his way across the room in the direction of the hall, the contents of which he had not yet inspected in any detail. He did remember that there was a stag-head on the wall.

Fourteen

James strode across the pasture, came to the gate, and continued on up through the deer park toward the house. He had verified what he had already suspected: it was the middle of the morning and Fred Baines hadn't yet milked the cows. He himself had no real idea how to milk them and he was damned if he was going to do it anyhow. He resolutely shut the whole matter out of his mind and went on across the rough grass under the beeches and elms.

The trees were bare now; the grass under them was littered with leaves and touched lightly with a morning frost that had not yet burned away. When he came to the hedge at the end of the park he went through it, shutting the gate behind him, and turned down toward the river and the Mill Cottage.

Where the hedge ended, at the corner of the of the stone mill, he stopped and looked around him carefully. There was no sign of anyone along the river or across it in the meadow that led up to the forest. In the other direction, to his left, he could see the Val curving gracefully over the riffles just beyond the house and then disappearing from sight in the bend toward Pense Coombe a mile or so away. The whole landscape was deserted; he was alone with his possessions and with the virtually unspoiled, the Wordsworthian nature that surrounded them. He stood for a minute contemplating all this, then he turned the corner of the Mill Cottage, past the decrepit statue and the pond now full of fallen leaves, and went quickly to the museum.

With a final glance around him he entered noiselessly and switched on the lights. The presses were exactly as they always were, standing solidly and blackly with the light beating down over them. Although they might have seemed similar to anyone else, he recognized them all and could have called them by name as a hunter does his dogs: Albion, Stanhope, Chandler, Blaeu, Winterthur. In the middle of the room, surrounded by the iron machines, the old mill wheel lay like a beached whale.

He had half expected to find someone else in the room; he had come here frequently in the last few days and switched on the lights abruptly without announcing his presence, in the belief that when he did so he caught a glimpse out of the corner of his eye of something that wasn't supposed to be there. He was cautious about this belief and only skirted around it in his own mind, and certainly he wasn't going to tell anyone else about it. As a matter of fact, Bonner had set up his workroom in one of the small stone rooms now, and if he had seen anything it was probably only his elbow or ankle, or the last of his ginger-colored head, disappearing back into his room from the museum where he had been skulking around doing something or other in the dark. Heaven knew what it was; perhaps he was trying to print the book he was writing on one of the presses. Of course, there was never any sound from the room beyond the door. One of Bonner's self-willed eccentricities was that he refused to use a typewriter and wouldn't say why; whatever composition he did took place in the silence of the tomb.

He decided not to open the door and see if Bonner was in there, although a part of him was strongly drawn by this impulse. He held back from this act out of a kind of holy dread, connected with Bonner's oddness and with the special sanctity owing in James's mind to deep activities of the intellect, such as writing recondite books about old medieval texts. Of course, it might not have been Bonner that he had seen. In that case, he preferred to explain the fleeting apparition as something that had happened in his own mind rather than a glimpse of a real person. If it had been a real person and not Bonner, he reasoned, then this person would have to be confronted and dealt with somehow; he would have been an invader of his daytime waking life rather than a figment of his dreams, a trespasser on his property who would have to be chased away or even physically subdued. I probably just imagined it, he told himself without conviction, but the formula comforted and reassured him anyhow. If not, it was probably Bonner he had seen. Of course he had not seen anything at all today. The connections between these thoughts circled in his mind like a ring of dancers who, stretching out their hands to one another, still don't quite connect. He switched off the lights and left the museum.

Outside there was still no one in sight. The grounds and the land along the river were curiously deserted today for some reason. Over his head a rook took wing and, with a raucous caw, flapped off in the direction of the Long Barrow and the forest. The only other sound was the flustering of the Val running over its riffles. Crossing the lawn, still looking around him reflectively, he went up to the house and entered through the orangery. It struck him for the first time that there was a flaw in the design of the house. Its eighteenth-century planners, chiefly Sir Fellows himself, had assumed that people would mostly enter the house from the carriage drive, near the present graveled terrace and garage. But nowadays, because people walked and weren't taken about in carriages, they came in through the orangery door which had been added only in the nineteenth century and was intended only as a side entrance. Perhaps he could have the orangery door removed, or simply make a rule that whenever possible everyone should enter through the main door to the hall. He doubted that anyone would obey it.

Cassie and Rhondda were puttering in the kitchen as they usually did in the morning, and Tita was in the morning room. She had left her French *Vogue* facedown on the coffee table and was pacing up and down before the windows with her cigarette.

He told her, "Fred Baines didn't milk the cows this morning. He didn't turn them out into the pasture either. They're still in the barn."

"Why didn't he milk them?"

"He and I are having a difference of opinion. It's been going on for some time. I want to pay him in milk and he doesn't want milk. If he took half the milk as I've suggested, that would be about twelve gallons. If he'd only realize it, the fool, it would be worth far more than the money."

"What was your arrangement before?"

"I've been paying him in cash. But there's no sense to that. We have more milk than we can use. But if we have to pay him to milk them, we might as well get rid of the cows and buy our milk in the village."

"Then why don't we?"

"Because," he said patiently, "the farm would no longer be an agricultural enterprise and the rates would go up."

She sighed and crushed out her cigarette. "Well, I can see it from Fred's point of view. He's been doing it this way for years. Since long before you came here."

"I don't care for his ways. Have you noticed? They all look alike, these locals. The people in the village. Old Mrs. Thrane in the bakery. The farmers hereabouts. They all have dark hair and eyes set in caves, and they skulk around without saying very much. They all stoop a little and look at you sideways. They won't look at you directly in the eye."

"I've never noticed it."

"You can't see it because you're a Cromlech. You're half one of them yourself."

"I don't have dark hair and I don't stoop. I don't have eyes set in caves."

"I mean you grew up here. You're accustomed to them. You can't see them in the way someone coming in from the outside can."

"There's a lot of Celtic blood in the district. They can't help it. It's just the way they are."

"No doubt. But I don't like it."

Long-chinned Cassie came into the room drying her hands on her apron. "James, Fred didn't leave the milk this morning. Rhondda and I were going to make butter."

"I know. Fred didn't milk the cows."

"Then what shall we do?"

"You won't be able to make butter, will you?"

"Cassie, remember we're having a guest for lunch," said Tita.

"Well, he won't have butter on his bread. Why don't you speak to Fred?"

"I have spoken to him, and he has spoken to me. As a result of our conversation together, he didn't milk the cows."

"Well good heavens. It's because you won't pay him, I suppose. It's only a few pounds a month. You're both behaving like children. Besides, if they're not milked it's not good for the cows. Imagine if you were a cow, your udder full of milk that you couldn't get out, and no one would do it for you."

"I refuse to imagine I'm a cow."

"Why should you imagine you're a cow, James?" Stasha entered the room with her slouching insouciance, slumped down onto the sofa, and took up the magazine that Tita had been reading.

"James and Fred Baines are being cruel to the cows, owing to a dispute."

"And in a little while they're going to start making a horrible racket," said Cassie. "They did it one winter when there was a blizzard and we couldn't get to them."

James said, "If you don't like it, why don't you all go down to the barn and milk them yourselves?" He left the room angrily, crossed into the gallery, and disappeared through the door into the hall.

"What's the matter with him? He *is* in a state."

"Your father," said Tita, "feels that he is surrounded by a conspiracy of Celts. They look at him sideways out of their dark eyes, and they won't carry out his commands."

"You never asked me whether you ought to marry an American," said Cassie. "You never asked any of us. You were so headstrong as a girl. Americans," she said, "always believe they'd like to live in the country, but when they do it makes them nervy. I don't see that it's doing Bonner any good either."

"Cette Saison, Prè-Mamans en Toutes Couleurs," Stasha read from the French magazine. "What an idea. Here's another one. Agrandissez Votre Poitrine Immédiatement Sans Peine."

"Your chest doesn't need aggrandizing, dear. Shòw it to Sylvie. Here she is. Or la voilà as they say."

Sylvie entered the room followed by Bonner. Bonner had not, as James thought, been writing his book in the room in the Mill Cottage. Instead during the morning he and Sylvie had gone for a walk along the Val in the direction of the village. It was the other way from the dairy barn and he hadn't heard about the cows or James's quarrel with Fred. It had to be explained to him.

He had been born and raised in the city and it hadn't occurred to him that if cows weren't milked it could be damaging to them and hurt their udders. He had thought it was something like semen; it came out if you wanted it to, otherwise it was just stored up in there until needed. Now it seemed it was more like urine. He didn't really care for either idea. In his mind, milk came in milk bottles and one thought about its animal origins as little as possible.

"Sylvie and I walked almost to the village. Then we saw there were some people there, so we turned and came back."

"On the way back he kissed me," said Sylvie. "There's a certain poplar tree that we're fond of for that purpose."

"Well," said Stasha, "what a fascinating insight into marriage."

Tita said, "You shouldn't reveal such details to your unmarried sister. It might give her ideas. In old-fashioned times, it wasn't thought proper for a married sister to divulge such things. Maidens were kept in suspense. Their married sisters wouldn't tell them a damned thing. It frustrated the hell out of them."

"Well, Sylvie really hasn't told me an awful lot."

"If she did," said Tita, "it would surely be an histoire sans surprises."

"Well, I think the affection of our young pair for each other is touching," said Cassie. "They're behaving just as people did when I was a girl. In fact, they used to kiss under that same poplar."

"Oh, do you know the one?" said Sylvie, coloring slightly.

"There's a bench by it, and an oddly shaped stone to put your feet on."

"That's the one." She was pleased and flustered by the turn the conversation had taken. Bonner was not quite so much at ease. He shifted about, put his hands in his pockets, and took them out again. Sylvie prattled on, "We were going into the village for some honey. Bonner is very fond of honey. It comes from his having read the poem about the owl and the pussycat at a very young age.

> *'They took along some honey*
> *And plenty of money,*
> *Wrapped up in a five-pound note.'*

Now with inflation, of course, the prices have gone up and you'd need a Krugerrand."

"Cut it out, will you?" said Bonner irritatedly.

James entered the room abruptly and said, "There's something missing there in the hall. Something that used to be there."

"Where?"

He disappeared again, and they all followed him one after another throught the gallery into the hall.

"What is it, James?"

"I've told you. There's something wrong about this room. Something has been changed. Something has been moved around, or something is missing that should be here."

"Well, what is it?"

"I don't know. But there's something."

They all looked around the room with the mechanical indifference of members of a family who have been asked to help look for something by someone who has lost it. Bonner could clearly see a large oval spot on the wall, a lighter color than the rest, where the mounted stag-head had been. Facing it on the opposite wall, the crossed shotguns and the hunting prints were in their usual places.

"Well, I can't imagine what it is," said Cassie. "It must be all in your imagination, James. Nothing in this room has been changed for ages. Hardly anyone comes into the room these days. Rhondda dusts it now and then. Probably she's moved something or other."

"It's just because she's dusted," said Tita. "You're used to it dusty and now it's been cleaned."

"Old Cromlech creepies come in here," said Stasha. "I don't like it at night."

Sylvie sat down on the sofa and pulled Bonner after her. They held hands. "This old sofa has a hole in it." She thrust her finger into the leather. "But that's always been there."

"There's something missing that used to be here," repeated James.

No one responded to this; the conversation expired out of lack of interest.

"I'll have to go out and buy some cream to churn," said Cassie. "We can't have lunch without butter."

"Why don't you just buy some butter?"

"The store butter is full of dye and preservatives."

The rest of them dispersed too except for Bonner and Sylvie, who sat on the old leather sofa conversing in whispers. James felt left out of things and isolated in his own house; no one paid any attention to his opinions or bestirred themselves when he asked them questions. Through the window he saw Cassie getting into the Daimler with Miles at the wheel, going in to the village to buy her cream. In a mood between irritability and depression, he went into the kitchen, which, as a source of nourishment and a place where there was light and warmth at all seasons of the year, always consoled him. Rhondda was alone, cutting up smoked mackerel with a knife. The dark and pungent odor of the fish, which some might have found offensive, filled him with a primitive pleasure.

"What are you doing, Rhondda?"

"Getting ready for lunch," she said crossly. "Who would if I didn't."

"Rhondda." He came and slipped an arm around her as she worked at the cutting board, sliding the hand forward until it enclosed her warm and firm breast with its soft yielding button in the center. The crisp black stuff of her dress crinkled under his fingers. There were two reasons for doing what he was doing; first it was sexually stimulating, a sensation he still enjoyed, and second it gave him a sense of manorial privilege, a feeling that he was following in the tradition of centuries of landowners who had behaved in this way with their sullen and acquiescent domestics. He manipulated the soft fruit under his fingers. Her had forgotten the feel of the thing, the simple and elemental satisfaction of such acts. My God, why should people imagine that such things were sinful or wrong—instead they recalled the child's deep sensual pleasure of intimacy with the mother, or of a father with a daughter—here his thought strayed a little and became muddled. With difficulty he steered it back onto the correct track.

It's too much work for you when there's a guest. Perhaps we could get a girl from the village to help you."

"You say that when you've got your hand on me. As soon as you take the hand away you'll forget."

"Rhondda."

She allowed him to caress the other breast while she finished chopping the mackerel. Then, disengaging herself, she went to the vegetable bin in the pantry for the potatoes.

In the bedroom at the side of the house, Bonner stood looking out the window while Sylvie sat at the dressing table putting on her eyes. She wore more makeup now that they were married. In fact, he couldn't remember her wearing any at all before. Through the window to the extreme right he had a view of the garage, the graveled drive, and the kitchen garden and orchard beyond. Everything was dull now under a grayish sky and the trees in the orchard were leafless. As he watched a gray Jaguar sedan came down the drive, slowed, and circled to a stop on the gravel in front of the garage. A bison-shaped man with thick spectacles got out of the car, an attaché case in one hand and a raincoat slung over the other shoulder. Because of his two burdens he had to shut the car door by pushing at it with his shoulder, an awkward gesture that almost threw him off balance. When he turned Bonner recognized him abruptly, as he already had, he now realized, in a subliminal way.

"It's Lovejoy."

"What?"

"He's just driven up in his Jaguar."

"Yes, he's been invited to lunch."

"By whom?"

"By James, I imagine. He's James's friend."

"I thought he was a friend of the family."

"Not really. *You're* a friend of the family. Or you were until we got married." She came to him at the window, still carrying her little black brush. "Would you like some eyes? Or some carmine lips?"

"No thanks. Why is he coming here anyhow?"

"I just told you. He's been invited to lunch."

"Of course he has to eat lunch now that he's here. But why has he been invited?"

"Oh for heaven's sake, how do I know? You're as suspicious as a leopard."

"I don't like it. I wish I didn't have to go down to lunch with him. Sylvie. You didn't by any chance tell anyone about . . . the Little People?"

"Of course not."

"You didn't tell James?"

"I wouldn't tell James. He wouldn't believe in it anyhow, would he?"

"No, but he might think it meant that I'm not well."

"Well you're not. I won't tell anybody, Bonner. It's our little secret. Which we believe in and don't believe in at the same time, don't we."

"You don't believe in it?"

"Of course I believe in it but not really."

"You said you did."

"No I didn't." She turned and set the things back on the dressing table, while he followed her with his eyes. Was this a quarrel?

With her quick pouncing nervosity, her abrupt changes of mood, he could never be sure.

He thought a little more. "I can't help feeling that Lovejoy . . ." The bulky figure had disappeared into the house now. "Maybe I told somebody. Maybe I told James. Or perhaps James himself saw me when I—" But this was impossible and didn't make sense. He didn't know where his thoughts were taking him anyhow. He felt a need to be reassured, to be reconciled with the concrete and affectionate solidarity of things. "It's just that . . . will you kiss me or something?"

"Only briefly. I have to go tinkle."

"Is that what you call it?"

"We did when we were children. What did you say?"

"I have to go wee-wee." They were pleased with themselves, like children together, naughty children, talking about things their elders wouldn't want them to.

He got through lunch with a minimum of discomfort, mainly by the expedient of not talking much and making an effort not to catch Lovejoy's eye. There was a fish pie, which seemed to be the specialty when there was a guest for lunch. It was what they had had for Bonner on his first day in the house. They were eight at the large oaken table: Tita, Drood, and Cassie, who helped Rhondda serve as she always did and then sat down herself; James, Sylvie, and Stasha, Bonner, and Lovejoy. Lovejoy drank a good deal of bottled ale and wiped his spectacles, which steamed up as he made his way through the meal. He appeared to be in a jovial mood and was enjoying himself. Perhaps food was his vice. When he got the glasses back on he rotated them around the table with a rectangular smile, taking in each face in turn.

"Well, you're a member of the family now, Bonner."

"M'mm."

"And are they taking good care of you? Ha ha." A roguish glance in the direction of Sylvie.

"Oh, Bonner is no trouble to take care of," said James roundly. He seemed to have missed the innuendo. "You wouldn't know he's around. He's always got his nose in a book."

"What *have* you been reading, Bonner? I hope you haven't been burying yourself in those old medieval texts."

"Oh no. The latest French criticism. Lacan and Derrida."

"Well, there can't be any harm in that."

The rest of the conversation was about trivialities, and there was no mention of unmilked cows, conspiracies of Celts, Bonner's illness, or anything else that might lead to unpleasantness. However Bonner still felt uncomfortable and had a mildly stifled sensation; the dining room seemed to have shrunk in size. Perhaps Lovejoy had hidden his attaché case under the table with magnets or something in it. At the end of the meal he excused himself with a murmur and escaped out the orangery door onto the lawn. He felt better as soon as he was out of the house.

He heard a rhythmic thud behind him and Lovejoy caught up with him, glinting jovially. He even slapped him on the shoulder. "A little digestive walk, eh? An excellent idea." In his hurry to pursue Bonner he had left his coat behind, and he clenched his teeth resolutely. It was bitterly cold. He still smiled with his blue lips.

"What a lovely place. Impressive, isn't it?"

"You haven't been here before?"

"No. Of course the Boswins only moved here last spring. I never knew the Cromlechs, you know. Except for Tita of course. What a dear she is."

"She's very affectionate. She must have been a striking woman at one time." He was pleased with himself. He felt these two contrary statements, colliding violently in the intersection so to speak, summed her up perfectly, deftly avoiding terms like aging nymphomaniac and yet getting at the same sense.

Lovejoy appeared not to notice this minor literary achievement. Walking along beside Bonner, he thrust his hands into his pockets, still speaking through clenched teeth on account of the cold. "It's very pleasant here in the country. It's so quiet and peaceful. It takes your mind off your troubles."

"Is that why you've come here?"

"No, as I understand it that's why *you've* come here. I've come simply because I was invited to lunch."

They had reached the Mill Cottage now and Bonner saw that the door had been left open. He would have to speak to William about that; James would detect instantly if something was different and it would make him suspicious.

"What's in there?"

Bonner was anxious that he should not poke about in there and somehow discover William. "Nothing much. It's an old mill. Abandoned now. This path ends a little farther on. You can't go up the river on this side. You have to cross to the other bank."

He hoped that the bulky and unstable Lovejoy would not attempt to follow him across the footbridge, which seemed unsafe even to him with its wobbly railing. But when he started across it Lovejoy followed, moving his hand inch by inch along the railing, clenched and frozen, still smiling in his fixed way. When they reached the opposite bank, Lovejoy lurched rather than stepped onto solid ground and clutched Bonner's elbow for support. He disengaged himself and started off along the path across the meadow. The path was too narrow for them to walk side by side and Lovejoy tagged along behind him, swerving up to his side now and then to address remarks to his cheek, his city shoes thrashing in the tough cold grass. The exercise had warmed him now and he trailed a little private cloud of steam as he went.

"This all belong to the Cromlechs? That is to James."

"Not on this bank. It belongs to the National Trust."

"And that's the Long Barrow."

"Yes. Who told you that?"

"Someone. I don't remember. There's a forest too. That must be it up ahead." Lovejoy seemed to be blithering. Anyone could tell it was a forest. "Seems there's a lot of archaeology around here. Old artifacts. Digs. Sacred places. Standing stones. Drood knows all about that sort of thing."

"Yes." He thought of something. "You said you didn't know the Cromlechs. But Drood told me that he had met you."

"He did?"

"Yes. He said that he had come to London and the two of you had talked about me."

"I didn't know he was going to tell you that."

"Do you tell a lot of lies to people, Lovejoy?"

"Now listen Bonner. You needn't be offensive. We're just having a friendly chat."

"I'm not. I'm going for a walk. You're the one that's chatting."

"I wonder if we ought to go any further. Where does this path lead to anyhow?"

"I imagine you must know all about that. Since you've been interrogating Drood about these things."

"Interrogating him? I don't know what you're talking about. Suppose we cut back here and go down toward the river."

They had reached the first of the trees. Bonner was moved by a spirit of malice, a recklessness. "What's the matter? Don't you want to meet my friends?"

"Your friends?"

"That's what you've come along for, isn't it? I must have let slip to James or someone that I have friends in the forest, and you're coming along now because you suspect I'm going to them."

"You're very mysterious today, Bonner. What you say doesn't make sense. I'm a little concerned about you. I wonder if you shouldn't go and have another stay with *my* friends in Wimbledon."

"Do you have the power to do that?"

"Oh, power, power. We're not speaking of power. I'm only thinking of your best interests. No one is going to force you to do anything you don't want to do. I think we should stop right here and go back, Bonner." He came around him on the path and blocked the way with his bulky body. The bottleglass spectacles caught the gray light. "If you go a little farther you come to the sarsens, and then you come to the Fairy Ring, and God knows what you'd come to next."

"The Fairy Ring?"

"It has a very simple natural explanation. They're Horse Mushrooms, *Agaricus arvensis*. Every year they grow out a little further from the center. After a while they've formed a circle in the grass."

"What's the other explanation?"

"This is all nonsense, Bonner. It's not good for you to chase around like this after will-o'-the-wisps. I want you to come back to the house now."

"I thought you said nobody was going to force me to do anything I didn't want to do."

Lovejoy only glinted at him. Bonner attempted to pass him on the narrow path and there was a tussle. Lovejoy was solidly built but he gave the impression of not being very stable, like a building with imperfect foundations. He tottered and trembled. Bonner thought he could easily push him aside. He imagined him falling into the forest floor, gazing straight upward through his glasses like a collapsed puppet. The two of them pushed and prodded at each other, Lovejoy's large arms around him and Bonner's elbow digging into the other's chest. In spite of his bulk, and in spite of the steam that trailed after him, Lovejoy's body was curiously cold. The weather had evidently penetrated him to the bone; it was like clasping a side of beef in a butcher's cooler. Bonner struggled. He didn't feel very strong himself; the cold had made his bones stiff and a drop of water clung to the end of his nose.

"Whatever are you two doing? Bah. You're like a couple of schoolboys."

Bonner looked over Lovejoy's shoulder. The small bony form of Cassie had appeared on the path, and on the wrong side of them; she was coming not from the house but from beyond them in the forest. Yet they had left immediately after the meal and Cassie had been still at the table. Her sudden appearance had a quality of legerdemain to it. Bonner broke off tussling, and Lovejoy too lowered his arms and sighed. His glasses were clouded and he took them off and wiped them with his handkerchief.

"Where did you come from anyhow?"

"Don't worry. I can walk faster than either of you. I went along the Val, and then there's another path you don't know about. I like to take a brisk walk after lunch sometimes, to visit my friends."

Lovejoy put his glasses back on and gazed at her curiously. Bonner, his heart in his mouth, said, "Your friends?"

"Just the deer."

"There aren't any deer in the forest."

"Don't be coy, Bonner. You know there are as well as I."

"James says there aren't."

"James," she said, "is not the final authority on all matters pertaining to the wildlife of the region."

Lovejoy stayed for dinner and then left, glad to get back into his heated Jaguar. The fire at tea-time hadn't really been enough to warm him up. After he was gone they all went back to gather around the hearth in the gallery. They had chattered a lot at dinner but now they all fell silent. James poked at the coal in the fireplace and broke up the larger chunks so that they fell apart all glowing and thrust up clouds of sparks. It was a practice that annoyed Drood and Cassie, since it wasted fuel and really made the room too warm. They had never really agreed on the proper temperature for the gallery. James as an American wanted it to be comfortable, and the Cromlechs preferred an English chill in the air that kept the wits alive and didn't dry out the leather furniture. As for the hall, nobody had laid a fire in there since the nineteenth century.

The coal stopped hissing and grumbling and the flames died down. It was very quiet now. The old house crepitated in its sleep, Rhondda in the kitchen opened the water tap and then shut it again, the grandfather clock in the hall struck eleven with a dirge-like slowness. Thinly over the fields they could hear the sound of the lowing cows, an irregular chorus of moans that slid down the musical scale, like many nauseated baritones complaining.

No one said anything for some time. Then Cassie, looking at James and then away again into the fire, said, "I told you they would. It's exactly the same sound they made in the blizzard."

Sylvie bit her lip. "The poor creatures."

"You might telephone to Fred," said Tita, "and tell him that they're suffering."

"I wouldn't telephone to Fred to tell him an asteroid was headed at his house."

Stasha said, "Why can't they just squirt it out?"

"Has your own spectacular bosom ever produced anything so useful as milk, dear?"

"No, but—"

"Then you don't know what you're talking about," said Tita.

"Do *you* know how to milk, Drood?" asked Cassie.

"I'm damned if I do."

"We used to milk the cows when we were children."

"You did?" Drood grinned. "Who?"

"Perse and I. Your father loved animals of all kinds. He used to take me to the dairy barn when I was no bigger than a finch. I was his little sister of course. He was ten years older. We would squirt the milk into the mouths of the cats. I don't know if I could do it now. I've forgotten how. Still we could try."

"Damned if I will," said Drood. "The cows belong to James."

Tita said, "Oh dear. We must do something. It's such a dreadful racket."

"Let 'em roar," said James doggedly.

"How *do* you do it? You know. How do people get milk." Stasha was all innocence. "I'd like to squirt mine at the cats."

"You have to have a husband first."

"Then Sylvie could do it."

"Oh shut up, you tiresome creature. I'm tired of your vulgar witticisms. I'm so glad I don't have to sleep in the same room with you anymore. I put up with it for twenty years. Your chirping drives me out of my head. Oh, if only someone could make that noise stop."

"Sylvie. Get a grip on yourself. And Stasha, you do chatter." Tita sighed. "Whatever must Bonner be thinking of us."

"Why don't you all put cotton wool in your ears," said James.

"I believe we do have some cotton wool upstairs. It's in the cabinet in the bathroom."

Whenever there was a lull in the conversation they could hear it again, a ragged repetitive moaning, not very loud but clearly audible across the fields. It made Sylvie wince. A crease had appeared in her forehead and remained there, like a wound laid bare. Bonner was surprised. He would not have expected her to associate herself so strongly with anything so bovine as cows.

"I for one am going up to bed," said Cassie. She and Drood exchanged a glance. They hardly seemed bothered by the pathetic chorus from the barn. They seemed to be sharing some private joke which neither of them had expressed aloud. It appeared only in the set of their little mouths, that rabbit-look which was beginning to annoy James more and more.

"Why don't you all go to bed," he said. "Put the pillows over your head."

Fifteen

Bonner woke up and found himself in the darkness lying on his back in the narrow bed, his customary posture when he was sleeping in a room with Sylvie. He must have been awakened by the preliminary strumming of the grandfather clock downstairs, because now it began solemnly striking the hour.

One.

Two.

Three.

Four.

When it had finished, and subsided with a little catarrhal rustle, the house was silent again. Across the fields he could still hear the lowing of the cows. The sound sank away, then grew louder, then sank away again, perhaps through some atmospheric effect, or because the cows themselves oscillated in their suffering. The only other sound was the stifled mewing of Sylvie, who was scrunched up into a ball in her own bed with her knees against her chest.

"Sylvie?"

No response.

"Are you awake?"

She only sniffed for an answer. As James had recommended she had put the pillow over her head. He slipped out of bed and went to the window. The customary scene below was exactly as it always was: the garage, the white gravel in the darkness, pools of deeper black to indicate where the orchard and the kitchen garden were. He could hear the groans from the dairy barn more clearly now that he was standing next to the glass.

"Sylvie. I'm going out. Come with me, won't you?"

Her voice came muffled from under the pillow. "Oh, I couldn't bear to go near the poor creatures."

"It's just that—*they* might be able to help us. I can't explain it to you. If you'd just come along with me then . . . "

"Oh I can't."

"Sylvie. Please come with me."

When she didn't answer he stood for a moment by her bed, then quickly got into his clothes, fumbling with the buttons and zippers in the dark. He put on a sweater with the corduroy jacket over it and found his stout walking shoes, which would at least keep his feet warm. Then, with a final glance at the balled-up figure in the bed, he opened the door and left.

Stealing silently through the house, he went out of the door of the orangery onto the lawn. It was a thick overcast night, still cold but not for some reason as chill as it had been in the daytime. He crossed the slope down toward the Mill Cottage, his shoes crunching in the grass. There was really no light at all under the low metallic sky; things on the horizon were visible in silhouette and everything below the level of his waist was an inky pool. He had to be careful not to trip over a stone or the outstretched root of a tree. When he reached the hedge he trailed his fingers along it until he came to the corner of the Mill Cottage, which was visible through a faint stony phosphorescence.

He stopped and looked out across the Val, attempting to evoke their appearance through the sheer force of his will. For the moment there was nothing. The night lay wrapped in silence except for the distant lowing of the cows and the almost inaudible plash of water over the riffles. He could make out the two banks of the river, the darker band of water between them, and the dim outline of the weir and footbridge. The slope across the river, off toward the forest, sparkled with tiny silver pinpricks.

He went a few steps farther and then hesitated, reluctant to cross the narrow and precarious footbridge on so dark a night. At that instant he saw something outlined against the sky on the hillside near the forest, a line of tiny black dots like ants on a grassblade. He lost them occasionally and then caught sight of them, each time nearer. They appeared finally on the other bank of the Val, enlarged now to soft fluttering gray shapes like moths. The pinpoints he had seen were the buttons of their clothing sparkling

faintly in the darkness. After some delay, as though they were con-
ferring in a cluster, they came across the footbridge with the small
figure in the topper at their head.

Is that you, John Greene?

Aye, who else would it be?

I thought you'd come.

It's a feer-ful sound the poor creeturs are making, isn't it. The
suffering innocents.

They had all crossed now and were gathered at the corner of
the Mill Cottage. He was conscious of fluttering forms all around
him, at his elbow, behind him, just out of touch in the darkness
ahead.

He said softly, Then you could hear them in the forest?

Aye, we could hear them. We roam about at night, you know,
and we hear a lot of things.

And in the day too.

Yesterday, said a voice he recognized as Flicka's, we saw you
wrestling on the path with a wicked giant.

This provoked titters from the others. He smiled and looked
around him.

Who else is there? Is Lara there?

Oh, we're all here.

A gray shadow approached and circled around him; he felt the
brush of a shawl and Lara's soft fingers trickling over his shoulder.
He reached playfully for her, but there was nothing but a peal of
laughter in the darkness.

Come on, then.

He set off with them past the Mill Cottage and along the hedge
to the gate. He himself groped for the latch in the darkness and
opened it, since they couldn't meddle with metal locks or fittings.
In the deer park Flicka and Lara sprang ahead and the others followed. Bonner was about in the middle of the band; he was afraid
he would lose them and tried to keep the hurrying shapes ahead in
his field of vision. At the second gate they came together in a cluster, whispering and flittering, while they waited for him to unlatch
it. When he pushed it open they streamed across the pasture to the
dairy barn.

The anguished lowing from inside was painfully loud now. He
had no idea how to open the large door of the barn. He felt along it

with his fingers. Reaching up to the top, he found it was fitted with rollers that slid back and forth along a track. He tried to push it to the left and then to the right; it was solidly locked into place. From the inside of the barn came a din like a set of bass viols being played by demons with tin ears.

Can't one of you help me?

The men explained while the women giggled.

No, we can't help you.

That's what we have you for . . .

Hee! Hee!

To open gates and things.

Infernal nuisances they are.

Teehee!

No more levity now, all of you, John Greene told them. The sweet creeturs are paining.

Levity. Heehee! John Greene, you learn these long words from Bonner.

He's a Clark, a learned man.

At last he found the catch and the door slid open. A tiny cheer arose. He felt rather than saw the flitting shapes pouring past him into the opening; they brushed his shoulders, their hair tickled his cheeks, their elbows softly bumped against his arms. He followed them into the heavy sweet stench of manure and sour milk. There had to be an electric light in the place somewhere. In the winter Fred Baines had to milk them before daylight. He groped around in the logical place, at the side of the door, and found the switch. A white glare leaped out and filled the barn. The Little People were startled; they sprang back nervously from the fiery globes overhead, then looked around at each other and blinked. He smiled at them reassuringly, concealing his own dislike for the white violence of the electricity.

He slid the door shut, cutting off the flood of light that spilled out into the pasture. The six cows were arranged in the stalls with their rumps out. They were still bellowing in their ragged rhythm. Now that the lights were on the nearest cow looked around, stretched out her neck, thrust her lower jaw out, and crooned.

To work now, quickly, said John Greene.

Some of them made for the row of gleaming aluminum pails on the bench; others brought up boxes to sit on, since there was only

215

one stool. Bonner, being the largest, was given the three-legged stool. He set it by the nearest of the cows and felt for the large pink candles under the hairy bag. The smell from the floor under his nose was gagging. He thrust his forehead into the warm flank, careful to stay as far as he could from the black blubbering cunt at the end. He pulled with both hands for a while but nothing came; the cow only roared with indignation. Then cunning Flicka, putting her hands over his, showed him the trick. It was a squeeze, a pull, and a sideways wrench at the same time. A white thread sprang out and rang in the pail, then another, then others, one-two one-two in quick succession. It was easy with her small cool fingers guiding him.

No one spoke now and there was no more laughter, although the women were still smirking and simpering. For a while there was no sound but the pingle-pangle of the milk squirting into the pails and the moaning of the cows, which gradually subsided until it was no more than a series of sighs, smelling heavily of fermented hay. Then these too stopped and the cows only blinked, looking around to gaze with their large damp eyes at these fellow creatures who were alleviating their pain.

The first pails were filled and the women ran for more. Bonner's fingers were tired from the unaccustomed squeezing and he turned his cow over to old Quare with his stubble beard, who sat down frowning on the stool and soon had a pair of darting streams pinging into the pail. Lara, with a glance at Bonner and a dreamy smile, took up one of the pails and tipped it to her lips. He was surprised that so slight a creature, only an ethereal wisp, could lift the heavy load so easily. The creamy foam plashed against her smile and stained her with a golden-white mustache. She never took her eyes from him. He too lifted a pail—the infernal thing *was* heavy—and sipped as he gazed back at her. The milk was warm, with a strong flavor of the barn, and as thick as oil. A gush of it sprang onto his chin and streamed down over his clothing. He smiled through the creamy mask that covered the lower half of his face. He heard Flicka at his side humming lightly, and then she broke into a fragment of song.

> *And drunk the milk*
> *of Par-a-dise . . .*

The others burst out in a soft peal of laughter. John Greene admonished them. Hush now. They'll be hearing you all the way to the town.

In only a short time they had filled all the pails in the barn. Elof and Alban, horseplaying, squirted the last of the milk into the mouth of simple Trig lying under a cow. Cobold sprayed some sideways in the direction of Bonner, who ducked. They had perhaps not milked them dry but the cows would be more comfortable for a time.

Bonner slid the door open again. A square tunnel of light streamed out illuminating the pasture and more dimly the hedge at the end of it. They all helped at carrying out the pails, Bonner and the men with two each, the women tottering along as best they could with one and sniggering with mirth. Bonner set his pails down and opened the gate and they all streamed through. He picked up his pails again and followed them

Beyond the gate they all stopped in a bunch, looking off into the park with sly expectancy. At their backs the glare from the open barn door streamed over the grass and penetrated dimly through the hedge. For a few moments nothing happened. Then the deer appeared as if by magic, drawn out of the darkness by the soft clinking of the pails. An antlered head took form, a great red rough neck, then a doe with a fawn. In only a moment there were a dozen of them. They stamped up delicately and without a sound to the pails, examined them timidly, and then stretched down their muzzles to drink. There was a sound of soft lapping, echoing in the aluminum pails. The Little People were pleased; they gazed around with smiles and the men laid their hands on their small neat stomachs.

This is a good night's work we've done, said John Greene.

But without Bonner, said another, we couldn't have done it. We can't open gates, you know.

And those fire-bottles overhead in the barn. That's a scary thing. We couldn't do that.

Oh, we could do it in the dark, said Trig heavily.

Flicka simpered. We can do everything in the dark.

A little peal of mirth trickled out into the night. They broke a soft chant, pumping their elbows.

In the dark.

The dark.
We can do it in the dark.
Hark hark! The Lark!
It barks in the dark!
You're all acting rather silly tonight, said Bonner.

They were gone. He sat on a fallen tree-trunk and surveyed the last two of the deer, the old stag and a heavy and solidly built doe, perhaps his mate if red deer were monogamous. He didn't know much about their ways. The stag had a milky mask over his muzzle, like his own, he realized. There was a strong smell of milk from his clothing and from one of the pails which had been kicked over. A trickle of light filtered through the hedge from the open barn. The stag raised his head, stared at him with a large-eyed tranquillity, and put his nose back in the pail for the last of the milk. His antlers rattled against the white metal.

Bonner saw the beam of a flashlight coming down the park. It was a disembodied instrument, carried by no one, preceded under the leafless trees by its bumping conical beam. At last, when it was only a short distance away, James took form behind it. The deer turned and fled, their hooves thumping in the dark. They were gone and the park was silent.

James came up to him and fixed the beam of the flashlight on him. He was sleepy and sulky, in a dressing gown and unshaven, his hair awry.

"What are you doing, Bonner?"

"I'm sitting here looking at these empty pails, as you can see."

"The noise of the cows stopped. I knew something had happened."

"You mean you lay awake listening to them all night?"

"No. I was asleep. But when the noise stopped it woke me up. That's often the way with a continuous noise. You don't notice it until it stops, and then it wakes you up."

With another glance at Bonner he went on with his flashlight through the gate and across the pasture to the barn. Bonner followed. James went in and looked around.

"Where's the milk?"

"Some of it I drank. The rest of it I gave to a the deer."

"Deer don't drink milk." He looked around again, more carefully, with his angular suspicious smile. "Who milked them?"

"I did."

"You couldn't do it all by yourself. Besides you don't know how."

He said nothing.

"Well," said James, "now that you've done it, you might as well clean up after yourself. These pails need scalding in hot water. I'm not sure how Fred does it. There's a boiler over there." He discovered three full pails on the bench that had not been carried out to the deer. "You might as well bring these up to the house. There are some milk cans somewhere. I don't know where they are. Maybe Fred carries them around in his truck. You are really a fool, Bonner. You do these things just out of craziness. The trouble is, you're a very clever fool. I wouldn't want to get rid of you. You're interesting to have around. Besides, you're married into the family now and I'm stuck with you. I just wish that you wouldn't take it into your head to do these bizarre things. You ought to find some more acceptable outlets for your imagination. You know, I was talking to Lovejoy about you."

"Yes. You had him come for that reason, didn't you?"

"I beg your pardon?"

"You had him to the country so you could talk to him about me."

"He came up for a number of reasons. I told him about this affair of your breaking into a shop and leaving a Krugerrand. He said you couldn't possibly have eaten all that honey by yourself. There were twenty-four jars of it. He said there must have been somebody with you. You see, Bonner, that somebody might have been all in your mind."

"How could somebody who was all in my mind eat twenty-four jars of honey?"

"I don't understand that very well myself. That's what I want to talk to you about."

"I am very fond of honey. And of milk too."

"I suppose you're going to tell me these same people helped you milk the cows."

"I didn't say there were any people. You're the one who said that."

"It was Lovejoy. He said you imagined all this probably. He said that if a person who was not in his right mind believed that non-existent persons were helping him, he might be able to do prodigious things under the delusion that these people were helping him."

"In that case, how is it a delusion?"

"I really don't care for your paradoxes, Bonner. You have this smartaleck way of turning every darned thing I say against me. I suppose you pick that up around the university."

He dutifully found out how to turn the electric boiler on and scalded the pails, except for the three that were still full of milk. He was unable to find Fred Baines's milk cans and carried two of the pails up to the house, where he dumped the milk into the separator under the direction of dark-eyed Rhondda, who came out sleepily in her gown to supervise. He started up through the park with the third pail, then he changed his mind.

It was daylight now; a light like a thin whitish fluid was beginning to seep into the air from overhead. He turned to the right along the hedge and carried the last of the pails, brimful of milk, around the corner of the Mill Cottage to the door. He glanced around. James had gone back into the house and there was no one in sight. Rhondda was probably looking out of her window in the kitchen but that couldn't be helped. He pushed open the door and went in, switching on the lights in the museum.

The light was on in William's room too. He was awake and sitting with the mounted stag-head on the table before him. He had taken off the oval hardwood plaque and was digging away at the interior of the thing with a spoon. It seemed to be full of plaster of paris; the table was covered with broken chunks of it and a dusty white powder had discolored the pelt. The stag, lying on the side of his head, stared at the ceiling with his dusty eye. There was a mug half full of tea on the table.

"I've brought you some milk, William."

"Oh, thank you. I don't drink milk much."

He looked around the room, which was fixed up quite cosily now. "I see you have some Weetabix. You could put milk on them."

"They're fine with just a little water on them. Some sugar maybe."

"Or you could put the milk in your tea."

"I don't take milk in my tea."

"I'll leave it here anyhow. You might find some use for it."

"Thank you very much," he said in his dull monotone. "You're right. I might find some use for it."

"I was surprised to find you awake. Don't you ever sleep, William?"

"I go to bed early. There's nothing much else to do. I wake up every morning at daylight."

"How can you tell if it's daylight when there are no windows in your room?"

"Oh I can tell well enough all right." He never looked up from the stag-head as he said all this.

"What are you doing there, William?"

"Mr. Miles says you've been accused of a crime."

"Who? Oh, Miles. I never knew whether it was his first name or his last name."

"It's his last name."

"Have you been talking to him again?"

"Oh, I have a chat with him now and then. When I go out past the garage on my way to Waldon."

"Skulking along under the hedge."

"He says you broke into a shop and stole some things. I was surprised at that, Bonner. A brilliant man like you, a professor. Someone who writes books."

"I'm trying to write a book but I have other things on my mind. You steal things yourself, William. Where did you get that stag's head?"

But he had a curious unwillingness to discuss this subject, as though he hadn't heard, or as though something prevented him from understanding what Bonner was saying, a form of amnesia. He continued to work slowly but patiently as he talked. It was a slow business because the plaster was hard and the spoon was dull and rounded. "Miles also said," he went on after an interval, "that you have some troubles with your mind. He said you had been in an institution. That surprised me, because I always thought you were a sensible chap. He says you're not quite well yet and you roam around the countryside getting into mischief if you're not watched."

"Watched by whom?" When William didn't answer he hesitated for a moment, then he broke out recklessly, "William. Did I ever tell you about my—my friends in the forest?"

"I don't think you did."

"But you remember, in Maidenhead we talked about the derailing of the train. You said you applied the brakes because of a little chap wearing a topper on the tracks."

"I didn't say that."

"Yes you did. William, did you by any chance tell Miles about that? About all of these things that are supposed to be secrets between us?"

"The train derailed because I applied the brakes too hard. It was a human error as they call it. I don't know what you mean by secrets. I don't like to have secrets with people. Everything should be aboveboard is my idea."

"If you told Miles he might have told Drood. And Drood might have told James."

"I don't know what you're talking about. Evidently these are some friends of yours. I really don't care to hear about all these things, Bonner. I'm snug in here and I've got my books and I've got everything I need. If you're having trouble with your friends, that's your business. I'd rather you didn't tell me about it. I've got my own things to do and I keep busy." He had hollowed well into the base of the mounted head now and he had to bend down to look inside it as he worked.

"His name is John Greene."

"Who?"

"The little chap with the topper."

"I've told you I don't know any of your friends, Bonner."

Sixteen

Sunday afternoon in London: the Wigmore Hall. The seats were not reserved, so James and Tita, coming early, had laid their coats down in the front row center, on what they imagined were the best seats in the hall. Drood, Bonner, and Stasha had joined them at first, then after ten minutes or so Bonner had got up and crept away quietly with Stasha to seats on the left about a third of the way back, the proper choice seats at a piano recital, where they could see the performer's hands on the keyboard. Aunt Cassie, of course, was not present; she came into London only when she needed a new umbrella, which was about every quarter century or so. Scattered around the hall were various representatives of the Sundays which the family used to give in Wilton Crescent: the Chelsea poet, the BBC programmer with her solemn alabaster face, the sheepdog of a landscape painter, and Aylesworth and Doggenbank, the two London University lecturers, who caught Bonner's eye and beamed simultaneously. For the rest, the hall was only about half full.

To pass the time while waiting for the recital to begin Bonner examined the fanciful polychrome bas-relief in the alcove above the stage: a nude god offering mankind rays of the sun or something of the kind. Two dark varnished doors with brass fittings, like those in a funeral home, gave onto the stage from the room behind it. The tone of the place was Edwardian; the piano was an enormous dark Bechstein that seemed to date from the same period as the hall. There was a large vase of tuberoses on either side of the piano, included in the price of hiring the hall. He turned to the rectangle of glossy paper on his knees.

PROGRAMME

CHACONNE from the Partita in d minor for violin BWV 1004	**BACH-BUSONI**

BUTTERFLIES AND BIRDS OF PARADISE (1920)   BOHUSLAV MARTINŮ
1   Butterflies in Flowers
2   Butterflies and Birds of Paradise
3   Birds of Paradise above the Sea

PRELUDE, CHORAL AND FUGUE   CÉSAR FRANCK

INTERVAL

VALSES NOBLES ET SENTIMENTALES   MAURICE RAVEL

ETUDE EN FORME DE VALSE Op 52 No 6   CAMILLE SAINT-SAËNS

He wasn't a music expert, but it seemed to him a difficult program and one that was probably too formidable for her. The barrel-vaulted ceiling overhead, along with the odor of tuberoses, gave the place even more the air of a church decorated for a funeral. Bonner now made out a second-string music critic from the Times who had once been induced to attend a Sunday in Wilton Crescent and was now to pronounce his professional judgement on the proceedings. There were probably other critics present too; James had hired a press-agent for the recital. He felt a little chill. Sylvie was not really a professional concert pianist and she had not been adequately trained. She was really only a clever schoolgirl who had taken piano lessons, and now she was to be thrown to the London critics, as keen as angels and as pitiless as wolves.

"I hope she's practiced enough," whispered Stasha, echoing his thoughts.

"James says—"

"Nigel says she hasn't practiced enough."

"Shhh."

The door on the right opened and Sylvie came out to a little patter of applause. Following her was her page-turner, who was identified by a murmur of Stasha as her teacher Nigel Farrington. An odd arrangement, thought Bonner; he couldn't be a very prominent teacher if he was willing to sit there on the stage and turn her pages. But perhaps he intended to whisper encouragement to her in the difficult places or something of the sort. Sylvie had told him once that a serious concert pianist didn't read from music; he was supposed to watch his fingers on the keys. Sylvie was in the same antique gown in which she had been married in the chapel at Pense Coombe, an ivory-colored affair with lace down the front. She smiled thinly at the audience and bowed slowly to left and right. So far she seemed in command of her usual lucid self-possession. She sat down and adjusted the bench. Nigel helped her to fix the music, which rose up and threatened to fold itself as piano music always does. Lifting her chin, she stretched her fingers to the keys.

Stasha, glancing at him, made a little moue, an expression of mingled alarm and delight like a child watching another child about to do something forbidden and dangerous, slide down the roof or tightwalk along a fence: *here she goes.* Sylvie launched into the Chaconne, an intricate lacework of counterpoint and fugal motifs. She played with confidence and competence as far as he could tell. Her mouth was tightly set with a little crease on either side of it. Her fingers flew. The Times man stirred and examined his program again although he must have known it by heart.

At the end of the Chaconne there was a polite little cascade of applause. All went well too in the Martinů; the butterflies fluttered and the birds of paradise circled gracefully over a tropic lagoon lined with bougainvilleas and hibiscus. The Times man no longer consulted his program; he had folded his arms and his chin rested on his chest. Bonner found that his own glance was fixed on the little crease in Sylvie's forehead, which could be seen only when she turned her head slightly. She did this whenever her right hand fled up to the top of the keyboard. Each time she did it he looked for the crease and found it still there, as though she were a schoolgirl frowning over an algebra problem. This was painful to watch and he raised his eyes instead to the polychrome bas-relief over the stage. He saw now that the godlike nude had careless garlands falling conveniently over his genitals. His hands were raised toward a kind of brass mandala over his head, from which streamed rays dispensing all light, learning, and knowledge to humanity, including a raptured violinist and a Dante scribbling onto a scroll on his knees. This work of art was so bad that it took your breath away; it was stifling and it was difficult to pay attention to anything else, for instance to a young woman playing a piano, while it was in your frame of vision.

The Martinů ended and he heard another little patter of applause. Lowering his eyes to the stage, he found Sylvie standing with one hand on the Bechstein, smiling at the audience in a kind of stiff rictus. When the applause died away she sat down again, adjusted the bench, and began on the César Franck.

It was really quite beautiful, like classical music reflected in trembling water. He didn't think he had ever heard it before, which was curious since she must have rehearsed it in the house while he was there. Perhaps she only played it when he left the house, for some reason connected with its powerful appeal to the senses, its coolly erotic delicacy, its way of nakedly and almost embarrassingly revealing the innermost sentiments of the performer. It was Sylvie personified, her soul laid bare in harmonies, plangent cadenzas, and trills as fragile as hummingbirds. It evidently took considerable skill; her fingers flew and her frown deepened. A kind of wild tremor had appeared at the corners of her mouth. The audience sat motionless, hesitating almost to breathe. The Times man removed his chin from his chest and gazed at her fixedly. It seemed to Bonner that she fluffed at least once and missed a note. The thing came to an end at last, with a flurry of notes in the treble. Sylvie gave a kind of gasp and stood up abruptly, as though the bench were hot. The applause was about like that for the other two pieces. Nigel, standing behind her, smiled wanly.

It was the interval as it was called in Britain. "Oh, I've got to have a drink," said Stasha.

"I believe there's a bar."

The aisle ahead of them was jammed and moved at a trickle. "All these people. Why won't they move along, the elephants."

"Where are James and the others?"

"Oh, I don't know. Lost in the crush. The whole thing's so boring."

Stasha was wearing black velvet trousers, a mauve blouse with ruffles, and a sheepskin coat. The narrow coat had been cut by a Paris designer and was probably very expensive. Her electric-bronze hair sprang from her head like wire. As they shuffled forward in the crowd he accidentally bumped into her rear and immediately felt a little twinge of desire.

They came out into the foyer and she made directly for the bar. "Oh merde, it's closed."

"It's because it's Sunday."

"England is such a bore. Can you imagine? A concert with no booze."

She pulled him after her down the long dark-wood vestibule leading out to the street. People were standing around drinking coffee from paper cups, but she smiled grimly to indicate her contempt of this.

"Where are we going?"

"There's got to be a pub."

"Not in Wigmore Street."

"Well, somewhere around."

They came out onto the street. Even though it was only the interval the critic from the Times was leaving, turning up his coat collar and watching carefully for traffic as he crossed in the direction of the Bond Street Underground station. It was a wintry December afternoon, the sky gray and the air chill.

"I don't think you're going to find a pub open on Sunday. Not in this part of London."

"Well I've got to have a drink or I'll expire. Did I ever tell you that I hate piano music? I also hate Sunday."

They hurried down Wigmore Street to Marylebone Lane and turned up it. The street were deserted and the shops were closed.

"There are no pubs, as I told you. We'd better go back to the hall."

"Oh, Bonner," she pouted.

She pulled him along by the elbow, making a circle on the pavement and turning back toward Oxford Street.

"We're going to be late," he warned.

A taxi came by and she went out into the street and stopped it. She got in, pulling him after her. He allowed himself to be led in a kind of paralysis of the will, distracted by her odor of something like patchouli or lavender. Slumping onto the seat of the taxi, he crossed his legs to conceal the rigid spell she had cast over him.

"Wilton Crescent," she told the driver.

In the flat she poured him a cognac in a balloon glass and took one for herself, gazing at him thoughtfully, with a gravity unusual for her, over the rim of the glass.

He told her, "It was only a year ago that James wouldn't let you drink and you only sipped from other people's glasses."

"That was rude, wasn't it? This is ever so much nicer."

"Stasha. We've got to go back."

"It's too late now. They will have started."

"Of course they will have. It's awful."

"So we can't go back until the end. We might as well wait here. They'll all come here afterward anyhow."

"What did you mean when you said that you didn't like piano music? Do you mean that you don't like Sylvie?"

"Oh, I just love Sylvie. We're the best friends in the world. It's just that binkle-bonkle noise that the thing makes. It's so mechanical. Singing is ever so much nicer. Sylvie has a lovely voice, did you know that?"

"I've never heard her sing. I think we ought to go back now, even if they won't let us in until the music is over."

She sat down on the sofa and immediately sprang up again. "Oh, it's so hot in here." He watched in fascination as she took off the sheepskin coat and dropped it on the floor, and then began unbuttoning the mauve frilled blouse. She was wearing nothing whatsoever under it. Off came her shoes, and the velvet trousers, and the tiny triangle of nylon which she wore under them.

She smiled at his shock, raising her arms and rotating before him like a dancer. Her pubic hair was the same stiff glowing electric bronze as that on her head. The rest of her was an even apricot hue without a blemish. "Why don't you take off your clothes too and we'll do something," she said in her squeaky fluted voice.

He was subject to Homeric symptoms, like Hector struck a mortal wound or Achilles confronted by a goddess; the air about him darkened and his limbs grew weak. In the field of spots that afflicted his vision her pale limbs glided like sea creatures. As she strode around the room her narrow thighs dipped and crossed against the tuft of bronze. He fumbled with his necktie, dropped his corduroy jacket to the floor to join her sheepskin, and hopped about the room dealing with his trousers. She giggled, eluding him. When they finally fell onto the sofa he still had his underwear on and she helped him with this.

"You're so *clumsy*. Good heavens."

"Stasha. Stasha."

He fell into her with the ease and velocity of a stone dropping into the sea, and felt the same sense of oblivion, of waving his arms and legs slowly under unfathomable depths. A great piercing hotness emanated from the center of his body and excited him madly. Stasha giggled. Her own writhing seemed to arise more from mirth, or from gaiety of spirit, than from any excitement on her part. Much too soon came a series of shocks and spurts like a stock of fireworks exploding before the spectators are quite ready for them. He lay stranded on her for some time, totally thoughtless, while the warm twitches gradually weakened and diminished.

"End of the line. Everybody out please."

He extricated himself from her and sat on the edge of the sofa, his bottom against her thigh which in some way was cool and warm at the same time.

"We've been very bad."

"Very bad. Do want to do it again?"

"No, not right away. After a while perhaps. Stasha, do you think it's possible for a person to have several characters all at once?"

"I haven't the slightest idea what you mean by character. A character is just what a person does, that's all. If he does different things, then he becomes a different character. You add them all up and that's his character."

"But what if the things he does aren't consistent?"

"Then his character is not consistent. That's perfectly normal. Pass me my pants, will you?"

He found the wisp of nylon for her. The room looked like a photograph of a tornado-stricken town, clothing and cushions strewn around in it, and a vase was knocked over. Together they searched out their clothes and put them on.

"And we've left a spot of something on the sofa."

"Well I know what it is if you don't. Good grief, it's only ten minutes since we got here. The rest of them won't be back for an hour. I'll make us another drink."

Knotting his necktie before the glass, to his surprise he felt curiously content and guiltless. Male lust, he thought while she moved around the room humming to herself and filling the glasses, is vastly and widely misunderstood by people who do not suffer from it, small children, women, old men have forgotten and are

prone to condemn it as a form of madness. All the pejorative ab-
stractions are marshaled against it, selfishness, egotism, and so on.
But in fact it is a form of powerful and overwhelming poetry. It has
all the marks and powers of the transcendental; in spite of all reason, in spite of all previous experience of its transitory nature, it
seems to rise before us in the moment of its power like a bright and
radiant angel, offering us an ecstasy like that promised by religion.
Arising from the body, demanding the contact of another body, it
is not bodily at all but spiritual; it transcends the body and raises
us to a pitch of electric understanding that lasts only for an instant
but blinds us with its eloquence, like the aura of an epileptic. So
meditated Bonner, finishing the knot in his necktie while a kind of
bruised and contented memory throbbed in his trousers. Was this
rationalization? Very probably. But was not rationalization itself a
form of poetry? It transformed the world by applying a trick of
language to it. The world is my idea, said Schopenhauer, the world
is my metaphor, says the poet. He smiled at his face in the glass,
seeing another person smiling back at him, more powerful and
more gross, a healthy animal.

An hour later the flat was full of people. Some had apparently
come who were not at the recital; the rooms were so crowded that
people were elbowing through them sideways. The minor poet
from Chelsea chatted with the sheepdog painter; the BBC programmer was moonfaced and silent with a large glass of whiskey.
Lovejoy was sitting exactly on the spot on the sofa, effectively concealing it. Bonner wandered around contented through the throng
with a glass in his hand, the second cognac given him by Stasha
which he had not yet finished. He felt very vigorous. The illness
that had dogged him for months had left him. He picked up a
poker from the hearth and tested its weight; he felt capable of attacking a dragon with it or compelling a powerful enemy to do his
will. He balanced it in one hand and found himself confronted
with Sylvie, who was still wearing her ivory gown. She greeted him
with a marmoreal smile.

"Oh, hello," he said cheerfully.

She was furious. "Where were you?"

"What?"

"You left with Stasha at the interval. And you didn't come
back."

"How could you see from the piano?"

"I turned around to look. When I saw you weren't there I muffed that horrible valse by Saint-Saëns."

"I'm sorry."

"It ruined the whole recital."

"The Times critic didn't notice. He had already left."

"But where did you go?"

"We went out for a drink, but we couldn't find a pub open, so we came here."

"But why didn't you come back? What were you doing all that time?"

"Well, what do you imagine?"

Her face went pale. She snatched the poker from his hand and struck him in the face with it rather ineptly; it only bounced off his cheek. The iron clattered to the floor and she turned and fled. In the crowded room this was hardly noticed; by the time people turned their heads the poker was lying on the floor and she had disappeared. He followed her out the door and down the passage to the bedroom, the big one that had been Tita's, the room where they had spent their wedding night.

He closed the door and leaned back against it, feeling the bruise on his cheek. "Look, Sylvie."

"I don't want to speak to you. I don't want to hear about it. How long has this been going on?"

"It was the first time. I swear it was. Oh Sylvie, God, this is awful. I swear it was the first time."

"But I imagine you'll be doing it again."

"I probably will. Just think, Sylvie. It didn't hurt you, did it? You're still my wife. I still love you."

"Love!" she spat. "You haven't the least idea what the word means."

"It means several things. It means what I feel about you and what I do with Stasha. Sylvie, can't you see, there's a logic to it. A logic that's been there all along, but I've only just seen it now."

"Stop! I don't want to hear this." She clawed the velvet ribbon from her hair and the soft and silky mass fell, covering her face. Beginning to sob, she bumped against the wall, spinning around slowly so that first her back struck, then her elbow, then her forehead.

"Oh God! Sylvie. You've got to listen to me. Even you can see that it's right. There's something inevitable about it. You're half of love and she's the other half. When you're put together you're a whole woman, what every man wants. Why does the idea make you so wild? It's just convention. If we were the last three people on earth, or if we were on Mars, you wouldn't give it a second thought. It's only because we're here on earth and other people know about it that you object."

Through the hair that covered her face she gasped in a stifled tone, "Bonner, if you are right, I am so wrong that I'd better kill myself."

"Nonsense. That too is a convention. You read that in some book."

She emitted a sharp scream, a noise so ear-splitting that he could hardly believe she was capable of it. She pushed over the lamp on the nightstand and it shattered. Then it was the turn of the bibelots on the dressing table: the Dresden figures, the jars for powders and pins. She yanked the curtains from the window, struggled hysterically to roll them into a ball, and flung them across the room. "Oh God in Heaven how could you do such a thing. Oh God I'm so unhappy." Her face a distorted mask, streaming with tears, she began tearing her hair. He had thought that tearing one's hair was only an expression, but she was pulling out great chunks of it and throwing them onto the floor.

"Please, my darling, oh God Sylvie, don't go on in this way, I'll do anything you say."

She flung herself onto the bed and lay sobbing. "No you won't. You'll promise you won't do it again but you will. You've already said so." Lying on the bed with her hair over her face, she broke into a hoarse keening, a ululation like a wounded animal. It made his blood run cold, not that she felt grief and anger but that she was capable of making such a sound.

He came to her and set his hands gently on her shaking shoulders.

"Don't touch me!" She writhed away from him and got up on the other side, keeping the bed between them. She was still sobbing at intervals but the animal-like howling had stopped. "Oh, I must look a fright. I'll have to do something." She found a tissue and mopped her eyes, then took the powder-puff from the table littered with broken porcelain and patted over the blotches on her face as best she could. She was still whimpering at intervals, although she was trying to control it. "Oh Bonner."

"I do love you both."

"Who?"

"You and Stasha. You in one way and her in another. Since you don't want to—you know—I can't see my loving Stasha in that way hurts you."

"You call that love?"

"It's half of love. What you and I have is the other half."

"Oh, it's so hateful, I don't want to hear about it."

"The two of you are dividing me up. You're sharing me in a sisterly way. Stasha might object to what you and I do, but she doesn't."

"What do we do? We don't do anything."

"Yes we do. We do all kinds of things that I couldn't do with Stasha. We talk, and we take walks, and we're tender and caring, and we understand each other deeply and we console each other about life and its difficulties, and sometimes we kiss a little."

"Yes, it's so nice. And you know so many things and explain them to me. You're Professor Twist."

"Yes, and now I'm explaining this to you. I—"

"I'm not sure I want this explained."

"It's just that—you see—men are different from women. People are always saying that men don't understand women, but women don't understand men either. Men are lustful animals. It's not their fault. It's just the way we are. A man can be tender and understanding and loving and caring and all those things with a woman, and he can offer her a devotion that's pure poetry. At the same time there's a beast in him that demands to be let out from time to time, otherwise it'll claw his insides. I feel so much better after making love to Stasha."

"Do you indeed?"

"Yes, I'm not afraid of iron anymore and I could slay monsters and dragons. You saw me swinging the poker. It's made me a lot better and I can be a better husband to you too."

"I don't understand," she said, cool and a little distant, even getting vexed again. "In what way?"

"Well, I'm not sure in what way, but I'm sure I can be a better husband. I'm not the old mixed-up Bonner anymore. I'm well now and I—"

"But I liked the old mixed-up Bonner. That's the one I was in love with."

"Well that one is still there, but—"

"And I'm mixed-up too, so we fitted together better when you were mixed-up."

"You want me to go back to being mixed-up?"

"Well, why not?"

"Because then I wasn't well."

"No, you were Professor Twist, you were so odd and funny, you did funny things and explained things to me in such a lovely way, and I loved you so much." Here she began to cry again and looked around for a tissue.

"Sylvie."

"Did it ever occur to you that what you are doing is terribly egotistical?"

"Of course."

She looked at him soberly, seeming to ponder over this. A little cloud passed over her brow. "Then you don't think you can leave off?"

"Leave off?"

"With Stasha."

"I don't know. I doubt it. Not if she's willing, and I think she will be." With noble chivalry, he refrained from explaining to her that Stasha had taken the initiative in this whole thing and he was only a passive victim. And wasn't it lovely, he reminded himself again.

"Then if I—put my foot down and say you can't do it with her—I'll just lose you and you'll go on doing it with her?"

"I'm afraid that's right."

She sniffed and said, "Well, I don't know. If that's the only way I can have you."

"You're fond of her too."

"Yes I am."

"The three of us—"

"Yes I know. Don't explain it again." She sighed and said, "We've had such lovely times. Do you remember when we went for a walk in Kensington Gardens and found the Peter Pan statue? And that tea in Brown's. It was so nice. We—talked about whether things were all in your mind or—"

"Really happened, and you explained to me about Coleridge, that he—"

"Might really have heard the song from the Little People, which would mean that—"

"I heard it too, I really learned it from them, and I wasn't just remembering it from when I was a student. We were so much in love that we walked out of Brown's without paying for the tea, and we—"

"Forgot the car and walked back to Wilton Crescent. Oh Bonner."

She pressed the tissue to her nose a last time, threw it away, and smoothed out the creases in the ivory gown; there was nothing she could do about the tear-stains on it. She combed out her frazzled hair and tied it again with the velvet ribbon. Bonner came to her; she gave him an uncertain smile and then pressed her mouth on his. They embraced and went out to the party.

The fracas, of course, had been perfectly audible to the other people in the flat only a thin wall away. When the two of them came out heads turned, then people went on with their conversations. Bonner and Sylvie melted away into the crowd as inconspicuously as they could.

"I know what it's about," murmured Tita to James. "It's because he wanted to—you know. And she wouldn't let him. You should have married him to the other one."

"When there are two sisters, a man courts the elder daughter first. Otherwise he's a cad."

"I know. You read that in Jane Austen. But it's not the eighteenth century anymore, James. You'd like it to be, but it's not." She found another Marlboro in her bag and lighted it. "And they made it up, did you notice. There was a horrible racket for a time, as though he was throwing her against the walls or something, and then afterward they were perfectly quiet for a quarter of an hour. I think that's sweet."

"Here in the bedroom? While there are guests?"

"Oh well. When I was young," said Tita.

It was Tuesday night and Bonner was lying awake in his bed in Byrd Mill. They had all stayed over in London on Monday after the recital and then come back to the country the next morning.

During the day they had all been tired and they had loafed around the house not doing very much and not talking very much to one another. Nothing was said about Sylvie's recital or the reviews of it which had appeared in the Monday papers. Sylvie was asleep now, the others had gone to bed too, and the house was dark; there was no sound but the creaking of the old roof overhead and the occasional scuttling of a mouse in the walls. He lay for a long time thinking, and then he got out of bed carefully, one limb at a time, in order not to awaken Sylvie in the other bed only a few feet away.

Outside the sky was clear with only a few broken clouds, and the pinpoints of the stars blazed brilliantly. It was cuttingly cold, much colder than in London; he wrapped his scarf another turn around his neck and tucked his chin into it. Down by the river the Mill Cottage was a white block in the starlight. He crossed the footbridge with care, keeping his hand on the railing; there were clinking shards of ice at the edges of the water now. He set off along the path through the gate of trees, continuing on toward the vast gloomy shape of the forest. He knew the way thoroughly now and went on with confidence although he could see almost nothing. The Long Barrow was only a lump in the darkness. When he came to the sarsens he at first couldn't make them out, then caught sight of their dim blue glow in the undergrowth. The path turned steeply upward; he climbed like a sleepwalker, sure of his footing in spite of the dark chasm around him on all sides.

In the second clearing he stopped and stood motionless for a long time, listening. There was the cheeping of some night-insect, a soft hush of breeze in the branches overhead, an almost inaudible clicking that was perhaps only the cold clutching the dead leaves and the twigs of the trees. Overhead in a gap in the branches a single star pricked like a needle. In its rays he could gradually make out the details of the clearing: the tree-trunks standing solidly in a circle like elders at a council, the lacework of bare branches, the tiny pale points of the mushrooms in the grass at his feet. It was so quiet that he could hear the sound of his own breathing and the bump in his chest from the exertion of climbing.

Gradually his breathing and his pulse subsided. There was nothing. He knew there was no point in going any farther into the forest. The Little People were not there. There was no trace of them. He knew they would not appear again, at least for a long time, and it was on account of what he had done with Stasha. That memory came back to him now in a flash like an obscene movie, flaring brightly. He saw every detail, every pink organ, every whitish spurt. It was as though this scene in his head, radiating into the clearing, drove the Little People away into the darkness. He felt no aura or sign of them now and it was as though they didn't exist. They had been only feverish visions, fleeting goblins of sickness. With his regret at their disappearance came a great clarity, a cold lucid mastery of himself and the world about him, dark and freezing as it was; it didn't terrify him and he understood and dominated it in its last detail. This is what it is to be sane, he thought; this is how scientists have felt as they discovered the secrets of atoms, astronomers probing the skies, mathematicians adding confidently to their intricate and infinitely complex systems of signs. Now I am like the others. Now I am well. I won't see them again. He felt empty.

Seventeen

A small but persistent cloud hung over James's thoughts these days: the reviews of Sylvie's recital, especially the one in the Times. He felt a sense of betrayal—that this inconsequential person, this journalist of the kind he had hired and fired all his life in America, who had been a guest of the family on its Sundays, who had eaten caviar sandwiches and Ritz crackers with double Gloucester cheese, and had chatted amicably with James himself and smiled benignly when told that Sylvie was a pianist—the man had known why he was invited and shouldn't have accepted if he was going to write the kind of things he wrote about the recital. But James was accustomed to the treachery of the world and told himself that he ought not to be surprised by it. If there was blame to be placed, it was on Sylvie, or on James himself for not motivating her to practice enough. It was clear now that Sylvie was not to be a concert pianist. He had to acknowledge now that she lacked the drive and flair, the hard iron core of determination, that distinguished the genuine artist from the mere dilettante. Still he was determined that she should go on with her practicing; to give up something too easily was bad for the character, especially in women. Her teacher Nigel Farrington said that she was technically unprepared for Saint-Saëns and Martinů and advised returning to a regimen of classical piano composers: Beethoven, Brahms, Clementi, and Shumann. She had the strength in her fingers, Nigel said. What she lacked was the strength of will. That was all right, he, James, could provide that himself.

Of course for a woman, all hypocrisy and feminist tosh aside, being a pianist was in the end only an attribute to catch a husband. Since Sylvie had caught Bonner now, there was no reason to go on with the charade that she was going to become a concert pianist. The scheme had worked—a good part of her attraction, of her marriageability in the eyes of Bonner, had no doubt been her exquisite talent at the keyboard, where young women are displayed so gracefully, and where the requirements of their art oblige them to keep their mouths shut while bewitching their swains with the seductive graces and harmonies invented for them by other men, the Mozarts and Chopins who in this way performed a valuable service to mankind and the continuation of the race. These were not fashionable ideas, he knew. But James had no desire to be fashionable. Fashion was for women; it was found in the unimportant parts of newspapers, which he himself, when he had been a newspaper magnate, had turned over to women to write and edit. He, James, had something more important to concern himself with than fashion: a sense of the past, of tradition, a defense of the values that constituted civilization in its broader and more permanent sense. And, paradoxically, along with this came, as a correlative, an awareness of the ephemerality and unimportance of events reported in newspapers, the things that he himself had purveyed as a newspaper owner, the very things that had, in effect, provided the substance which he now used as a bulwark to protect his family from the harsh reality of the world of things reported in newspapers.

He did this selflessly and with only their interest in mind, and the interests of tradition and the ritual of the past, embodied in its purest and finest form in the English country house. Here at Byrd Mill he had created and now fiercely defended an enclave of security and peace remote from the buffets of the world; it was he, James, who enabled Drood to go on collecting his shards and bone needles, Cassie to fuss with her butter-making, Tita to tend to her exotics and tropicals in the orangery, Bonner to write his book, and the girls to gambol on the lawn in white dresses—all of them obsolete activities and not economically viable, to be enjoyed only if subsidized by an external source. And that source was James; this they did not recognize, to this they were blind. They were children. Very well, that was perhaps in the nature of the situation; if you insulated people from the cruel reality of things you had to expect them to remain in a sense children. The First Couple too were children, happy children, before they sinned and were driven out of Eden by the Angel. And the Lord God did not look very good in that story either. Part of the price of lordhood was that you did not figure as the hero of the story in the eyes of those you lorded over for their own good. He too was now victim of this cosmic irony. While Byrd Mill prospered and the others went about their innocent occupations, all was not entirely well with James himself.

He didn't know precisely what it was that was the matter with him, but it was connected in some way with his role as keeper and defender of Byrd Mill, its grounds, and the family it contained. It involved his defense of these values against forces which were no less inimical for being invisible, intangible, and perhaps non-existent, or existent only in a figurative or metaphorical sense. He was careful to conceal his condition from the others, since people were quick to interpret a legitimate concern about invading menaces, when these were invisible and intangible, as a sign of some spiritual malaise or a derangement of one's grasp on reality. Or, to put it in clear language, if he told people the things he had been seeing lately they would think he was off his head, like Bonner. Of course he didn't see them; that was the worse of it. If he saw them he could put an end to them, with a bare bodkin as the Bard had it, or at least drive them off the property with slashes and blows. But there was no use swinging at the empty air; that would only call attention to his inward disquilibrium, the thing he wanted to avoid above all. The thing to do was to maintain aplomb. It was all a matter, he told himself, of the angle at which you held your head. In the last few weeks, since the odd things had started happening, he had made a constant effort to hold it upright with the chin slightly raised and to look people straight in the eye. Because, if you formed the habit of looking furtively out of the corner of your eye, of holding your head a little bent as though you were listening to something, like Bonner . . . in short, that way lay madness, or at least the appearance of madness, which was just about as bad.

These flits and flurries, these quick-disappearing shadows, these shapes that melted instantly when you turned the light on, he connected in his mind, first tentatively and then with more conviction, with the presence of Bonner in the house. They hadn't happened before he came. And then things began to turn queer. He didn't mean the honey, or the milking; these were only schoolboy pranks. In some obscure corner of his mind he suspected Bonner, he accused Bonner, of somehow summoning spirits from the vasty deep (he knew his Shakespeare well enough, even though some people thought they were the only ones who had a right to be intellectuals), of surrounding himself in some way with a swarm of invisible cohorts who were perhaps only the emanations of which he himself complained. That is, James reasoned, if Bonner was afflicted with magnetic symptoms, then perhaps there was some way he could turn these into magnetic *powers* which could affect others as well if he so commanded. The cells of the brain had tiny magnetic spots on them. He had understood Lovejoy to say something of the sort. (Lovejoy had said that Bonner could not drink twenty-four jars of honey, but perhaps you could with magnets.)

Although he didn't accuse Bonner himself of being the primary source of the things he had seen out of the corner of his eye, he knew that he sometimes got up late at night and left the house for mysterious purposes. He, James, had ears as sharp as a fox and he could hear the slightest rustle in the house even when he was asleep or believed himself to be asleep. He knew, for instance, from tiny and almost inaudible sounds that he apprehended through the walls, that Bonner and Sylvie lived as brother and sister in their small room down the passage and did not observe their conjugal duties. That was their business and they could do as they pleased. He even preferred it that way; the important thing was that Bonner, a professor, had been captured and made a member of the family, to shed a soft and dimming scholarly glow over its bright new money, and that Sylvie was provided for. Who stuck what part of his or her body into what part of someone else was none of his concern. He had even overheard a conversation on the lawn between Tita and Bonner in which she had generously offered to compensate for Sylvie's shortcomings in this respect, and this too bothered him not in the least, even though it had included a number of comments on James himself not flattering to him. He, James, was magnificently indifferent to all such groveling and weasely plans that others made, in secret as they thought, to dispose of each other's bodies. Let them stew in their incestuous sheets. If Bonner should start to tamper with Stasha, of course, that would be something different. But he wasn't capable of that.

Daybreak rustled softly outside the window. He got up from his bed, bundled an overcoat around his pyjamas, and slipped out into the passage, where he checked first to be sure that Bonner was still asleep in his room with Sylvie. Through the door he could clearly hear the two breathings, Bonner's little snort like a timid locomotive, and his daughter's gentler and more melancholy sighing, the night-breathing of a sentimentalist. He stole out of the house through the orangery door, the same one that Bonner used for his nocturnal sallies, as he had verified by dusting it with talcum. Nothing stirred. A grayish dawn attempted feebly to rise over the forested hills across the Val, and a touch of frost lay on the grassy slope that led down to the water. His quick eyes, narrowed in the twin prisms of his frown, flickered over the elms and beeches, along the hedge, and down to the white block of the Mill Cottage at the water's edge.

And then he saw it. Or he didn't see it, as had so often happened in the past. A flicker of nondescript color against the hedge, something that didn't belong there. He felt a void inside him, not very large but terrifying all the same. For if what he saw . . . it was not so much that there were antlers on the end of it, since this was what he had detected or suspected before. It was the stance of the thing. The human mind was programmed to distinguish instantly between vertical animals and horizontal animals, even when they were glimpsed only fleetingly. It was an ocular reflex as ancient as the species. The horizontal were one's possessions: cows, sheep, faithful hunting dogs; or saber-tooth tigers, woolly mammoths, and other outlines that while inimical were still inferior creatures subject to man's domination, his skill at hunting. The vertical ones were kin, or if not so, more formidable enemies and competitors, stealers of daughters, ravagers of camps, equal in cunning to one's own primordial but complex mind. Some of these vertical animals too might be one's possessions, but they were more elusive, more difficult to handle, more vexing and annoying in their refusal to obey, to conform to one's plans for them. What he had seen, in a glimpse as brief as a single frame of a racing movie-film, was a vertical animal with antlers on its upper end. That was what disconcerted him and made this hollow form under his ribs. For, if these antique spirits should come out of the forest and assail a man's house, his property, all that he had built as a bulwark against the void, then it would be an end to everything.

No use chasing the thing. It had disappeared upstream along the Val and he had only caught a glimpse of it out of the corner of his eye anyhow. It was the kind of thing that afflicts you when you are alone in a room with the wind blowing; you think there is something moving there at the edge of your eye; you wheel toward it and it is only a curtain rustling at the window. He went back into the house and prowled around through the rooms, opening and shutting doors as he passed without making a sound. He had some notion now what it was that was missing from the house. It was not something from the hall. (He looked around; the shotguns on the wall, the hunting prints, no everything was there.) It was something in the gallery. He went in, turned on the light, and inspected the glass cabinet. He felt hot and flustered; his hand left a sweaty mark on the glass even though the house was chill.

He would have been disturbed and uneasy if he had found the carved horn gone, but perversely he felt a little shock of surprise that it was still there. Someone may have moved it an inch or two, but it was still arranged correctly so that the primitive stick-figures on it were visible through the glass. The virile leader cursed or blessed with upraised arms; the others bowed to the ground. He took a deep breath. He got out his handkerchief and wiped the perspiration mark from the glass.

Early-rising Rhondda, observing these antics from her vantage point in the kitchen, sighed.

Eighteen

On the long and freezing night of the winter solstice Bonner lay clasped in the arms of Stasha in his workroom in the Mill Cottage. There was quite enough room for the two of them on the narrow wooden cot which dated from the eighteenth century. William had been made *au courant* and kept his door shut; in any case he was busy with his own affairs and not curious about what other people did. It was a little after ten o'clock. In the official view of things Bonner was in his workroom writing his book and Stasha was in her own room in the house, the small bedroom that had once been Bonner's, preening herself to go to the Night Fair.

Stasha was draped on top of him, her customary position, and Bonner lay passively under her with one hand dangling on the floor. She had just finished eliciting from him his third ejaculation of the evening, which was an unprecedented event in his life and one which he would not have thought possible. It made her laugh, a silvery tinkle which rang hollow in the old stone walls.

"Funny Bonner. So soft and chubby, with a prong of solid rock."

"Only when you're around. Stasha, what makes you go anyhow?"

"Go?"

"Yes. What makes you the way you are."

"I'm just myself. I don't think much about why I'm the way I am."

"Do you ever think about whether things are right or wrong?"

"Of course."

"Do you think this is right or wrong?"

"It feels luscious."

"But is that really true? You see, I have the feeling that you don't really enjoy it all that much. That you just do it for me."

"Well, what's wrong with that? You should count yourself lucky. I do think," she said, "that I'm rather good at it."

"You certainly are. But it's not supposed to be a thing that one's good at. If you love somebody then it's good. If you don't, it's supposed to be wrong."

"Oh, I just love you, Bonner. I could eat you up."

"You just about have. Get off me, will you?" He found that it was difficult or impossible for him to move while she was lying on him. He felt stifled, as though the middle of his body was pinned to the cot by an immense spider while he waved his arms and legs ineffectually. God! was this what it was like for women? If so, how could they stand it?

He made a final effort and spilled her off to the side. She gathered herself together like a cat, laughing again in her tinkling way. When she kneeled on the cot the bronze tuft sprang like a mane from the vee of her thighs. There was an electric fire on the floor by the cot and its red rays inflamed the points of her body, elbows, knees, cheeks, breasts. Seeing that he was contemplating her, she said, "*You* look like a teddy-bear that's lost its hair."

"That's what I am. A senile teddy-bear. Pass me my underpants, will you?"

They repeated the usual game they had fallen into, sorting items of clothing from the heap on the floor and flinging them at each other. Her narrow velvet trousers, his checked shirt, her moccasins, one of which still bore a trace of headline from its passage through the printing-press. The trousers fitted her legs closely, but she could come out of them as though she were peeling a banana. Such dexterities always surprised him, although it was really only what you would expect from her if you thought about it.

"You're sure you don't . . . "

"No, we don't have time."

"It would only take a minute or two."

She was probably right, damn her. He dressed hurriedly before he fell under the influence of this pernicious suggestion.

* * *

Eleven o'clock. The two cars rolled through the frozen night along the Canal Road, the Daimler in the lead with Miles at the wheel and the Boswins—including Bonner himself who was now a kind of Boswin—distributed on the cushions and the two jump seats, and the old estate wagon following with Drood, Cassie, and dark-eyed Rhondda. The Night Fair, like the Venetian Carnival, was an event without class distinctions at which masters and servants became equals. James explained to Bonner that it took place only in Pense Coombe and nowhere else in the world. Such allegedly unique festivals were the most common events in Britain; every village had one.

"And what happens exactly?"

"Oh, nothing much. People put on costumes and drink beer and set off fireworks. If they didn't the sun wouldn't come back from the North Pole and there would be no summer."

Both sisters had made up their faces; Stasha's eyelids were orange and Sylvie's were mauve, and they had drawn elaborate orange curlicues on their cheeks with concentric circles around their eyes.

"Of course," said Sylvie, "we've none of us been, we weren't here last winter, so we don't really know. We got it all from the Cromlechs."

"We went to it when I was a girl," said Tita. "It's a silly thing. Nothing to it, really. It's only kept alive by the National Trust. They're very keen on preserving traditions, even when they're pointless."

It wasn't just the National Trust, said James. The farmers had been doing such things for ages. "On Midsummer Night they burn bonfires on the hills to wake up the earth. We saw it last summer."

"Why wake up the earth in midsummer when the crops are already grown?"

"I don't know. You'd have to ask Drood."

They reached the square and parked the two cars, and they all got out. Bonner had felt perfectly comfortable in the Daimler and no one had noticed that he was willing to ride in the car in spite of its iron carcass. This was lucky, because he could hardly imagine himself explaining the reasons for his sudden cure, his almost daily dallyings with Stasha in the stone room in the mill. As they shut the car doors he saw a billow of red flame on the farther side of the square; perhaps these were the fireworks described. There were several hundred people in the small square which had always been deserted before when he had visited it with Sylvie. They were the only representatives of the expensive classes. The others were villagers (he recognized old Mrs. Thrane from the bakery), local farmers, and factory workers from Waldon. Children were walking about carrying sparklers as though they were the sceptres of kings, and their parents lighted small fiery fountains and then walked away and left them burning on the stones. The fountains spouted whitely, illuminating the undersides of people's faces. The adults in the crowd, at least the males, were carrying beer from the Arm & Hammer, and many in the crowd were in costume. The Boswins and Cromlechs themselves were in a motley kind of attire. Drood was wearing his gamekeeper disguise, and Cassie was in her usual Diana-the-Huntress outfit of mannish coat, felt hat, and walking shoes. James was also in *bal-masqué*, disguised as an English gentleman, in a tweed jacket with patches on the elbows, a foulard, and flannel trousers, with an old trenchcoat thrown on over them. Bonner was in his old corduroy jacket and sweater, and Tita wore an astrakhan coat that came down to her ankles. Sylvie also had a long coat on, and her ivory wedding-gown under it, her only festive garment. As for Miles and Rhondda, they had come as parodies of themselves, Miles in an old-fashioned chauffeur's livery with black gloves and a black visored cap, and Rhondda in a black taffeta maid's uniform with a white apron.

It was Stasha who attracted curious glances. She wore the same nylon nightgown she had worn at the wedding, silver shoes with tiny spike heels, and white nylon stockings. Over the gown she wore only a short black bolero that scarcely covered her shoulders. The gown was lightly translucent to the glow of the fireworks, and in the eyelets around the waist her pale apricot complexion was visible in little dots. It was so cold that the ends of Bonner's fingers were numb, but she seemed not to notice; she laughed and prattled, sang snatches of song, and pointed at things as though still warmed by the afterglow of her play with Bonner, or by an electricity generated by her bronze-wire hair. Her breath, like everyone else's, condensed instantly into frozen steam.

In front of the row of shops facing the square there were food stands and kiosks selling fireworks, lighted with strings of glaring electric bulbs. The Boswins and Cromlechs wandered about through the crowd looking at the various spectacles. They encoun-

tered a black man wearing a white mask, white gloves, and white
shoes. The rest of his costume was black; he looked in the dark like
five disembodied and loosely connected organs, a face, two hands,
and two feet, drifting about the square. He floated with jerks and
undulations through the darkness, the organ at the top grinning
hideously. Another black man, a Jamaican, was skillfully playing a
set of chromium-plated steel drums which he beat with hammers.
The clangor of this melodious savage industrial music filled the
square and rang from the stones; it seemed exactly suited to the occasion, to the darkness and freezing cold, to the excited crowd
drifting about drinking beer and eating cheap fried food.

People stared at the sisters in their odd eye makeup, and at
Stasha's nightgown and bolero. Led by James, they moved through
the throng like a miniature royal family, full of aplomb and smiling at people stiffly and condescendingly. On the quay at the far
end of the square they found out what was making the intermittent
flares of flame. A grimy-faced young man in black clothes was pacing back and forth holding a bottle. With his coat and collarless
shirt, and his morose air, he had the look of an itinerant country
preacher. He took a swig out of the bottle, grimaced, and puffed
out his cheeks. Motioning to little children to stay back, he held a
stove-lighter to his pursed-out lips and spewed. A vast tongue of
flame leaped from his mouth and sprang across the square. The red
glare echoed off the faces of the spectators and shuddered on the
store-fronts across the way; for a moment everything was illuminated as though by daylight. It died away and the grimy man spat
with contempt. He paid no attention to the spectators except to
motion them away from the flames.

"Why, that's only Tom Wenn," said Drood. "He's the blacksmith here in Pense Coombe, and his father before him. Nowadays
of course he mostly mends cars."

"An insolent fellow," said James with equanimity.

"They're like that. All the Wenns."

"All the locals."

"Oh, the Wenns are not locals. They came here from Waldon
in the eighties. It was less than a century ago."

"Yes, they're town folk," agreed Cassie. "No one in the village
would be a blacksmith. The village was here before there were
blacksmiths. You can't be a local if you came here only a hundred
years ago. The Wenns have never really been accepted, you know."

"What about me then?"

"Oh, you don't count, James. We accept you. You're only a foreigner. A visitor."

James only snorted at this good-natured family joke.

Separated from the others by the confusion, Bonner and Sylvie wandered about through the crowd hand in hand. The square was a jumble of moving shadows, glare from the lights on the stands, and stygian prisms of darkness where the light was cut off. There was a raucous din from various kinds of music in addition to the steel drums: a blind man with a violin, led by a little girl holding his belt; a gypsy who played distracted fanfares on a cornet, accompanied by his wife beating a tiny tambour no larger than a saucer; a dwarf who sang in a powerful basso, without accompaniment, to a throng that was totally ignoring him.

> "Hence vain deluding joys,
> The brood of folly without father bred . . ."

They came to the edge of the water. Across the canal there were more houses but no shops. People were straggling along the road on the opposite bank, dimly visible in the light from the square. He and Sylvie stood on the quay hand in hand. There was no wind and the surface of the canal was absolutely still, a sheet of glass. In it the objects on the other bank were reflected with a vivid precision, illuminated by the fireworks and the glare from the lanterns: parked automobiles, a row of small cannons set into the stone, the moving and ghostly strollers. He thought how strange it was that he should see this other race of people, inverted like Chinamen and walking with their shoes pressed precisely against the shoes of the ordinary people walking above them. They lived in their own reality under the water, all moving, colored, having all the attributes of people in the ordinary world, and yet they didn't exist. They were only a trick of optics. Still how real they seemed. He could see every detail of this inverted subaqueous world clearly, yet he could never be admitted to it. How fragile it all was; it could be destroyed by the least disturbance, a pebble flung into the water, a breath of air. And could they—the others—see us in the glimmer on the underside of that skin that lay over the water? Undoubtedly. He felt that if he could pass into that realm under the canal he might find some unknown joy laid up in store for him, some fresh and inverted vision of the nature of the world and our fate in it. He was just wondering whether he would be able to explain all this to Sylvie when she remarked, by one of the thought transferences that had become common between them, "When I was a child I wanted to go there under water and see if I could touch them."

"But someone always threw a stone into the water and they disappeared."

"How did you know?"

"I imagine all children have much the same thoughts."

"But tonight, no one has thrown a stone."

They turned back and worked their way through the crowd looking for the others. They found them at the row of food stands that had been erected in the lane before the shops with glaring lights hanging from them. The food was prepared and sold by the ladies of the village Women's Institute: sausage rolls, meat pasties, fries in cones of newspaper, whelks, jellied eels, and roasted chestnuts. A little farther on a whole sheep was roasting in a spit with jacket potatoes in the embers below it. There were no crêpes, pizza, Coca-Cola, or any of the other international fare sold in the streets of London; he suspected that this too was an arrangement of the National Trust to keep the Night Fair as falsely authentic as the village itself. Someone handed him a sausage roll. It was the kind of thing that disintegrated as soon as you bit into it and sprayed greasy crumbs all down your shirt-front. James ate his with dignity, ignoring the fragments that cascaded onto the pavement. They all got beer from the Arm & Hammer and carried it out into the square, where it too was spilled in the bumping of the crowd. Its smell mingled with that of fried food and the cold winter-odor of humanity, different from the sweat of summer and faintly sensuous, like a rare kind of musk. Carrying their glasses, and keeping together with difficulty in the press of the crowd nudging and pushing against them from all sides, they made their way back to the canal again.

At the water's edge there was a clear space around Tom Wenn and his bottle of petrol. Led by James, they pushed themselves to the front of the crowd amid murmurs of disapprobation.

"Bloody toffs. Who in fucking hell do they think they are."

"It's the Yanks from the Mill."

Tom Wenn waved them back with a grimy hand; they were too close. James remained where he was, with his smile of grim resolution, and the others did the same. They finished their beer and set the glasses down on the stones. Bonner was with James and the others, and Stasha was standing a little apart from them at the edge of the quay.

Tom stared resentfully at them for a moment. He strode back and forth with out taking his eyes from them. Then he drank his swig from the bottle, grimaced with white eyes bulging, and spat his enormous torch across the square. It billowed over the stones, leaving a puff of smoke and a nauseous smell of petrol behind it. A few coins fell onto the blanket at his feet. He shook his head, spat onto the square, and blinked. Taking the petrol into his mouth evidently made him slightly sick.

Stasha laughed, a small tinkle that could be clearly heard over the music from the other side of the square. The flame had come so close to her that it had singed the nylon gown; her face was flushed and hot. Tom Wenn stared at her and waved her back with more violence that before. In the glare from across the square her naked body was silhouetted in the flimsy dress.

"It's not so hard. Anybody could do it." She mimicked the fire-eater, posturing and blowing an imaginary flame from her mouth.

"Stasha," said James mildly. He was amused by her antics.

"Maybe he'll let me try. Will you, Tom Wenn?"

Tom Wenn seemed consumed with hostility. He glared at her, his blackened face contorted. His muscles swelled and his eyes started from his head with anger; a lock of hair fell over his face. He uptilted the bottle to his mouth and then set it on the stones, working his lips. He never took his eyes from Stasha. This made her laugh again.

When the flame sprang out it struck her full in the body and engulfed her. The nylon gown took flame instantly; a white pillar of fire sprang up in the darkness, illuminating the appalled faces of the crowd. She began screaming in high intermittent peals. There was a sickening odor of burning petroleum and plastic. Bonner was paralyzed for an instant, then he leaped forward taking off his jacket as he went. But she was flinging herself around the square in a kind of ghastly dance, the gown still burning brightly. He attempted to catch her, following after her swerves and jerks with the jacket held ready in his hands. The high-pitched frightening screams continued.

Out of the darkness plunged a man in a black coat and tieless shirt. Striking against her, he knocked her violently off the edge of the quay. There was a splash; the upside-down ghosts across the water were shattered. After a moment something came to the surface and hands reached down to pull it out. It was laid on the stones, dripping and still emitting a wisp of smoke here and there. In front of Bonner's eyes was an object he did not recognize, a pig or a sheep barbecued for a feast like the one across the square. The gown was almost burned away; only the scorched bolero over the shoulders remained. Tiny pinpoints of blood sprang out and grew on the flesh.

The man in the black coat and tieless shirt, a young farmer, confronted him angrily. "You gentlemen have no pity for a girl. Too nice to get your hands dirty, aren't you? Afraid you might burn your fingertips, is that it?" He went on for some time. "Sod me if I'd knock you into the water if you were afire."

A pair of constables appeared and seized Tom Wenn by the arms. He paid no attention to them. He was still staring at the scorched body on the stones with a kind of contempt. Shaking off the constable on one side, he raised his arm and wiped his mouth with the back of his hand. Then he allowed himself to be led away.

A blue van pushed through the crowd with a blue light pulsing on top of it, and then a police Rover. Tom Wenn was put into the car. A pair of attendants got out of the van and made their way through the crowd to the edge of the quay. A third opened the doors at the rear of the van.

Nineteen

Stasha lay for several weeks in the King Edward VII Hospital in Waldon, swathed in bandages which were removed daily to the sound of her weak screams so that the nurses could spray her with medicinal fluids. She made periodic trips to surgery to have skin cut off some places of her and sewed back on other places. Then after she came home to Byrd Mill she spent several more weeks lying in her room in the house, attended by Rhondda and Sylvie, groaning like an arthritic old man whenever she turned on the bed.

The bandages had come off now but the bedclothes were still changed every day, stained with serum. When the sheets were drawn back a very unpleasant spectacle was revealed. The former apricot skin was now a mass of oozing pink oak-gnarls and welts with tracks of stitching crossing it here and there, ugly black ladders on a background of scarlet. Skin had been taken from her legs and transferred to her breasts, her abdomen, and the lean and obtuse points of her pelvis under the hips. One nipple had been burned away and could not be restored by the cleverest surgeons. Her bald head and bald pubic mound both shone pinkly, as though melted with a hot iron. The bronze-wire hair would grow out again in time, but her looks were ruined. Her face was seared beyond all recognition; the eyebrows were gone and her mouth was pulled to one side by a scar. When she talked her voice was a croak, hoarse from the flame she had breathed to get the necessary air to scream while her gown was burning.

Her temperament had changed too. Her easy wit was gone,

and her insouciance; now she was waspish, irritable, and complaining. She was given to long gloomy silences which she would break only to voice a petty complaint: that somebody had left a window open and caused a draft, or that she couldn't bend to clip her toenails. Although she might have been carried downstairs to take her meals with the others, she preferred to stay in bed. Anyone who wanted to see her could come to her room. She had no objection to the others contemplating her ravaged body, in fact she even invited it. She would mutely throw back the sheets and show herself naked to anyone who inquired, and indeed the gesture was perfectly chaste; the spectacle did not inspire concupiscence. Bonner came several times, impelled by a kind of morbid curiosity. He could not look upon her without revulsion, in which there was a good deal of pity, but even more revulsion. If only suffering were not so ugly it would be possible to sympathize more with it. The Stasha he had held in his arms was only a fleeting vision, a mirage. He hardly remembered what he had felt toward her or what she had looked like then. It was as though it had not really happened. When he dreamed, or when he closed his eyes, what he saw was the present-day Stasha, throwing back her sheet in grim silence to reveal her object-lesson in the vanity of the flesh, a network of gnarls, flaring angrily, crawling like worms. He thought about this as little as possible but the image persisted at the back of his eyelids.

At night he and Sylvie slept chastely in their two narrow beds, lying on their backs with their arms at their sides like that old entombed Crusader and his wife who were their conjugal avatars. The life of the house went on as before. James was his usual self only more so; he had become more stiffly dignified, more wry in his angular smile, more inclined to chatter and less consequential in his speech. He was given to standing up abruptly from the dinner table and going to the window out of which he stared with a twitch at the corner of his cheek, sitting down and taking up his napkin again without a word of explanation. He never referred to Stasha except to inquire nightly whether her dinner had been sent up to her and nodding when he was assured that it had. Tita morosely read fashion magazines and chain-smoked Marlboros in the gallery. Drood polished prehistoric bone implements with an old toothbrush, and Rhondda busied herself as usual in the kitchen.

Now that the dairy service was restored she and Cassie made butter once a week, on Fridays.

After the first of the year a period of rain began and went on for weeks. There were never strong downpours but the sky dripped continually, or sent down a fine cold haze that shimmered over the fields and blurred objects in the distance. The pasture was muddy and Fred Baines sank to his ankles cursing as he drove the spattered cows into the barn. The sound of the rain on the roof night and day was a murmur like distant surf over the house. The drops spattered on the windows and slid down in a distorting film.

Then in March the rain stopped abruptly. In a single night the weather turned mild and the sky cleared. Bonner was awakened in the night by the unaccustomed silence and lay listening in the dark for a while before he grasped what it was. The patter on the roof overhead had ceased; there was only the creaking of the old house and the occasional drip from a spout. When he got up and went to the window a single star hung in the black sky framed in a gap in the clouds.

He opened the window and stood motionless, listening. The tepid night air sifted over his limbs and stole into the room behind him. After a time, straining intently for sounds, he thought he could hear from the park the faint knock of an antler in the branches, the pad of a hoof on the sodden ground, a snuffle in the leaves. Probably it was only his imagination.

Outside everything was still soaked from the rain but the sky was clearing. It seemed to be about four o'clock. He stood at the edge of the lawn for a minute or two, then he moved down stealthily with his feet hardly touching the grass toward the Mill Cottage and the Val.

At the edge of the water he stopped. The Val murmured, full of rain and tickling sleepily at the grass along its banks. At this time of the year it was still pitch dark at this hour; there was no sign of graying to the east. As the clouds left the sky the stars came out and gleamed brilliantly in the clear night. In the thin phantom-light he could see everything dimly: the white bulk of the Mill Cottage, the naked branches of the trees, the black weir and the footbridge across the river. There was nothing else, even though he stared at the opposite bank of the river trying to make out something against the forested slope. He was sure they would be there now that he was chaste again, but he was reluctant to go in search of them for fear he might be wrong.

He waited for a long time. When he first saw something moving it was not on the opposite bank, where a thick blackness still hung over the meadow and the path toward the forest, but on the footbridge itself: a stirring and a set of grayish bumps as though the bridge had come to life and was sending little pieces of itself scurrying over to the land. On the bank these phantoms coalesced, solidified, and gathered into an irregular line, weaving down the path toward them. They metamorphized at last into the familiar faces and shapes: the square-topped hat, the swirling shawls of the girls, a long knitted cap that belonged to Bork, the demure smile of Lara floating slowly past his field of vision.

He called softly, John Greene.

How are ye this lovely night, Bonner?

Are all of you there?

Aye, we're all joyous and set for the task.

I've heard the deer in the park. They're awake.

They don't sleep, Bonner. And your Sassenach friend, the master of the house with his crooked smile. Would he be awake at this hour?

He often gets up at dawn and prowls around the park and grounds.

At dawn. We've got a bit of time yet then, said John Greene. Coming closer, he appeared in his familiar guise, the topper at an angle and a smile on his square friendly face. From all sides he felt small stubby hands touching him, John Greene's at first and then, he thought, those of the girls. He wheeled and laughed, but he couldn't catch them. The fingers slipped over his shoulders and face, brushing coolly, lingering to tickle here and there. Then the Little People turned and whisked away along the hedge, one after another, and he followed them.

At a brisk trot, their feet moving noiselessly over the soaked grass, they swept along in an irregular, swelling and shrinking, softly bumping band. When they came to the gate they piled up in a bunch and waited for him to catch up to them. He unlatched the gate and they all streamed through. Inside in the park they spread out into a long sideways line like beaters on a hunt; each one could see his mate to right and left, and together they combed the trees and the stiff grass so that no small animal, no tuft of weed or rock, escaped their sharp eyes. Bonner was in the middle of the line next to John Greene, with Lara at his side and Flicka just visible in the starlight at his left.

They came upon a young stag first, a sentinel set out to warn the others of anything moving in the night. He made a small snuffling noise, tossed his antlers, and trotted away a few feet. Then he turned and stopped, a dark silhouette in the starlight, the complicated black tree on his head trembling slightly.

Ho, Cos, said John Greene. Easy now.

You know their names?

Of course. The old stag, he's Rab. His wives are Ata and Ubi. Cos, said Bonner.

He moved tentatively toward the shadow. The stag shook his head and pawed nervously but made no motion to flee. He seemed to recognize Bonner; an eye gleamed in the darkness and he made a toss of his head like a greeting. Perhaps he remembered the milk in the aluminum pail. Then he set off under the trees and they all followed, Bonner and John Greene in the lead. Those who had straggled out to right and left now gathered together again in the loose band. In only a short time they came upon a pair of does, and then the rest of the herd, a set of moving wraithlike shapes in the starlight. Stamping, the deer drew back around old Rab, who tossed his head and snorted softly.

Hush, child. Come along now to your folk. There's a good soul.

Ho, Rab, said Bonner. Smiling in the dark, he advanced toward them. Ho Cos. Ho Ata and Ubi.

They seemed to recognize him as the one who had given them the milk. They padded up to him and nosed into his clothing, softly and noiselessly. He laughed. The touch of their muzzles was warm and damp and as soft as cotton; their nostrils snuffled out a babylike breath into his hands. Old Rab was so moved by the encounter that he stretched out his hindquarters slightly and sent down a splashing thread onto the grass. A woodsy odor of urine, not unpleasant, rose in the cold air.

The others snickered in the darkness.

It's that Bonner's filled him full of milk, said Flicka.

That was months ago.

It was a lot of milk.

They giggled again.

You drank some too as I remember, he told them.

Ay, but we peed that away long ago. If you can find where we do it, Bonner, there's a gold piece at every place.

Another little silvery tinkle ran through them, coming mostly from the women.

These gels, they're all foolishness, intoned Trig in his basso. It's a mistake to bring 'em along.

They'll be breaking into their song next, agreed old Quare, more tolerantly than Trig.

Let's get on with it afore they rouse the countryside.

Ho Rab, said John Greene. Come to me, child.

The old stag moved up, stamping delicately with his fore-hooves, tossing his head with a snuffle. John Greene held the topper on his head with one hand, reached up to the creature's neck with the other, and vaulted onto his back. Setting the hat straight, he arranged himself onto the bony spine on top.

Go, Rab! Go Cos, go Dar and Nik! Go all!

The great stag moved forward with John Greene on his back. The others followed, with Bonner and the Little People trotting at their sides.

John Greene called softly over his back to the does. Come Ata! Come Ubi, come Ifi and Esi! He reached forward to pat Rab's neck, again almost losing his hat.

They crossed through the park quickly, the deer at a trot and Bonner and the Little People loping along with them. A frightened doe almost lost them in the starlight and fled up trembling to nuzzle in with the others. They came to the gate and stopped with a soft clashing of antlers. He opened it again and waited while the deer padded softly in twos and threes. When they had all passed through he hurried after them down the lawn, leaving the gate open behind him.

He was not sure how the Little People would get the deer across the Val. The footbridge was narrow and precarious even for a person. But John Greene, patting old Rab reassuringly, steered him down to the water and then to the left along the ragged weedy bank. They were directly in front of the house now; anyone in the morning room could have looked out and seen them clearly in the starlight. A little farther on was the shallow ford that had been there before the mill, the place where according to Drood primitive men had crossed the Val on their way to the sarsens. Here the river was only a foot or so deep; it floated over the stones murmuring sleepily and breaking into riffles at its surface.

Ho, Rab! Go, boy! Courage!

The stag reluctantly entered the water, prancing delicately. The others followed. They snuffled, stepped sideways, and bumped into one another and into the Little People; the stags tossed their antlers. Bonner stepped into water to his knees; it was shockingly cold. A thousand tiny needles pierced his shins and turned them numb. The Little People followed. When the cold water struck them the girls broke into laughs like tinkling glass.

Oh you sillies, rumbled Trig. A little water don't hurt.

Doesn't hurt, but it's mortal cold.

They all giggled again. They streamed up the opposite bank, deer, Little People, and Bonner in an irregular cluster. Dripping, they formed up into their band again. A nervous doe broke wind in a little flutelike trill. Then they set off swiftly up the ley in the direction of the forest. Bonner glanced behind him at the house. It was still dark and there was no sign of life.

It was almost daylight now. A murky gray crept up from the hills to the east, but the path along the ley was buried in the darkness. Come Rab, come Cos! Faster, faster they flew along the path. Bonner strained to keep up with them, running precariously at top speed over the pasture full of holes and hummocks. They flew along the magic track of the ley like wraiths in a dream, making no sound but the soft drumming of hooves, the snorts of the deer, the whisper of the wind streaming over the antlers and over the flowing hair of the women.

John Greene ahead was a swaying figure in the dim light, holding comically onto his hat.

Fly Rab! Fly Cos and Dar! Fly all! Fly Ata! Fly Efi and Esi!

He urged old Rab along with a thump of his heels. They were all racing along together, deer, Little People, and man, feet and hooves touching lightly on the path. Bonner was not sure where they were; he had lost his bearings in the excitement of the mad gallop. He didn't remember passing the sarsens but they were deep in the forest now. They turned to the left with a lacework of branches over their heads and came out into a clearing. Here they slowed, and John Greene put out his hand to caution them.

Easy now all. Softly. Make no sound.

For a few seconds there was nothing but the panting of the deer and the softer breathing of the Little People. Bonner's own heart pounded in his chest. Then, in absolute silence, other reddish particles and fragments slowly took form in the thicket across the clearing; here a muzzle, there the tip of an antler, there a reddish flank. The deer from the park detected the movement and tossed nervously, still panting from their run. Their noses quivered and the hairy tassels stirred on the penises of the stags. They stirred and stamped their forehooves softly.

John Greene dismounted from old Rab and gave him a tap. He restored his precarious topper to the horizontal.

Go now, Rab. It's your own folk it is. Go.

The stag started forward and the others followed him. The Little People watched, the women with suppressed smiles and the men gravely. The park deer crossed the clearing cautiously, stopping now and then to paw the ground hesitantly with their forehooves. As they approached the thicket the forest deer appeared and nosed the air ahead with their muzzles. Like a play of slow dancers they wove together and merged into a single band, then they turned away into the thicket. One moment they were there and the next moment there was only a mosaic of textures in the branches, a patch of reddish coat, a glimpse of antler. Then these too simply dissolved like wetted crystals and disappeared into the forest. It was as though they had never been. Bonner was not sure he had seen them at all.

When he looked around the Little People too had disappeared. He was bewildered and full of conflicting emotions; he was still panting a little from the exertion of the run into the forest. It had all happened only a few minutes ago.

He had no idea at all of where he was. In their mad dash into the forest they had passed none of the familiar landmarks—the circle of mushrooms, the sarsens in the clearing. From the loom of daylight to the east he thought he could establish the direction where the house and the village ought to lie, over a thickly forested slope. He found a crude path tangled with roots and boulders and made his way up to it to the crest of a hill. Here, surrounded by the great trunks of beeches and oaks, he looked out to the north. On the horizon was the silhouette of Waldon, with the spire of Lady Church standing out conspicuously like an indicating finger. Looking lower, he could see the black thread of the Val winding through the fields, meandering toward a clump of trees that hid the village of Pense Coombe. There was a glimpse of white through the branches that ought to be the Mill Cottage. The house on the lawn next to it was invisible from this point.

Aligning these two marks of the ley, the church spire and the mill, he followed them down through the forest. There was no path and he had to push aside branches and struggle through waist-high bracken as he went. He came out after a half an hour into the clearing with its mushroom circle. There he regained his old path, and in a short time he had passed the sarsens and the Long Barrow and was striding across the open meadow toward the gate of trees. Here he hesitated. Then, instead of turning down toward the Val to cross to the house on the footbridge, he continued on along the path on the right bank of the river. In another few moments he came out onto a point on the grassy slope directly opposite the house and grounds.

He stopped, half sheltered by a clump of yew. The pale-green leaves were thick and glossy even in March, and the tiny red globes of its blossoms were hanging from the undersides of the branches. Through a gap in the foliage he could clearly see the house and a glimpse of the Mill Cottage at the side. The tiny figure of James was making its way down the lawn toward the water. It was too distant to make out the features, but the jerky intent pace and the cut of the clothing were unmistakable. The figure stopped at the river-bank, looked around from one side to the other, and went on down the bank a few yards toward the Mill Cottage. Then it turned and came back, stopping on the lawn to gaze across the river exactly at Bonner's clump of yew.

He stole away from the gap in the branches and went back to the path. He didn't think James had seen him. The opening in the leaves was small and only the upper part of his face had shown through it. The path on this side of the river, leading along a curve to the village downstream, was sheltered by trees for a short distance, and then it descended into a long grassy hollow separated from the river by a ridge. A person walking in it was completely obscured from the view of anyone across the river. Following this for a mile or so, he came out onto the Val again. The first house of Pense Coombe lay just ahead, on his side of the river. There was a footbridge over the canal. He stole through the village, encountering nobody, and crossed the Val on the road bridge on its outskirts. He set out toward the house on the Canal Road, going back the way he had come but on the opposite bank of the river.

A little way beyond the bridge he heard the sound of a motor behind him, and turned to find a bakery van coming out from the village along the road. It was green and it had the word *Thrane's* painted on the front. As it came abreast of him it stopped.

The driver was a dark-eyed young man in a cloth cap, as pale and handsome as a girl. "You're out early, aren't you?"

He said nothing. The driver looked curiously at his muddy shoes and his trousers wet to the knee.

"It looks like you're Mr. Foley from the Mill."

"That's right."

"Like a lift to the house?"

"Thanks, I would."

He went around the van and got in on the passenger's side. The back of it was full of paper bags with the word *Thrane's* in green on them, neatly arranged in plastic baskets. The driver started up without a word and drove on down the road. He was in a friendly and talkative mood.

"I'm Ken Thrane."

"Related to old Mrs. Thrane?"

"Grandson."

"My mother-in-law used to steal money to buy cream-cakes from her."

"That would be Tita. She was wild as a girl, they say. She later ran away from home, you know. Went to London and married an American."

"Of course. James Boswin. That's my father-in-law."

"Oh yes. We know who you are. Mr. Boswin took Miss Tita away with him to America, and then years later they came back and had a flat in London. About a year ago he moved here from London with his family."

"Why are you telling me all this? I know it as well as you do."

"And now you've come here too. You Americans seem to have quite a fascination with our little corner of the world."

"Not exactly. I came here because of—"

"The girls." He made a quick grin.

"It wasn't really that. I was a friend of the family." They were just passing Bonner and Sylvie's kissing-place under the poplar. It seemed to him that Ken Thrane took particular note of it. Everything they did was observed by the people in the village, he suspected. "I'm married now to Sylvie of course. As for Stasha ..."

"Yes, I know. A terrible thing, wasn't it. I was there and saw it. You know, the Wenns are not really village people. We've never really taken them. They're town people really."

"That's what Drood says."

"Tom has been in trouble before. Bought stolen cars and changed the numbers, that sort of thing."

"You seem to know a lot about things around here." An idea occurred to him; perhaps he could sound out Ken Thrane about something. He had never before really talked to a local of the region, apart from Drood and Cassie. He proceeded cautiously.

"It's pleasant here, isn't it. The countryside is so beautiful. The forest. Everything so unspoiled; protected by the National Trust."

Ken Thrane only nodded non-committally.

"Do you ever go to the forest?"

"Not much. I used to when I was a kid."

"Do you know there are people living in it?" Ken Thrane turned and looked at him curiously. "Little. I mean people who—"

"What?"

"Nothing much. Just something I heard."

Ken Thrane glanced at him again with a little smile and then went back to looking out at the road ahead. He had probably heard that Bonner wasn't well. The rest of the poplars along the river-bank went by, and then the house loomed up ahead. "Here's your lane." He brought the van to a stop. "Say, would you take in these two bags for me? On your way, as they say."

"I didn't know that Thrane's delivered to us."

"Oh I don't, usually. If we bake a little extra sometimes I leave off a bag or two. Miss Sylvie likes scones." He passed Bonner a bag of scones and another full of rock cakes. "You know, that old chap has been seen walking along the river. You'd better tell him to be careful."

"What old chap?"

"The one with the horns on his head. Well, I'll be on my way. Ta ta."

"Have a nice day," said Bonner. He thought as long as he was an American he ought to offer a little of the vernacular. On his way in to the house he took two scones out of the bag and put them in his pockets. Carrying the bags, he went down the gravel past the garage and entered the house through the hall without anyone noticing him. He carried the two bags into the kitchen.

"Hello."

Rhondda looked around from the counter at him without particular curiosity.

"I've been for a walk in the village. I've brought the scones and the rock cakes from Thrane's."

"Ah." She looked at him again. "You look as though you've been wading."

"The grass was wet along the road."

"Everything is soaked. Better weather coming, though."

She took the bags from him and Bonner went into the morning room. It was deserted except for Sylvie.

"You're up early."

"Oh, not really. The others have had their breakfast. James is out for a walk." She didn't ask him where he had been, nor did she seem to notice his soaked trousers and shoes. He gave her a scone from his pocket and put one on a plate for himself, then he went to the sideboard for some butter and jam and sat down at the table.

"The rain has stopped."

"Yes." She reflected, and said, "I feel as though something's changing. There's something new. A different time has started, and things are going to be different."

"It's just the weather. It's almost spring."

"I do love scones. You're not eating much. There's some kidneys."

"I think I'm turning into a vegetarian. I don't mind fish. Perhaps I'll try a kipper, a small one."

He started to get up to go to the sideboard, then James abruptly entered the room. He sank back into the chair again, concealing his wet trousers under the table, and went on eating his scone.

"The deer are gone," said James.

"What?" Sylvie stared placidly at him over her teacup.

"They're not there. I've searched the park. They're all gone."

"Somebody must have left the gate open."

"No. They wouldn't leave the park. The gate's been left open before but they didn't run away."

Drood had entered the room silently behind James. He poured

himself a cup of tea and sat down. Although he had come in in the middle of the conversation he seemed to follow it perfectly.

He said, "Then someone let them out deliberately?"

"Not let them out. Drove them away. You can see hoofprints down by the river where they were driven across the ford."

"But who would do that?"

"I don't know. I have my ideas." He turned sharply to Sylvie. "Has Bonner been with you all night?"

She said demurely, "Of course."

Bonner was amazed at how easily and naturally she lied. She hardly seemed interested in James and his deer. She hadn't even turned around to look at him; she went on buttering the scone and eating it delicately.

Cassie came into the room now. She too had been for a walk; her boots were as wet as Bonner's shoes.

"Left the gate open, did you James?"

"No, I did not leave the gate open."

"I was walking across the Val. There are hoofprints on the other bank too. As though someone drove them across the ford."

"I know. Don't tell me what I already know. What I want to know is who did it."

Sylvie said, "Whodunit I think is the proverbial expression. It's like a Dorothy Sayers book. Country house. Something stolen. Everyone sitting around trying to identify the criminal in their midst."

"The deer *are* valuable," said Drood. "You know what you paid for them, James. It was quite a lot. Perhaps someone stole them to sell to another would-be gentleman."

"Don't be funny, Drood."

Sylvie finished her scone and poured herself more tea. *"Le Bourgeois Gentilhomme* by Molière. Monsieur Jourdain. Didn't know he was speaking prose. Must I have deer? You must have deer. Very well, I'll buy some."

James ignored her japes, which were beginning to resemble Stasha's now that Stasha no longer made them. "These locals are not friendly to us. This should be obvious to all of you by now." He tossed his head to indicate the upper floor of the house where Stasha lay in her room. "What will they do next? Burn down the house? But none of you mind. It's all just a joke to you."

"We don't think what happened to Stasha is a joke," said Sylvie, her lips tightening. "That's not fair, James."

"I didn't mean that."

Now Tita entered the room, in a silk wrapper over her nightgown and a cigarette dangling. "Well, what's all the fuss about?" she drawled negligently.

"Someone let the deer out. They're gone."

"Not let them out. Drove them out," said James irritably.

"Well what on earth does it matter. They only left their dung about in the park so that we all stepped in it."

"James says the locals did it. He says they'll burn down the house next."

"They won't burn down the house," said Drood. "At the most they might throw stones through the windows. They're a simple enough folk. It's true they don't like outsiders."

Bonner spoke for the first time. "Some of them are friendly enough. I met Ken Thrane on the Canal Road and he gave me a lift. He seems like a decent chap."

James turned to him sharply. "When was that?"

He remembered that he had spent the night with Sylvie and had just got up. "Last week, I think." He glanced out the open door of the room to see if Rhondda was listening from the kitchen.

James hardly paid attention. It was the name Thrane, a village name, that had set him off. "Damn their black hearts."

"It's true their eyes are black. Some of them have black hearts, others different colors." Drood with his small rabbit-smile sipped his tea as if he was enjoying the conversation.

Cassie said, "I can see another local folk-tale in the process of formation. They'll tell it at the Arm & Hammer for years. Deer disappear mysteriously from the park of the local manor. Probably stolen by the Little People. Drove them into the forest, where they live hidden with their stock of gold coins."

James turned to her with an annoyed frown on his red-lined face. "Oh don't talk nonsense, will you. Can't any of you take this seriously?"

Bonner got up from the table hurriedly and left the room. The irritated James, glancing at him, didn't notice his soaked trousers and shoes. Behind him he heard Cassie saying, "They love to collect tales like that in the village. They're encouraged by the National Trust. It's a local heritage."

Later in the morning, after he had changed into dry clothes, Bonner looked out the window of the bedroom and saw a police car standing on the gravel by the garage. James was talking to a constable in uniform, who was looking dubiously in the direction of the park. James gesticulated and pointed first at the park, then at the still open gate, then at the lawn and the soft ground beyond it at the river's edge where the tracks were, all in dumb-show since Bonner couldn't hear anything through the glass. His fellow-mime the constable looked around to follow each direction of the pointing hand and then reluctantly got out his notebook.

Sylvie came quietly into the room. He turned from the window and looked at her carefully. She was her usual cool and demure self.

"Why did you lie for me?"

"You mean about your being with me all night? Because I knew you hadn't done it."

"Done what?"

"Set free the deer. And if you hadn't done it, there was no point in putting suspicion in James's mind. It would only drive him into a frenzy."

"How do you know that I didn't do it?"

She smiled as if privy to his secret in at least a part of her mind. "You couldn't drive a herd of deer across the river all by yourself."

"Suppose *they* helped me?"

"But that's just in your head, isn't it?"

"Yes, and the missing deer are just in James's head. And I'm just in your head. Must we go through all that again?"

"Do you know, Bonner, I just love you. I always have. And what I love about you is your imagination. You live in a different world from the rest of us, and sometimes you can invite us into that world for just a little while. You should have been a poet, like Keats or Shelley. Why are you writing that dry-as-dust old scholarly book anyhow."

"Who do you think stole the deer?"

"I have no idea. Perhaps it was Ken Thrane the baker-boy."

"No. You believe in them too."

"What?"

"The Little People."

"Wrong you are, Professor Twist. I don't believe in them, so they're not there. If I believed in them, they would be there. I might like to but I can't. For you it might be different. You believe they're there, so for you they are." She came to him and kissed him.

"You don't want me to be well, do you? You told me so once."

"I did? When did I say that?"

"In the flat in Wilton Crescent after the recital. We had a big fight and I said that because of what Stasha and I had done together I wasn't mixed-up any more, and you said you liked me better when I was mixed-up. You said you were mixed-up too, so we fit together better when I was mixed up."

"Oh, why do you hold me to old things I said months ago. You know," she went on, becoming thoughtful, "when I think of what happened to Stasha it's just dreadful. Oh God, I feel awful about it. It's the most horrible thing I've ever heard of . . . I do love Stasha and I feel so sorry for her. And yet it's . . . it's nicer for us, now that we're together as we were before—before," she finished off lamely. Here she blushed and seemed angry with herself. "I'm sorry, Bonner, but that's the way I feel. Why should I conceal it? We're not responsible for our emotions."

"Aren't we?"

"I don't think so. I read in a magazine that we aren't. And so I'm—happy now that you're mixed-up again. If you think in your mind that the Little People helped you set free the deer, that's the imaginative poetical side of you that's so wonderful; that's why I love you. I wouldn't want you any other way. Maybe, instead of writing that dull old medieval book, you could write a story about the things you've seen in the forest—a funny odd book, poetic and . . . full of wonderful strange things . . ." Her voice trailed off and she became dreamy, looking past him into the room; then she caught him by the shoulder and turned him to her. "You're a poet, Bonner. That's why I love you."

Bonner looked out the window again. James was still explaining things to the constable. He had him down by the river now and was making gestures to indicate where the tracks were in the soft ground by the ford. The constable looked around. All he could see was deer-tracks. If there were tracks of people too they had been totally obliterated by the hundreds of neat little forked depressions in the mud. Probably the deer had got out by themselves and run away. The two of them were having a big argument on this point. James's thin face was getting red, and he gesticulated even more vehemently and pointed off into the forest. The constable, with a dubious smile, shook his head.

Twenty

It was a month later. James had become resigned to the loss of the deer now. The police had found no trace of them; there were some tracks on the other bank of the Val but they soon dwindled away in the grass of the meadow. The police, finally persuaded that the deer would not have escaped by themselves, were of the opinion that someone had put them into a cattle lorry on the other side of the river and taken them off to another part of the country. It was only about a half mile down the river-bank to a road where the thieves could have brought up a lorry, they pointed out. James wasn't so sure. He himself had never been able to get within fifty yards of the deer, even when they were his own possessions, and he didn't see how anyone could walk up to them and persuade them to get into a lorry. At least so he told the police. He had ideas of his own. James had lots of ideas that he kept stored away in his head, conveniently at hand for when he wanted to examine them or turn them over now and then, in the way you might pick at a pimple or an infected hair follicle, partly to hurt yourself and partly to see what kind of a thing it was. He was careful to tell no one else about these explanations he had generated about the events around him in the world. Everyone's thoughts were bizarre inside their heads; so James told himself. It was only when you confided them to others and embarked on the task of trying to explain them and justify them that the trouble started. Keep your troubles to yourself, hold your head upright, and look them straight in the eye, that was the trick.

Although the weather had turned fine now that it was April, a melancholy cast seemed to have fallen over the house, coming first from Stasha's misfortune and then from James's moodiness and frustration over the stealing of the deer. Drood went for long walks and showed up only for meals, where he sat at the table with little to say; he made his little leporine smile only infrequently and in a polite way as something someone else had said. Cassie and Rhondda made their bread and churned their butter. A stray lock, these days, often sprang from Rhondda's head and hung in front of her face as she worked. Stasha, who could wear a gown and a wrapper now, stayed upstairs on her bed reading; she could no longer tolerate fashion magazines and someone had given her a book about animals with pictures. Tita was morose and smoked too much. She was developing a hacking cough and would probably get cancer or emphysema if she kept it up. As for Bonner, a curious sort of torpor or numbness had fallen over his life. He went through all the motions but he didn't see the point of most of the things he did. He was happy enough, he supposed. He loved Sylvie and was happy being married to her in the curious way they had of being married. He had always been an early riser but now he slept in the morning, or rather he lay in bed and lazed while the others got up and went about their business. He would lie hidden under the bedclothes with one eye half open while Sylvie got up, yawned, stretched, went to the window and looked out, and then disappeared behind the screen from whence he would presently hear the thin tinkling sound into the chamberpot. He knew why she did this now; she had confessed to him that she didn't like to sit down on a toilet that a man had used. After she went down to breakfast he would lie in bed listening to the sounds from the morning room, the clink of tableware and china, the murmur of conversation, the rustling as James unfurled his morning paper and read it. Then, when they were all gone except late-rising Tita, he would come down and chat with her in a desultory way while he had his own breakfast, usually only a piece of dry toast and tea.

"Lovely weather we're having, isn't it."

"Oh bugger the weather."

"We're finally having a spring after all."

"Most godawful month of the year as the poet said."

"Oh, you mean Eliot. He just said that April was the cruellest month."

"Whatever."

From the music room he could hear Sylvie practicing the piano. She had dropped it for a month or two after her recital and then she had taken it up again, but she had abandoned the difficult and insubstantial show pieces, the Martinů and the Saint-Saëns, and she was working her way doggedly through Beethoven's sonatas, the *pons asinorum* of the third-year piano student which she ought to have left far behind. He listened as she played over and over again a piece that began with three loud chords, then entered a pathetically tender lyrical passage that for some reason depressed him and gave him an intimation of just how it would be that a person might contemplate suicide. Then this was broken by a loud crash of chords again. He and Tita exchanged a glance. Sylvie made a mistake and started over; the violent opening chords that must hurt her fingers, then the soft and moving lament, then bang! again. He found it painful to listen to this; he dropped his napkin on the table and excused himself, then went down to the Mill Cottage to spend the rest of the morning working on his book on the *Ancren Wisse*.

In the afternoon he and Sylvie went for a walk. As usual they left the house by the lane and strolled lazily down the Canal Road, she stopping to pick a crocus or an early daffodil, he walking a little apart from her with his hands in his pockets and kicking stones. They stopped at their usual rendezvous under the poplar tree, sitting on the bench and putting their feet together on the oddly shaped stone. There were riverine bushes of some sort, willows he thought they were, that hid them from view from the road.

Usually she kissed him at this point, a quick and cool touch of the lips no different from that she had offered him before they were married, and now giving him only a general sense of affection, of intimacy, totally devoid of desire. But today she turned away with her chin on her fists and stared with a frown at the gently running water pulling at the weeds along the bank. She had been moody and silent during their walk too.

"What's the matter?"

"Nothing."

"Is it something I've done?"

"Oh no. I'm out of sorts."

Perhaps it was the time of the month again. He didn't inquire. He stood in awe before these feminine mysteries which in her, with her heightened delicacy and sensitivity, assumed the significance of Delphic rites forbidden to the profane eyes of men, secrets that turned her all distant-dark and complicated. But she dispelled this explanation by remarking fretfully, "I can't get Stasha out of my mind. What happened to her—I think about it all the time."

"Yes. It's terrible."

"Of course it's terrible. But it's not that. It's that I can't get rid of the thought that in some strange way it was I who did it to her."

"You? Surely not." There were a number of candidates for guilt in this matter, starting with Tom Wenn and going on to Bonner himself, who couldn't rid himself of the notion that Stasha's burning was in some way a punishment for that happy and feckless sin that he and she had committed so many times and enjoyed so much. He and Stasha fell, and only she was punished. Along came retribution in the form of Tom Wenn, the poor beggar, he was in prison now for being an unwitting tool of fate.

"That's nutty. You're not to blame in any way. How could you be?"

"I don't know. If I had—you know—if I had let you into my bed. Then you and she wouldn't have had to do it together, and she—wouldn't have been burned." This was exactly his own theory; he felt a little chill to realize that she had thought of it too. "Oh Bonner, everything is so complicated."

"Things *are* complicated. If they weren't, life would be even more boring than it is now."

"Oh, don't be clever just now when I'm trying to explain something to you. I had a dream in which I looked in the mirror and saw that I was all scarred. And I turned and Stasha was standing beside me with her perfect skin, just as she used to be. And she didn't say anything; she just smiled."

"Dreams are so banal. Their meaning is obvious. They're all alike."

"And I said something terrible to you. You know—the day the deer got out. I said I was sorry about what happened to Stasha but that it was better for us. But now I think about her lying upstairs—it's not worth it. And you ... you're not happy. It's not enough for you. Our living in this way without—being really married."

"Sylvie—"

"It isn't. And I can't bear to ride in the car anymore."

"You what?"

"Not the Daimler. When I get into it I feel as though I'm suffocating. It's like an iron prison on wheels, always taking me to places I don't want to go—to the village and back, to Waldon for clothes, to a stupid chamber concert—always the same, two violins, a viola, and a cello. Squeak squeak squeak. Oh God, my life is so pointless. Why am I doing all this? All these things I don't want to do. Going to concerts that bore me. Buying clothes I don't want. Practicing on the piano. James says I have to go on with it, even though I'm not going to be a concert pianist now."

"How is it that James can tell you what to do? I'm supposed to be your husband."

"Well, *you* tell me what to do. He says it's not good for my character to give up on things. The piano has become my enemy. It's like a big hostile machine that I have to master and dominate, a machine with a great iron frame. The strings have a pull of thirty tons, did you know that? Oh God, I'd so love to sing. I can't sing very well but I'd love to do it. Singing is natural. But a piano is a machine that's made in a factory, it has eighty-eight hammers that beat on steel wires, and I have to struggle with every hammer and make it do what I want. I'm so tired."

Her dwelling on the wires and the iron frame, and her remark about not liking to ride in the Daimler, made him wonder if he had infected her in some way with his own phobic view of the world. He didn't think that having little particles of iron on your nerve-ends would be contagious, but it might be. He was of two minds what to think about this possibility. On the one hand he didn't wish her any more trouble than she already had. On the other hand he suffered from the loneliness of being isolated in this private and unreal, slightly ridiculous illness, and the idea of someone joining him in it was a novel and not unattractive notion. He said nothing and only listened thoughtfully, not looking at her directly.

"And Beethoven," she went on, frowning and throwing a pebble into the water. "How I hate that German brute. He's so violent and male."

"Of course he's male. I don't see what you mean."

"He's like a great brutal unfeeling man making love. He always starts off with a big bang, a chord that grabs you by the neck. Have you noticed?"

"Yes. And then comes a little quiet passage."

"He remembers that he's supposed to be tender, but after a while his passion overcomes him and he bangs you around some more." It was a good description, he thought, of his own behavior on their wedding-night. "Then finally, having got you knocked flat, he set himself to going in-and-out with a certain amount of tenderness, but it's for himself, not for you. He's got what he wants so why shouldn't he be tender?"

"Are you really still talking about Beethoven?"

"Yes. It's a metaphor, don't you see. And what is the point of all this tenderness? He's sorry for himself, that's all. He's so Germanic, so brooding and tumultuous. He's terrified of life and takes it out in violence on his music. Everything about him is death, deafness, sterility, and unfeeling egotism. The horror of death's black softly pulsing wings."

"You're a little distraught about Beethoven. Perhaps you ought to try some other composer."

"James won't let me. Nigel told him that I ought to go back to Beethoven and start over. Nigel is cross with me because—of what I did, you see—at the recital at the Wigmore."

"What do you mean?"

"I let everybody down."

"But it wasn't you. It was my fault."

"Your fault? Oh no. I just didn't practice enough."

She seemed genuinely surprised at this idea. And yet earlier, when they had had their great fight in the flat in Wilton Crescent, she had told him it was when she had looked out into the hall and found him and Stasha gone that she had muffed the valse by Saint-Saëns. She had put it out of her mind. He himself had little doubt that he was responsible for the failure of her recital, and thus at the bottom guilty of everything that had happened after. He had a whole collection of these guilts now that he had accumulated one by one; he ought to put them in a glass case like Drood's bone needles.

"Sylvie," he said, "I do love you. I'm sorry about—about everything. The recital, and Stasha, and the way I—you know. Behaved like Beethoven."

"Yes, I know what you mean. But it doesn't matter."

"Yes it does. I want to make it up to you somehow."

"Oh, you can never make things up."

"I want to try. I want you to be happy, Sylvie. You're not

happy now. You don't like to live in this world you're caught up in, you know, the one you don't like. There are other worlds—worlds where we can go together, where there are no pianos, where people are friendly and loving—you say you want to sing—well you can. You—" He stopped, feeling that he was speaking incoherently. "You can choose the world you want to live in. It's just as you yourself said. If you would just believe, only for a moment—"

"Believe?"

"If you would just—just come with me to the forest." He stammered and went on. "You've never been there, have you? I've just realized. You've lived here for a year and you've never been across the river. Why? Why don't you go there? I want you to come with me, Sylvie. I've told you about my friends. *They're really there, they really exist.* I want you to meet them."

Her lips were fixed in a brilliant smile. She ignored him. "It's such a lovely day, isn't it."

His enthusiasm left him and he felt suddenly foolish. It was as though a cloud has passed over the sun. He looked up and saw it was still shining brilliantly, although some clouds were building up in the west. "Would you like to go back? What would you like to do?"

"I'd like to fling myself in the river," she said.

At seven in the evening the family was gathered for dinner around the oaken table in the morning room. The sun had set but it was not dark yet; the medley of spring greens faded only gradually from the trees on the lawn outside. Aunt Cassie, with the aid of Rhonnda, had prepared an old-fashioned springtime meal that was very English but a little too heavy for Bonner's taste: a joint of lamb, stewed cabbage, and boiled potatoes with parsley. As usual Cassie helped Rhondda serve and then sat down at her own place at the table.

"Has Stasha been taken her tray?"

Cassie said, "Yes."

James nodded stiffly. They proceeded into the meal, dominated by light conversation between Drood and Tita, who were arguing about whether it had been colder in the country when they were children. It was colder then, said Tita. The canal used to freeze over and people skated. They don't do that anymore. Nonsense. The canal froze over only last year and people skated. Well I wasn't here last year. Well then. All I say is that it isn't so cold in the country anymore. Well, offered Drood, we always remember the weather as more severe when we were children. Children are more affected by the weather. The same thing with heat. Tita said yes, when I was a child it used to be hot as hell in the country. In Pense Coombe the children used to take off their clothes and get into the horse-trough. They still would, said Drood, except that they've taken the horse-trough away. No, corrected Cassie, joining in for the first time, it's still there, except the National Trust has moved it around behind the chapel and planted it with petunias. Is that what that thing is! I never recognized it as the old horse-trough.

And so on. To finish off the meal there was a trifle of custard, jam, and spongecake, which was delicious but also a little heavy. Bonner only dabbled at it. He was still preoccupied with his riverside conversation with Sylvie and was feeling floaty and a little unreal; perhaps he was going to be unwell in some way, although it didn't seem to be a way that was particularly unpleasant. James didn't have much appetite either. He took a spoonful or two of the trifle, laid the spoon down, and looked across the room as though he were studying a spot on the wall. After a moment he got up and went to the window overlooking the lawn and the river, still holding his napkin.

No one paid any attention. They went on with their conversation, and after a while James came back and sat down again, tucking his napkin around his knees. Cassie and Drood went on talking as they had two years ago when the Boswins had not even moved into the house.

"It's a lovely quiet evening."

"Yes. Usually the starlings are chattering on the lawn. Especially at this time of the year."

"It's perhaps because it's clouding up for a storm. That always makes the birds quiet."

"Except the swallows. They race around in the sky barking when a storm's on the way."

"They're just catching gnats," said Cassie. "You can't see the gnats but you can see the swallows chasing them. When there's a storm coming it makes the gnats rise up out of the lawn. The swallows know that, so they come out in droves and race around barking, as you put it."

"I don't know that we really need all that much ornithology," said Tita. "Is there going to be coffee?"

James got up again and went to the window, this time leaving his napkin behind. He stood for some time looking at the lawn leading down to the Val and the Mill Cottage over to his right. From the table they could see a little muscle working at the corner of his jaw. Then he started violently. Turning from the window, he hurried past them without a word and left the house through the orangery door.

Bonner and Sylvie exchanged a glance. The others continued with their conversation as though nothing had happened.

"It's hard to see how the swallows can see anything as tiny as a gnat."

"It's the only thing swallows are good at. They're not particularly clever in other ways."

Only Tita took notice of the obvious. "What's the matter with James?" she inquired petutantly, working her mouth.

She looked from one to the other around the table. Nobody else said anything. Bonner pushed away his trifle which he had only half finished. Sylvie hadn't touched hers, he noticed now. Although it wasn't hot the evening air was slightly oppressive; perhaps it was something about the humidity. A kind of stickiness hung in the room so that the spoon clung to Bonner's fingers; there was a film of moisture on the goblet that held the trifle. It was a half an hour now since the sun had set. Through the window the objects in the distance, the far bank of the river and the hills, were losing their color minute by minute.

James bolted back into the house, banging the glass door of the orangery and leaving it open. Through the door they saw him crossing the gallery into the hall. An instant later he crossed by the door in the other direction, this time carrying the shotgun from the wall.

Drood and Bonner stood up from the table. The women remained seated; Sylvie frowned into her lap and Tita lit a cigarette with a sigh. Only Cassie remained unperturbed. After a moment of hesitation Bonner left the table, moved quickly through the gallery to the orangery, and came out through the open door onto the lawn. There he began to run. Out of the corner of his eye he sensed that Drood was behind him.

In the distance James was standing on the bank of the Val,

holding the shotgun in one hand with the butt resting on his hip. He pointed. "It's across the river," he shouted up to them. "It was coming in this direction and then it ran away."

He was still a good distance away from them and there was no point in shouting back. They exchanged a brief look and then slowed to a walk. They made their way down the lawn a little apart from each other as though they were setting out to catch a nervous escaped animal. Before they could come up to James and ask him what he was doing, he turned and ran away down the river-bank, still holding the gun in his hand. He moved in a steady jog, remarkably nimble for a man of his age and one who customarily took no exercise. Bonner started to say something to Drood and then changed his mind. They both broke into a run, loping down the lawn after the fast disappearing James. When they came to the water in front of the Mill Cottage they turned along the bank. In this direction the path continued for only a hundred yards or so and then dwindled away into ferns and clumps of willows on marshy ground adjoining the dairy barn. James had gone past the end of the path into this miniature jungle. Occasionally they caught a glimpse of his head in an opening in the leaves. When they finally caught up to him he was standing waist-deep in the ferns, panting and holding the gun in the same military position with the butt on his hip. He was looking out through the willows at the other bank of the river, wearing his usual grim smile, a little exultant now.

"You didn't see it, did you?"

They both shook their heads. They were all three out of breath after their thrash through the ferns. James breathed in and out in a curious deliberate way, as though he were making a statement: *Ha. Ha. Ha.* He continued to stare at the opposite bank, glancing at them sharply now and then, still with his little smile, as if asking them to confirm that there was nothing there and that this was a highly suspicious sign.

"James . . ." said Drood.

James glanced at him in irritation and said, "Shhh." He went back to staring across the river. For a while there was nothing but the sound of their breathing. Then he was galvanized again and gave a little start. The path over the meadow on the other bank of the river was obscured here and there by clumps of small trees. In a gap between the trees an upright figure had appeared with something convoluted, familiar, and yet strange on its head. It was only a dim shape in the gathering darkness. It hurried along with an undulating gait, disappearing at intervals behind small trees and then appearing again.

James's mind moved rapidly. All the things that had been mysterious and baffling to him in the weeks before assembled into a picture that blazed fiercely and precisely in his mind, as though it had flame at its edges. He knew now who had led away his deer into the forest, an enemy wraith, a god out of the old darkness. The courage to oppose such things, once you had detected their presence, required an effort of the will which he supplied instantaneously and with the full power of hysteria. He raised the gun and fired. There was an earsplitting crack; Bonner had not realized that a small shotgun could be so deafening. The figure across the river broke into a run.

Drood threw himself on James and grappled for the gun. James turned to him with a kind of fierce determination, hissing through his teeth. He wrenched himself away from Drood and began thrashing through the ferns in the direction of the Mill Cottage, carrying the gun. He fell several times in the soft prickly leafage but flung himself up and ran on. Bonner and Drood, following after him, also fell. The footing was uncertain and there were puddles of water in the ferns. There were nettles too; the large soft leaves that slapped them in their faces stung like insects. After a half-minute or so of thrashing and struggling the three of them came out onto the path.

James was a few paces ahead of them with the shotgun at his shoulder. The antlered figure was crossing on the footbridge, wobbling and groping at the handrail for support. James fired again. The figure drew into itself like a slug sprinkled with salt and then stumbled on to the end of the bridge. It fled up the bank with flailing limbs; it seemed desperate to reach the shelter of the Mill Cottage. It staggered past the ruined pond and disappeared into the door. James, running hard, was immediately behind it.

Drood and Bonner hurried after him, past the dilapidated statue in the abandoned leaf-filled pond, and pressed through the door. In the darkness inside they made out James who seemed to be groping or wrestling with something and reaching into the air overhead at the same time. Over his shoulder jerked the shadow of the antlered head, canted at an angle as though it was looking down at the floor. James found what he was groping for, the light switch. But the lights didn't go on; instead there was a metallic clanking, and at the same instant the antlered head lurched down behind his shoulder and disappeared.

It was Drood who found the right switch and turned the lights on. Down below the Winterthur press was still groaning and clanking. The overturned stag-head lay on the floor behind it. Bonner caught a glimpse of William's body in a tangle of crumpled paper, still moving jerkily an inch or two into the press. Then it stopped, the head crushed by the feeding-arm. A bright red paint leaked out through the framework and fell in sticky threads to the floor.

"For God's sake, James."

"It was only bird-shot." He looked at Drood rather than at the press below him in the museum. "It couldn't have hurt him. It was—"

Drood ran down the steps to the floor of the museum. He stayed a short time, then quickly came back.

"What in the devil did you think you were doing?"

James stared at him. "I thought it was real."

"You what?"

"Real, you see. That it was something—my God, that it was something—I'm trying to tell you." Drood looked at him fixedly as he babbled on. "It had . . . you saw it." He realized that he was still holding the gun and he set it carefully down onto the landing.

"It was only the stag-head from the hall."

"Yes. I see that now."

"Everyone but you saw that it was gone from the wall weeks ago."

Sylvie arrived with a pale face, drawn by the sound of the gunshots, but Drood blocked the way so that she couldn't see into the museum. "Police," he told her briefly. "And an ambulance."

"But who is it?" Her voice squeaked, terrified. "Is it Bonner?"

"No no. It's someone we don't know. Do as I say."

She ran away to the house. Cassie appeared with Tita trailing after her. Cassie pushed past Drood and took a long look at what was in the museum.

"You murdered him, James." He stared back at her with a manic smile. "We wanted the house back but not this way."

James seemed not to understand what she was saying. His

mouth pursed and his jaw worked as though he were chewing something. Then he swallowed what he had chewed and understood what it was. In silence he looked first at Drood and then at Cassie.

Bonner stood in a buzz, conscious of the gun at his feet, the iron press below still clutching its half-swallowed victim, and the lighted room full of iron machines. A vertigo came over him and he felt unbalanced, as though he were standing at a slight angle to the vertical and couldn't recover it. Turning away from the museum, he went outside to the river-bank. He stared for a moment at the pitted and black Eros on its pedestal illuminated by the glare from the open door, then he sat down at the edge of the water with his head in his hands. After a while he vomited into a little depression in the leaves between his feet. It went on for some time, in waves alternating with periods of relative calm. Everything came up; the trifle, the cabbage and the potatoes, and the mucoid little lumps of lamb. When it stopped it didn't make him feel any better.

There was a soft rustle. He turned and in the light from the open door he saw Sylvie approaching from behind him. She half-knelt, half-bent, and touched his shoulder, then crouched down to enclose him in her arms.

"Bonner?"

"It's the engine driver."

"What?"

"I killed him."

"What are you saying? Don't talk nonsense," she said, frightened. "It was James. He had a gun—"

"I know. I brought him here. He was perfectly harmless. A harmless lunatic."

She lifted him gently to his feet and they went up to the house together. On the gravel by the garage a police car and an ambulance had already appeared, the rotating blue lights on their roofs thudding silently in the darkness. The beams fled across the garage, the trees of the park, the façade of the house, and their own faces. In the flash he caught of her Sylvie's face was blue. The first black drops of rain thumped onto the gravel around them. It was a spring rain, warm; it would make things stir in the earth and push them out into the air, the corpses of last year's plants.

Twenty-One

The trial was over and James had already been in prison for a week. The trees on the lawn outside the morning room had turned into their summer green, darker and more uniform than the hundred subtle variations of April. The birds sang piercingly in the trees and the robins stalked spraddle-legged over the empty park stabbing for worms. The flowers in the untidy garden by the orchard sprang forth in profusion even though no one was taking care of them; phlox and lobelia, day lilies and stocks nodded in the sunshine and alyssum ran riot in the borders.

The household, recovering from its shock with a resiliency that is common in such cases but always surprises a little, was already falling into a new routine. The Cromlechs, symbolically and practically at least if not in the full legal sense, resumed possession of their estate, the marshy patch of land at the bend of the Val where men had come to cross the river before Roman times. Tita, a Cromlech once again after her quarter-century of thralldom to the foreigner, took over the financial affairs of the family and discovered that James still held large quantities of common stock in eighteen American newspapers, even though he no longer took an active hand in running them. There would be plenty of money if only she could figure out how to evoke the dividends from across the Atlantic. Through the open door of the study she could be seen uncertainly pushing the buttons of the telephone machine one after the other, like the incompetent commander of a space ship.

With the coming of the soft warm weather Stasha arose from her bed and dressed herself. Moving stiffly like a mummy inside her toughened skin, she put on a shirt and a black tie, a shabby man's jacket, corduroy breeches, and stout walking shoes. Considering further, she pulled an old felt hat over the frizzled cap of her hair. She wore no makeup; her face was the color of dried mud.

Downstairs she took a stick from the umbrella rack and followed Cassie out onto the lawn. Their voices could be heard filtering up from the river through the tepid air, Cassie's thin and clear, Stasha's a throaty scarred wheezing.

You know girl, I saw a stoat down here by the water just a week ago.

Are you sure it wasn't a marten?

No, it was a stoat all right enough. White throat, little ears, carrying a river-rat in its mouth.

Maybe I'll see one.

See them all if you keep your eyes open.

They crossed the Val on the footbridge and disappeared rapidly down the other bank, moving in the same rhythm with scissors-motions of their legs. It was hard to tell them apart except that Stasha was taller.

"So what are you going to do, Drood?"

"Do?"

"I mean now that James is gone. You're the head of the family now. You're the oldest male. Are you just going to go on collecting things from the Long Barrow and putting them in the cabinet? It doesn't seem like much of a life."

"It's true there's not much future in it. I don't expect there's much more in the barrow. Might find a scrap of pottery or a bone needle. Got all the gold and all the erotica out of it long ago— that's what most people are interested in."

It was late in the morning after Cassie and Stasha had gone off for their walk. The glass top of the cabinet was open and Drood, with infinite care, using a pair of tweezers, was arranging four tiny pierced pebbles on the green felt surface, all that remained of a necklace that had adorned some twelve-year-old bride in Aurignacian times. The other objects of the collection were the familiar ones that had been there since Bonner came to the house. The incised stag-horn, which had been subpoenaed by the court as evidence of William's contorted and fatal delusion, was now restored to its place in the cabinet.

"Did you ever think of going to the university? You could take a degree in paleontology."

"Oh no. I don't think those chaps know very much, you know. Dons in their robes. Never did a real dig, most of them. And anyhow I'm tired of mucking about with the past. I'm thinking of getting married."

"Do you have someone in mind?"

"Oh yes. Rhondda I think."

"But . . . I didn't think that you. Um."

He grinned engagingly. "Oh, if you mean that sort of thing. Beast with two backs. I'm not interested in that, you know. Never have been. It's just that a chap needs to settle down sooner or later. She's an excellent cook and she's no trouble. Very clean. Doesn't chatter like most women."

"Have you asked her?"

"Oh no. Not yet."

"Do you think she'll have you?"

"Oh yes. I imagine she will. She usually falls in with most things people suggest to her. She's had a hard time, you know. Life hasn't been easy for her. Grew up on a farm just down the other side of the river and her father molested her. To get away from that she went into service with a judge in Waldon, and he laid his hands on her too. Then we took her, and it was fine for a while, but then James came along and started bothering her like all the others."

"Did he really."

"Yes indeed. I came on them once in the kitchen, James all hot and beady and poor Rhondda stoically resigned to her fate."

"I don't imagine she thinks much of men after that."

"She doesn't. But I don't care for women either, so we'll make a good pair."

"What will you do? Go on living here?"

"Oh no. I'm thinking of opening a pub in Waldon. I'll preside in a striped shirt with garters on the sleeves, and Rhondda can do the cooking. We'll hire Miles to wipe the tables and mop up after closing. Call it the Cromlech Arms. We do have arms, you know. Ancestor was knighted in the eighteenth century."

They stopped to gaze at the pictures of Sir Fellows with his long upper lip, staring at them with a frown of annoyance out of the cracked varnish.

"Not a hereditary title though."

"Unfortunately not. Still we've got the arms. Gold two lions passant sable, looking backwards." Bonner saw for the first time that there was a small gilded shield with two lions on it in the lower corner of the picture, twined about with ribbons and almost hidden in the ivy. "Put it on a sign and hang it in the street. People like to be served by a publican with some sort of distinction, you know. Former prizefighters, Spitfire pilots, that sort of thing. With me they can rub shoulders with the past. Page out of England's history. Have a pint with the lord of the manor."

"I'll miss you."

"Oh, you'll be coming in to the pub for a drop now and then. Besides we need you to stay here and take care of things. Keep after Fred Baines to be sure he milks the cows. I wouldn't get any more deer if I were you. They're an infernal nuisance. You'll find the footbridge on the weir is a bit shaky and needs mending."

Bonner inspected the portrait again. "Since I'm married to Sylvie, does this mean that I can use the coat of arms too?"

"Oh no. You're not a Cromlech. We've acquired dozens like you as we've gone along. Your son would inherit if you had one though."

"I don't think that's very likely."

Bonner woke up in the middle of the night, attracted by something fluttering dimly and pinkly at the corner of his closed eyelid. He went to the window and opened it. It was a clear warm night, absolutely still. In the distance a hilltop stuck up out of the farmland, the only protuberance in the otherwise flat landscape. On the top of it a bonfire was throwing up a long tail of flame, so bright that its light was reflected into the room and left a quivering shadow on the wall behind him. Although it was several miles away, he could see the tiny black figures like ants moving around it, silhouetted in the fire. It was St. John's Eve, he remembered, exactly six months after the Night Fair. Someone had remarked at dinner that it was the shortest night of the year. There was a hieratic grace and elegance about this tiny cameo scene in the distance. It excited him and filled him with a thrill of longing, a general and unspecified craving for something or other, perhaps merely to go out and caper around the bonfire in bare feet like the others.

"Sylvie?"

He called softly to her, no more than a whisper. In the uncertain flicker of the bonfire he could make her out dimly. She lay asleep on her back with her hands on her waist, breathing rhythmically. Her lips had fallen open and a little wheezing puff of air came from them every few seconds. Perhaps her nose was stuffed up. As he came closer and kneeled by the bed he was aware of her fragrance, milk and scented talcum, the odor of a baby. Her features were delicate, her small nose patrician and narrow, her closed eyelids like pink marbles. A faint smile lingered on the partly open mouth. She would not want to go to the bonfire. She slept in the deep and sensual oblivion of an animal or a small child. She did take a delight in the sensuous, he now saw, and it was in sleep, in dream. He felt deeply protective and would have allowed himself to be cut in pieces rather than disturb her. He would never have imagined that he could love anything so hotly and fiercely that gave no satisfaction to his own body, that his own body regarded quite without desire, with the dumb and selfless tenderness of a father for a child, or a brother for a sister.

Moving stealthily so as to make no noise, he lay down again on his own bed and imitated her posture, lying on his back with his wrists crossed on his small plump waist. He wasn't sleepy and he lay for the rest of the night with open eyes. The flickering on the wall from the distant bonfire gradually paled and dimmed, and then disappeared. Nothing disturbed the absolute silence of the room. From the hall downstairs he heard the hours from the old grandfather clock: one, two, three, and four. At four-thirty he dressed himself and crept downstairs. Rhondda was not up yet. He put the teakettle on and brought some water to a boil, found some scones and warmed them, and put them on a dish with the butter. Then he carried the tea and scones back upstairs like an acolyte with his censer, trailing by the crisp fragrant odor of fresh bread.

He pushed open the door. She was still lying in the same position, her recumbent form silhouetted in the grayish light from the window.

"Sylvie?"

When they finished their breakfast they left the teapot and the dish with the crumbs of scones on it and stole downstairs. There was a light under the kitchen door now and they heard small sounds; the murmur of running water and the knock of a pan. They avoided that part of the house and left through the door of the orangery.

Halfway down the lawn he looked back and saw Rhondda's head, a dark lozenge or a nut, framed in the lighted window of the kitchen, following their progress like a compass.

Everything was gray with the morning green just beginning to seep up through it, still very dim. A mist lay along the surface of the Val, blurring its contours and giving the impression of a stage-river of smoke sifting slowly downstream. Although it was not cold there was a touch of winelike crispness in the air, the champagne that rewards those who get up early in the summer. They went on down across the grass to the Mill Cottage.

"Sometimes I think his ghost is still in there."

"I'm sure it is. Poor old chap. He knew they were there in the forest but I don't think he ever saw them, even though he was chaste. He couldn't have been able to see much anyhow from inside that fool stag-head."

"Do you have to be chaste?"

"Yes."

"What else do you have to do?"

"Have no iron with you, and make no noise until you see them."

She took off her wristwatch and dropped it behind her in the grass.

"Are you sure they'll be there?"

"Not entirely. I think so. I hope so."

"What must I do?"

"Nothing. Behave naturally. Don't try to touch them until they touch you."

On the footbridge he looked back and found her following him with small steps, gripping the railing timidly. He reached and took her hand to steady and reassure her. On the opposite bank she smiled bravely.

"It's the first time you've crossed the bridge. You've never been to the forest."

"No."

"I wanted you to come so many times. Why wouldn't you?"

"Oh, I don't know. I didn't have the proper shoes."

The shoes she had on now were most improper; they were flimsy narrow slippers like dancing shoes of soft leather. They were already damp and muddy from the path. She smiled and took his hand again. She was wearing a simple frock with a low waist and a pleated skirt; at the top it came to her throat and was fastened with a brooch, the Diana-figured cameo she had bought for herself at Harrods. They passed the Long Barrow, which she gazed at without curiosity, and went on up through the trees into the clearing with the sarsens.

"Oh, those stones. Drood and Cassie are always talking about them."

"What do they say about them?"

"That they're very old."

"If you pry up the one that's fallen, there's a sack of gold under it. But you have to have someone to help you."

She laughed. "Oh, Bonner."

"Be quiet now because we're getting near."

"Near to what?"

"Shhh."

On the steep path up through the cleft, with the giant trees arching overhead and glowing now dimly with the green of daylight, she showed signs of getting tired but still smiled at him cheerfully. The path leveled and they came out into the grassy clearing with its odor of rotting vegetation. The circle in the grass was almost obliterated; there was only discoloration to mark where it had been. He wasn't sure about the habits of mushrooms but he imagined the circle of pale white buttons would appear again after the summer thundershowers, a little farther out from the center.

Without speaking he halted her by stretching out his hand. They stood in silence for a few minutes with no sound but their own breathing and the rustle of insects. He kept his eyes fixed on the curtain of vegetation on the other side of the clearing. It was motionless; only a leaf nodded as a drop of water touched it or a beetle fell to the forest floor.

Then he saw something. In the interstices of the leaves a fleck of reddish brown appeared and vanished, and reappeared again in another place. It was joined gradually by others. He caught a glimpse of a soft brown candelabrum with a lighter gold at its tips, then a shaggy throat appeared and moved past an opening in the branches.

He took her by the hand and drew her stealthily after him across the clearing. When they pushed their way in through the branches they found the deer all around them in the thicket.

Clearly visible only a few paces away were a young stag and two does.

Ho Cos, he said softly. Ho Ata and Ubi.

The others were forest deer; he didn't know their names. They gazed at him without fear out of their liquid brown eyes. Then they turned and wove their way up the slope farther into the forest with their stiff-legged swaying grace.

He and Sylvie followed. He turned to look at her and she made a kind of silent laugh of delight. He smiled too and they followed on after the swaying rumps with their small neat tails. The way through the trees here was steep. The deer scrambled and lunged delicately, tapping with their forehooves, leading the way for the two humans into this part of the forest he didn't know very well. The valley was far behind them; they caught only occasional glimpses of it through the openings in the trees. Then they came out into a kind of cirque, a miniature valley enclosed on three sides by higher ground. Broad-limbed arching trees spread their limbs overhead and there was a floor of leaves. Here the deer melted away into the maze of green shadows and they were alone.

They stopped without making a sound. Sylvie turned to him once with a little questioning look; when he said nothing she became solemn and stood with a little suppressed smile on her lips.

He had expected to hear voices, but what he heard was the thin fluting of Bork's wooden pipe, strained through the trees, a plaintive and playful melody on three or four notes. He advanced a pace or two with Sylvie following.

Bork? Is that you?

But it was the women playing tricks on him again; they had cleverly imitated the sound of the flute with their voices. Instead of Bork it was Lara that appeared, slim and dreamy in her cobweb dress tinged with magenta. She pirouetted slowly, stretched out her hands, smiled over her shoulder, and drew away with beckoning motions. Flicka in violet appeared at her side imitating her gestures in reverse. The two of them, a pair of pastel shapes in mirror-image, moved playfully away from them across the cirque.

He turned to look at Sylvie.

Do you see them?

Of course.

He felt a joy of triumph, a private little exultation. She was trembling a little, either from fear or from excitement, he couldn't tell. Her expression was calm. As though entranced she moved forward, taking the lead now; Bonner followed at her shoulder.

Elof and Alban appeared, and then Bork with his pipe, and then the other women: Jenny Stone, Penny, and serious May Brown. Flicka, pirouetting in her slow dance, sang a fragment of song in a voice so low it was almost a sigh:

Weave. A. Cir. Cle.

And Lara, taking her hand so that the two of them pranced lightly around the newcomers, joined in with her in the mocking little chant:

Round. Him. Thri-iiiice . . .

They broke off in a tinkle of laughter.

Good day to all, said Bonner in the best of spirits and barely suppressing a grin. Where's John Greene?

You found your way then, said John Greene, appearing abruptly from one side with his topper at an angle.

It was your forest chums that led us. Cos and Ata, and Ubi.

Ah, the good creeturs. They love to guide people in the forest and bring them to us.

This is Sylvie.

Ah, we know you, Sylvie, said John Greene, glancing at the others for confirmation. It's a kind soul you are and a loving creetur. You're welcome to us.

Sylvie. What a pretty name, said Lara.

It means forest girl, said Bonner.

Does it now. Well I never knew that, said John Greene. You see, I don't—

I know, you don't know Frinch.

John Greene smiled broadly. The others grinned too. Well, you're a learned man, a Clark, he agreed. We need you to tell us about these hard things, Bonner, what words mean and so on.

There are some things that even a learned man can't know, said Bonner. About himself. I mean—for instance, are you really here or am I only imagining you?

If you're imagining us, Bonner, it's the best thing you've ever done, said John Greene.

The laughter died down. They stood in a ring watching the two of them intently, smiling and full of mirth, with special attention to Sylvie, who seemed to attract their sly curiosity. He caught the eye of Flicka on the edge of the band, and then the other women.

Won't you sing?

Sing?

Sing and dance. I've told Sylvie about it.

John Greene shook his head. Ah, its a sad thing we have to sing about today, Bonner, he said with a twitch at the corner of his mouth.

Sad thing?

Without explaining John Greene turned and led the way out of the cirque along a green corridor through the trees. After him the Little People formed into a procession two by two. They were all solemn too; they trudged along like small soldiers, lifting their knees in rhythm. Puzzled, Bonner followed them through the forest with Sylvie at his side. The Little People began chanting softly in a kind of dirge, men and women together.

> *Did you ever think, when a hearse goes by,*
> *That someday you are going to die . . .*

They came out into a small clearing with John Greene still in the lead. He stopped and the others trailed up behind him in a little band, looking at something on the ground before them. Bonner came up to see what it was. At their feet Gondal was lying on a pallet made of saplings bound together with twigs. Her small stubby body seemed even more short-limbed and odd than when she had walked and sung among them. Her face was gray and she lay motionless with her eyes closed; a fly walked over her brow. The pink tint of her dress appeared somehow to have faded. The Little People gathered wildflowers and strewed them over her, and then they stood with their hands clasped looking at the effect. Four of the stronger ones—Cobold, Hern, old Quare, and simple Trig— came forward and lifted the rustic bier.

Come Bonner and Sylvie, said John Greene gruffly.

Bonner had a vague feeling of foreboding. He took his place at the end of the double line with Sylvie; the procession started up, led by the bearers carrying the swaying litter, and they followed after it. Sylvie glanced at him questioningly but he looked straight ahead. The Little People wound through the forest after the bier, with wildflowers dropping from it onto the path. They went on with their dirge, fitting the rhythm to the slow pace of their march.

> *They'll wrap you in a wooden shirt,*
> *And cover you over with grass and dirt.*

They sang all this with the utmost gravity, as though they scarcely understood the meaning of the words. He tried to read the expressions on their faces, but this was hard because he was following behind them and their eyes were fixed on the pallet of saplings with its burden at the head of the procession. Lara turned her head once, and then Bork. Their expressions were blank; only a trace of a little malicious smile still lingered on Lara's lips.

> *The worms crawl in, the worms crawl out,*
> *They crawl all over your face and snout.*

They stopped. They had arrived at a tiny open place in the forest with the twisted limbs of the trees providing a ceiling overhead. Here they scooped out a hollow in the dry brown leaves. The four bearers set the litter down in the hollow and stepped back. Gondal lay motionless with the wildflowers scattered on her face, one of them touching her closed eyelid. The Little People came forward one by one and scattered brown leaves over her, almost covering her.

> *The worms crawl out, the worms crawl in,*
> *The worms play pinochle on your chin.*

In their thin sweet voices they sang the grotesque words solemnly and mournfully, as though it was a deep and tragic funeral lament. Bonner, bewildered, pushed them aside and knelt by the lifeless form of the girl almost buried in the leaves.

John Greene, what's this? You told me—

The little man in his topper smiled. Bonner stared at him, then was distracted by a rustling in the leaves before him. Gondal sprang up from the rustic littler scattering leaves. She laughed and flung herself around in a circle, strewing leaves over all of them, over Bonner and Sylvie, John Greene, and the other Little People. Then she sat down on the litter again, her legs crossed tailor-fashion and a pleased smile on her face. The pink tint shone again in her dress; her gray face had been only a trick of light. The four bearers picked up the litter. They were smiling broadly too.

Bonner made a foolish grin.

We only do this as a joke, you see, said John Greene. We like to copy the Sassenachs' ways, for fun.

And the song?

Ah, the song. We learnt that from the children in the village.

Wooden shirt!

Pinochle on your chin!

They burst out in their tinkling laughter. They were all smiling, flushed and pleased with themselves at the joke. Bonner caught Sylvie's eye and took her hand. She had been tremulous and fearful during the procession through the forest, but now she smiled with the others. The litter bearers started back down the path the way they had come, and the others followed. Bonner still held Sylvie's hand, and on the other side of him was Lara with her little curving smile. With one hand she twirled her shawl, which floated about her shoulders as she went.

He asked her, Do you know what the thing was that they were pretending?

Oh yes. Her smile faded and she looked at him fixedly. The shawl sank to the ground and trailed behind her. But we don't fear it, you see, because—

Don't talk of such things, John Greene interrupted roughly, marching along at his side. You're here among us now and you're our friends.

Their friends. The word rang queerly in the small man's mouth, as though it had a private meaning among them here in the forest. An idea struck him.

You said you knew Sylvie. Do you know the others then?

The others?

The people in the house at Byrd Mill.

Some we do and some we don't, said the small man, assuming a furtive caution.

Some of them come to the forest. A fellow dressed like a game-keeper.

Oh aye, we've seen him.

And an old woman in a man's hat, and a young woman with her, dressed the same.

Ah! the old dame in her boots, said John Greene. She's a good thing. And the other one who comes along with her now. He shook his head and smiled. Would they be friends of yours now?

The young one I—knew well at one time. He was a little embarrassed. But not anymore.

John Greene understood perfectly what he was referring to. Don't talk of that, he said shortly. It's a mortal thing, Bonner.

I knew a man who said the same thing. A doctor. He said it's because of doing that thing that we must die.

If you're our friend, Bonner, you won't speak of it among us.

Bonner exchanged a glance with Sylvie. He wasn't sure whether she was following all this. She smiled back at him thinly with a distant look.

Then he thought of something else.

And those two. Do they see you?

The old dame and the girl who was burnt so horrible? Ah no. They can't see us, even though they look right where we are. Because look you, Bonner—

Is it because they—

They see only what's there. They have no vision in their minds—no spirit to make up things. They see all that's there. And that's many a thing—all the creeturs of the forest, tiny as they are. But that's all they see. There are many like that down below. Good people they are, but we don't show ourselves to such as them. But you and Sylvie—

Down there in the world they say we're not well.

So they do. And you're not. Not well for them. But there's well and well. If you're well in their way, there are things you don't see, and things you don't hear. It's true you've only imagined us. But everything there is is imagined by somebody. Otherwise it wouldn't be. He gave a tap to his topper. It's fortunate you are, Bonner, you and Sylvie. We're glad you've come. You can't stay and live among us, but you can come to us often and enjoy a visit.

Bonner's a beloved soul to us, said serious May Brown. He's someone special.

Fed on . . . crooned Flicka.

Honey-dew! They all tittered.

Leave him be now, said John Greene mildly. You gels must always be joking and bantering. But it may make him sore in his mind.

I'm not sore in my mind. He grinned. You wouldn't have a bit of honey here in the forest, would you?

No, it's all gone. But we know where to get more. With you to help us. We don't break things. We don't fiddle with locks. We don't open doors. We don't touch iron. You wouldn't happen to have a bit of iron with you, my dear? he inquired, turning to Sylvie.

No, I dropped my watch in the grass.

That's well. We're pleased you've come among us and we welcome you.

All this time they had been trudging along the path following Gondal perched on her litter. Bonner hadn't been paying attention to where they were going. They were in an unfamiliar part of the forest. Flicka was at his side and Sylvie had fallen behind, whispering and flustering with Bork who was showing her his flute.

Then are you going to sing your song?

Our song?

Woodland dark.

Flicka looked at Lara, and Lara looked at Norn and Jenny Stone. The procession stopped; Gondal sprang down onto the path and the men threw away the litter of saplings.

The women began to sing, taking up the procession again. It was the same odd oblique melody he had taught to Sylvie, the one she had played on the piano at Brown's.

> *Wood-land dark, wood-land deep*
> *Shel-ter now my love a-sleep.*
> *Let the hid-den fire-fly gleam*
> *In the for-est of her dre-eeam . . .*

After they had sung the four verses through they began again, and a new voice joined them. Sylvie was flushed and excited; her eyes glowed and her small mouth hung open birdlike as she sang.

Her voice was thin and high, not a trained voice but faultless in pitch, the voice of a musician who was skilled in some other instrument. A light veil of perspiration as fragile as lace covered her face.

> *Make her clad in rai-ments fair,*
> *Gold her gar-ments, gold her hair . . .*
> *Pearls are dew-drops in her ears,*
> *Pre-cious dia-monds are her tears . . .*

She had learnt the words perfectly after listening to them only once. She looked at the others only now and then for a hint or for encouragement. All smiling and exchanging glances, they slowed in the last verse until each word was delicate and distinct.

> *Let. Her. Slumb-ber. Till. She's born.*
> *Wake. Her. With. A. Shep. Herd's horn!*

The song ended and they all burst out into soft hurrahs and cheers which trailed away into laughter and titters. They seemed to be enjoying themselves and were pleased to have Sylvie join in their singing.

Ah, she has a sweet voice, said John Greene. Not like the others but sweet.

Sylvie loosed her hair and let it fall over her cheeks. I want to be like the others, she said. How must I sing?

Ah, sing like your own sweet self, Sylvie girl. We want you only as you are.

The procession trudged on; they had stopped climbing some time ago and were descending now through the forest. Bonner was still bewildered about where they were. Through the branches he caught a glimpse of the Val below winding through the valley floor. Then the way became more familiar; they descended through the ravine with the shadows of deep green on both sides, across the circle of grass with the traces of mushrooms, and down the path which still descended steeply. Abruptly they came out into the clearing with its three sarsens, two erect and one fallen in the ferns and bracken. They were all smiling. Bonner and Sylvie were panting and perspiring from the exertion in the warm summer morning; the Little People were restless and energetic, breaking out of their procession and flitting around playfully in the ferns. John Greene glanced about him, considered, and signaled to the others with a toss of his topper. The four strong ones—Cobold, Hern, Quare, and Trig—ran off into the thicket for poles and branches.

Bonner put his arm around Sylvie. They're going to give us Krugerrands, he laughed.

Oh Bonner. They are not.

Wait and see.

Dreamy Lara, clever Flicka, Gondal in her pale pink cobwebs came to them and joined them in their embrace. In a kind of circle in which each body touched the others, in which arms and hands, cheeks, breasts, knees, brushed in the softest of caresses, he and Sylvie swung with them through the ferns around the three old stones. An energy suffused him, a soft wild delight of limbs and soul, an ecstasy of spirit that struck deep into his blood, into the dark joy of his entrails. He laughed and felt Sylvie's unbound hair brushing his cheek, a touch as light as moonbeams. Flicka and Lara began a soft chant, their fingers wandering lightly over his limbs, his face and his chest.

Beware!. . .
Beware!

He felt in the sunlight around him, grasping and groping for their soft hair even softer than Sylvie's, their evanescent limbs that coiled under his fingers. They eluded him, laughing, and sang on.

His flash-ing eyes . . .
floating hair . . .
Weave a cir-cle . . .
round him thrice. •
Close your eyes with . . .
hol-y dread,

Even in the middle of the song his mind was filled all at once with the thought of the old poet a century and more ago, hearing these voices in a lonely farmhouse at night and writing them down. He had been mad; Coleridge was mad. Sylvie joined in with them, her stronger voice overriding and dominating the others.

For he on hon-ey . . .
dew hath fed,
And drunk the milk . . .
of Par-a-di-iise . . .

He felt his eyes brimming with tears, but they were tears of joy, of a nameless emotion that was beyond joy and suffering, a keen knowing of what could never be known and which lay always just beyond the yearning grasp, the elusive hunger, the longing for an invisible bliss that he sensed in the air about him, and was as thin and elusive, as untouchable, as air itself. Through his blurred vision he saw the reflection of his own expression, the same bewildered and yet knowing bliss, on Sylvie's face. He was certain now that he was no longer isolated in his strangeness, in the dark and blissful disease that had made him an outcast among men, that she was with him and would always be there, and that these happy and insubstantial, melodiously singing figures were to be their constant companions.